KEEPING PROMISES

Books by Gina Marie Coon

~ : ~

Silver Springs Settlers Series
Building Fences, Mending Hearts
The Right Choice
Mail Order Bride

~ : ~

Silver Springs Contemporary Series
Elizabeth's Hero
Cowboy Dad
Winter Awakening
His Leading Lady
Running Out of Time
The Cooper Kids
Keeping Promises

~ : ~

No Regrets

~ : ~

The following multi-book volumes are also available in e-format.
Silver Springs Settlers – books 1-3
Silver Springs Contemporary – books 1-4

KEEPING PROMISES

A Silver Springs Contemporary Novel

by

Gina Marie Coon

Copyright © 2013 Gina Marie Coon
All rights reserved.
ISBN: 1484943988
ISBN-13: 978-1484943984

Dedicated to the Lord – He was with me every step of the way.

Many thanks to Kay Coon, Jeanne Dandridge, Cheryl Gilroy, and Katy Vining for enduring the rough drafts of this book. As always, your insight and editing skills were invaluable. Also, a big thank you to my husband, Mike, for being my sounding board and providing advice on some of the more masculine aspects of the story.

Jer. 29:11 'For I know the plans I have for you,' declares the LORD, 'plans to prosper you and not to harm you, plans to give you hope and a future.'

Chapter 1

'Shots fired! Officer down!' Spence barked the words into his radio then dropped to the asphalt in agony.

Excruciating pain held him in its iron grip. His shoulder screamed; fingers of white-hot fire raced down his right arm. Blood soaked his shirt. Darkness loomed around the edges of his vision, threatening to engulf him. He shook off the shadows and pushed up on his left elbow. Adams needed help. The agony intensified as he dragged his broken body across the rough pavement toward his partner. Sharp reports from multiple weapons fire reverberated across the space between the buildings. He paused and listened, trying to pinpoint their origin. Somewhere in the distance, a phone rang...

Carl Spencer emerged slowly from the nightmare, tugged from its hold by a high pitched buzzing. Pushing the pillow aside, he reached blindly for the phone and pressed it to the side of his head.

"Spencer here," he mumbled.

"Someone's looking for you."

Rolling to his back, Spence scraped a palm over his closed eyes and shook his head, hoping to dispel the remnants of the terror that plagued him whenever he slept. His pulse still hammered a staccato beat, and his chest heaved painfully.

"You there, Spence?"

The voice on the other end of the line was familiar, known to him. It was work related, but he was on leave. Why would the Bureau be contacting him?

"Yeah, I'm here, Jefferson," he rasped then cleared his throat. He'd never been much good before a cup of coffee. What had the guy said? His instincts warned that it was important. "Say again?"

"I said, someone's been looking for you," Jefferson repeated with mild irritation. "Your name popped up on a couple of search engines we monitor."

Spence's brain shifted into gear. The hair on the back of his neck prickled. In his line of work, he'd made a few enemies.

"Hold on," he barked into the phone, tossing his sleeping bag aside. He grabbed a pair of wrinkled jeans from the pile on the floor and yanked them on over his boxers. A grey sweatshirt followed. Even this close to summer, mornings were cold at the cabin. He reached for the satellite phone that never left his side. In this part of the country, cell phone coverage could be sporadic. The FBI liked to keep tabs on its agents, even when they were off-duty.

"Okay," he said, all business now. "How do you know it's me?"

~ * ~

Jordan hit the print screen button and waited. One after another, three sheets of paper slid into the printer tray. She grabbed the small stack and dropped into her swivel chair, discouraged. Nearly fifty names were printed on the pages. Her already overwhelming life just took a turn for the worse. How could she possibly track down this man when his name was so common?

"Buck up, girl," she mumbled to herself. "Remember how hard you thought it would be to get this far?"

She nodded absently, responding to her own question. Yeah, she remembered. When she started this search, all she'd had to go on was her nephew's birth date, and a fervent prayer for God's help. Her sister had never mentioned the guy's name.

And help He did. Jordan contacted her sister's best friend from high school. Sandy and Tanya were inseparable in those days and for a few years afterward. Then, Sandy married and Tanya had Caleb, and the two drifted apart.

"Hey, Squirt!" Sandy had said when Jordan introduced herself.

Jordan cringed, glad the older woman couldn't see her annoyed expression through the telephone. She'd always hated that nickname. Tanya only called her 'Squirt' to irritate her, and it worked, especially when her friends started doing it, too.

They got through the preliminaries in about fifteen minutes – age, marital status, kids or no kids, etc. There wasn't really much to talk about. Sandy had heard about Tanya's death last year and offered her condolences. Finally, Jordan got to the point of her call.

"Do you know who fathered Caleb?" She could tell by the silence on the line that her question surprised Sandy.

"Wow, I guess I wasn't expecting that."

"Sorry," Jordan said.

Naturally, the woman was curious. After all, the boy was thirteen. A lot of years had gone by since Caleb was conceived. Sandy and Tanya were only nineteen and determined to test their wings in a big way. Tanya had always been the more outgoing of the two. Trolling around Southern California's beaches and under-21 clubs was a weekend ritual. The places were always teeming with good-looking Marines and sailors from Camp Pendleton and San Diego.

Jordan's head pounded a little more with each question. Stress headaches were becoming a regular occurrence. She didn't want to go into all the details of why she needed to find this man. If anyone had told her a year ago that she'd be raising her niece and nephew now, she would have laughed and said they were crazy. Her sister was finally grounded. Tanya had married a wonderful man; John was an excellent father and a good provider. But Jordan wasn't laughing now. In fact, she hadn't laughed in a long time.

"I'd like to know his medical background," Jordan hedged. "You know how those forms at the doctor's office are always asking for the parents' health history. It'd be nice if I could actually check a few boxes on the paternal half of the page." It was a flimsy excuse, but Sandy seemed to accept it.

"Yeah, I know what you mean," she replied. "But I can't help you. I was seeing someone back then and didn't go to any of the same places as Tanya."

Jordan's heart sank. She'd never known most of Tanya's friends. There were nine years between her and her sister. She couldn't think of anyone else to call.

"What a sec, Jordan," Sandy added excitedly. "Jackie Cavanaugh might know something. In fact, she married a Marine later that same year." She rustled through an old address book. "Her last name is Jenkins now," she said then recited the phone number.

Jordan thanked her and disconnected. A few days later she had a name – Carl Spencer.

"Everyone called him Spence," Jackie told her. "I remember that much. I had my ex look him up in the military database." Jackie's now ex-husband, Bill Jenkins, was a sergeant in the Marine Corps. "Spence finished his second tour of duty and didn't reenlist," she added. "Bill doesn't know where he is currently. He joked that Spence is probably dead. The guy's favorite part of being a Marine was jumping out of airplanes. Bill said he was wild, even by Marine standards – you know hang gliding, bungee jumping, that sort of thing. That's what Spence did with his time off."

"And get my sister pregnant," Jordan muttered with a sigh. She hadn't considered that he might be deceased. What would she do if that were the case?

~ * ~

With his second mug of coffee gripped firmly in his right fist, Spence stood on the wooden porch appreciating the scenery and considering what he'd just learned. Jefferson's information was accurate. Someone was searching for *him*, not some other guy who shared his name. They had his birthdate and years of military service. Who knows what else?

He scanned the rolling hills in front of the cabin. The dirt road from the highway was in clear view. No one could approach from the front without him noticing. The woods behind the cabin and to its right were another story. Easy enough for someone with a little hiking experience to get in there without being seen.

His gut told him there was no danger today. All the same, after breakfast he planned to hike the hills surrounding the cabin and take a closer look.

Raising his mug to his lips triggered a painful reminder of his last assignment — as if the nightmares weren't enough. He stifled a groan as a phantom knife blade stabbed through his right shoulder. The drug running operation was supposed to be fairly innocuous as far as they go, mostly a bunch of high school kids carting marijuana between New Jersey and Pennsylvania. The only reason the Bureau was even involved was because the drugs were crossing state lines. That made the crime a federal matter. During the three month investigation, no major gang involvement was detected.

Spence and Adams were outside a warehouse in one of the seedier parts of Trenton, ready to make the bust. They were just waiting for the local cops to get into position. Adams' radio crackled, and all hell broke loose. Gun fire erupted from every direction. They were caught in the middle. Before Spence could find cover, searing pain exploded in his shoulder where a hollow point struck. He'd taken bullets before but had never felt anything like this, and never wanted to again. The force of the shot slammed him into the side of the building, and the pain brought him to his knees. He shoved the shock down deep and got himself under control. Adams was face down on the ground a few yards away, blood pooling under his head. Spence crawled to him intending to render aid, but there was no hope. A bullet to the head ended his partner's life that day.

That was nine months ago.

After three surgeries and countless hours of physical therapy, Spence still couldn't lift his right arm above shoulder level. He exercised daily, did everything, just as he'd been instructed. Still, the experts predicted that he'd never regain full mobility. That put him out of commission, at least from the field. There was a desk and a filing cabinet awaiting his return. Spence just couldn't see a future for himself in a swivel chair.

He downed his lukewarm coffee in one gulp and stepped inside the cabin.

~ * ~

Jordan's hand quivered as she pushed through the office door of Washington Middle School. As though she were the one in trouble, her insides trembled and her stomach did a flip. In all her years of school, she'd never once seen the inside of the principal's office. Never! Jordan did her homework, read classic literature, and hung out with the other members of the chess club. She behaved herself. In the last six months, she'd been through this routine no less than six times. She'd dealt with stealing, cheating, cussing, and fighting. This was visit number seven.

Jordan checked in with the secretary and took a seat in one of the plastic chairs in the waiting area. The woman's disapproving scowl did not escape her notice. Except for the ringing phones, the office was fairly quiet. Occasionally, a student would come in with a note or a question. A concerned mother dropped off a brown paper bag. Apparently, her son had left home without his lunch. If only Jordan's visits were that simple.

"Ms. Gray."

The stern voice dragged Jordan from her thoughts. She looked up at the now-familiar face of Principal Becker. 'Ms.' again, she noted with annoyance. She'd always disliked that title. Having never been married, she certainly didn't want anyone assuming she was divorced. His furrowed brow warned about the nature of the impending meeting and pushed aside her irritation. She nodded and followed the stout man to his private office.

As the door shut behind her, Jordan became aware that she wasn't the only person present. She'd expected to see Caleb, but he was strangely absent. A uniformed police officer stood and extended her hand.

"Mrs. Gray, I presume. I'm Officer Yates."

"It's M-Miss Gray," Jordan stammered as she shook the officer's hand.

"Ms. Gray is Caleb's aunt and legal guardian," Principal Becker interjected as he moved behind his desk and gestured to the chairs opposite. The police woman nodded, and the three of them sat down.

"What's this about?" Jordan asked. Her pulse raced, concern for her nephew welling up inside her.

Jordan learned that Caleb was caught fighting again. The other boy claimed Caleb shoved him, and several people corroborated the statement. Jordan wondered briefly about the officer's presence. Fighting wasn't usually an offence that got the police involved.

"He had this in his pocket," the principal said, pointing at a plastic bag on the desk.

As Jordan stared through the clear bag, a chill trickled down her spine. She'd never seen the pocket knife before.

"Bringing a weapon to school is grounds for expulsion, Ms. Gray. Caleb claimed this belonged to his father, and that he didn't know it was in his pocket," Becker explained.

Jordan swallowed hard and clamped her shaking hands in front of her. Three infractions in one incident – fighting, bringing a weapon to school, and lying – would the boy never learn?!

"Is there any truth to your nephew's story?" Officer Yates gently asked. She'd dealt with many distraught parents in her time. Usually, in a situation like this, they were furious and ready to give their kid a thrashing. This woman looked close to tears.

Jordan's throat closed up as she stared at the knife. *No, none.* What was she going to do?

Chapter 2

Spence spent many sleepless nights deliberating what to do with the information Jefferson provided. Being searched for and not knowing who was doing the searching was disconcerting, at best. He wouldn't risk the lives of the people around him.

After his injury, when Spence knew he'd be taking an extended leave from the Bureau, he'd been at a loss. He didn't relish spending months cooped up in his tiny condo; being in the city wasn't to his liking. He lived in New Jersey only because it was near his office. As a field agent, he rarely spent time at home.

Five years ago, his job had reacquainted him with Jack Summers, a former commanding officer. They'd served in the Marine Corps together in what felt like another life. Spence was sent to Jack's Montana ranch on an undercover assignment. The case ended and the two men went their separate ways, intending to keep in touch. That didn't happen. Jack was busy raising a family. Spence was just plain busy.

His current unexpected leave of absence reunited the men again. Spence thought about the old cabin on Jack's ranch. They'd once stopped a not very nice man from attacking Jack's wife there. Spence wondered briefly if his friend would have torn down the place. Would the cabin serve as a reminder of that frightening period in his life? He called Jack and asked if the cabin was available for rent.

After learning about Spence's injury and the tragic loss of his partner, Jack offered the place rent free. He even offered to give Spence his old job back. They'd had a good laugh. Unbeknownst to Jack, Spence had posed as a cowhand for several weeks. All the while, he drew his regular FBI paycheck, along with the small salary Jack paid. To both men's surprise, Spence actually found the idea of working on the ranch appealing. Since arriving four weeks ago, he'd helped out often, even covering a weekend shift so Jack could take his family on a short vacation.

Now, Spence worried about those same people. What would happen if this person tracked him to Silver Springs, or worse, to the ranch? Jack's wife and kids could be in danger. A week ago, Spence made the decision to meet his adversary head-on.

Jefferson used his computer expertise to trace the searches back to the original IP addresses, then to the location of the computers themselves. Two different computers were identified, both located in Southern California. Spence hopped on a plane and a few hours later, landed at John Wayne Airport. *Yep, you know you're in California when the airport is named after a movie star,* he thought with a wry grin.

He rented a non-descript compact and went searching. When he pulled up across the street from the first location, a jolt of surprise rocked him. A church? Spence fished out the paper on which he'd written the address and checked it against the number on the building. They matched.

He looked the place over. The mid-sized chapel facing the busy street probably held no more than four or five hundred faithful worshipers each Sunday morning. Not a mega church, but definitely not small either. The parking lot was decent sized and only partially filled at this hour. Obviously, Thursday mornings weren't rush hour for God's folks. Spence made a U-turn and entered the lot, choosing a parking space at the back, next to a fenced playground. After rolling down the windows to let in the fresh air, he switched off the engine. The spot he'd chosen allowed an unobstructed view of the main doors to a building located behind the sanctuary.

Ten minutes passed and all remained quiet. Spence was on the verge of giving up when unexpected noises filled the air. He turned to the left and watched as a stream of young children poured through an open door at the rear of the building. The previously empty playground was suddenly filled with laughter, shouting, and the general mayhem only a mass of preschoolers could create. A smile replaced the stern scowl on the FBI agent's face.

Spence watched the children for several minutes, chuckling at the antics of two boys negotiating who would use the swing first. Clearly in a stand-off, each held onto one chain until a middle-aged woman entered the scene and decided the dispute. He shook his head in amusement and reached for his keys. This was a lost cause. The person looking for him wasn't going to be here.

"Excuse me, sir."

Startled by a feminine voice so near, Spence looked up. His right hand automatically slipped inside his jacket to his shoulder holster. A young woman stood a couple of yards away staring at him from the opposite side of the chain-link fence. His practiced gaze quickly sized her up – mid to late twenties, slender, very attractive. He smiled appreciatively as his gaze reached her face. She didn't smile back.

He cleared his throat. "Yes, ma'am?" he asked through the open window. "Anything I can do for you?"

She folded her arms across her chest and frowned. "I was about to ask you the same thing." The words were brisk, businesslike, stern – a teacher's tone.

Crap! Spence wanted to kick himself. He'd stayed too long watching the kids and now looked like some sort of pervert.

"Uh, no, ma'am," he stammered nervously. Good heavens, what was wrong with him?! He should have had a ready reply. "I'm just waiting for my...wife. She went inside to inquire about your ladies' Bible study classes," he said, thinking fast and grasping the first thing that came to mind. A banner on the front lawn announced a summer Bible study starting soon. Thankfully, he'd noticed.

Spence watched a small tremor quake her body and goose bumps break out on her forearms. He'd frightened her. Damn! Well, it couldn't be helped now.

"I'll just park over there," he said, gesturing to the farthest corner of the lot, near the street and away from the playground. "Have a good day, ma'am," he added sincerely as he started the car. He'd park where he'd indicated and remain there a few minutes, until the preschoolers and their teachers went back inside or the police arrived, whichever came first. He didn't look forward to dealing with the locals, and fervently hoped he hadn't alarmed her enough to call them.

~ * ~

Spence stood inside the apartment's darkened front room and pulled the drapes apart a couple of centimeters. Peering through the narrow gap, he could just see the door to unit number six across the courtyard. The person hunting him was inside, or would be soon.

He was fortunate this conveniently located apartment was vacant. Earlier, when he'd inquired about availability, the manager was more than happy to show him the place. Leaving a rear window unlatched before the tour was concluded had provided the necessary access.

He moved to the back of the empty unit, extracted his phone, and punched in a preprogrammed number. Maybe Jefferson had a description to go with the address. He was tired of playing cat and mouse, especially after the near disaster at the church this afternoon.

"Jefferson here."

"It's Spence. Listen, I was hoping you had more information. Who am I looking for?"

"Let me take a look." Jefferson punched a few keys on his computer. "Would a name help?"

"A physical description would be better, but I'll take whatever you've got," Spence replied.

"The guy's name is Jordan Gray. I found a few local listings under that name and a whole lot more using the first initial only. If you want me to narrow it down, it'll take longer. I might have a photo in thirty minutes."

"Fire it off to this number as soon as you can," Spence said.

"Will do," Jefferson replied. "And Spence – watch your back."

Spence returned to the window. A light was on inside the apartment now. Damn! He'd missed them! He must be getting rusty. Spence remained at his post, noting the comings and goings of the people who lived in the complex. An elderly couple carried several bags of groceries between a green sedan parked on the street and an upstairs apartment. A heavy-set woman left the unit next door, walking a small, leashed dog. A young man came, stayed briefly, and then left with an attractive girl on his arm. Date night, Spence figured. Twenty minutes later, he watched a skinny teenaged boy enter the small gate at the front of the courtyard. It was at least seventy-five degrees outside, yet the kid wore a heavy hooded sweatshirt and oversized sagging jeans. He exuded attitude. Spence chuckled, wondering if the boy was sweating under the ridiculous outfit.

Dumbfounded, Spence could only gape mutely when the kid opened the door to apartment six and stepped inside. What in the world? What was a kid doing involved in this? A brief vision of his last assignment, and the dozen or more teenagers moving the drugs, flashed across his mind. A connection between that case and whoever was looking for him now seemed highly unlikely, yet he couldn't discount it completely. Loud voices drew his attention back to the apartment across the courtyard. The boy stood outside the door holding an empty laundry basket.

"I know, Jordan!" he shouted impatiently through the apartment's open door.

Well, at least that confirmed he was on the right track. Jordan Gray was inside. He continued watching. When the boy reached inside to close the door, a little girl came into view. They spoke quietly then stepped outside. The boy started walking away, the plastic basket dangling from one hand. A few seconds later, he passed in front of Spence's window, followed by the skipping girl.

Spence assumed they were headed for the laundry room which was on this side of the small complex. With two kids in the apartment, he knew he'd be smart to take a step back and think about things. He couldn't go charging in there without a warrant or a plan. At best, he'd scare the kids, the little one for sure. He had no idea what the older kid might fear. At worst, someone might get hurt. He didn't like the possible outcome of any scenario that came to mind. He needed to catch this Gray character alone. No kids, no witnesses.

Spence waited the five minutes it took for the two kids to return. The boy carried nothing this time, not even the empty laundry basket.

"But what about my jammies, Caleb?" the little girl asked as they approached Spence's hideout.

"Jordan can get them when they're dry," the boy replied. "I have homework."

"I wish I had homework," the youthful voice faded as the two kids got farther away. "Jordan says..." The little girl followed the boy inside apartment six, and the door thudded shut.

Kids and homework - what else could go wrong? How was he going to get this guy alone?

An hour passed before Jordan remembered that the laundry was still in the dryer. She didn't usually try to wash clothes on weekdays, but Ally had wet the bed last night and her sheets couldn't wait. Jordan had to run home on her lunch break and start the load. It was seven already. Where had the day gone? After tucking her niece into bed, she hurried out the door.

She stepped inside the laundry room and flipped the wall switch. The single overhead bulb flickered off and on a few times before remaining off. Heaving a sigh, Jordan grabbed the laundry basket Caleb had left on the floor and pushed it in front of the dryer. As she reached for the door, the air in the room shifted. With a sudden stab of fear, she started to turn. A large hand closed over her mouth from behind, and the fear exploded into full-blown terror.

In a one fluid, well-practiced movement, Spence stepped out of the shadows, clamped one hand firmly over the mouth of the person in front of him and the other around the chest, pinning his quarry's arms to his sides. With the weight of his hard body, he pressed the surprisingly smaller person flat against the stacked washer-dryer, kicking the laundry basket aside.

"Jordan Gray," he breathed through clenched teeth. "You found me."

Jordan's heart slammed into her chest wall; her voice screamed inside her head. She squirmed and fought, tried to kick at her attacker, terror giving her a strength she normally wouldn't possess. All of it was for nothing. A brick wall pressed her flat against the machines; a steel vise held her arms. Visions of Ally and Caleb skittered across her mind. She choked back tears, could barely breathe.

'Please, God,' the desperate voice in her head called. 'Help me! Please, help me!'

Amazed by how easily he was able to subdue the man, Spence held fast. His breathing was sharp and raspy, his adrenaline pumping hard. He sucked in a breath and, all at once, inhaled the scent of flowers. Immediately following that unexpected surprise, he became aware of the small stature and slim figure of his adversary. A woman? As the thought sliced through his mind, his grip loosened slightly, and then tightened again. He'd fought women before, not often, but it happened. Bad guys came in all shapes and sizes...and genders. A couple of fellow agents were female. Despite their smaller size and seeming fragility, he had no doubts about their ability to challenge him. However, this person was much smaller than those gals. All these thoughts raced through his mind in seconds.

The light bulb chose that moment to flicker back on, and Spence found himself squinting at the top of a head that didn't quite reach his chin. Strands of light brown hair caught in his two-day stubble. A sense of foreboding washed through him. Did he have the right person? How could he have screwed this up so badly?

"I'm not going to hurt you," he whispered in the most soothing tone his racing pulse would allow. At this point, he only hoped she wouldn't press charges. *You've really stepped in it this time, Spence!* he berated himself. He loosened his hold. "I'm letting go. Don't scream."

The gentle voice of her attacker yanked Jordan from her fervent, non-stop prayer for rescue. When she felt his arms slacken, she immediately lunged for the door. A thick bicep halted her escape.

"Let me go, please," she pleaded, turning to her captor.

At the same instant, recognition dawned on both their faces.

"Oh my God!" Jordan gasped, her voice quaking with fear. It was the man she'd caught watching her students today. *He was watching me!*

Spence stared in stunned surprise. The young woman from the church playground stared back at him, her eyes rapidly widening with shock. As her words registered in his mind, Spence watched her inhale a deep breath. Before the intended scream could escape, he clamped his hand over her mouth again.

A moment! I need just a moment to think. No police, no screaming or hysterics, please. I need to think! This was no coincidence. It couldn't be!

"Are you Jordan Gray?" Spence asked, his tone much gruffer than he'd intended.

Tears streamed from the terrified woman's eyes, and she tried to shift away from him. The toe of her slipper clad foot slammed into his shin. He didn't flinch. Her fingers wrapped around his forearm and squeezed. She fought him, and he held on.

"Dammit!" Spence growled as her nails dug into his skin. "I'm not going to harm you! Answer my question. Yes or no, are you Jordan Gray?"

Jordan was crying in earnest. She'd never been so frightened in her life. With one last heavenly plea, she nodded 'yes.'

Spence swallowed hard. Could someone else be utilizing her computer to search for him? "Do you have a computer in your home that others can access? A husband, boyfriend, anyone at all?"

Jordan shook her head 'no' then remembered Caleb. She blinked and nodded.

"Who?"

Now, she was getting annoyed. He wanted questions answered – personal questions that were absolutely none of his business. She placed her palms against his chest and shoved, nearly falling in surprise when he actually stepped away. With her mouth finally uncovered, she considered yelling for help. If the guy hadn't looked so confused and worried, she would have, but for some reason, she no longer felt threatened.

"What do you want?" she asked angrily, her voice quivering with the aftermath of the incident. "Why were you at my job today? Who are you?"

Spence stared at the irritated woman and almost laughed. She wanted to be in command now. Soaking wet, she couldn't weigh more than 120 pounds. At nearly twice that and probably eight inches taller, there was no way she was taking control without his permission. He leaned against the counter behind him, carefully positioning himself between her and the door, and folded his arms across his chest. He'd let her think she had the upper hand, for now.

"I'm looking for someone who is poking into my life," he replied coolly. That ought to send a chill down her spine. If someone was sneaking into her apartment…

"My nephew and I are the only people who use my computer," she replied huffily. "You obviously have the wrong person." She speared him with her sternest glower and made for the door.

Spence shifted to block her path. "Someone, using your computer, both at home and at your job, is plugging my name into search engines, and I damned sure want to know why!" he growled, matching her withering glare.

Jordan stared into a pair of brown eyes that seemed all too familiar, especially attached to a scowling face that she was certain she'd seen before – many times. The air in the room felt suddenly thin.

"Carl Spencer," she whispered. Without warning, her knees gave out, and she sank to the floor.

Spence watched the woman wilt before his eyes. He reached out almost too late, grasped her upper arms, and lowered her gently to the cold vinyl floor. He wasn't sure what to make of this, only that he'd found the person who was trying to find him, and she wasn't at all what he'd expected.

Thirty minutes later, Spence sat across a booth from Jordan Gray at a mostly empty Denny's restaurant. She ordered hot tea, and he ordered dinner. He hadn't had a thing to eat since this morning and was starving. 'We need to talk,' she'd muttered from the laundry room floor. Not much had been said since, but whatever it was they needed to discuss, he figured he'd handle it better on a full stomach.

Spence studied the woman – pretty was an appropriate word. He'd almost say cute if it wasn't such a pansy word. Her milk chocolate colored hair was gathered loosely in a ponytail. Tired, blue-green eyes gazed back at him, no doubt making a mutual assessment. The whites were bloodshot, and dark shadows spoke volumes. What happened tonight wasn't the only thing that wearied her.

The minute Carl Spencer's plate was set down in front of him, he attacked it with determination. Jordan suppressed a smile. His son ate with the same gusto. They also had the same rich brown eyes, the same stubborn set of the jaw, the same angry scowl. Their hair was different. Caleb's was light, almost blonde, with a hint of red and a slight wave – just like his mother's. Carl's thick hair was dark brown, and more unruly than curly. He was a good-looking man. No wonder Tanya chose him. Laugh wrinkles around his eyes were the only indication of his age. She knew he was nearly thirty-five, which put his age at twenty-one when Caleb was born. Her curious gaze moved to his broad shoulders and wide chest. He was fit, obviously worked out regularly. Except for the hair cut, or lack thereof, he still looked the part of the soldier.

Spence propped an elbow on the table, his hamburger half gone and his hunger satisfied, for the moment. He raised his eyes to Jordan's, noted her appreciative inspection, and smiled.

"Like what you see?" he asked, half joking and wondering if she'd be offended. He never used to worry over such things, just said what he wanted to say. He'd had an occasional drink tossed in his face as a result, but usually the benefit outweighed the risk. Most women preferred the direct approach.

Jordan pointedly ignored the suggestive remark as she shifted her gaze to his smug expression. She smiled, and felt a bit sorry for him. He was about to have the proverbial rug yanked out from under him, and she was the one who had to do the honors. In that sense, she felt sorry for them both – and Caleb, too. *Please, God, look out for my nephew's heart,* she prayed one last request before doing what needed to be done.

"I like that there are so many similarities," Jordan replied cryptically to his question. "That might make what I have to tell you easier."

Spence's mind worked at deciphering her riddle. Similarities to what? A past assignment? Someone he'd helped put away? His guard slid back into place taking his smile with it. Had he been fooled into thinking her harmless? For the second time today, his hand automatically moved toward his shoulder holster. He should have trusted his instincts. Something was about to go wrong.

"What do you mean, Ms. Gray?" he asked evenly.

Jordan was taken aback. She'd just watched his mood do an about face, after only one innocent comment. What did the man think she was going to do? Wondering if some photographs might help put him at ease, she reached for purse.

Quick as lightning, Spence grabbed her hand and snatched it away from her bag. "No you don't," he grunted. His accusing gaze drilled into hers.

"Ouch, let go," Jordan rasped, yanking her hand from his not too gentle grip. "What is wrong with you?" Anger mixed with tears, and she fought for control of her emotions.

"What do you have in here?" Spence asked, surprised once again by her response. He jerked open the bag and did a hasty inspection. The small purse didn't seem to contain anything dangerous.

"My wallet, my photos, my car keys!" she seethed, adding furiously, "Oh, and some feminine protection items that you might want to inspect."

Spence's teeth clamped together, his jaw hardened. She was right to be annoyed. He was acting like an ass. But still… "Why were you looking for me?"

Jordan reached for her purse, her heated glare focusing on his face, daring him to refuse. He gingerly handed it back. How did she tell him about his son? Before today, she figured she'd find him first, and then formulate a plan. Now she was left to scramble, completely unprepared.

Blanching under the man's intense stare, Jordan slowly withdrew her wallet. He never took his eyes off her hands. She flipped through the vinyl photo section until she came to the most recent school picture of Caleb. It was taken last year, seventh grade, before his parents were killed. He'd refused to have his picture taken at school this year. She gazed at the photo, tears welling in her eyes, and slid it across the table.

Spence watched her eyes fill and wondered about the reason. This whole situation was bewildering. Her emotions teetered between sadness and anger, but he hadn't detected an ounce of animosity. She didn't appear to be a threat. He shifted his attention to the photo in front of him, picking it up. The boy who looked back seemed oddly familiar. Then he remembered; he was the kid with the laundry basket. Didn't Jordan say he was her nephew?

"Should I know him?" he asked hesitantly, warning bells suddenly clanging in his head.

"No," Jordan replied. "His name is Caleb. He's my sister's son. Her name was Tanya Tanner – Tanya Gray when you met her."

Spence's brain shifted backwards. Tanya Gray. He couldn't honestly remember ever meeting anyone by that name. But then, in his youth, he'd done some crazy things, met some wild women. He glanced at the photo again, and something clicked. He didn't get a good look at Jordan's nephew, but the kid in the picture seemed...

"Caleb has his father's eyes," Jordan said softly. "I didn't know that – until today."

Realization dawned, and Spence felt a wave of anxiety sweep over him like a tsunami. Cold sweat drenched his back and underarms. Goosebumps prickled the skin over various parts of his body. Every emotion a person could feel washed through him in seconds, leaving him suddenly weak and gasping for air. Without conscious thought, he stood and headed for the door.

For a beat or two, Jordan stared in surprise at his retreating back. His muscles were bunched beneath the light jacket he wore, evidence of the shock brought on by her news. When he reached the foyer and didn't stop, she hastily fished a few bills from her wallet, tossed them on the table, and rushed after him. By the time she got to the parking lot, he was gone. The black Corolla was nowhere to be seen.

"You certainly handled that nicely," she mumbled to herself as she opened her purse and dug out her car keys.

Chapter 3

With no particular destination in mind, Spence drove around for an hour, eventually finding his way to the beach. He parked in a metered spot that faced the Pacific and sat for a long time staring through the windshield. The lights of a few boats bobbed in the distance. Moonlight shimmered and danced on the water then disappeared into the blackness near the horizon.

What he'd discovered tonight shook him to the very center of his being. *I have a son.*

Those four words had raced through his mind a thousand times since he left the restaurant. With each acknowledgment, the world as he knew it tipped, and his head spun. As the shock lessened, his emotional condition began alternating between elation and stark terror. His physical state was just as precarious. Most of the time, he felt sick to his stomach. He wished he hadn't eaten.

After a while, he got out of the car and started walking. His feet took him toward the damp sand, and his slow pace turned to a jog, and then a run. Mile after mile, he raced down the beach, until his chest heaved with the exertion, and he could barely catch his breath. Then he dragged his weary body up to the dry sand and collapsed onto his back.

He had no idea how long he lay there staring at the star-filled sky and thinking about his knew status. He was a father. If there were other things Jordan said or tried to tell him, he didn't recall. He'd have to find her later, talk some more, meet his son. The sound of waves crashing on the beach soothed his battered soul long into the night.

~ * ~

Jordan held the door leading to the playground, and her preschool students hurried outside. This was the final recess of the day. The sky had grown dark earlier, and everyone hoped the rain would hold off until school let out in another hour. Jordan followed the last kid, drawing the door closed behind her. As she automatically scanned the nearby parking lot, her surprised gaze landed on a black compact car parked in the same spot as yesterday. Caleb's father was back.

As she moved toward the fence, the driver's door opened and Spence climbed out. Her smile faltered. He wore the same clothes he'd had on yesterday, and they looked – well, slept in. Where had the man stayed last night? He watched her approach through dark sunglasses.

"Hello, Mr. Spencer," Jordan said evenly. He looked even more disheveled up close. His rumpled hair and unshaven face matched the condition of his outfit. The unexpected urge to touch him, to offer comfort, was strong.

"Ms. Gray." The greeting accompanied a brisk nod.

The clear, deep tone surprised her. She'd expected his voice to be raspy, tired sounding. "Are you okay?" she asked hesitantly.

"I'm fine," Spence replied. "When can I meet my son?"

The frank request reminded Jordan once again of just how unprepared she was for this situation. She hadn't considered that he'd want anything to do with Caleb. At times, she'd imagined just the opposite. She pictured herself having to convince him that the boy needed a father figure. Heat reddened her cheeks at the way she'd misjudged the man.

"Um, well...I think we should talk first," she stammered. "You left so quickly last night and there's a lot you don't know."

Spence studied her flushed face. Why would she be embarrassed? What could she want from him? Was this about money? And, where was the boy's mom? Numerous questions flashed through Spence's mind, but before he could ask any, thunder boomed overhead.

Jordan glanced over her shoulder, checking to be sure her class was mobilized. Sand toys and bicycles needed to be put away before the children went back inside. She returned her attention to Caleb's father. "I have to go." A rain drop chose that moment to splash across her nose. She blinked in surprise then frowned as several more landed around her.

"When and where, Ms. Gray?" Spence urged, knowing she was about to make a run for the door.

"Can you come to my apartment at two o'clock?" she asked as she pulled her windbreaker hood over her hair.

Spence nodded. "I'll be there." And she was gone, running toward the building and herding the youngsters along. He waited until she was inside then left to find a hotel and a much-needed shower.

~ * ~

Spence slowly turned the pages of the photo album, hoping to glean something about the first thirteen years of his son's life. Most major holidays were represented, including Caleb at different ages sitting on the laps of various mall Santas, hunting Easter eggs, trick or treating in costume. He slowed and studied his son at about five or six wearing a cowboy hat. Propped on Spence's mother's mantel in Abilene, Texas was an almost identical framed picture. It was the third or fourth time he'd seen himself in the boy. A paternity test wouldn't reveal anything he hadn't already figured out. This kid was his.

Before she handed him the photo album, Jordan had shown him a few pictures of Caleb's mother. He recognized her. She'd called herself Tonnie, not Tanya, and they'd had a pretty wild couple of weeks before he shipped out to parts unknown. No profound feelings surfaced. It was a fling, for both of them.

"Where is she now," Spence asked. Somehow, he knew he wasn't going to like the answer.

"She died a year and a half ago," Jordan replied, a touch of sadness in her tone. "She and her husband, John. They'd gone to the river for the weekend. Their speed boat collided with another." She stood suddenly and walk to the window, her back to him.

Spence knew she was struggling with her emotions. He didn't push, just waited until she'd restored her composure. There were more questions. After a moment, she cleared her throat and returned to the chair she'd been occupying.

"Alcohol and speed are a volatile combination," Spence said. He remembered going to the Colorado River when he was stationed at Camp Pendleton. He knew what went on there.

Jordan nodded, and then gave a soft half-laugh, half-moan. "Funny thing was, she'd given up drinking. It was the people in the other boat who were drunk." She swiped at an errant tear and looked away.

"So Caleb came to live with you and your daughter," Spence said.

Jordan started in surprise. "N-no. Ally is Tanya's daughter – Caleb's sister."

Spence added that piece to the puzzle that was his son. *The boy has a little sister, and a very young aunt.* "How old are you, Jordan?" he asked curiously.

"Twenty-six."

"So you were what, twelve or thirteen when Caleb came along?"

"Twelve," Jordan confirmed.

"How'd they end up with you?" He leaned forward, propping his elbows on his knees, and watching her. She was much too young to be raising a teenager. Why hadn't other relatives stepped up to the plate?

"I'm all they've got," she replied matter-of-factly. *Until now,* but she didn't voice that thought.

"No grandparents? No in-laws?" he asked with a hint of unbelief.

"Our mom died in a car accident when I was nine. Dad passed away seven years ago from a heart attack. Tanya was my only sibling. She and her husband, John, had known each other a little over a year, and Tanya never met any of his family. Since neither of the kids were his…" She trailed off, staring at her hands, waiting and wondering what would happen next.

While Spence looked through the album, Jordan finished folding last night's laundry and started dinner. She discretely watched the man, spotting a mixture of smiles and sorrow as he flipped through the photos. Her throat tightened, and sympathetic emotions surfaced. This wasn't easy for him.

At five o'clock, Ally came home. At Jordan's urgent request, her friend and co-worker, Deborah Olsen, had kept the little girl after school with the kids who stayed for day-care. Jordan had hoped to have the introductions over with by then, but Caleb chose this, of all nights, to exercise his strong will. By six-thirty, she was beginning to worry. What was keeping the boy?

Fifteen minutes later, he sauntered through the front door.

"Where have you been?" Jordan cried, unable to hide her irritation.

Caleb knew he was late and expected his aunt to give him crap for it. Turning on his practiced scowl, he grumbled, "I told you I was going with Trent to the library." Self-conscious of the lie, he dropped his gaze to Jordan's shoulder and hoped she wouldn't come too close and catch a whiff of the cigarette smoke that probably still clung to his sweatshirt.

"And I told you to come straight home after school," Jordan retorted, aware that he wouldn't meet her eyes and disappointed with his attitude, especially with their present audience. Though she didn't take her gaze from the boy, every nerve in her body told her that Carl Spencer was watching and listening. She crossed her arms over her chest and waited for an explanation. None came.

"I have homework," Caleb mumbled and turned away, intending to blow her off.

"We have company," Jordan said, quickly reaching for the boy's arm and stopping him.

Caleb spun around. A man stood beside the couch on the other side of the living room, staring at him. His mouth was drawn into a straight, disapproving line.

Great! Caleb thought disgustedly. Jordan finally has a date, and the guy was probably about the give him an earful. Feeling his aunt's hand gently squeeze his forearm, he turned and noticed her red-tinged cheeks. His tough mood deflated slightly. He'd embarrassed her.

"Caleb, I'd like you to meet Carl Spencer," Jordan said haltingly. Unanticipated panic rose suddenly in her chest. Her heart rate ratcheted. *How do I do this? What should I say?*

Spence walked slowly toward his son. The uncertainty in Jordan's voice skated across his mind, and he shifted his eyes to hers, holding her gaze for a long moment. She looked almost frightened. *I'll handle this,* his thoughts whispered. He cleared his throat and extended his hand.

"Hello, Caleb."

The look Mr. Spencer gave her put her instantly at ease. With utter relief, Jordan watched father and son shake hands. For a few minutes, she stood by and listened to the exchange of pleasantries, two men meeting for the first time. She nearly jumped out of her skin when Caleb asked her when dinner would be ready.

They chatted throughout the meal, Ally carrying on the majority of the conversation.

"Evan found a frog, Auntie," she said with awe. "Miss Deborah let us go on the playground when the rain stopped, and he found it in the bushes by the slide."

"Oh, that's neat," Jordan uttered, barely covering her nephew's insensitive, 'Big deal.' She shot a censoring look his way, but Caleb ignored her.

Spence listened and watched, annoyed by the boy's attitude. Jordan hadn't explained much about why she'd been looking for him, only that she felt Caleb ought to know his father. Now that he'd seen the kid in action, he suspected the open defiance and disrespect were major reasons. If he'd spoken to his mother the way his own son had to Jordan, a trip behind the woodshed with his uncle would have cured him of ever doing it again.

"Did you ever see a frog, mister?"

Spence dragged his thoughts back to the present, to the little girl asking him a question. Her wide eyes and sincere expression sent unexpected warmth diving into his heart. He smiled. "A frog? Yes, ma'am. There were frogs in abundance around the ranch where I grew up, especially after a storm. Sometimes I'd catch one and keep it in a shoe box until my mom made me let it go."

"Like a pet?" she asked eagerly.

"Yup, just like a pet," he replied. Okay, cute was the only way to describe her, sissy word or not. Blonde, bouncy curls, blue eyes, freckled nose – she looked a lot like her brother.

"Eat your spaghetti now, Ally," Jordan quietly urged. The short conversation alerted her to an area of concern she'd completely overlooked in this venture. She knew nothing about this man, other than his name and his obvious parentage of her nephew. She was on the verge of initiating further inquiry when Caleb entered the conversation.

"You lived on a ranch?" the boy asked with interest. "What was that like?"

"It was a great place to grow up," Spence replied, pleased that something had finally penetrated the sullen boy's armor. He'd barely uttered three words throughout the meal. "We rode horses, herded cattle, mucked out stalls, everything." He chuckled when the boy wrinkled his nose in understanding. "I grew up planning to be a bull rider on the rodeo circuit, before eventually joining the Marine Corps."

"Cool, a bull rider! Did you ever do that?"

With each question, Jordan watched Caleb's surly indifference morph to avid interest. She listened to Mr. Spencer tell his son about riding wild broncos in the junior rodeo, going on trail-rides, and helping at branding time.

When Caleb asked about his experiences in the military, the animated expression grew more serious. This was evidently a less carefree period of his life.

"It was during my first tour of duty that I met your mother," Spence said, grasping what he hoped would turn out to be a convenient opening in the conversation.

Caleb's mood subtly shifted to match his father's. "You knew my mom?" he asked softly.

Spence nodded. "I did."

The words hung in the air for a long moment. No one quite knew what to do next.

Jordan's attention was drawn away by Ally's soft, even breathing. She'd fallen asleep. Standing, Jordan gathered the little girl in her arms. "Caleb, why don't you and Mr. Spencer go into the living room to chat, while I put Ally to bed?" she suggested, thankful that the child had offered her a way out of this awkward situation.

Caleb looked from his aunt's odd expression to the guarded one on Mr. Spencer's face. He'd assumed the man was Jordan's friend. But why would she refer to him as 'Mr. Spencer,' and where did his mom fit? "Sure," he said with a touch of uncertainty.

Spence watched Jordan make her escape, the little girl cradled in her arms. As he carried his plate to the sink, he suppressed a smile. She'd been wise to leave this up to him. Even though she'd been the one to initiate the search, it was only fair that the difficult task of telling the boy fell to him.

Five minutes later, he sat on the sofa beside his son with no idea where to begin. Caleb saved him by asking, "Hey, why is this old photo album out?" He reached for the binder and flipped it open. The first page held a half-dozen baby pictures, all him.

"Your aunt was showing it to me," Spence replied.

Caleb flipped to the next page, then the following, effortlessly walking through the first few years of his life. "Why?" He glanced toward the man, and a strange sensation settled around them. *Who is this guy? Why is he here, looking at these old pictures of me?*

Spence knew the time had come. The boy's curiosity was quickly turning to caution. His lighthearted smile had vanished. "There's no easy way to say this, s..., uh, Caleb," he began. "Your mom and I met about fourteen years ago." He hoped the hint would lessen the shock Caleb was about to receive. Recalling his own response just the night before, he tried to prepare himself for the worst.

"That was before I was born," Caleb said evenly.

Spence nodded. "Yeah, exactly nine months," he added gently. He waited, counting slowly to ten inside his head, wishing with all his heart that he didn't have to put his son through this.

Caleb stared at a photo of himself at about three years of age, wearing a dinosaur costume and a toothy grin. *Happier times...* The stranger's words slowly penetrated. His general science class had recently finished the biology section of the textbook. Nine months was how long it took for a human baby to grow inside its mother's body. Chills raced across his skin. He turned suddenly and stared at the man beside him.

"What do you mean?" Anxiety and fear made his voice shrill.

Spence reached across the distance between them and gently grasped Caleb's forearm, just as he'd seen Jordan do earlier. An anchor, a touch to lessen the shock. There was never going to be an easy way to say the words, so he just laid them out there.

"Caleb, you're my son."

Chapter 4

Jordan returned to the living room at that moment. She stopped as Caleb jumped up from the sofa and turned toward his father. "That's impossible!" he shouted. "My father is dead."

Spence stood too. He reached for the boy, but Caleb shook him off. Without another word, he turned and bolted for the hall. A second later, his bedroom door slammed shut. The air in the room stilled, everything seemed frozen.

"Damn," Spence muttered, shoving the tense fingers of his left hand through his hair.

Jordan gazed at his face, the ache in his eyes. He was hurting and upset. "I'll go talk to him," she offered quietly.

"No, let him be," Spence said, striding across the room to block her path. He stood between her and the entrance to the hallway, facing her. "He needs time to think. He won't want to hear anything we have to say right now."

Jordan stared at his pained expression. He understood what Caleb was feeling better than she. After all, he'd suffered a similar blow just last night. She nodded, and laid a gentle hand on his arm. "Are you okay?"

Spence stared into her blue-green eyes, her open expression so filled with compassion. He couldn't remember the last time anyone was genuinely concerned about him – probably because no one except his mother ever was. The thought was not a pleasant one. He'd rarely opened up to anyone, so why would anyone open up to him?

The warmth of her hand on his arm seeped through his sleeve, and the look on her face left him feeling suddenly exposed, unable to hide from what had just occurred. Emotion pooled in his chest and thickened his throat. Without warning, he dragged her soft body against his and wrapped his arms around her, an aching groan tearing from him. He hadn't cried since he was a child, and he wouldn't now, but it took all his strength to hold the tears at bay.

It would be a grave understatement to say that Jordan was surprised by this turn of events. How was it that this strong, capable man, who seemed to be made of steel, would need or want the little bit of comfort she offered? There was desperation in his firm hold, a hunger for security. She slid her arms around him, hugging him back, holding him tight. No words were spoken, none were necessary. His world had been shaken in the past twenty-four hours. It wouldn't right itself any time soon. He and Caleb would have to navigate a path neither had ever trod before. It wouldn't be easy. She understood well, having done so herself during the last eighteen months.

Spence held tight for several long minutes. His deep breathing stayed the treacherous emotions but, at the same time, drew in her heavenly aroma. The sweet, floral fragrance of her perfume blended with the exhilarating scent of wind and rain saturating her hair. The potent mixture awakened long buried needs and sent his nerves spiraling. Letting go was suddenly not on his list of things to do today. He needed a woman to alleviate his stress, to numb the pain. His hand moved to the back of her head, catching on the band that held her hair. His fingers drew it down and off, then plunged into the silky strands.

Jordan felt the subtle change. His gentle hands stroked her spine marking trails of fire along her skin. Warm and enticing, his breath whispered across her ear. She felt herself softening beneath his touch, her thoughts growing dim. Her resolve weakened. Everything about him felt good – his strong back under her palms, the muscles rippling as his arms moved, his hard chest and warm body. It would be so easy...

Stop! Jordan's unwavering will reasserted itself, compelling her to think about what was happening. Blinking rapidly, she forced her head to clear. His need for comfort had shifted to a desire for something she couldn't and wouldn't give.

She withdrew from his embrace. Her heart pounded and her nerves thrummed. She moved away, anxious to put a few feet between them. How could she have let that happen? Her already heated skin reddened more. She didn't even know this man!

Spence groaned inwardly when she pushed away. His body burned; his soul ached. He didn't know which was worse. There was no denying she'd felt it, too. He wanted to pull her back into his arms and keep her there. An iron will, the invisible force that had saved his life on many occasions, kept him from doing so. She looked mortified! He'd been turned down before, but usually with laughter or anger, never with embarrassment. Damn! This situation was baffling on all fronts.

"I'm sorry," he mumbled. "That, uh...I didn't intend for things to get so personal." He cleared his throat and gave her a hopeful look.

Jordan dragged her gaze from the floor, where she'd been busy trying to bore a hole in which to disappear. When her eyes reached his face, she noted a repentant expression. That was good, right? "Me neither," she whispered. She couldn't let him shoulder all the blame. His embrace, after all, had felt very nice.

Her hands clasped together in front of her, trapping the remaining warmth. Something niggled at the back of her mind. His warm body, his back...as she pulled away, the fingertips of her right hand had bumped against something, a hard lump under his jacket. What was it? What was he hiding?

Spence watched the emotions on her face. Embarrassment gave way to confusion, and then alarm as her eyes widened. When she lunged toward him, he didn't step back soon enough. She grabbed his jacket front and yanked it apart.

"A gun!" she hissed, her eyes riveted on the weapon, absolute proof that she'd guessed correctly. Her stunned gaze moved to his face just as his large hands closed over hers, capturing them to his chest.

"Jordan," he began, holding her gaze. He didn't want her to run screaming from the apartment.

She tried to pull away, but he held fast. "Why? Who are you?" All the questions that she should have asked yesterday zipped across her mind. How could she be so stupid, so trusting?

Spence nodded toward the sofa. "Let's sit down."

Because he was bigger and stronger, and she really had no choice in the matter, she let him guide her across the room. As she sat down, he removed his wallet from an inside jacket pocket, opened it, and handed it to her. Jordan held the leather billfold and examined the heavy bronze badge. His photo identification faced her from the opposite side of the wallet.

"You work for the FBI?" she asked in surprise, handing the wallet back with trembling fingers.

Spence nodded. "I've been an agent for the last eight years."

"That's how you found me," Jordan stated. This felt surreal. She'd initiated a search in which she'd gotten almost nowhere, only to have the person she was hoping to find show up on her doorstep. Why hadn't that oddity registered with her before now?

"Right," he confirmed. "You started looking for me, which put me on alert. I had no idea what or who was doing the looking, so I had to come and find out."

~ * ~

The following day, Spence picked up his son and drove to a local outpatient clinic. The day before, he'd contacted the physician in charge to inquire about paternity testing. Initially, Spence was told the results would take a week. After a small cash down payment, the doctor agreed to rush the procedure, and Spence made an appointment.

During the ride to the clinic, the boy stewed silently. Other than barking an angry, "I can't believe you're going to let me go with a total stranger!" directed toward Jordan, he hadn't said a word in Spence's presence. From the stressed look on his aunt's face, Spence deduced that those weren't the first words they'd exchanged this morning.

Spence pulled into a parking slot and switched off the motor. As Caleb reached for the door handle, Spence leaned across the seat and grasped his arm.

"Caleb, I don't want to start our relationship off on a negative foot," he began calmly.

"What's that supposed to mean?" the boy replied defensively, pulling at his arm.

Spence tightened his hold, and the boy shot him an angry scowl. He matched it with a firm stare. "It means, even if I wasn't your father, I wouldn't stand by and allow you to disrespect your aunt," he said, his tone low and serious. Releasing the boy's arm, he added, "Don't do it again."

"You're not my father," Caleb muttered. He didn't care what this guy thought. He'd submit to this stupid test because Jordan insisted, and that would be the end of it.

Twenty minutes later, Spence and Caleb entered a small examination room. Caleb watched as the man shrugged out of his jacket and tossed it over the back of a chair. He stared at Spence's thickly muscled bicep and thought of his own skinny arms. Would he ever look like that? As the man turned, Caleb's gaze fell on the leather shoulder holster stretching across his back. His eyes grew wide in surprise when he realized there was a hand gun under Spence's left arm. Why did the guy carry a gun?

Spence heard the sudden intake of breath and knew Caleb had spotted the Glock. Before he could offer an explanation, the door opened and a middle-aged nurse entered.

"Hello, gentlemen," she said cheerfully. "Who's first?"

"You didn't tell me I'd have to give blood," Caleb groused as they exited a short time later. He inched down the sleeve of his thick sweatshirt, careful to lift it over the cotton ball and elastic bandage at the bend of his elbow.

Spence chuckled.

When the nurse stuck the needle in Spence's vein, the boy's face had gone white as a sheet. She'd insisted Caleb sit down for his turn, then pressed a cup of orange juice into his hand afterward.

"Don't you dare let your son leave until his coloring returns," she'd admonished Spence.

When Caleb grunted something about them not being father and son, she'd laughed. "Anyone with eyes in their head can see the resemblance, sweetie," she'd said to the boy. Then, to Spence, "You're wasting your money on this test."

Spence placed a hand on the boy's shoulder, directing him to the rental car. "How did you think they were going to do it, kid?" he asked.

"I don't know," Caleb mumbled. "Pee, I guess."

Patting the boy's back, Spence said, "I'm starving. Do you want to get some lunch?" He rounded the car and stuck the key in the lock.

Caleb studied his father over the top of the car. Could people really tell just by looking? He couldn't see any resemblance. His stomach growled loudly, and Spence laughed.

"Is that a yes?"

Caleb felt the tug of a smile and dropped his gaze. "I guess so," he muttered.

~ * ~

Late that night, Spence lay in his cold motel bed and thought about the day. It hadn't gone too badly. He and the boy had a nice discussion over lunch. He'd asked about school and found out Caleb was taking geometry.

"In eighth grade?" he'd asked, surprised. He'd had the course as a sophomore. "I didn't think they offered geometry until high school." When the boy shrugged, Spence asked how he was doing in the class.

"Okay, I guess. I'm getting a B. It's easy," he replied indifferently.

Spence's eyebrows rose at the smug statement. "If it's so easy, why aren't you getting an A?" he asked, his intention to challenge the boy into thinking about his actions.

Caleb shot a bitter look toward the man across from him. "Maybe if I'd had a dad all these years, I would!" he seethed. Tears filled his eyes, and he pushed away from the table.

Spence watched the boy stomp off to the car. Heaving a sigh, he gathered his and Caleb's trash, dumped it in the nearest can, and joined him at the car.

"I didn't know about you, Caleb," he said, once they were inside. "Your mother never contacted me."

"Then how do you know now? My mom's been dead for over a year."

Well, at least they'd surpassed the need for the paternity test to confirm things. It seemed Caleb had come to terms with the inevitable. "Your aunt initiated the search, son. Otherwise, I still wouldn't know you existed."

"Jordan found you?"

~ * ~

Spence was a little worried about the boy's reaction to the news that his aunt had been the one looking for him. When they returned to the apartment, Caleb had brushed past her almost like she wasn't there.

"How'd it go?" she'd asked.

"Fine," Caleb grunted. Then he headed to his room, shut the door, and didn't come out again. When she checked on him later, he made some excuse about having a big assignment to work on that was due Monday.

The following morning, Spence pulled into the parking lot of Jordan Gray's church for the third time in the last four days. He found a space in one of the farthest rows and parked. He was not a church going man, not since his dad skipped town when he was twelve. He'd loved attending prior to that pivotal event. Afterward, only his mom's tears and the occasional bribe could make him go. Yet here he was, preparing to attend a service. Willingly!

Jordan had invited him.

"We attend the first service at nine-thirty," she'd said unapologetically. "After losing their mom, the kids need to feel the Lord's presence now more than ever."

"I'll try," he'd fibbed. He had every intention of sleeping until at least ten. Church was the last place he wanted to be. His mother's God had abandoned him long ago and since then, Spence had managed just fine on his own.

But he'd awakened at six o'clock this morning and hadn't been able to go back to sleep. He'd tossed and turned, punched his pillow, stared at the ceiling, flipped to his back, but nothing worked. Eventually, he'd gotten up and showered, and then paced. He clicked on the television and turned it off just as fast. The certainty in Jordan's tone coupled with the sincere invitation warred with his desire to avoid all things religious. Finally, he'd given in to the compelling pull. What could it hurt? Besides, he'd like to see his son.

He walked toward the building behind the sanctuary, entered the main doors, and headed up the stairs. He looked for the room number Jordan had given him. She taught a Sunday school class prior to the regular service. He passed several classrooms, each filled to capacity with eager young students. Suppressing an internal scoff, he continued until he stood outside room 208. Children of about nine or ten years of age occupied rows of student desks. Jordan's pleasant voice drifted through the doorway.

"Who can tell me why the centurion's faith in Jesus was significant?" she asked, her tone excited and interesting. "Thomas?"

"Because he was important?" Thomas replied hesitantly.

"That's part of it. What else?" She paused then called, "Dane."

"Because he was a Roman military officer," Dane said with certainty.

"That's right. He was a commander with one hundred subordinates under him. Were the Roman's Jewish?" Jordan asked the class.

Answers of 'no' came from several people. "That's right. They hadn't grown up hearing about the Messiah, as the Jews had. In fact, the Romans and the Jews didn't even like each other. The man had no good reason to adopt a faith in Christ. The Romans were Gentiles. It was significant that this important man, this Gentile, was a believer. His faith was so strong that Jesus himself is described as being *amazed*."

Spence stood outside the room and listened to his son's aunt talk eagerly about faith, as though it were of utmost importance. *What am I doing here?* It was a valid question, one for which he had no answer. His gaze traveled down the hall toward the stairs, escape on his mind.

Jordan's words drifted through the open door. "That is the kind of faith we're called to have, the kind we'll need when dark times come, a faith that is so strong, our Lord will be amazed. Let's pray."

A bell rang somewhere in the building, and Spence stepped away from the door. A cold sweat drenched his body. He couldn't do this, not today, maybe not ever. He turned suddenly and strode to the stairs. A few minutes later, he drove away from the church, feeling like a coward.

Jordan gathered the Sunday school materials and filed them in the appropriate drawer. A feeling of urgency made her hurry. She had the strangest sensation that Caleb's father would be waiting in the hall. She'd told him where to find her but, until just now, she honestly didn't think he'd come.

She stopped in the doorway and glanced around, craning her neck to see. Her heart beat quickened when she spied a dark headed man. She was about to call out when the man turned, and she realized she'd been mistaken. The hallway slowly emptied until only a few stragglers remained. Carl Spencer was not among them. She sighed, unaccountably disappointed.

Chapter 5

Spence telephoned later in the afternoon with an invitation to take his son out to dinner.

"Can't," Caleb mumbled into the phone. "I'm leaving right now for a friend's house to work on a group science project."

Jordan listened to the excuse, guessing that it was just that. She couldn't imagine a weighty assignment being given this late in the school year. Her internal speculating was interrupted when Caleb pushed the phone into her hands.

"He wants to talk to you." He flashed a dark look before disappearing into his room.

Jordan hesitantly lifted the receiver to her ear. "Hello, Mr. Spencer."

"Hi, Jordan," he replied. "And it's Spence, please."

"I'll try to remember," Jordan promised.

"So, what do you think?" he asked. "Does he have a school project to work on?"

"I doubt it," she softly replied.

Spence heaved a ragged sigh. "That's what I figured. Do you have any suggestions?"

Jordan considered his request. He clearly wanted to get to know the boy better. She couldn't begrudge him that. "It's a school night. He's required to be home by dinnertime. Why don't you come over then?"

"That sounds fine," Spence said, adding, "I'll spring for a couple of pizzas, if that's okay with you." What kid wouldn't soften up over pizza?

"That would be nice," Jordan agreed. She hadn't gotten around to thinking about the evening meal. This crazy weekend had her head spinning. Agreeing to let him provide the food wasn't a hard decision.

Caleb sauntered out of the room, tossed a scowl in his aunt's direction, and headed for the door.

"Hold on!" Jordan blurted into the phone. Pulling it away from her face, she called to her nephew, "Caleb, please be home by 5:30."

"I was planning to eat at Drake's," he replied, as he pulled open the door.

"Not tonight," Jordan said firmly. "You need to come home for supper."

Keeping his eyes averted, Caleb asked, "Is *he* coming?"

"Yes," Jordan replied softly. She silently counted to three, waiting for his angry response. When he only nodded and walked out, she felt a mixture of relief and concern. Was that an affirmation of his decision to obey, or merely an acknowledgement that he understood her reasons for making the demand? She wouldn't know for sure until later. She raised the telephone to her ear.

"It's all set," she said, adding in an apologetic tone, "I'm really sorry about his bad attitude. It has been a problem lately."

Spence nodded. He'd already figured that much out. "Why don't I come a little early so we can talk about it," he offered. Getting some insight into Caleb's recent past would help him know the best approach to take with the boy.

A few hours later, Jordan sat in her swivel rocker across from Caleb's father explaining what she could about his son. She began by outlining the troubles he'd had at school over the past year.

"Was he a problem before his mother died?" Spence asked from his place on the sofa.

"I'm not sure," she replied. "My sister moved away for a while. I didn't see either of them for a couple of years. She'd only been back about a year before her death."

"You never witnessed him back talking his mom, or acting defiant?"

Jordan shrugged. "I was mostly Tanya's babysitter. I didn't see them together for longer than a few minutes. Caleb was usually in a good mood when he came over." She added hesitantly, "I think...he liked getting away from her." With the unflattering comment, heat infused her cheeks. She shouldn't have verbalized such a selfish observation.

Spence watched the deep blush creep up her neck and into her face. Cleary, she wasn't the type of person to make disparaging statements about another.

Feelings of regret whispered through Jordan. She should have made an effort to mend the rift between herself and Tanya. Instead, she'd immersed herself in school and ignored the problem. How could she know the effects such a decision would have on her impressionable young nephew?

"I'm sorry," Jordan blurted. "I shouldn't have said..."

Spence held up a hand. "It's okay, Jordan. I want to know everything you can tell me about my son. Your observations, however critical they might be of his mother, are important. Obviously, his home life wasn't perfect." She nodded but remained silent. It was time to change the subject. "Why were you trying to find me?"

Oh, boy. Jordan inhaled a fortifying breath and silently prayed she'd be able to articulate what she needed to say. "I'm doing this alone," she said. "Trying to raise a teenaged boy...well, it isn't easy. I don't have much to offer him, particularly when it comes to training him to be a man. My friend's husband – he's talked to Caleb a few times, even took him fishing once. It isn't enough." She looked at him, imploring him to understand that she wasn't rejecting her nephew.

"He needs a man's influence," Spence stated, reading her loud and clear.

"Yes!" Jordan exclaimed. "I'm not asking you to take him away, Mr. Spencer. However, he needs more than I can give him. I started looking for you...well, because I feared he was heading down the wrong path, and I was helpless to stop him."

"What made you think I would want to help?" Spence asked out of curiosity. "This mission of yours could have ended badly. Caleb's father could have been a lowlife creep, for all you knew."

"I had hoped to find you first, sort of look you over without your knowledge," she explained, her face growing pink again at the inference. "Sorry, that didn't come out right."

She'd already checked him out in Denny's the other night, or at least that was his impression at the time. He stretched his arms along the back of the sofa, and grinned at her discomfort. Jordan was a very attractive woman – silky hair, flawless skin; the sprinkling of freckles did nothing but add to her innocent beauty. The modest, flowered skirt and sleeveless top she wore hugged a slender figure, disguising her shape enough to intrigue any man. He wouldn't mind inspecting more of her, if that's what she wanted.

Jordan's skin flushed further under his intense scrutiny. Though discrete, she felt the feather-light touch of his gaze skimming over her. When his eyes met hers, she turned away, fearing he'd read her thoughts, discern the frightening attraction she was experiencing.

The air between them crackled with energy. Impulsively, Spence leaned forward and then stood. On the verge of closing the distance between them, he halted when she looked up. Her wide eyes were brimming with fear and uncertainty. Surprised, Spence's usual headlong determination faltered. She wouldn't welcome his advances. He turned away, feathering his fingers through his hair. *This isn't some nightclub,* he reminded himself; and Jordan Gray wasn't a woman he could avoid seeing again. His heart pounded as he stepped away and checked his watch.

Clearing a roughness from his throat, he said, "It's almost five. I probably should get that pizza ordered."

Jordan breathed a sigh of relief. "Y-yes," she agreed then hurried past him to the refrigerator where she kept a magnet for a local pizza restaurant. Without meeting his eyes, she handed it to him and escaped to her bedroom where Ally was playing with her dolls.

With a jumble of regret and relief, Spence watched her run away. It was just as well, he assured himself. He'd be smart to maintain a cordial association with her and nothing more.

Caleb returned at six, half an hour late. Jordan remained silent on the tardiness. The strained meal was accomplished with little conversation. Once again, Ally dominated the discussion at the table, talking about her Sunday school lesson.

"Jonah got swallowed up by a big fish," she said between bites of cheese pizza.

"Why did that happen?" Jordan asked. She liked to see how much Ally understood the lessons, but the discussion also filled the deafening silence in the room.

"Cuz he was naughty and didn't want to do what God said," the little girl replied matter-of-factly. "I won't ever do that. I don't want to go in a fish."

Spence listened to the exchange and couldn't help smiling. The kid was entertaining. He glanced at his son. The boy had quietly devoured four slices of pepperoni pizza but hadn't said a word.

"How's your project coming along?" Spence asked, eyebrows arched in curiosity.

When her nephew continued eating and appeared to ignore the question, Jordan nudged him under the table.

"Huh?" Caleb looked up at his aunt. She nodded toward his father, and he turned that direction.

Spence repeated the question for the distracted boy.

"Oh, yeah...fine. We, um, got a lot done," Caleb replied haltingly.

"Anything I can help with?" Spence asked. "I was a fairly decent science student in my time."

"Oh, uh...no. We're pretty much finished," Caleb said, his cheeks growing pink under the man's scrutiny.

Spence watched the color creep into the boy's face. His instincts told him the kid was lying. What was he really up to today? Jordan was right. The boy was rebellious and needed a man to take him in hand.

The rest of the meal passed quietly. While Jordan herded her niece to the bathroom for a bath, Spence and his son watched the last couple of innings of a baseball game on television. When it was finished, Caleb said he needed to shower and get ready for bed.

"I've got school tomorrow," he said, scuffing his tennis shoe on the carpet and looking away.

Spence stood and nodded, though he wasn't pleased with the apparent dismissal. The boy was being evasive. There wasn't a thirteen-year-old on the planet concerned about getting enough sleep on a school night, or any other night, for that matter.

Taking the hint, he replied, "All right, I'll say goodnight then. I'll be by tomorrow after school. You and I need to talk."

"I'll have homew..."

"I'll help you with it," Spence replied pointedly. This was going to happen whether or not the kid agreed.

"Fine," Caleb grumbled. "See you tomorrow." Without another word, he turned and disappeared around the corner. A moment later, his bedroom door thumped shut just a little harder than necessary.

Spence exhaled a pent up breath. He needed to find a way to reach the boy. Before leaving, he spoke to Jordan for a few minutes, explaining his plan to come by the following day. She agreed.

~ * ~

Jordan glanced at the clock on her nightstand. It was a few minutes before midnight and still, she couldn't sleep. She absently spun the small silver ring adorning the third finger of her left hand. It felt good, right again, after all this time. After the intimate embrace she and Caleb's father shared the other night and the odd sensations that seemed to permeate the air around them earlier, she needed the reminder.

At the tender age of fifteen, during a youth rally at her church, she made the commitment to remain pure until marriage. Dad was so proud! He'd indulged her strong faith by letting her choose any promise ring she wanted. A sterling silver, long-stemmed rose curved around her finger, its closed bud resting on top. A Bible verse was engraved on the band. For a long time, she'd worn the ring sincerely, not once regretting that promise.

Because so many people mistook the delicate ring for a wedding band, she'd stopped a few years ago. She'd never find a husband, godly or otherwise, if they all thought she was spoken for. The ring lay in her jewelry box, ignored – until yesterday. Her intense reaction to Carl Spencer had both frightened and exhilarated her. Her thrumming nerves evidenced the need to be reminded continuously of her vow.

An image of Carl Spencer drifted across her mind again, setting her pulse humming. She felt so silly, so foolish. The man was Caleb's father! Had he chosen to accept her invitation and attend church this morning, it would have been because of his son, not because he wanted to be there. That reminded her of another part of the promise she'd made on that long-ago evening. She wasn't waiting for just any man. The partner God chose for her would be a God-fearing man who would be the spiritual leader of the home they'd make together. She'd seen nothing indicating that Carl Spencer would fill such a role.

Giving up trying to sleep, Jordan pushed the covers aside, careful not to disturb the slumbering angel by her side. Ally and she shared the room, so Caleb could have his own. Except on the rare occasions when she wanted to read in bed, she didn't mind.

Jordan made her way into the hallway and stopped. The air was cold here and felt damp. A cool breeze whisked across her bare feet from the direction of Caleb's room. He must have left his window open again. Walking to his door, she quietly turned the handle and pushed into the room. Sure enough, the curtain wafted around the open window. She hurried across the room. When she pushed the curtain aside, she faced an empty space that should have been covered by the screen. Leaning through the opening, she spotted the frame propped against the outside wall of the apartment. Anxiety flushed her skin. Turning suddenly, she stared at the empty bed and groaned. He'd snuck out!

~ * ~

"Do you have any idea where he might have gone?" Spence asked, his agitation rivaling that of the woman seated on the sofa. He'd come as soon as he'd received her panicked phone call. That was two hours ago. Now that the two o'clock hour had rolled around, he was beginning to worry. At this time of the night, a boy could find nothing but trouble.

"No," she whispered anxiously. Before putting in the call to his father, she'd phoned all of Caleb's friends. They were all accounted for, and none of the parents seemed pleased to be telling her that at midnight. She'd apologized profusely.

"Obviously, you don't know all of his friends," Spence pointed out.

"Obviously," Jordan agreed. "I should have guessed he was running with a new crowd. The boys he hung out with last summer never seemed like trouble makers." Why hadn't she inquired during her visits to the school principal?

"When did you begin to notice things were getting worse?" Spence stopped pacing the room and moved to the chair opposite hers.

Jordan shrugged. "A few months ago, I guess. The last time he got in trouble at school, he was nearly expelled," she explained, angry tears near the surface.

She told him about the pocket knife, a detail she'd overlooked when they talked earlier in the day. "I begged them not to kick him out of school, promised it wouldn't happen again. They bent the rules, only because the knife never came out of his pocket during the fight."

Spence slowly nodded. She'd covered for Caleb, pleaded for mercy on the boy's behalf. That might be part of the problem. He knew from his own tumultuous youth that some lessons needed to be learned the hard way. Otherwise, they'd be repeated. A knock on the front door ended further discussion on the matter.

Jordan opened the door and froze. Shocked and suddenly weak in the knees, she stared at the police officer. The last time an officer of the law stood on her step, she'd received news of her sister's accidental death. *Please, God!* she prayed fervently. *Please, not Caleb.*

Spence felt more than saw Jordan's reaction – the sharp inhale, the heavy silence that surrounded her. "Come in, officer," he said as he gently cupped her quivering shoulders and guided her to a chair.

Straining to hear over the thundering pulse in her head, Jordan watched the scene. The officer explained that they'd picked up Caleb and two other boys after getting a call about broken shop windows. Apparently, the teens had been caught vandalizing a vacant strip mall.

"Several windows were smashed," he said gruffly. "There's been no theft but they'll probably have to pay restitution. I've got your boy in the cruiser," he added throwing a thumb over his shoulder in the general direction of the street.

"He's with you!" Jordan jumped from her chair, the color returning to her pale cheeks. "Oh, thank God! Can I see him?"

"Sure, ma'am," the officer replied.

At the same instant, Spence barked a firm, "No!"

Jordan's gaze slid from one man to the other, settling on the hard planes of Carl Spencer's face. His mouth was set in a rigid line; a pulse ticked in the taut muscle at the side of his neck. She stiffened her spine and prepared to argue. Before she could utter a word, he turned his back on her.

"I know it's a lot of work for you guys, but I want the kid booked," he said in a tone that only a fool would dare to challenge.

"What?!" Jordan all but shouted. "No, Mr. Spencer! Please...."

"Yes, Jordan," Spence said firmly, turning to face her. Then gentling his tone, he added, "It's what the boy needs, and certainly what he deserves."

"But..."

He grasped her rigid shoulders and held. "He'll be fine. It'll only be for the night, and the lesson he learns will be invaluable."

She started to pull away, angry now and weeping. Spence let her go. He spoke to the arresting officer for a few more minutes then saw the man out. He walked all the way to the curb, and made sure his son saw him. Emotion thickened in his throat as he watched the police cruiser drive away. It was the hardest thing he'd ever done, his initiation into the toughest job he'd ever have – fatherhood.

~ * ~

Caleb lay in the narrow bunk crying silently into a thin pillow. The hot tears were a caustic combination of anger and fear. Anger because they'd betrayed him. The arresting officer said that his father declined accepting responsibility for him. Declined! And, no doubt, the decision was rubber stamped by his aunt. They'd taken him home, after all, and Jordan had to be there. How could they do this to him?

"Shut up!" the kid in the bunk above mumbled.

Caleb immediately stopped breathing. He'd heard stories about juvenile hall, about the angry, violent teenagers who ended up here. What would happen to him now? Morning was only a couple of hours away. He prayed that Jordan would come get him.

~ * ~

Jordan finally slept toward morning, her anxiety spent. Before going to bed, she telephoned her supervisor's office and left a message that she'd be out today. Carol was good about stepping in when one of the preschool teachers couldn't be there. When she finally awoke, it was after ten o'clock. The sound of cartoons playing on the television drifted through her partially open door. Ally was up and fending for herself? Jordan dragged on her bathrobe. After a trip to the bathroom, she headed toward the kitchen.

Blue's Clues played on the television as she passed. Ally sat on the sofa, her favorite doll tucked at her side, and her eyes glued to the screen. The smell of perked coffee filled the apartment. Jordan was surprised to find Carl Spencer seated at her kitchen table sipping from a steaming mug. When she'd gone to bed, she'd left him dozing on her sofa. He must have stayed there all night. Ally's empty cereal bowl sat on the table across from him.

"Good morning," his deep voice boomed.

Not quite awake, Jordan mumbled, "Morning," and headed straight for the coffee pot.

Spence waited several minutes while she'd poured herself a cup, added a spoonful of sugar, and indulged in a fortifying drink. "Sit down, Jordan," he said gently. "We need to talk."

Jordan's first instinct was to tell him just what he could do with his orders. She was an adult, after all, and didn't appreciate being told what to do. Annoyance at the way he'd taken over the night before simmered in the back of her mind. No, she didn't appreciate his manhandling ways one bit! Cupping her mug between both hands, she leaned casually against the kitchen counter and speared the man with a look of irritation.

"What do we need to talk about?"

Spence nearly chuckled at her open defiance to his suggestion. She was obviously still angry about last night. He'd assumed Caleb's rebellious nature was a direct result of the Spencer family genetics. Clearly, the Gray side of the gene pool also boasted a stubborn streak. *The kid is doomed*, he thought with a faint grin.

"Is there something funny about all this?" Jordan asked sarcastically, noting his amused expression and becoming even more incensed.

"Nope, nothing at all," Spence said, clearing his throat and behaving suitably chastised. Still, he could barely conceal his mirth. "I already checked with family court. There's going to be a hearing this afternoon." Hopefully, a subject change would deflect her attention away from him.

"There wouldn't need to be a hearing if…"

He held up a hand to stop her, his jaw already tightening at the reprimand he knew was on the tip of her tongue. "It's no longer up to you, Ms. Gray, to decide what happens to my son," he reminded her firmly. When her cheeks flamed with embarrassment, Spence wanted to kick himself. His words had sounded insensitive, and that hadn't been his aim.

"So you're going to step in and take over," she said, snapping her fingers angrily, "Just like that!"

"Jordan..."

"It's *Miss* Gray, to you, Mr. Spencer!" she hissed heatedly.

Spence stood and approached her, reaching out to touch her shoulder. She shrugged away, stepping back farther into the kitchen. "I'm sorry," he said sincerely. "I didn't mean that the way it sounded." Damn, he'd really botched this. "Look, to be completely honest with you, I'm not in a position to take over, much as I'd like to. It rankles that I've missed out on my son all these years, but there's nothing to be done about that now. All we can do is start from today and move forward. And *today* doesn't look too rosy for Caleb."

Feeling completely deflated, Jordan nodded her agreement. He was right. Caleb had been a problem for over a year, nearly the entire time he'd been in her custody. The trouble he'd gotten into had grown steadily more serious with each offence, with last night's arrest being the worst, so far. If something didn't change – soon, there was no telling how much damage he'd do to his life, his future.

Spence watched her blink away tears, fight for control of her emotions. Gently, he took her arm and guided her to the dining table. They spent the next hour outlining a plan of action that they hoped would do the trick.

Chapter 6

Jordan released the latches on Ally's car seat and lifted the girl out. Ally bounded up the curb and straight for the familiar double doors to the Sunday school building, with Jordan following close behind. Though she was glad to be back at work after three days away, she wasn't looking forward to explaining the reasons for the unexpected absence. The excuse of a family emergency would satisfy most of her coworkers, but Deborah would expect more. Her friend would be concerned.

The two women had met in college and a close friendship developed during the subsequent years. Deborah was the first person Jordan called when she got word of Tanya's accident. She never would have survived that horrible period without her good friend's support. Deborah was aware that Jordan's search for Caleb's father had been successful. She knew the man had shown up, but had no knowledge of Caleb's most recent troubles. Before the end of the day, Jordan expected an inquisition that would make the Spaniards proud.

After checking in at the office, Jordan took Ally to Deborah's classroom. Her friend taught one of the classes of three-year-olds. Jordan's pupils were all four or five and starting primary school the next year. Her job was to get them ready for kindergarten. With just a few minutes remaining before the children began arriving, she took the opportunity to pray. Her head still spun from the events of the past few days.

Caleb had spent not one night in juvenile hall, but two. At Mr. Spencer's request, the hearing was rescheduled for Tuesday, giving him time to attain the results of the paternity test. They attended together, but Caleb's father did most of the talking. As soon as he was able, he presented the judge with the document verifying his relationship to Caleb. He also laid out his plan to pay for the damages Caleb had caused and then take him to Montana for the summer.

"So, you want to reward the boy with a vacation?" the judge asked incredulously.

"No, sir," Mr. Spencer replied. "I've got a friend there who owns a cattle ranch. The boy will be expected to work off his debt." He described the recent events leading up to the discovery that he had a son, adding that he hoped he and Caleb might get to know each other better over the summer.

After verifying that the plan was acceptable to Jordan, the judge agreed. Caleb would be required to work a minimum of forty hours on the ranch – the amount of community service time the judge had planned to assign. Immediate payment of restitution to the strip mall owner was required, along with a letter of apology written and signed by Caleb. The boy was given a pen and a sheet of paper, while his father wrote the check.

A very solemn Caleb was released to Jordan's custody. He barely said a word the remainder of the day. Wednesday morning, Jordan contacted Caleb's school and explained what was happening. With only two weeks left in the school year, Caleb was given permission to complete his remaining work at home and mail it to the principal. Caleb and his father flew out later that evening.

Jordan made it all the way to noon before Deborah caught up to her. Thankfully, the other two teachers were handling lunch duty with the kids today. She and Deborah took their sack lunches to a private picnic table, where she explained what had transpired during the past week.

"Wow, so Caleb's in Montana with his father," Deborah finally said after the whirlwind explanation. "That must be nice for you."

"To tell you the truth, it hasn't really sunk in yet," Jordan replied. It all felt surreal to her. Caleb and his dad had left just last night. She'd yet to recover from the anxiety of the last few days. She didn't want to think of Caleb's absence as being 'nice.' She loved her nephew dearly. She would miss him – eventually.

"What are you doing this weekend?" Deborah asked.

"Absolutely nothing," Jordan replied. She wanted only to relax and spend time with Ally. The little girl had also suffered because of this week's craziness. Jordan planned to put in some quality time playing with baby dolls and having tea parties.

"Well, when you're sufficiently recovered, Gary and I are having you over to dinner," Deborah said with a smile. "It's been a long time."

Jordan realized the truth of her friend's words. Prior to becoming Caleb and Ally's guardian, she and Deborah spent lots of time together, even double dating on occasion. Between Jordan's new responsibilities and Deborah's recent marriage to her longtime sweetheart, free time had become even scarcer. If they didn't make it a point to get together, they risked drifting apart. And Jordan really needed her friend right now.

~ * ~

Barefoot and shirtless, Spence stood on the narrow porch in the early-morning sunshine and pondered the recent events. He'd returned to Montana a week ago, a very recalcitrant Caleb at his side. The boy hadn't wanted to come, that was clear. He'd resisted vocally and physically, even shedding a few tears. His efforts, both genuine and contrived, had proven fruitless.

Spence suspected the weeping was for Jordan's benefit. He'd watched the boy turn tear dampened eyes on his aunt, begging her not to make him go. When her eyes filled with matching moisture, Spence figured she'd give in to her nephew's pleas. He'd been pleasantly surprised to the contrary.

"I'm sorry, Caleb," she'd said, holding the boy gently by the shoulders. "Your father and I are only trying to do what's best for you."

Caleb's mood instantly transformed from apologetic and solemn to angry and defiant. Fuming, he jerked out of her grip.

"He is not my father, and never will be!" he'd shouted, gesturing toward Spence standing a few feet away. Spence was poised to intervene if the boy stepped over the line with his aunt. The minute the words "I hate you!" erupted from Caleb's mouth, Spence was at his side, gripping him by the hood of his ever-present sweatshirt and hauling him to his bedroom.

"Pack!" he ordered, shoving a large duffel bag into the red-faced boy's hands. "And don't even think about going out that window again." As he turned around and exited, he tossed over his shoulder, "Leave the door open."

Jordan stood in her small living room, in the exact same spot where he'd left her. Her hands covered her face, and she was weeping. A burning sensation stabbed his heart as he went to her. He resisted the urge to pull into his arms, recalling her reaction, and his, the last time he'd done that. Emotions ran too high to risk further complications and confusion. Instead, he slipped an arm around her shoulders and gave her a light, reassuring squeeze.

"He didn't mean that," he said, rubbing her upper arm softly. "He's angry, and when a boy's angry, sometimes he lashes out where he knows his words will do the most damage." *Where were these words of wisdom coming from?* Spence wondered. He wasn't known for being either sensitive or eloquent.

She nodded and took a few deep breaths, slowly bringing her emotions under control. "He's been through so much," she whispered brokenly, leaning heavily against Spence's side. "When Dad died, he was devastated...we both were. I was nineteen and Caleb was only six. Dad was our rock, the only stability we'd ever known. We mourned together. Then, Tanya and John – Caleb was only just beginning to get to know his step-dad. That marked the first time in his short life that Tanya had ever brought a decent guy around him. It's just so unfair!"

Spence digested these few hints into the upbringing his boy had received...or endured. Was his mother as bad as it sounded, exposing her young son to unsavory boyfriends? Was a long-dead grandfather the only man to provide the child with a positive male influence? Clearly, the boy liked and missed his step-father. That explained the crack about his father being dead.

Spence felt a jab of jealousy. What if he'd been around all these years? Would he have been there for the kid, teaching him how to be a man, coaching his Little League games? A part of him wanted very much to say 'yes.' However, in all honesty, he couldn't imagine the wild young man he'd been settled down or caring enough about anyone else to make that sort of sacrifice. A feeling of self-disgust left a bitter taste in his mouth.

Spence returned to the cabin, switching off the generator on his way past. The loud rumble slowly subsided. His laptop battery should be fully charged by now. He moved to the electric coffee pot, which had also benefited from the power source, and filled a large mug, taking a long swallow of the hot brew.

Spence smiled, remembering Caleb's initial reaction to the rustic cabin. Apparently, the boy had been looking forward to lounging in front of the television while his handheld video game console recharged. When he walked inside and discovered that neither wish was about to be granted, he'd been livid, turning accusatory eyes on Spence.

"You did this on purpose," he'd seethed.

"Yes, I did — two months ago," Spence replied unperturbed. "I chose this place intentionally, to get away from the rat race, the noise, the garbage. I needed a break from all that, and it appears you're going to get one, too."

Caleb's face had reddened; his shoulders tensed. He spun around and, without thinking, hurled his video game against the log wall. The device hit hard. Plastic shards flew in every direction, the main part dropping to the wood plank floor with a thud.

When the boy uttered a curse word followed by an exclamation point, Spence decided to let it slide. Caleb had learned another important lesson today, not his first and certainly not his last. There'd be time later to deal with his foul mouth.

"Do you have to run that thing every morning," Caleb grumbled from behind Spence, dragging the man's mind back to the here and now.

Spence turned in time to see the boy yank the sleeping bag over his head. "Time to get up anyway, lazybones," he said with a chuckle.

"Go away," Caleb mumbled through the thick covers.

"All right. Guess I'll go shooting without you," Spence said, hoping the manly pursuit might pique his son's curiosity.

The covers flipped open and the boy sat up straight, smacking his head on the plywood above him. He slept on the bottom of the narrow built-in bunk unit.

"Ouch!" he grumbled, rubbing his scalp.

"Seems like after a week, you'd remember that was there," Spence pointed out with amusement.

"Yeah, you'd think," Caleb agreed. "We're going shooting?"

Spence noted the eager glint in the boy's eyes just before his customary indifferent expression returned. He figured the kid was working hard at maintaining the aloof act. He took another swig of his coffee and smiled. "I'm going out for a little target practice in fifteen minutes. Whether there is a 'we' or not depends on how motivated you are to join me."

An hour later, after hiking into the hills behind the cabin to a clearing Spence found a few weeks ago, he was teaching the boy the proper way to handle and shoot a 22-caliber rifle. During the trek in, they'd gone over safety until Caleb could recite everything back verbatim. Spence wouldn't take any chances. If the kid was going to handle a gun, he was going to learn to respect it first.

"A gun is not a toy and should not be treated as one. Never point a weapon at anything or anyone you don't intend to use it on," he warned. That opened the door to numerous questions, some of which Spence was reluctant to answer.

"Have you ever shot anyone?" Caleb asked.

This wasn't the first time they'd discussed Spence's job. Last week, as their airplane coasted toward the terminal in Bozeman, Montana, Caleb's MP3 battery had blessedly run out of juice. With nothing else to do, the boy was forced to communicate. While collecting their bags from the luggage carousel, he'd asked why Spence carried a concealed weapon, a long-overdue inquiry considering he'd seen the gun for the first time several days previously.

"I'm an FBI agent," Spence had matter-of-factly replied, grabbing his duffel and slinging it over his shoulder.

"Yeah, right!" Caleb retorted sarcastically, hurrying to match his father's long strides as he pushed through the double doors and made his way across the parking lot.

Spence stopped beside a sleek, black Porche and pressed a button on the key fob. The alarm beeped twice indicating it was disengaged, and the trunk popped open. Spence tossed his bag inside and held the lid for Caleb to do the same. When he turned to look at the boy, the expression of surprise made him almost want to laugh.

"This is your car?"

Spence nodded. "Yeah, I got it at a government auction. We FBI agents get first crack at the best stuff," he said, patting the boy on the shoulder and giving him a push toward the passenger door. "It was confiscated in a narcotics bust. The former owner is doing twenty to life in a maximum security federal prison for dealing drugs to high school kids," he explained as he climbed behind the wheel.

Caleb had stared at him for a long moment but said nothing. Spence figured, like himself, the boy needed time to adjust to each new piece of information thrown his way.

Now, a week later, he wanted to know if Spence had ever shot anyone.

"I've had to use my weapon many times," he replied solemnly.

"Did you ever kill anyone?"

Spence inhaled a deep breath and nodded.

"More than one person?"

"Enough, Caleb," Spence replied in a quiet, firm tone. "It's never easy to take a life, even when the person is one of the bad guys."

After thirty minutes of target practice, they found a shady tree and sat down. Spence dug around in his backpack. He tossed a prepackaged Danish to his son, followed by a carton of orange juice. For himself, he unscrewed the lid from a thermos and poured black coffee into its plastic cup, then tore open the cellophane wrap of his Danish. They ate in silence for several minutes.

"What happened to your shoulder," Caleb asked. He'd seen the ugly scar for the first time this morning. He'd also watched his father shoot his handgun. When Spence used his right hand, his left always supported the arm just above the elbow. He also shot using his left hand, but not with the same accuracy. "Did you get shot?"

Spence nodded, unexpected emotions slicing through him at the memory. "Yeah, we were doing what should have been a routine bust. Things went south."

Caleb watched the anguish drift across the man's face. Spence was the toughest person he'd ever met, even tougher than that mean guy his mom dated before

Ally was born. Whatever happened must have been pretty bad to make him look so tormented.

~ * ~

Jordan parked along the curb in front of Deborah's 'new' forty-year-old house and opened her door. She smiled at the sight of her friend's prolific flower beds. Colorful marigolds and snapdragons lined the cement walkway, and several attractive shrubs stood guard on either side of the front door. The new additions did wonders for the previously drab front yard. The lawn Gary had planted was coming in nicely, as well.

They'd only made the major purchase a couple of months ago. Nearly every penny they earned went toward the mortgage. Needless to say, the luxury of dining out was now a fading memory. Instead, they entertained at home. Jordan had managed to put off her friend an entire week and a half. Before finally relenting, she'd warned Deborah that Ally would be coming with her. Her budget was tight too, and hiring a babysitter was simply out of the question.

"That is no problem at all," Deborah had assured her. "Kiera will be here Friday night to help." Gary's daughter from his first marriage was nine and loved playing with Ally. The shared custody arrangement meant she was with her dad every other week.

With a warm hug, Deborah ushered them inside her cozy home, then took Jordan's purse and sweater, hanging them on a rack behind the front door. When deep voices filtered from the living room, Jordan eyed her friend suspiciously. Why did it sound like Gary was talking with another man? The appearance of Kiera saved Deborah from answering the silent question.

"Hi, Ally, do you want to come play in my room?" the girl asked excitedly. "I have a new little pet shop toy."

Nodding eagerly, Ally tugged at Jordan's hand. "Can I?"

"May I, please," Jordan corrected, emphasizing the last word.

"May I, please," the little girl repeated impatiently.

"Yes, you may," Jordan replied, giving her niece a quick kiss on the forehead before she scampered off.

The girls dashed down the hall and before Jordan could reclaim her earlier thought, Deborah guided her into the living room. Gary sat in his recliner talking to another man who was seated on the couch. Both men looked up and then stood as the ladies entered. Gary came forward and drew Jordan into a friendly embrace.

When he stepped back, he turned to his friend and said, "Jordan, this is Chris Oliver. Chris – Jordan Gray, one of my wife's dearest friends."

Jordan pasted on a smile and extended her hand to the stranger. "I'm pleased to meet you, Mr. Oliver," she said, then glanced over her shoulder at her friend. Deborah stood back with a satisfied expression on her face.

"It's Chris, if you don't mind," he replied, taking her hand.

"Chris then," she said. "And I'm Jordan."

He held her hand for a long moment before reluctantly letting go. His smile was genuine, not at all like Jordan's forced, uncertain one. He'd known about this set-up beforehand.

"Gary, come help me in the kitchen," Deborah said, reaching for her husband's hand. "You don't mind keeping Chris entertained for a few minutes, do you, Jordan? Dinner will be ready shortly."

Turning her back to Chris, Jordan shot daggers at her friend. As she pulled her husband toward the kitchen,

Deborah had the good grace to look sheepish. Jordan inhaled a deep breath, mentally preparing to make small talk. A throat clearing behind her brought her back around.

Chris Oliver smiled. "I gather you didn't know about this."

Jordan's face flushed in embarrassment. "Is it that obvious?" she replied with a sigh.

"I'm afraid so," he said, waving to the sofa. "Well, we're both here now. Why don't we make the best of it?" he suggested. "I've been told I'm not bad company."

With her pink tinged face brightening even more, Jordan nodded. "Okay, and I'm sorry if I made you feel unwelcome. It's just...well..."

"You don't like blind dates?" he said, chuckling.

Jordan laughed with him, and the ice was broken. He was friendly and personable, putting her instantly at ease. They chatted about their jobs and interests. Like Gary, Chris was an engineer working for the same large aeronautics firm. Jordan learned that he was thirty years old, hailed from San Diego, and liked surfing and anything else related to the beach.

Not for the first time, Jordan wished she had interesting things to share about herself. Most men weren't impressed with her preschool teaching job, and it had been so long since she'd had time to pursue any hobbies, she could hardly remember what she enjoyed. The kids were usually a favorite subject, but she refrained from dwelling on them. She mentioned her sister's death and that Ally was now hers to raise but left Caleb for another time. Though she wouldn't lie, neither did she feel full disclosure was warranted at this point. She hadn't been on a real date since Ally and Caleb became her legal charges. There was no point in squashing her chances prematurely.

"Isn't he gorgeous?" Deborah asked in a quiet tone as she and Jordan cleaned up the supper dishes later. The men had retreated to the back patio with beers. Their deep voices could be heard through the door off the kitchen.
"You're not supposed to notice such things, *Mrs. Olsen*," Jordan teased her still newly-wed friend. "And I don't appreciate the underhanded way you set me up!" Though her earlier annoyance had all but disappeared, she wasn't about to let her friend off the hook so easily.
"Oh, you're not still mad!" Deborah exclaimed in a whisper. "I can tell you like him. Besides, if I'd told you ahead of time, you wouldn't have come."
Probably not, Jordan conceded silently. Deborah was right. With his pale-blonde hair and blue eyes, Chris was a good-looking guy in a boyishly cute sort of way. He was not exceptionally tall, only a few inches above Jordan's five and a half foot height, but what a nice body! His shoulders were broad, his chest and stomach firm beneath his light-blue golf shirt. He obviously kept in shape. His manners were impeccable. When he offered his arm to escort Jordan into the dining room, she felt like she'd stepped into an old-time movie. When Jordan introduced Ally, he'd smiled and joked with the little girl, even making her giggle.
"I met him at Gary's company picnic last month and when I found out he was single, I immediately thought of you," Deborah explained, as she set the last glass in the dishwasher and closed the door. She turned and reached for Jordan's hands, suddenly serious. "When he asks you

out, do yourself a favor and accept," she urged. "You need a nice guy like Chris."

Jordan chewed her lower lip and nodded. There was still much she didn't know about him. Important things, like if and where he went to church. Caleb hadn't come up either. One or two dates should sort it out, she reasoned.

~ * ~

Spence brought Caleb to the Summers Ranch a few days each week. Working on the ranch served several purposes. Spence helped out his friend in order to stay in shape and repay Jack for the use of the cabin. The four hundred dollars in restitution Spence forked over for his son's share of the vandalism was the other reason for the workdays.

"How're things going?" Jack asked, hoisting the heavy hay bale onto the tailgate of his beat up Ford truck.

With a grunt, Spence grabbed the bale and dragged it farther into the bed, then turned back for the next. "Not too bad," he replied, surprised to realize he meant the words. "I took him shooting, like you suggested. The kid loved it."

"I thought he might." Jack grinned, recalling the first time he'd taken his nephew out. Jeremy and Caleb were the same age. Naturally, they'd like doing similar things.

The men finished loading the truck and Jack whistled for the teenagers. A few minutes later, Jeremy emerged from the barn followed closely behind by Caleb. They'd been assigned the job of mucking out the horses' stalls, a skill Caleb wasn't too thrilled to learn. Jeremy was given the task of teaching his new friend.

Jeremy strode quickly to the truck and jumped into the bed. The baggy jeans Caleb still insisted on wearing slowed him down and made climbing onto the tailgate a comical and cumbersome task. A snicker from Jeremy earned a dirty look from Caleb. The boys found comfortable seats on the bales of hay for the ride.

A couple of hours later, after depositing their load at various feeding sites on the range, the four hungry men returned to the homestead. Delicious aromas met them at the back porch. They quickly shed their mud encrusted boots and sneakers, leaving them outside. In the utility room, they took extra care to wash away the grime of the day.

Spence stepped into the dining room in time to see Jack planting a kiss on the back of his wife's neck. With an adoring smile, Elizabeth pushed a large serving dish into her husband's waiting hands. Spence grinned and shook his head incredulously. Nearly fifteen years ago, Jack was one of the toughest Marine commanders Spence had ever known. He was still tough, Spence realized, but marriage to a good woman had revealed his softer side.

A few minutes later, seated at the Summers' long, dining room table, Spence was surprised once again at the changes in his friend. Jack held the hand of his wife on his left and his two-year-old daughter on his right. Each person at the table reached for the hands of those on either side of them, and Jack led his family and friends in grace. Spence bowed his head and listened as the man asked a blessing on the meal and included a few special words for the 'guests with whom we are privileged to share our table.' Spence realized it was himself and Caleb Jack was talking about and experienced a twinge of humility. Though he'd sat through grace many times, never before had anyone verbally prayed for him.

A vision of his mother's face slid across his mind. No doubt she'd often brought up his name with God over the years. In fact, many times when he was young, he recalled watching her raise closed eyes heavenward in exasperated petitions. He'd often wondered if she was asking to be rescued or begging the Almighty to smite him. A grin tugged his lips. As a newly minted father for only the past two weeks, he was beginning to understand. How had she managed it? Caleb was a copy of himself in many ways.

After dinner, the kids took themselves off to other pursuits. Jeremy and Caleb were upstairs playing video games. After being shooed from Jeremy's room, Jack's niece, Emily, was entertaining the two youngest children in the downstairs playroom. Youthful voices, mixed with the music from a kids' movie, filtered down the hall.

"So, what do you think of fatherhood, Spence?" Elizabeth asked as she set a mug of coffee on the end table beside him. Jack had filled her in on the latest developments.

Spence rolled his eyes. "It makes me realize I owe my mom an apology," he replied humorously.

Jack's robust laughter filled the room. "I can only imagine!" he exclaimed, recalling the younger man during their military days. How many times had the MPs thrown Spence into the brig for being a general pain in the rear?

"They are a handful," Elizabeth agreed, sipping her tea. "If you recall, our initiation into parenthood wasn't much different from yours."

Spence remembered. Jack's brother and his wife were murdered five years ago, leaving their two children orphans. Jack married Elizabeth, a virtual stranger and the best friend of his brother's wife, in order to keep the kids together. Now, their niece and nephew were well adjusted, and the marriage was filled with love and affection. They'd even added two children of their own to the mix.

"I just wish it hadn't begun in his teenage years," Spence commented earnestly. "Caleb is so cynical and angry, much like I was at his age. I doubt he was like that as a youngster."

"Parenting isn't for wimps," Jack agreed, adding, "Especially with teenagers."

"God knows what we need and gives it to us when we need it," Elizabeth's soft voice intoned. "Right now, the boy needs you. Perhaps the Lord knows that you need him, too."

Spence lay awake later, considering his friends' wise words. Jack's assessment was totally accurate. This job wasn't meant for the faint of heart. He wondered how Jordan Gray had managed it for the last year and a half, being thrust into motherhood without warning or preparation. Spence pushed Elizabeth's observations to the back of his mind. Right now, he couldn't face a God who would allow such things to happen. In some ways, he agreed that the kid needed him. However, him needing the kid – that just didn't make any sense at all.

Chapter 7

Jordan retrieved her mail from the community boxes at the entrance to the complex and headed toward the apartment. Ally followed, skipping in the carefree fashion of the young. Juggling her purse and two grocery sacks, Jordan managed to get the door open. She set everything on the kitchen table and dropped to the nearest chair.

"Can I watch TV, Auntie?" Ally asked.

"For a little while, sweetheart," Jordan replied distractedly, as she sifted through the mail.

She set aside the grocery flyers, tossed several credit card offers for which she'd never qualify into a pile to be shredded later, and tucked the electric bill in the wooden rack hanging near the phone. Her hand stilled over the last item – the Social Security check. She heaved a worried sigh. What would she do when these quit coming? Money was tight, even with the supplement. When the government eventually learned that Caleb's biological father had been located, they'd probably cease sending the checks. Since Caleb was no longer an indigent orphan, the money would have to be stopped. And precious Ally – no funds would come on her behalf.

Jordan's thoughts drifted back to the time of her sister's accident. She'd been babysitting the kids while Tanya and John were at the river. They'd gone to Laughlin to celebrate their first anniversary with gambling and watersports. When they departed, they still weren't sure at which Nevada hotspot they'd end up. How many times had Jordan wished they'd chosen Vegas instead?

Setting the mail aside, Jordan focused her attention on preparing supper. Meals were simple fare since Caleb left with his father. Ally was easy to please, and Jordan was rarely excited about cooking for only two.

She still worried about her nephew. He'd been so angry! Even now, nearly two weeks later, memories of the hurt expression in his eyes haunted her. Would he ever forgive her? Daily, she had to remind herself how difficult he'd become. She'd begun looking for his father because she feared the poor decisions Caleb was making would continue to escalate. His arrest confirmed that her concerns were not ill-founded.

Thank God Carl Spencer was in the picture by then. While she'd stood frozen and mute, he'd stepped right in and taken over. She hadn't been too thrilled at the time but now realized what a blessing the man had been.

Caleb had called twice since he left. The conversations were short and offered little insight into his time with his father. Jordan gleaned that Mr. Spencer was making sure Caleb worked off his debt. That was good. He mentioned cleaning horse stalls and hauling hay at the ranch of his father's friend. Most of her questions were met with one word answers or indifference.

The one high point was when he spoke to Ally. While the little girl brought her brother up to date on all the important details of her daily life, Jordan listened discretely, pleased when Ally's chatter paused to let her brother speak. Whatever he said made her smile and laugh, and for that, Jordan was grateful. At least he was tempering his sullen attitude around his sensitive little sister.

~ * ~

"You ever ride a horse before?" Jeremy asked, while demonstrating the proper technique for oiling a saddle. The dull leather immediately began to shine as he smoothed a soft cloth over its surface.

Caleb recalled his one and only time in the saddle. When he was five years old, he'd ridden a pony around a circle at the county fair. His grandpa had walked alongside the animal, his comforting hand resting on Caleb's thigh. Caleb almost laughed, wondering if Jeremy would be impressed.

"No, not really," he finally replied. He took the greasy rag Jeremy held out and started rubbing it on the worn saddle in front of him.

"You want to learn?"

Caleb shrugged indifferently, but inside his heart beat faster. He'd seen several of the ranch hands ride in after checking the herd. For the most part, they looked like real, old west cowboys. He liked the creaking sound of the leather when they climbed down, the smell of wind and sweat from the horses, the scuffed cowboy boots and tall hats. But he wasn't about to tell this country boy any of that.

"I guess it couldn't hurt to know how," he replied. "I probably won't ever do it again after I go home. More likely to be riding a surf board than a horse in California," he added, a touch of boastfulness in his tone.

Jeremy grinned. "That sounds pretty cool. Maybe I'll talk Uncle Jack into coming to visit your dad; and you can teach me how to surf."

Caleb blinked in surprise. "What? Oh, wait, I don't live with him." He still couldn't quite figure out what to call his father. 'Dad' didn't feel right, but neither did 'Carl' or 'Spence.'

"Who do you live with?" Jeremy asked curiously. Uncle Jack had told him that Caleb's mother was dead. He also heard that Caleb and Spence had only recently learned about each other. He figured Caleb had jumped at the chance to be with his father.

"Me and my little sister live with my aunt," Caleb explained. "We're orphans."

"Well, now you got Spence," Jeremy commented cheerfully. "That's pretty cool."

Caleb stared at the boy for a long moment, unexpected annoyance rising in his chest. "It ain't cool at all," he replied heatedly.

Jeremy shrugged, surprised at the other boy's sudden ire. "I think it is," he replied, memories of his own beloved father flashing across his mind.

"My mom's dead! Then, *he* suddenly appears out of nowhere." His eyes flashed with anger. He threw down the polishing rag and stomped a few feet away. "What do you know?" Caleb growled. "You live on this nice ranch, with a perfect family!"

Jeremy stared at Caleb's back. At only thirteen, he understood better than most adults what his friend was going through. Caleb's hurt was deep. He was angry and bitter. Jeremy remembered struggling with the same emotions, though at a younger age.

"I didn't always live here," he said quietly. "My sister and I came to live with Uncle Jack and Aunt Elizabeth after our parents died. That was five years ago."

The words seeped into Caleb's churning thoughts. He turned surprised eyes on his new friend. "How'd they die?" he asked hesitantly.

"Plane crash," Jeremy said, swallowing the thickness in his throat. He didn't want to cry in front of this kid. "Y-you're lucky you have Spence. I'd give anything to have just one more day with my dad," he added tightly, swiping at his damp eyes.

"Oh," was all Caleb could manage. He watched as Jeremy struggled with tears and turned away. They had more in common than he realized.

~ * ~

Two days after the revealing conversation with Jeremy Summers, Caleb finally worked up the nerve to ask, "Can you teach me to ride a horse?"

Spence nearly missed the softly spoken question. He and Caleb sat in a booth at the Bread Basket Café, enjoying cheeseburger dinners with a chocolate shake for Caleb and a glass of lemonade for Spence. The boy hadn't said two words on the drive into town, or uttered more than his menu selection since sitting down. Spence glanced up in surprise.

"Sure, I'd be glad to," he replied. A pink blush skated up Caleb's neck, alerting Spence to his son's discomfort. This was the first time he'd asked for anything that wasn't an absolute necessity. Spence suspected, in order to make the request, the boy was forced to push aside a huge chunk of stubborn pride. "I'm sure we can borrow a couple of horses and saddles from the ranch."

As they headed toward the car later, Spence noted his son's awkward gait and suppressed a chuckle. Without ever having been on a horse, the boy had already mastered the bowlegged, cowboy swagger. The oversized waistband of Caleb's pants was cinched with a belt around his narrow middle, and the crotch hung nearly to his knees. The getup would never do.

Spence drove down Main Street and stopped a few minutes later, much to his son's surprise.

Caleb glanced through the windshield. They'd parked in front of a men's clothing store. "What are you doing?" he asked suspiciously.

"I need a hat," Spence replied casually. "Come on."

Once inside, Caleb realized the shop carried mostly western wear. He affected an uninterested air and glanced around. Spence had walked over to the cowboy hats and was examining the broad selection of headgear. Caleb's eyes roamed to the back wall where an enormous collection of cowboy boots was displayed. He wandered in that direction.

While looking over the hats, Spence kept a subtle eye on his son. After several minutes passed, he joined the boy. Caleb's interested gaze bounced between a stylish black boot and a more traditional two-toned brown. Both boasted a basic, old west flavor.

The proprietor appeared at Spence's side. "Would your boy like to try on a pair?" he asked nodding in Caleb's direction.

An hour later, Caleb staggered outside, a large bag clutched in each hand. The boots were the initial draw. After he'd decided on the black pair, the store's owner suggested trousers.

"You'll never be able to mount a horse in them jeans you're wearing," the man commented.

Caleb glanced down at his unusual attire, his face reddening. "I guess not," he replied.

Two pairs of Wranglers, several plain T-shirts, and a three pack of thick socks were added to the growing pile. Caleb had drawn the line at the western style, snap front shirts the older man gamely attempted to foist on him.

Spence decided he'd like a new Stetson, so he and Caleb tried on hats for twenty minutes. After making their selections, the proprietor rang up their purchases, and Spence handed over his credit card with an internal groan. Though the total was painfully high, the undisguised happiness on his son's face more than made up for the sacrifice. Besides, he hadn't paid child support for the first thirteen years of Caleb's life. He was probably getting off cheap, he reasoned.

~ * ~

The run to the store triggered an as yet unexamined area of his son's recent existence. Spence had neglected to inquire with Jordan about her financial state. From his brief experience, he'd come to the startling conclusion that kids weren't cheap to have around. He could only imagine how hard it must have been for the boy's aunt. How much did a preschool teacher make?

In the excitement of finding out he was a father, Spence had forgotten his previous concerns regarding who might be searching for him. While he was busy getting to know his son, his colleague, Jefferson, had continued delving into Jordan Gray's background. At first, Spence considered tossing the faxed pages into the nearest shredder or campfire. Instead, he'd tucked them away.

Now, as he perused the report, his suspicions were confirmed. The woman's salary was pathetically low, barely above poverty level. In addition to her weekly paycheck, her bank records indicated another monthly deposit. Jefferson had made a notation beside the figure, 'social security benefit.' Without that extra money, he doubted she'd be able to afford both rent and groceries. He frowned at the disturbing thought.

There were several additional pages that outlined her personal history. A copy of her transcripts from Cal State Fullerton confirmed she'd earned a bachelor's degree in early childhood education a few years ago.

Feeling like a peeping Tom, Spence started to set the packet aside when something caught his eye – an Arizona birth record. Upon closer inspection, he discovered that Jordan Gray had given birth to a daughter three years ago. He stared at the papers in surprise. Jordan had said that Ally was Caleb's sister, Tanya's daughter. This paperwork told another story.

~ * ~

As her friend predicted, Chris asked Jordan out before they parted that first evening. Tentative plans were made to have dinner the following Saturday night. When Deborah heard about the date, she offered to babysit Ally, even though it was Gary's weekend without his daughter. Jordan accepted without remorse. Missing out on spending alone time with her husband was Deborah's payback for tricking her.

By Friday night, Jordan knew she wouldn't be keeping the date. Ally had not been herself all day. When Jordan checked her temperature that evening, the thermometer read ninety-nine degrees. The following afternoon, the number was a little higher. She called Chris.

"I'm terribly sorry," she apologized, hoping he'd understand. He did, even offering to pick up takeout and come to her. Jordan debated only a moment before deciding against the suggestion. Ally was fussy and needed Jordan's undivided attention. It wouldn't be fair to either of them to stretch herself so thin. The date was rescheduled for the next weekend.

Ally's fever lasted two more days then abated, leaving only a runny nose and mild cough. She returned to school on Tuesday. Chris called on Wednesday afternoon.

"How is your niece today, Jordan?" he inquired.

"She's feeling much better, thank the Lord," Jordan replied. She told him that she was back at school.

"Excellent! How about if I treat you both to pizza tonight?" Chris said, adding meaningfully, "I don't think I can wait until Saturday to see you."

Jordan smiled to herself. He sounded sincere and eager. How could she refuse?

Chris came by the apartment and took them to an old fashioned pizza parlor. The boisterous celebrating of a little league team marking the end of their season made conversation a bit challenging, but they managed.

Jordan had hoped to ask him some of those important questions for which she still needed answers. When Chris asked whether she'd like to go to the beach with him on Sunday morning, she took advantage of the opening.

"We go to church on Sunday mornings," she explained.

"Of course," Chris replied. "Gary said you attend the same church as he and Deborah. I guess I forgot. Maybe someday you could go with me on a Saturday evening," he suggested. He told her the name of the mega church where he worshiped.

Jordan's heart leapt with relief. She really liked Chris but couldn't justify a second date with a man who didn't share her faith.

"That would be nice," she said. "I usually teach Sunday school, but perhaps down the road."

She decided against telling him that the teaching schedule was on a monthly rotation, and June was her month off. In another week, July would begin, and she'd be teaching every Sunday. By the end of that month, she ought to know whether she wanted to continue seeing him, she reasoned.

~ * ~

Thursday afternoon, Jordan rushed inside to the sound of the ringing telephone. She glanced at the caller I.D. and smiled.

"Hello, Caleb!"

At the sound of her breathless words, Spence's heart did a little flip. Half wishing the joyful tone was for him, he replied, "It's Spence. How are you doing, Jordan?"

"Oh, Mr. Spencer!" Jordan exclaimed, embarrassed. Why hadn't she waited to see who was on the line? "I'm so sorry. I just assumed..." she stammered.

Spence chuckled. "Don't worry about it," he said, adding not for the first time, "And it's Spence, not Mr. Spencer. Please."

"I'm sorry," she said sheepishly. "I keep forgetting."

"No problem. Listen, there are some things we need to discuss." Spence felt a stab of worry. How was he supposed to broach a sensitive subject like money, especially when he was privy to personal information? He'd need to choose his words carefully.

Jordan's pulse instantly accelerated. She fully expected him to demand custody of Caleb. He had every right to do so, she kept telling herself. *But he lives so far away*! She'd always been close to her nephew, even prior to becoming his guardian. How was she supposed to just give him up? And what about Ally? Would they lose touch with each other?

"Jordan? Are you still there?" Spence asked worriedly. What was she thinking?

"Y-yes...yes, I'm here, Mr. Spencer," she said, forgetting that he'd asked her to call him Spence. "Sorry, I was just...distracted."

Spence sighed, relieved. "Good, that's good. Jordan, I'm going to need to get back to work at the end of the summer. I've been thinking, I don't really know what you were expecting from all this..." he trailed off, suddenly afraid she'd believe he was rejecting his son.

"I wasn't thinking anything, Mr. Spencer," Jordan replied softly. "My only hope was that Caleb might know his father."

"That's exactly what I want, too," Spence agreed. "I want to maintain a relationship with Caleb, but I really need to get back to work soon. I'm not in a position to take him with me. Not right now, at any rate. For the time being, I was hoping he could continue living with you."

Jordan's heart soared and tears banked behind her eyes. He wasn't going to take Caleb away. *Thank you, Lord,* she silently prayed. She swallowed rapidly and took several deep breaths, bringing herself under control, then suddenly realized the man was still speaking.

"...visit often. Maybe he could come to me part of the time, and I'd fly there occasionally."

"That sounds fine," Jordan eagerly agreed.

A visitation plan was a great idea. She'd be able to provide him with a list of school holidays around which they could schedule.

"I'll be sending you a monthly check, Jordan," he said briskly. "I'm sure supporting a teenager is stretching your budget thin. I was thinking..." He named a figure he knew to be substantially higher than the supplement she currently received.

Speechless, Jordan could only nod at first. She'd been fervently praying about this very situation. God knew just how dire the situation was and had answered so very quickly!

"That sounds fine," she said, relief evident in her tone.

All at once, she started babbling. Her fears and concerns about keeping the apartment, continuing to accept the Social Security money she didn't think she qualified for anymore, and Ally's relationship with her brother spilled out in a tidal wave.

Spence listened carefully, surprised and pleased that he'd been able to relieve her mind. By the time she finished talking, he could hear her sniffling and knew she was wiping away tears.

"You don't need to worry about paying for anything related to Caleb's care," he assured her. "If something comes up that isn't covered by the support I'll be sending, please let me know right away."

"Thank you, Mr. Spencer," Jordan said softly.

"Spence," he reminded her.

"Right, Spence," she repeated.

They spoke for a few more minutes. Jordan asked after Caleb and discovered that he was off riding with Spence's rancher friend, learning to be a cowboy. She laughed. When Spence mentioned that he'd finally gotten the boy out of those awful clothes, she felt nothing short of elation. How long had she fought that battle? She told him how she'd once presented new clothes to Caleb, only to have him return them to the store and buy the baggy jeans with the refunded money.

"I'm afraid he's too smart for his own good," she suggested.

"My mother used to say the same thing about me," Spence replied thoughtfully. "I've noticed that he's very good at math, another trait he probably inherited from me."

"I'm glad you two have so much in common, even if it is mostly genetics," Jordan replied. "He needs you. He may not realize it, but God surely did. Your presence in his life is an answered prayer."

After disconnecting a few minutes later, Spence dwelt on the last part of their conversation. *Imagine me – an answered prayer to anything!* The other things Jordan said were similar to Elizabeth Summers' observations a few days before. Spence had spent most of his adult life avoiding pious women. The fates must be working against him because now there were two in his life telling him things he didn't want to hear. If they weren't so lovely, kind, and thoughtful, he'd tell them where to stuff their ridiculous comments.

Chapter 8

A few days later, Spence sat on a camp chair in front of the cabin soaking up the afternoon sun and watching Caleb wander aimlessly around the yard. Hands shoved in the pockets of his jeans, the boy kicked at the occasional dirt clod and stared off into the distance, frowning. Spence opened his pocket knife and reached down to retrieve a small hunk of oak from the ground beside his chair. As he whittled, he kept a discreet eye on the boy. Caleb was obviously troubled about something. Spence stretched his legs out in front of him, crossed his ankles, and waited patiently. It didn't take long.

Caleb slowly approached, halting a few feet from the chair his father occupied. Spence stopped chipping away at the wood and looked up. "Something wrong?" he asked, careful to keep his voice even.

"No, not really," Caleb replied hesitantly. He abruptly turned away and then back again just as quickly. "Jeremy invited me to a youth group meeting," he blurted anxiously. "Can I go?"

He had no idea where this man stood on church, just that he obviously didn't go. At first, to be honest, Caleb was glad to be out of the usual Sunday ordeal. However, it felt sort of weird, not attending church. After three Sundays in a row, he realized he missed going.

A youth group meeting, Spence repeated silently. That's what has been bugging the kid? Spence gazed at his son's red face and uncertain expression. Did Caleb think he'd object?

"Sure, when and where do they meet?"

"Tonight at seven o'clock, at Jeremy's church," Caleb replied, relief in his voice. "They meet every Tuesday."

"Okay, I'll drop you off at seven." The boy remained standing in front of him, still kicking at the dirt nervously. "Something else you wanted to ask?"

"Well, the thing is...it's sort of a father-son thing," Caleb explained quietly. When his father said nothing, he continued. "They start off with the guys and the dads having separate meetings, and then they get together for the last half hour or so. I think that's how Jeremy explained it."

Spence processed his boy's words with no small amount of unease. Caleb wasn't merely in need of transportation. He was asking him to attend the meeting *with* him, more than one meeting, from the sound of it.

"Well, I'm really not the type..." Spence watched as the previously hopeful expression faded from his son's eyes. His heart twisted as the boy's customary guarded look returned.

"Yeah, that's sort of what I figured," Caleb interrupted, unable to fully hide his disappointment. "I told Jeremy not to count on me bein' there."

"Now, wait a minute," Spence said hastily, raising his hand to stop Caleb's words. "I didn't say no, just that it's...different, that's all. I'd be glad to go with you tonight and check it out." He paused and inhaled a calming breath, then added, "I suppose, if we both like it, we can give it a try." Spence's heart raced thinking of the commitment he'd just made.

A few minutes before seven, Spence pulled into the parking lot of the Friendship Christian Church and parked. He'd barely turned off the car when Caleb hopped out and shut the door. Spence did the same.

"Hey, there's Jeremy and Mr. Summers," the boy said, pointing across the lot. A small group loitered in front of the chapel.

Spence smiled at the sight of the quaint building and recalled his last time inside this church. Part of his undercover assignment five years ago involved keeping a close watch on the Summers family. That meant attending a couple of church services. He'd diligently stuck to his duties, the sermon and the music barely registering in his thoughts. Clearly, this visit would be different.

"Hello, Spence," Jack called as they approached. "Jeremy said you and Caleb might be here tonight."

The two men shook hands, and Jack introduced his friend. "This is Dan Edwards, our fearless leader," he said good-humoredly. "He monitors the men's group."

"Call me Dan. Glad to have you with us, Mr. Spencer," the tall man said, shaking hands.

"Thanks, Dan," Spence replied self-consciously. "And it's just Spence."

Jeremy introduced Caleb to Mr. Edwards' son, Jeff, and the three teenagers headed off toward a building behind the sanctuary.

The thirty minute Bible study that followed wasn't nearly as boring and uncomfortable as Spence had feared. The discussion centered on parenting and a father's role in forming his son's character. Everyone received a small pamphlet. Apparently, the study started last week and was to continue for the next four.

"We're all responsible for the examples we set," Dan summed up the discussion. "We need to do more than tell our sons how to behave. We need to show them what right behavior looks like, by treating our wives with love and respect, by moderating or avoiding alcohol, foul language, and other temptations, by being honest and forthright in dealing with everyone, even those we aren't overly fond of. Our boys are watching us; you can count on that."

Spence took notes in the section pertaining to this week's lesson, paying specific attention to the areas that concerned him. Since he wasn't married and had no immediate plans to enter into that particular form of captivity, he needn't worry himself with the marital bits. He left feeling good about the experience and was surprised to discover that he actually looked forward to the next get-together.

The second half of the evening was a sharing time in which the men and boys fellowshipped. A box at the front of the room contained slips of paper. Toward the end of the boys' half-hour Bible study, they were encouraged to write down a question or comment which would be presented when the two groups met together. In this way, the whole group could address issues with which a boy might be struggling, without a particular youth feeling singled out.

~ * ~

Ally followed the receding water a few inches only to turn back suddenly, shrieking as she ran away from the inbound surf. Seconds later, her feet were overtaken and she giggled, stomping on the bubbly white foam that surrounded her. She'd been playing this game for thirty minutes and had yet to tire. Jordan stood on the dry sand a few feet away, laughing at the girl's antics. She glanced up and smiled. Chris waved from his surfboard where he sat many yards out to sea waiting for an upsurge. The waves weren't great, but he seemed determined to catch something before giving up. She raised her hand in response.

It was the second Saturday in July, their third official date, counting the pizza parlor with Ally. Last week, Chris had taken Jordan to a nice Italian restaurant followed by a movie. They'd had a lovely time. Today's trip to the beach was somewhat last minute. They'd planned to go out Friday night, but something had come up and Chris canceled.

When he called this morning and invited her and Ally to spend the day soaking up the sun and playing in the sand, Jordan couldn't resist the tempting offer. She'd loaded a cooler with sandwiches and drinks, lathered both Ally and herself with sunscreen, grabbed her towels, and met him here. Chris had already been in the water for hours, catching the early-morning waves when they were best. The morning was overcast but not cool and by noon, the sun had burned through the clouds.

Chris body surfed into shore, bringing his board to a halt beside Ally. She squealed with delight and clapped her hands. Smiling, Chris patted her head and grabbed his board.

"How about some lunch?" he asked, stopping beside Jordan and planting a wet kiss on her cheek.

Jordan blinked in surprise and smiled. This was the first time he'd kissed her, mainly because she'd intentionally orchestrated their end of the evening goodbyes. Determined to keep the relationship on the slow track, she'd made it a point to shake his hand each time. Last week, he'd taken her hand and, instead of shaking it, brought it to his lips for a soft kiss. It was the most romantic gesture any man had ever shown her.

Not long after lunch was consumed, Chris announced that he needed to head home. With Ally beginning to doze off, the timing seemed perfect. While Jordan cleaned up the meal things and stuffed towels in her backpack, Chris helped Ally gather her sand toys and stow them in a large bucket. A few minutes later, the sleepy girl was strapped into her car seat and rapidly losing her battle to stay awake.

Jordan stood beside the car, hoping and wondering if Chris would ask to see her tonight. When he pressed a kiss to her warm cheek, she closed her eyes and leaned into him.

Chris wrapped his arms around her and whispered, "I wish I could see you later."

"Me too," Jordan replied. She waited for an explanation as to why he couldn't, but none came. Instead, he leaned back and cupped her face between his palms.

"I'll call you," he whispered and kissed her softly on the lips.

Jordan's brain had barely begun to register the light kiss, and it was over. When she opened her eyes, Chris was already striding away. She watched him for several minutes, thinking how much he reminded her of the boys she'd known in high school, with his surf board tucked beneath one arm and a towel draped across his tanned shoulders.

Smiling, she got in her car and headed home. It had been a good day.

~ * ~

Silver Springs celebrated Independence Day with an old fashioned parade and carnival by day. At dusk, the whole town moved to the high school football stadium for a professional fireworks display. The town had been doing it this way for years, and few people missed it. All the food booths were manned by local volunteers with profits going into a special fund, which paid for the event.

Jack Summers had agreed to flip patties at one of the food booths and convinced Spence to join him. Elizabeth's brother, Gage, who was also scheduled to work the hamburger and hotdog booth, arrived with his wife, Andrea, and their two youngsters. Spence greeted Andrea Nelson with a smile, remembering her from his last time in the area. How her life had changed since that time, he noted with satisfaction. He'd interviewed her in connection with a serious crime but, thankfully, she was cleared of any wrongdoing. Now, it appeared, she was happily married. Elizabeth and Andrea bade goodbye to their husbands and herded their youngsters to the kiddie rides.

"Is it okay if I hang out with Jeremy?" Caleb asked, catching his father's eye.

"Sure, go ahead," Spence replied, knowing the boy would stay out of trouble, as long as he was with his friend. When Jack pulled out his wallet and handed his son several bills, Spence did the same. "Make sure you eat something," he admonished the boy. "Don't spend it all on rides and carnival games."

"Yes, sir," Caleb replied, accepting the twenty dollars with surprise.

Caleb's mom had always been perpetually broke. If he got to ride two rides at any carnival they went to, he was lucky. His mom usually hung on to her cash for beer. Unfortunately, Jordan wasn't in any better shape financially, though she tended to be more generous. Last summer, when she took him and Ally to the Orange

County Fair, she'd purchased him a wrist band that got him on as many rides as he wanted. The tradeoff was lunchmeat sandwiches she'd brought for dinner, instead of the overpriced offerings in the food court.

"They can eat here for free," Jack pointed out. Then, to the boys, he said, "Make sure you come back before six, and we'll feed you. That's when our shift is up."

"Sure thing, Uncle Jack," Jeremy replied and the boys were gone in a flash of denim.

With Jack and Spence manning the grill, and Gage taking orders and money, the three hour shift flew. They worked nonstop and, according to Gage, likely took in enough money to cover the cost of the professional pyrotechnics display. As promised, at five minutes before six o'clock, the boys returned, bringing along Jeff Edwards. Jack prepared a half-dozen burgers and hot dogs. As Spence plated the food, several adults arrived to take their places behind the counter. The men and boys found seats in the picnic area and devoured their meals.

"What have you boys been up to?" Jack asked. He grabbed his unopened soda, popped the top, and took a long drink.

"We only had enough money for wrist bands, so we've been riding all the rides," Jeremy replied between bites of his burger.

"They have some really cool games and prizes on the midway," Caleb commented self-consciously. "There's a neat stuffed cat Ally would like."

"What do you have to do to win it?" Spence asked, honing in on his son's not so subtle hints. If the boy wanted to play some of the games, he'd indulge him. Caleb had worked hard these past three weeks and deserved a reward. Spence figured they were about even on the cost of the vandalism.

"It's a duck hunting game," Caleb replied. "You have to shoot like five, I think, to win the big prize."

"Rifle or hand gun?" Jack asked, tuning in to the conversation.

"Rifles, I think," Caleb replied, turning to his friend for confirmation.

Jeremy nodded, adding, "Yeah. They were airsoft rifles."

Elizabeth walked up then, pushing a stroller bearing her sleeping daughter. "You boys and your shooting games," she teased. Leaning toward her sister-in-law, she said, "Can you see the glazed look in their eyes?"

Jack gave his wife a playful swat on the backside and pulled his son, Matthew, onto his lap. The hungry boy immediately began finishing off his dad's hotdog.

Andrea nodded. "And I always thought those games were there for the kids," she agreed, slipping her arm across her husband's shoulders. She pushed a stroller too, though their one-year-old son, Benjamin, was far from sleepy. He was busily working his way through a cup of apple slices. Megan, their five-year-old daughter, sidled up to her daddy and reached for his bag of chips.

"Right," Gage said, slipping an arm around his little girl. "If us dads didn't play, they'd never make enough money to stay in business." Though he preferred basketball shooting over rifles, he wasn't about to let down his compatriots. Men had to stick together. He turned adoring eyes on his wife and added sweetly, "Can I have five dollars to play the games, honey?"

Everyone laughed and headed for the midway. Hawkers called loudly as they passed, trying to gain their attention and hopefully, relieve them of some of their hard earned cash. The group kept walking until they reached the shooting gallery.

Several rifles rested on a counter. At the back of the booth, a conveyor system glided rows of ducks and other targets back and forth at a fairly rapid clip. A painted sign indicated that three targets knocked down earned a small prize, four targets earned a medium prize, and five earned the largest, an oversized stuffed cat. Though not nearly as ostentatious as the big feline, the quality of the small and medium prizes, Spence noted, was actually higher.

"Six shots for five dollars!" the booth's operator called. "That's less than a dollar a shot! Come on, fellas! Win your gal a prize!"

Spence and Jack stepped up to the counter. Ignoring the man's cajoling, they each picked up a rifle and sighted down the barrel. Not surprising, every gun was designed to shoot slightly off center. If aimed directly at the target, the shot would veer to the left or right and usually miss.

Spence spoke to his son, trying to make him understand that the guns were imperfect, that it was part of the gimmick. The boy seemed determined to win a prize for his sister, so Spence helped him choose a rifle and counseled him on how to aim in order to hit the target. He handed the attendant a five dollar bill and stood back while the boy gave it a try.

His first time out, Caleb hit two of the ducks.

"That was great shooting, son!" the hawker exclaimed. "You nearly got them last two. I'll give you seven shots for a fiver if you want to try again."

Spence understood the man's angle, though he was reluctant to slap any more cash down for the rigged game. When Caleb turned away, his shoulders slumped in disappointment, Spence relented. "Give it another shot, Caleb," he said. "He's right; you almost hit four."

Caleb's face lit up, and he rushed back to Spence for the cash. Spence leaned down and whispered, "Line up your shot and hold it steady at that level. Aim a half inch to the left of the target. Take your time. There's no rush. Got that?"

Caleb nodded and went to pay the man. He did exactly as his dad said. His first shot missed, but the next two knocked over ducks. The fourth missed, the fifth landed on a bull's eye, knocking it down. With two shots left, his hands began to shake.

Spence stepped close to his son and reminded him to take his time. "Relax. You've already won a prize." He moved back and waited.

Caleb squeezed off his fifth shot and hit a duck, bumping it but not knocking it over. *That should count,* he thought, disappointed. Only one shot left. He took his time, aiming first at a duck and then a target. He pulled the trigger, and the target flopped over.

"Yes!" Jeremy yelled from behind him.

The game attendant handed him a medium size black and white stuffed cat. "I hit that other duck," Caleb said, pointed at the conveyor system.

"It don't count unless it falls, kid." The man gestured to the signs posted around his booth.

Spence put his hand on his son's shoulder. "Caleb, this cat is the perfect size for Ally." He leaned closer and whispered, "Besides, the big one looks like a piece of junk."

Spence reached up and squeezed the foot on the giant stuffed animal. The squeaky sound of Styrofoam balls rubbing again each other could be heard. Caleb looked up at his dad's serious expression then at the big prize. He was right. The gaudy stuffed animal was kind of ugly, too. Smiling, he accepted the smaller animal and gave it a slight squeeze – no squeaky noise.

"Ally's gonna like this," Caleb said as he moved off with his dad. When Spence draped an arm across his shoulders, he didn't try to shrug it off. The manly touch didn't seem to bother him this time.

Chapter 9

A wide river cut through the county, providing a much needed water source for the thousands of cattle and sheep that grazed her hills and valleys. Big Mouth bass and Rainbow trout were plentiful in its cool depths, beckoning a good many vacationers every year. One of the many branches traversed the Summers' property. After this week's youth meeting had concluded, Jeremy Summers suggested a fishing expedition at a nearby cove. Early the following morning, Caleb, Jeremy, and Jeff Edwards met at the ranch and headed eagerly toward the woods on horseback, poles and gear in hand.

With the wistful hope of a barbequed fish supper, Spence drove down the Summers' long driveway later that day to retrieve his son. As he neared the homestead, he was surprised to see a police cruiser stopped in front of the house. Had something happened? Jack and the sheriff stood on the front porch talking. Spence parked the Porche beside the official vehicle and got out.

"What's going on?" he asked as he climbed the steps.

Just then, laden with a large tray, Elizabeth appeared at the front door. Spence moved quickly to relieve her of the burden, setting it on a table between two sturdy wooden rocking chairs.

"It's just a shame," she said. "The poor woman."

While Elizabeth poured lemonade into glasses and handed them around, Spence learned that Mrs. Hill, an elderly widow, had fallen and fractured a hip.

"I'm trying to organize folks to look after her stock," Sheriff Davies explained. "Woman's got quite a menagerie out at her place." He shook his head and rolled his eyes. "She ought to have scaled back a decade ago but just keeps adding animals."

"How old is she?" Jack asked incredulously. "When I was a teenager, I remember thinking she was as old as Methuselah."

"Well, she's looked it for a long time now," the sheriff observed with a chuckle. "Fact is, back then, she probably wasn't all that much older than you are now. I think she's in her late seventies."

Jack guffawed. "Do I look that bad?" He'd recently celebrated his forty-first birthday.

Elizabeth sidled up beside him and whispered, "You look great, cowboy." Jack slipped an arm around his wife's slim waist and kissed her soundly.

Chuckling, Spence and the sheriff both cleared their throats and looked away.

Pink faced and a little self-conscious, Elizabeth asked, "Sheriff, how long do you suppose Mrs. Hill will be laid up? I've heard this type of injury takes a long time to heal."

"Don't know precisely," Davies replied, rubbing his chin thoughtfully. "I'm thinking several months easily. Once she's released from the hospital, I understand she'll remain in Bozeman at a long-term care facility."

Jack rubbed the back of his neck, frowning. "I'm not sure having folks stop by to feed the animals daily is going to be adequate," he said, adding, "Seems like they might need to be boarded elsewhere."

"Yeah, I was wondering about that, too," the sheriff agreed. "On the way here, I stopped by the place to check things out. The two horses were whinnying for attention, and their watering trough looked like it could use a good scrubbing. There're two dogs, one really old and the other much too young and rambunctious for an elderly lady to keep up with. Fact is, I had trouble matching that little fella's energy. Bird cage in the house needed cleaning and there wasn't much edible food left in their dish."

"So, two horses, two dogs, and some birds," Elizabeth commented. "That doesn't seem too bad. We might be able to take…"

"Hold up, Mrs. Summers," Davies said, raising a hand to interrupt. "That ain't all she's got. I spotted at least two barn cats, and there's that old mule she insists on keeping. Can't imagine why that ornery old thing is so important to her."

"Oh," Elizabeth muttered.

Spence listened quietly to the conversation. He was on the verge of offering to man an occasional shift, when the sheriff's radio beeped. A voice announced that he was needed at the station.

The boys returned about the same time. Grinning broadly and clearly proud of himself, Caleb held up a stringer with several fine trout attached. Dinner, Spence thought greedily, his mouth already beginning to water. Jack directed the boys to a spigot beside the barn and followed along to oversee the cleaning.

As the sheriff drove off, Elizabeth remained on the porch with Spence, but her thoughts seemed distracted. "How are things at the cabin," she finally asked.

"Fine," Spence replied. Then, with a smile, added, "The boy's not too thrilled about the bathroom facilities."

The outhouse, which Jack kept in good repair for his hunting buddies, took care of basic necessities. Spence had rigged up a solar shower for bathing purposes. The simple contraption was really just a large water-filled, vinyl bag with a tube and shower head attached. It hung from the low branch of a tree. Theoretically, the sun was supposed to heat the water inside the bag. In actuality, the temperature rarely reached lukewarm on the sunniest days. Showers tended to be fast and accomplished with little attention to detail.

"How long do you think you'll be in Silver Springs?" she inquired.

Spence glanced at her, noting her speculative expression. "Six or eight weeks probably. Caleb will be starting school about then, and I'll need to get back to work." He could almost see the wheels turning inside her pretty head. "Any particular reason you want to know."

Elizabeth smiled. "Well, it seems you might be the answer to a few yet to be uttered prayers, Spence," she replied. "Do you think you'd like a bed to sleep in and an indoor bathroom for the rest of the summer?"

Spence knew exactly what she was thinking. He wondered why it took him even that long to catch on to where the conversation was heading.

~ * ~

Two days later, he and Caleb met Sheriff Davies at the Hill homestead. Located close to town, Davies explained that in its prime, the small ranch boasted nearly a hundred acres. With the passing of her husband, twenty-odd years ago, Mrs. Hill had begun to sell off portions of the land in order to keep up the taxes and bills. The total had shrunk to just a dozen acres, including the homestead. The same branch of the river Caleb had fished earlier in the week intersected a corner of the property.

"Back in the late 1800s, Mrs. Hill's great-great grandfather, man by the name of Owens, operated a sawmill right there," explained the sheriff. "Some of the original structure still remains."

"Cool!" Caleb cried, his eyes bright with interest.

The sheriff smiled and gestured to the boy. "You can check it out sometime," he encouraged. "Just be real careful."

"Yes, sir," Caleb replied in earnest.

Spence hid his pleased smile. He made a mental note to commend Caleb for his respectful response later, when they were alone.

"Mrs. Hill's okay with this arrangement, Sheriff?" Spence asked.

"She said she trusted my judgment," Davies replied. "Told me to let you know to make yourselves at home, eat whatever you can find in her cupboards and freezer — which ain't much if her wiry figure is any indication. Woman's as thin as a rail, and looked awfully fragile lying in that hospital bed." He frowned, recalling his brief visit with the sweet old lady.

The sheriff showed them around, pointing out the various farm animals, the small garden patch in which green things were beginning to appear, and the barn and out buildings. They stopped in front of a fenced corral that held two horses and the ornery mule the sheriff had mentioned. The horses trotted over to watch the proceedings. Spence noted that neither horse was particularly young. One, black with white socks, was positively swaybacked and definitely geriatric. She *probably hasn't seen the saddle in years,* Spence thought. The other was a rust colored gelding with a white star on his forehead. The sheriff confirmed that the old mare was a longtime resident, while the gelding a fairly recent acquisition.

"I believe Mrs. Hill got Dancer through one of those rescue services a few years back," Davies offered. "I don't think he was in very good shape when she brought him home. Near dead, as I recall. Between her tender loving care and the local vet's knowledge, he bounced back. The woman just can't stand to see an animal suffer."

The old mare, who Spence learned was named Shasta, nudged his elbow. He obliged by rubbing her soft, grey-whiskered nose. The red wouldn't come near enough to be touched. Caleb would need to be warned to take care around the skittish animal. At the far side of the paddock, Buster, the mule, brayed a few times but mostly ignored the visitors.

From behind the house, they heard an intermittent labored sounding 'woof' mixed with nearly continuous barking. The dogs occupied a sizable backyard enclosed by chain-link fencing. Caleb immediately walked over and held out his hand for the dogs to sniff through the fence. Both seemed pleased to make his acquaintance. After determining that the boy wasn't a threat, the aged shepherd ambled away, heading for the shade of a large oak. The smaller dog, some sort of short-haired terrier mix, hopped around on his hind legs eagerly licking Caleb's fingers.

"What are their names?" Caleb asked, glancing over his shoulder at the sheriff.

"The big gal lounging under the tree is Lady," Davies replied. "That spastic feller is Butch. They're friendly, well loved, and current on their shots."

As the men turned toward the house, Spence noted that the half-stone, half-wood structure was on the smallish side, especially compared to Jack's rambling home. A small back stoop opened into the yard where the dogs were kept.

"The stone part at the front is the original house, built around the turn of the last century," the sheriff explained. "I believe Mr. Hill added to the back after he and the missus married. That would have been, oh…fifty or sixty years ago, I imagine."

"Gosh, does it have electricity?" Caleb blurted, dragging himself away from the fence and rejoining the men.

Spence chuckled along with the sheriff, though similar thoughts had been running through his mind. Was this going to be a better arrangement than the cabin, or just one that required more work?

"Course it does, son. The Hills upgraded regularly, from what I've been told," Davies explained. "Oh, nothing's been done recently, but it ain't ancient either."

It didn't take long for Spence and Caleb to move their few belongings into the house. They each claimed an unused bedroom upstairs, of which there were three. They both took note of the full service bathroom, and Spence wasn't the least bit surprised when the boy commandeered it immediately. When Spence dropped his duffel on the full-sized bed in his room, dust erupted from the bare mattress. He glanced around and realized a similar layer covered every surface. The rest of the upstairs appeared to be in the same condition – neither cluttered nor filthy, merely neglected.

Fortunately, the first floor had received better attention. He rambled from room to room. The cleaning wouldn't pass a white glove inspection, but it adequately met his expectations.

The living room at the front of the house held a variety of furniture, all of it old but in good repair. Six maple chairs were tucked around a matching oval table in the formal dining room. A china cabinet in one corner displayed fancy dishes and knick-knacks.

The kitchen, while not modern, was clean and well stocked with cookware and spices. Spence was pleased to note the microwave oven on one counter. Two budgies chattered from a birdcage in the corner; a bag of seed sat on a nearby shelf. After checking to be sure the birds' food and water dishes were filled, Spence headed for the opposite side of the house.

A sunroom at the rear of the house contained a prettily made up bed, a dresser, and an antique wardrobe. A quick perusal revealed ladies clothing and personal items. This was Mrs. Hill's bedroom.

The bathroom across the hall was fairly clean and recently used. The only thing out of order was the shower curtain and rod, both of which were lying haphazardly in the bathtub. Spence had been told that Mrs. Hill's accident occurred in this room. She must have grabbed the curtain during her fall. He picked up and secured the rod in its brackets. Empty spaces in the medicine cabinet indicated that some things had been removed. A Good Samaritan must have been in to pack a few basics for the recuperating woman.

"Tell me about your mom?" Spence asked later that evening. They'd finished supper hours ago and now sat at the kitchen table enjoying a late night snack.

Caleb glanced up from the apple pie he was in the middle of inhaling. "What do you want to know?" he asked indifferently.

"Whatever you feel like telling me, I guess," Spence replied, shrugging. "Was she a good mother?"

Caleb responded with a shrug of his own. "I guess so," he said. "As good as she knew how, I suppose."

Spence gazed at the boy's bent head. "What do you mean?" he asked softly.

Caleb set down the fork, several bites of pie still uneaten, and slowly pushed the plate away. Cleary, the territory they were approaching was sensitive.

"I don't know exactly," he said, his tone low. "I guess...well, it's just that, since I've been living with Jordan, seeing what kind of mom she is to Ally, I've come to realize my mom wasn't all that...motherly." He looked up at his dad, wondering how much he should share.

"So, Jordan's a better mom to Ally, than your mom was to her." he clarified.

"No, Jordan's a better mom to both of us. I know my mom loved me. But she didn't, you know, pay attention to me. Jordan does stuff my mom never even thought of doing, like checking my homework and helping with school projects. I remember once wanting to join Cub Scouts. Some of my friends were scouts, and it looked like fun. My mom took me to one meeting. After that, she said she didn't have time to deal with it or the money to pay the dues."

"How much did it cost?" Spence asked curiously, his heart aching for the little things he could have done for his son, things the boy was too old for now. How he wished he could go back in time and make things right in Caleb's childhood.

"I think it was a dollar a meeting," he replied. "Plus the membership fee, but the leader said we could apply for a scholarship for that."

"What kinds of things did your mom like to do?" Spence asked, though he suspected he knew the answer to his question.

"She liked to go out with her friends, dancing and stuff," Caleb replied vaguely. "Before Gramps died, I'd go over there and hang out with him and Jordan. My aunt was a lot younger then. We'd play games and watch movies. I slept over a lot."

"What happened after your grandfather died?" Spence asked. "Did you still spend time with Jordan?"

"Sometimes, but Jordan had to move into a room in someone's house. She couldn't pay the rent on Gramps' apartment," Caleb explained. "The lady who owned the house didn't like Jordan to have sleepover guests. If Mom wanted to go out with her friends, she'd usually ask Jordan to come babysit at our apartment. Then one day, my mom and Jordan got into a big fight. My mom yelled at Jordan, called her names, and said she was just like Gramps. Jordan didn't come around much after that." During the last few words, the boy's voice grew thick with emotion. The memory of that argument obviously still affected him.

"What was the fight about?" Spence asked gently.

Caleb took a moment to answer, inhaling a few deep breaths to get his emotions under control. Finally, he said, "It was about my mom's boyfriend, Wayne. I think he did something to Jordan, or tried to."

Spence felt a surge of anger. What had Tanya's boyfriend done to Jordan to cause such a rift between the two sisters? Several unpleasant thoughts came to mind. When Spence's anger increased, he shoved the unhelpful thinking aside and asked, "How old were you then, Caleb?"

"Eight, I think. I was in the third grade."

"Did they ever patch things up, your mom and your aunt?"

Caleb shrugged again. "I'm not sure. Wayne moved out right after that. I remember my mom yelling at him, telling him to go. Then, Mom got a new boyfriend, and we moved away."

Spence watched a shudder ripple through the boy's body and wondered about the cause. Was it because of the boyfriend or the move? Caleb stood suddenly and carried his plate to the counter. He remained at the sink for a minute staring out the window.

"I'm going to bed now," he finally muttered, turning and heading for the stairs.

"Caleb," Spence called softly. He waited until his son turned to face him. "I'm really sorry I wasn't there for you, son." His tone was deep with the sudden flood of emotion that held him in its grip.

Caleb nodded but said nothing. A few minutes later, the boy's bedroom door clicked shut.

Spence remained at the table for a long time, pondering all he'd just learned. He wondered why Tanya never bothered to track him down. It wouldn't have been that difficult. The Marine Corps would have helped her. Had he given her the impression he wouldn't want to be found? Even if he had, he deserved to know he had a child, and she was entitled to financial assistance. He couldn't have made the situation worse, could he? The answer to that question, he knew, would remain a mystery for all time. It was impossible to go back and fix a broken past. The lost years could never be recovered. Closing his eyes, Spence vowed to move forward with his son, to do everything in his power to help make Caleb's tomorrows better than his yesterdays.

Chapter 10

Recognizing Carl Spencer's number, Jordan answered the ringing phone distractedly. If the cherry pie she had in the oven wasn't taken out right now, the crust would burn. Thankfully, Caleb was more interested in talking to Ally than her. She handed the phone to her niece and hurried to the kitchen.

Almost immediately, Ally launched into a detailed description of the art project she'd done at preschool. Jordan smiled as she reached for the oven door and pulled it down. Poor Caleb wasn't going to get a word in edgewise.

Rescued in the nick of time, the pie safely rested on a trivet on the counter. She turned her attention to the stove top. The chicken stew she'd started earlier smelled delicious. She peeked under the lid. The broth bubbled nicely. Almost time to add the dumplings, she thought. Her thoughts wound back to Caleb. He sounded different somehow. Happy and content were adjectives that came to mind. And open, she decided. He'd been guarded and closed off for such a long time. She barely remembered the happy-go-lucky boy he once was. An excited squeal from Ally jerked her from that train of thought.

"I hear a dog barking!" the girl cried. "You got a dog! Are you gonna get to bring him home with you, Caleb? What does he look like? Did you get to name him?" The eager child fired off questions without waiting for an answer. She paused and listened for half a second, then exclaimed, "Butch is a neat name! I want to see him. Can I, Caleb? Can I?"

A dog! Jordan thought with alarm. She felt a twinge of annoyance. If Mr. Spencer couldn't take on a kid right now, as he'd suggested, he wasn't likely to keep a dog either. Plus, Caleb wouldn't want to leave his new pet. He'd want to bring it home. Only small, quiet, well behaved dogs were allowed in this apartment complex. If Ally could hear the dog barking, it probably wouldn't qualify. Not to mention the hefty deposit that would have to be paid. They simply could not have a dog! Why would Mr. Spencer put her in such a difficult position? She'd need to have a word with the man! Yes, she'd telephone him just as soon as she had the chance.

All these thoughts swirled through Jordan's mind as she set the table for dinner. By the time the call ended, she'd worked herself into such a state of irritation, she wasn't sure she dared speak to Caleb's father. She might say something she'd regret.

Later, after Ally was tucked into bed, Jordan ran herself a hot bath. Her nerves were coiled and she desperately needed to unwind. All through dinner and Ally's bedtime routine, the girl had yammered on about Caleb's dog, Butch. What a good dog he was, and how smart, and how much she was going to love him. Jordan exercised immense restraint by remaining mostly silent. Mr. Spencer's thoughtless actions were going to result in both children's hearts being bruised.

Refreshed but still perturbed, she'd just finished slipping on her nightgown and robe, when the telephone rang. Caller I.D. revealed Carl Spencer's number.

Careful not to make a fool of herself a second time by assuming the caller was her nephew, Jordan answered, "Hello?"

"Hello, Jordan."

Carl Spencer's deep, rich voice hummed over the lines and straight into Jordan's chest. Her skin flushed involuntarily and a tingling sensation skittered through her. Why did this man unnerve her so? For a few seconds, she forgot her annoyance with him.

"H-hello," she stammered, wincing inwardly. She sounded like a school girl!

"I'm sorry to be calling so late," Spence said, "but there's something I wanted to ask you."

Here it comes, Jordan thought. Well, she intended to cut him off at the pass. "I don't really see how we can manage it, Mr. Spencer," Jordan began, launching into the speech she'd mentally prepared. "I really wish you'd discussed this with me prior to acting. I mean, we're rarely home, so he'd be alone all day. Our back patio is tiny, so there's just no place to keep one. Besides, the management is really particular about breed and size…"

Spence listened to the obviously rehearsed discourse and wondered what on earth she was talking about. He let her hurried speech continue, finally figuring out that her concerns were somehow related to Butch.

"Jordan," he interjected, trying to get her attention.

"…can't really afford a dog, and…"

"Jordan, I didn't get Caleb a dog," he said rather forcefully.

Spence's words finally penetrated, and Jordan quieted, her heart still pounding with the aftermath of the frenzied conversation. "What?" she asked breathlessly.

"I said, I did not give Caleb a dog," Spence repeated clearly. "Butch, the animal you mentioned, is neither his nor mine. We're looking after him for a local woman who is in the hospital."

"Oh." Jordan closed her eyes and tipped her head back. A deep blush of embarrassment climbed up her neck and reddened her cheeks. She'd managed to do it again! *He must think I'm a complete idiot!* "I'm so sorry," she whispered, mortified.

Spence suppressed a laugh, knowing she wouldn't appreciate his mirth at her expense. "It's okay," he replied. He went on to explain the circumstances of his and Caleb's new living arrangements.

"That sounds much better than the primitive cabin Caleb told me about." Jordan was thankful he'd so easily pushed aside her misguided assumptions. "Is Caleb enjoying looking after the animals?"

"We both are, though it's a little lonely," he replied. Now that they had their own responsibilities, he and Caleb didn't get over to the Summers ranch as often as before. "That brings me to the reason for this call. I've been thinking, maybe you and Ally would enjoy a visit to Silver Springs." The idea had come to Spence a few days ago. Caleb mentioned how much he thought his little sister would like the dogs and horses, and how little time Jordan had for fun. The boy hadn't come right out and said he missed them, only hinted at it.

"You...you want us to come to Montana?" Jordan asked, incredulous.

She was having trouble shifting her thinking from the previous subject to this new one. A vacation sounded lovely. She hadn't been on one since the last time she and Dad took the boat over to Catalina Island. That was the summer after she graduated from high school, nearly ten years ago, she was surprised to note. Dad had always loved going there. It was the place where he and Mom had met. Two years later, Dad was gone and there were no more trips to the island. Yes indeed, a vacation sounded wonderful – but impossible. Her meager savings were unlikely to cover the cost of gasoline, let alone plane fare.

"Jordan?"

"I'm here. Um, th-thank you for the offer, Mr. Spencer," she stammered. "I really do appreciate your thoughtfulness, but I'm going to have to decline."

Unaccountably disappointed, Spence heaved a sigh. "Any particular reason?"

"I...well, to be honest, I can't afford to take a vacation," she replied self-consciously.

"I didn't expect you to pay for it, Jordan," he said tightly. He'd already considered her financial situation, knew she wouldn't have the money for a trip. "I'd be covering all your expenses."

Jordan's nerves jumped at the generous and unexpected offer. "N-no! I couldn't let you do that," she said in surprise.

"Why not!" Spence replied in exasperation. "You and Ally are my son's family."

"Well, it's just...I don't know...I just wouldn't feel right about you spending a lot of money on me...um, us," she spluttered, tripping over her words and sounding, once again, like a halfwit.

That's just what he'd figured, and he'd prepared for her argument. "It won't be that much money. I've traveled a great deal in the recent past and have a bunch of frequent flyer miles socked away. If they don't get used soon, I'm going to lose them. I was planning to use some to cover your airline tickets," Spence explained. "There's plenty of room in the house, and it's free. You don't have to worry about overextending my budget. Say you'll come, Jordan," Spence added, a silent 'please' remaining behind his lips.

A hint of eagerness spread through her chest. He wasn't really paying for it, not in real money anyway, she reasoned. She could accept, couldn't she? A vacation away sounded heavenly.

Except for Chris, a little voice in the back of her mind whispered. What would he think about her taking off to parts unknown? Well, he'd just have to understand. It wasn't as if they were serious. They'd only met a few weeks ago.

"You and Ally will have a great time; I promise," Spence coaxed. "Caleb is eager to show you his horseback riding skills. Ally might like to ride, too. What do you say?" He held his breath.

"Okay," Jordan said quietly, a flame of anticipation flickering inside her. Yes, a trip would be great fun!

Spence agreed to make the reservations for early August, a little over a month away. In the meantime, he and Caleb would get the house in tip-top shape for their guests.

~ * ~

Spence finished forking hay into the freshly cleaned stalls. As promised, Caleb was up and out earlier to release the horses into the corral and take care of the unsavory task of mucking out their living space.

Leaning on the pitch fork, Spence surveyed the interior of the barn. His eyes automatically noted several gaps in the outside wall where the boards had rotted away or become dislodged. He'd have to go into town to pick up lumber and hardware for the repairs.

They'd been here at the Hill place for nearly two weeks. Spence found himself looking forward to the regular chores and maintenance work. Aside from his brief stint on Jack's ranch five years ago, he hadn't lived this way since he was a teenager down in Texas. Discovering that he missed it surprised him.

The rumble of a car's engine drawing near brought him out of the barn. The sheriff's cruiser slowed to a stop in front of the house. Spence walked over to greet the man.

"Sheriff," he said, holding out his hand. "What brings you out?"

Sheriff Davies gripped the younger man's hand and smiled. "Came to see how you and your boy were faring," he said. "Everything going all right?"

"We're doing fine," Spence replied. "In fact, we're rather enjoying ourselves."

A few minutes later, the two men sat at the kitchen table with mugs of hot coffee. Spence opened a box of cinnamon rolls and set them on the table, along with a stack of napkins. The sheriff didn't hesitate to help himself to one. Caleb came in through the backdoor, waved hello the sheriff, and headed for the cabinet under the sink. Butch could be heard snuffling around on the porch, waiting for the boy.

"The feds still treating you right, son?" the older man inquired of Spence.

Spence nodded. "As well as can be expected," he replied noncommittally.

"I sure was glad you were here when that mess out at the Summers ranch went down a while back," Davies said with candor.

Spence took a swig of his coffee and nodded. "That's why I was here, Sheriff. Just doing my job."

"Of course," the sheriff said, reaching for his pastry. "I just wanted you to know, I was darned impressed. You're a natural leader and a good lawman."

"Thank you, sir."

As Caleb listened to the conversation, he was surprised by the sincerity in the sheriff's voice. Spence and Jack Summers usually talked about their days in the Marines, so most of what he'd heard about his father was what a screw up he used to be. Course, Mr. Summers never said it scornfully. They were always joking around. Whatever had happened five years ago at the ranch must have been really awful for the Summers family. No one ever talked about it. The sheriff's observations were new to Caleb. When the conversation lagged, he stood to go, the two dog biscuits he'd been looking for stuffed in his pocket.

"Me and Butch are going for a walk," he announced.

The little dog had come to expect a morning trounce through the fields behind the house. Caleb had taken Lady only once. She'd tired after just a few yards, and he'd been forced to come back. The extra biscuit made her happy and gave her something to do while he and Butch were gone.

"Okay," Spence said, gazing at the contented look on his son's face. Being here had changed the boy. "Be careful and don't go beyond shouting distance."

"Sure thing," Caleb replied.

The boy grabbed a package of toaster pastries and hurried out. The sound of excited barking continued until the side gate opened and closed. Once freed from captivity, Butch was too busy running and chasing flying things to make any noise.

Spence stood and reached for the coffee pot. The simple action reminded him just how much moving to this house had improved their living conditions. No more generator, no more outhouse or cold showers. He refilled his mug and topped off the sheriff's, returned the pot to its warmer, and sat down again.

Sheriff Davies glanced across the table. "I hear you're taking a leave of absence."

"For the summer, maybe a little longer," Spence replied noncommittally.

Davies sipped his coffee and eyed the younger man. "Heard you were injured."

Spence nodded, his left hand involuntarily reaching up to rub his right shoulder. There were no secrets in a small town like Silver Springs, even for newcomers and passers-through. "I took a bullet – a hollow point," he said quietly.

"They can do some damage," the sheriff stated matter-of-factly.

"Yup." The silence hung between them. The sheriff ate his cinnamon roll, and Spence swigged his coffee. He looked away for a long moment, emotions swirling in his gut.

Sheriff Davies watched as the younger man's brow furrowed and jaw tightened. He'd always been adept at reading people, a trait that served him well in his line of work. The man sitting across from him was hurting. Clearing his throat, he said, "I'm thinking there's more to it than that."

Mildly surprised, Spence studied the man. Davies was correct and, no doubt, saw right through his injured shoulder excuse for taking such a long break from the job. Without warning, ugly images – memories of things he preferred to forget, sliced through his mind. Suddenly overcome with anxiety, he stood and walked to the kitchen sink, his back to the table.

"You want to talk about it?" the sheriff asked softly. He watched the muscles tense in the young man's shoulders. Whatever had driven him to come here, to escape, was still eating at him. "Maybe you should get it off your chest, son."

Spence felt a wave of anger wash over him. "There's nothing to talk about," he growled.

Davies stood quietly. He took the few short steps to the younger man's side and laid a hand on his back. "You know there is."

Spence felt the gentle touch, heard the concerned words, and something broke inside him. His head dropped, and a sob tore from his throat.

Davies remained at his side while the tears flowed. "It's all right, son. You let it out. Let go of what's hurting you."

A few minutes later, Spence accepted the paper towel the other man offered and wiped his face. The sheriff regained his chair and waited. Spence stayed at the sink, starring through the window at nothing and remembering everything.

"I was supposed to be on point," he rasped through an emotion clogged throat. "My partner was bringing up the rear. The shots sounded like they were coming from behind us. I turned around. Next thing I know, I'm being shoved aside, stumbling toward a dumpster. By the time I steadied myself and turned back, Eric was facedown and not moving. A bullet tore through my right shoulder before I could get to him."

"Eric was your partner?"

"Yeah, Eric Adams. He was a good friend," Spence chocked out. "He left behind a wife and two kids."

"So, he didn't make it," Sheriff Davies stated, adding softly, "And you did."

Spence nodded. "It should have been me. He pushed me away and got shot standing in the same spot I had just occupied." His voice grated with barely controlled emotion.

"That doesn't make it your fault, son."

"He had a family!" Spence ground out.

"So do you," Sheriff Davies pointed out.

Dropping into his chair, Spence propped his elbows on the table and rested his forehead in his palms. "I didn't have a family then, and Eric did. Those two little girls..." His throat closed around the words.

"Man knows not his time," Davies quoted. "Son, you were no more in control of who was going to die that day, than me. Only God has a handle on that sort of thing. He knows the number of your days, Spence. God knew your partner's time was up. If the man hadn't been there in that alley with you, he might have been mowing his yard or driving to the store. It wouldn't have mattered a lick. Your friend's time of death was determined before his birth. God called him home."

"Why would a loving God do that?" Spence grunted, anger returning to his tone.

"I don't know the answer to that. Only God himself can tell you." The sheriff continued, "When my first wife got sick and passed on, I was angry. Angry at God, angry at the doctors who couldn't cure her, angry at myself for bein' so helpless. I never did fully understand, but I learned to accept it. God didn't make her sick, but he didn't allow her to suffer long either.

"My second wife is a loving woman. She's given me three terrific kids, two by marriage and one of our own. The youngest is studying to become a minister. Imagine that?! One of mine, preparing to teach the Lord's word. That boy wouldn't exist if my first wife hadn't gone to be with her heavenly Father. Do you begin to see, son? We don't know the future.

"From what I hear, you and your boy only just met. What would have happened to your son, had you been the one to die that day?"

The radio attached to the sheriff's belt crackled, his cue that their time was up. He patted Spence's sagging shoulder and stood to leave. "Don't blame yourself, son. And don't hold none of what happened against God. He's got a bigger plan for you and me than we can even begin to comprehend. If you'd like to talk again, you know where to find me."

Spence didn't look up. A moment later, he heard the front door open and close, and the engine of the cruiser start. His thoughts whirled, tumbling over one another. He'd always thought the sheriff of Silver Springs a simple man. He was wrong.

~ * ~

Jordan didn't see Chris for nearly two weeks, though they'd spoken over the telephone several times. On each occasion, she'd intended to tell him about her upcoming vacation. The brief calls all seemed to end before she had the opportunity. Finally, just when she was wondering if he was avoiding her, he asked her to have dinner with him on a Thursday night. She hesitated, worried about Ally getting to bed on time. He was going out of town for the weekend, he said, and really wanted to see her before he left.

Ally went home with Deborah that afternoon, freeing Jordan to take her time getting ready for the date. Excited, she rushed home to shower and dress. Feeling strongly that something significant was going to happen tonight, she paid extra attention to her hair and makeup. Sifting through her jewelry box, her fingers closed around the promise ring. She hadn't felt the need to wear the ring during the last month. Her thoughts turned to Chris and their developing feelings for each other. She was beginning to care a good deal for him. Was he the one God had chosen for her? Her heart leaned toward him. She left the ring in her jewelry box, certain she'd survive the evening without its reminder.

Chris arrived a little before six o'clock and escorted her to a car she'd never seen before. He usually drove an older sports car – nice but not luxurious. The sleek, black BMW parked at her curb looked brand new.

"Nice!" she exclaimed as she slid onto the leather seat. Chris closed her door and jogged around the front of the car.

"Thanks, I just bought it," he said, a note of pride in his tone, as he climbed into the driver's seat and started the engine.

As he drove to the restaurant, he talked about the car, pointing out the built-in global positioning system, the heated seats, individual temperature controls, and other luxury features. Jordan was suitably impressed. The only amenity her nine-year-old Ford Taurus boasted was air conditioning, an extra for which she was regularly grateful.

Their destination was a small seafood restaurant in Seal Beach. Every date they'd been on had taken them to the ocean, Jordan noted. Chris loved it. Her only complaint, if she had one, was the strong wind that often blew at the beach. As she got out of the car, a salty gust caught her carefully styled hair, undoing some of her earlier efforts. She reached back and flattened her hand across the back of her neck, pinning her hair down and hoping to salvage the remaining curls.

Over salad, they discussed their jobs, with the conversation moving to Chris's last trip to the beach as the entre was served. Apparently, he'd gone surfing the previous Saturday, spending the day with friends. They'd even had a bonfire that night. Jordan experienced a twinge of jealousy. She'd spent the day at home, cleaning and catching up on the laundry. Thoughts of her upcoming vacation sprang to the forefront of her mind.

The waiter cleared away their plates and asked if they'd like dessert. Jordan shook her head but requested a cup of decaf. He delivered it, along with the check. Jordan slowly stirred in sugar and a tiny bit of cream, while Chris told her about a Hawaiian surfing vacation he'd once taken. The topic provided the opening she needed.

"Speaking of trips," she said after venturing a hesitant sip of her hot coffee. "I'm going to Montana next week."

Chris looked at her in surprise, processing what she'd just said. "Whatever for?" he finally asked.

"My nephew is there visiting his father," she reminded him. She'd recently told him about Caleb and her responsibility for the boy. She also mentioned searching for and finding Carl Spencer. "Ally and I have been invited to join them for two weeks. They're housesitting at a small ranch with horses and other animals. Caleb has been learning to –"

"You're going to stay with the kid's dad?"

"Yes, we'll be staying at the house with them," Jordan replied, picking up her cup and taking another drink. "Mr. Spencer has assured me that there is plenty of room. Ally's already looking forward to playing with the dog Caleb told her about." She looked up in time to see Chris' jaw stiffen.

"Let's go, Jordan," he said, his tone oddly gruff. With sharp movements, he signed the credit card receipt and grabbed his copy, stuffing it in his pocket.

Jordan wasn't sure what to make of the sudden mood shift. Why would he be upset? Gathering her purse and sweater, she slid from the booth and followed him to the door, hurrying to keep up with his rapid stride.

Quiet music filtered through the car speakers during the otherwise silent drive back to her apartment. Chris pulled to a stop in front and turned, his mouth drawn in a firm line.

"I don't like this trip, Jordan," he said. "You and this guy staying together – it's not right."

"Chris, we'll be fine," Jordan replied in surprise. He was jealous! How sweet. "It's nice of you to be concerned. Caleb's dad is a decent guy, I assure you."

Chris turned away and inhaled several deep breaths then speared her with a fierce look. "I don't trust him," he seethed quietly, adding, "You're a pretty girl, and men are – well, men."

Jordan's heart melted just a little, pleased that he cared enough to be worried about her. She cupped his cheek, leaned forward, and kissed him softly. "Everything will be fine," she whispered. "I promise. The children will be there to chaperone. I would never allow them to be exposed to anything inappropriate." Jordan glanced at her watch and frowned. Ally needed to be picked up soon.

"Jordan..."

"Chris, I have to go," she said, unable to delay any longer. "I had a lovely time tonight. Thank you."

She pushed open the passenger door, got out, and hurried toward her car. Ally was her top priority right now, not Chris's unreasonable fears. Besides, they'd made no commitment to each other. They'd talk later, and she'd make him understand that everything would be all right. She laughed as she drove to Deborah's house.

She had no worries about either Carl Spencer or herself losing control and doing something regrettable. Didn't Chris trust her?

~ * ~

Spence reached for the study pamphlet and turned to the section marked *Week 4*. Last weeks' session was about getting into your son's world. He turned one page back and glanced over his notes. 'Find out what the kid's interested in and get involved.' He recalled the discussion last week.

"Often times we try to get our kids to adapt to our interests. That's okay, once in a while. A boy needs to sample a man's world, after all. However, if we really want to reach our boys, we need to meet them where *they* are. We need to step out of our world and into theirs. Does your boy love fast cars? Take him to a race track or a car dealership that sells sports cars, even if you don't care for that sort of thing. Sacrifice! I can't tell you the difference we saw in my son's attitude after I started playing his video games with him," Dan Edwards said. He'd gotten a little choked up in the telling, so Spence knew it was a big deal. "This week, I challenge you to discover one interest of your boy's, then act on it, if you can. Obviously, if he wants to learn to snow ski, that'll have to wait."

Spence went away with that thought in mind. He'd watched the boy, listened to him, but no interest he didn't already know about presented itself. Then, he recalled his first real conversation with Caleb. The boy had been impressed with Spence's rodeo interest. Bull riding! There was no way he was climbing on the back of a ton of angry hamburger to impress his son. His shoulder would never survive the experience.

A couple of days later, Spence found himself at the hardware store. Tacked to the wall outside the building was a poster announcing an upcoming rodeo being held at the fairgrounds. Spence took note of the dates – this weekend, and decided he'd found his son's unknown interest.

Early Saturday morning, they hopped into the Porche and headed for the nearby fairgrounds. During the thirty minute drive, Spence kept their destination a secret. A huge banner stretching across the entrance announced the event. Caleb's face lit up.

"We're going to a rodeo?" he asked excitedly.

"Unless you don't want to," Spence replied nonchalantly. "I can turn the car around, if you think it'll be too boring."

"No way!" the boy cried, his face split in a wide grin.

They'd had a terrific time. Every event was an exciting first for Caleb, and he learned quickly how the scoring worked. His favorite event, much to his father's surprise, was the calf roping competition. He loved watching the cowboys lasso the animal then dive off their horse and bring the beast down. The boy was on his feet throughout, bobbing and shouting excitedly. Spence was pleased just watching his son's reaction.

They ate corndogs, popcorn, and all manner of junk food, drank their fill of sodas, and went home happy at the end of the day. The boy chattered all the way back to Silver Springs. In fact, he'd asked for the use of Spence's phone when they were still ten minutes away. Spence listened to one side of a breathless conversation with Jordan. From the sound of it, she was almost as excited as Caleb, or at least made a good show of it for the boy's sake. Whichever it was didn't really matter. She was a great mom figure for his son.

That thought stayed with Spence throughout the evening. Father-figure was a modern term invented due to the huge ranks of absentee dads in today's society. Most kids had a mother, and often only a mother. For a time, Caleb had neither. Jordan filled that gaping hole in his life. Without warning, she'd been thrust into the position of playing both roles. It must have been overwhelming.

Spence felt a tap on his shoulder and glanced up as Jack Summers took the seat beside his. Jack was attending with his nephew, Jeremy. Spence knew of several other uncles in attendance, as well as step-dads, one grandfather, and an older brother. One boy, whose family was new to the area, had no adult male to accompany him. Word got out to the congregation, and a father with only daughters volunteered. The church made sure every boy who wanted to participate was included.

This evening's lesson was about girls. Spence hid a grin, thinking of all the interesting stories he could share. Most, however, would fit a barroom setting far more than this Sunday school classroom. *Equipping our sons to resist temptation*, the pamphlet read.

The discussion ranged from dirty magazines and Internet porn to the scantily dressed women and girls who drive men and boys to distraction.

"None of us is immune," one of the older men in the group pointed out. "We're bombarded with sexual images every day. I imagine it's even harder for the younger generation. After all, the only pretty girl giving me come hither looks is my wife of thirty years. Our sons are getting those looks constantly."

"That's right," someone agreed. "My boy is only fifteen and already girls are calling practically daily. He's obviously flattered, but it also makes him uncomfortable. I overheard my wife ask one young lady to stop calling."

"The teen girls are doing this same Bible study, designed specifically for their gender," Dan Edwards mentioned, adding, "A few years ago, when my daughter was still in high school, the church did a similar study. Maddie made a commitment to remain pure until marriage. It was one of the proudest moments of my life, I have to tell you. Part of a father's job is protecting his daughter's innocence. That means raising her to understand that she is beautiful even when no cleavage shows, encouraging her to dress modestly, reminding her that God has a life partner already chosen for her, that he is worth waiting for.

"Maddie has shared with my wife and me that many of her college friends regret undervaluing that part of themselves. They wish they'd waited. I don't want my daughter to have those kinds of regrets."

Another father joined the discussion. "You might be wondering how all this relates to our sons," he said. "Well, first of all, we need to encourage our boys to wait for the life partner God has set aside for them, same as the girls. But also, we need to teach our boys the proper way to treat the fairer sex. By the time they start dating, or courting, if you prefer, they should be opening doors for women, using common manners. We certainly need to make them understand why being married prior to intimacy is so important. There is immense responsibility involved in taking a girl to bed. Pregnancy and disease are only two of the risks. Fooling around with a girl's heart and reputation, or risking one's own for that matter, is just as dangerous as the physical stuff."

Spence wrote very little down in his notebook, but his head reeled with the information being presented.

He'd never considered that any of his past girlfriends gave two hoots about their reputations. Caleb's mother certainly hadn't seemed concerned. For the first time ever, he wondered what her father might have thought. A vision of little Ally slid across his mind. She wasn't his daughter, not by a long shot, but if she were, would he want some bozo using her as casually as he'd used her mother? His pulse rate ratcheted at the thought. If anyone ever did, child of his or not, he'd find the guy and have a few words with him!

Chapter 11

As they made their way down the narrow aisle toward the plane's open door, Jordan held tightly to Ally's small hand. The long journey, which included a two hour layover in Seattle, was finally coming to an end. Jordan had never known one small child could contain so much energy. Ally jabbered and fidgeted all day. That much excited vigor, trapped inside a tin can at thirty thousand feet, made for an interesting and tiring day. A long soak in a bathtub, followed by an early bedtime, sounded heavenly to her aunt. When the airplane finally started its descent, the little girl had squealed with delight, and every passenger within earshot breathed a sigh of relief.

"Gonna see Caleb soon!" Ally cried excitedly as they stepped onto the tarmac. She tugged eagerly at her aunt's hand.

"Yes, we are," Jordan agreed, glancing at the windows that lined the building toward which the airline representative was leading them. The tinted glass revealed nothing beyond a distorted reflection of their small, travel-weary group.

Inside, Caleb had no difficulty spotting his sister and aunt. "There they are!"

Patting his son's back, Spence smiled. He'd been right to invite the boy's family. Caleb missed them. The visit would do them all good. They'd had no trouble getting the house cleaned and readying bedrooms for their guests. Caleb's energy level seemed boundless.

The minute Jordan stepped through the door, Caleb swooped in, pulling her and Ally into a fierce hug. When he finally let go, he quickly dragged the back of his hand across his damp eyes. Jordan was wiping away tears as well. Ally immediately started telling her big brother about their flight.

"We saw the top of clouds, Caleb!" she exclaimed. "Did you ever see that? And the plane got all wobbly sometimes and…"

While the siblings got reacquainted, Spence approached, stepping up behind Jordan, who was watching the exchange.

Jordan's heart swelled at the touching scene. Caleb seemed so different, happier somehow. Getting him away from home and the negative influence of his peers had done him a world of good. Or, was it the time spent with his father? Probably a bit of both, she decided, and the thought made her throat tight with emotion. Suddenly choked up, she abruptly turned away from the sight of the happy reunion and collided with Caleb's father. Startled, she stepped away too quickly and stumbled. Two large hands clamped around her waist, steadying her.

"Please excuse me," she whispered, her face flushing pink.

Spence suppressed a grin. "Flying must have left you unsteady on your feet," he observed and her blush deepened slightly.

"I'm okay now," she replied quietly.

Taking the hint, Spence removed his hands, and gestured toward an adjoining room. "Baggage claim is over there." The small group headed in that direction. Spence held the glass door, and Jordan preceded him through the entrance, his hand at her back.

Jordan felt entirely too aware of the man beside her. Practically falling into his arms before they'd even said hello probably didn't help. She knew her face was bright red; she could feel the heat rolling off her skin. Why did she have to blush so easily?

Thankfully, during the drive to his temporary home, the kids chattered nonstop, freeing them from the seemingly arduous task of making small talk. She hoped the time was sufficient to recover her dignity, as well.

"Here we are," Spence announced a short time later, bringing the rented sport utility vehicle to a stop in front of a quaint, two-story house. As he removed the luggage from the vehicles hatch, Jordan hurried over to help, assuring him that she was quite capable of handling the bags. When he ignored her attempts, she began to realize he harbored the same pigheadedness as her nephew.

Caleb surprised her by saying, "Jordan, it's what us guys are supposed to do."

When had he figured that out? She could only stare, her mouth hanging open.

"Careful now," Spence said, leaning close to her ear. "We've got a fly problem around here."

Jordan promptly clamped her lips together. She could hear him chuckling as he bounded up the steps to the front door. Caleb was ushering his excited sister toward a corral where two horses grazed.

"Hold Caleb's hand, Ally," Jordan called. "And don't go inside the fence."

Caleb hollered back, "I'll watch her, don't worry."

Satisfied that the boy could handle things, Jordan grabbed her handbag from the front seat of the car and headed toward the house. She entered a nicely appointed, if dated, living room and looked around. She was alone.

"Mr. Spencer?"

"I'm upstairs. Come on up."

Jordan hurried up the stairs and found him standing in the hallway, suitcases resting beside him. "You'll be sleeping in the big rear bedroom." He pointed toward an open doorway.

He'd considered putting her downstairs in Mrs. Hill's room but felt that would be an invasion of the kind woman's privacy. Other than that first look, he'd left her room alone. He planned to bunk with his son during Jordan's visit. Caleb's room contained a pair of twin beds. The third bedroom, obviously Mrs. Hill's sewing room, held a daybed which they'd made up for Ally.

Through the doorway, Jordan could see a double bed covered in a colorful patchwork quilt. A pattern of large antique roses in various shades of pink papered the walls. Lace curtains fluttered in the open window. The decor was dainty, a lady's room, and Jordan fell instantly in love with it.

"This is beautiful," she whispered in wonder, moving farther into the room.

Spence leaned against the door jam, crossed his arms over his chest, and watched her move about the room, touching and admiring their handiwork. Caleb had discovered the vintage linens in an old steamer trunk shoved into a corner of his bedroom. It was his idea to do up the room this way. Now that Spence was witnessing Jordan's reaction, he was glad he'd gone along with the boy's plan. She was positively mesmerized.

With reverence, she smoothed a hand over the quilt then reached out to trace the hand-painted roses on a vintage pitcher. Her fingers tenderly brushed the wild flowers Caleb had plucked from the field just this morning, and she leaned in to sample their sweet fragrance. When she turned to face him, something flipped inside his stomach. Her glowing skin and wide, innocent eyes brought to mind an angel. For a split second, he forgot to breath.

"Thank you," Jordan said softly. "I don't quite know what to say. Everything is...lovely."

Forcing himself to remember who she was and where they were, Spence inhaled a calming breath. "You're welcome," he replied evenly. "It was Caleb's idea." He turned suddenly and walked away, eager to regain his equilibrium. "Ally's room is across the hall."

Jordan stepped through the doorway. "She'll share with me," she said, reaching for the two suitcases she'd brought.

Spence picked up the bags before she had a chance. "That isn't necessary, Jordan. There's plenty of room, and Caleb thought you might like to have your own room."

Shaking her head, Jordan turned and walked back into the pretty bedroom. She stood aside, while he carried the suitcases in and set them on the bed. He turned to her, eyebrows raised in question.

"That's very thoughtful though impractical. Ally might wake up and forget where she is," Jordan explained. "She might go looking for the bathroom or for me, and end up falling down the stairs. It's best if we share."

Spence yielded to her wisdom in the matter and left her to unpack. Besides, standing with her in her bedroom was more than he could deal with just now. His stomach still felt unsettled, and he really needed to get some air. He headed downstairs with the excuse of checking on the kids.

A short time later, as the sun drooped low in the evening sky, Caleb gave his aunt the official tour of the homestead. She listened to the brief history of the property, and promised her nephew she'd let him show her the mill another day. All the animals were introduced except for the two elusive barn cats, which rarely warmed to visitors, she was told. Dancer, the gelding, even favored her with a whinny and presented his muzzle for her to rub.

"He doesn't care for men," Caleb explained. "My da...um Spence, says he was mistreated before coming here."

"That's a shame," Jordan replied distractedly.

Her focus had instantly shifted to her nephew's stumbled over words and flushed neck. He'd nearly referred to Carl Spencer as his dad. Had they reached that point so quickly? With both fear and anticipation, her heart ached for the close relationship. While she wanted the boy to bond with his father, she wasn't eager to lose him. The man lived across the country. Should Spence choose to become Caleb's full-time dad, getting together would be difficult and costly.

Her gaze drifted across the yard to the man in question. He was squatting beside Ally as the little girl offered a biscuit to the old dog. The shepherd took it gently, seeming to recognize the fragility of the giver. Ally laughed, clapping her hands. Mr. Spencer's face beamed, and his arm looped around Ally's tiny back. Jordan watched him pull the girl onto his knee and say something to her. She clapped her hands again and nodded eagerly. He stood then and looked up, catching Jordan staring.

"We're going inside to feed the birds," Spence called across the yard.

When Ally reached for the tall man's hand and tugged him toward the back gate, Jordan conjured up a tremulous smile and waved. Spence raised his hand in response then disappeared around the house.

~ * ~

They'd only been here a few days, and Spence knew he was getting in too deep. Ally trailed after him like an attention starved puppy and, if he were being completely honest, he'd admit that he didn't mind. She was sweet and adorable, and had him wrapped around her little finger before the sun went down that first day. Since then, she'd dragged him all over the house and yard, inspecting everything, and explaining things from a small child's perspective.

She taught him that dandelions were flowers not weeds, and that he should let the lawn get tall because it gives the grasshoppers a nice home, and his favorite question, "Why doesn't you got a birdfeeder? We got two at the 'partment."

He'd spent the last half hour sitting in the living room, half-listening to Ally's chatter filtering down the hall, while Jordan helped her take a bath. The girls had commandeered the downstairs bathroom for the duration of their stay. He and Caleb continued using the one upstairs. A few minutes later, dressed in princess pajamas, Ally scampered into the living room toting a picture book.

"You can read it," she announced, climbing onto his lap without waiting for an invitation.

"Ally, you ask!" Jordan scolded, rushing into the room on the child's heels.

Ally looked at her aunt's admonishing expression and crossed arms. Turning back to Spence, she said, "Please?"

"Okay, sweet pea, but only because you said please," Spence replied. He caught Jordan's eye and winked. When she rolled her eyes, he chuckled and opened the book.

Jordan went to the kitchen to pour herself a glass of water and get away from this man who had won over her precious girl. First thing every morning, even before Jordan opened her eyes, Ally was off looking for *'Pence*, as she called him. She kept him in her sights all day long, even crying earlier when he'd run an errand without her. He read to her, gave her piggy back rides, and tucked her in at night. Without a doubt, the child was falling in love with Carl Spencer.

Jordan wasn't jealous, not really. Her thoughts tended toward the heartbreak her niece was going to suffer at the end of the visit. Would Ally be able to go back to the way things were?

When Jordan returned to the living room, Carl was closing the book, and Ally was slumped against his chest.

"She fell asleep," he said softly.

Jordan chewed her lower lip and nodded. "So I see." She reached for the book he held out.

"I'll carry her up." The words were unnecessary. He'd carried her to bed the past three nights. The active little girl hadn't lasted beyond eight o'clock since they arrived.

Jordan hurried upstairs ahead of him and turned down the covers. She stepped back and waited while Spence laid Ally down and then pulled the sheet and light blanket over her. The quilt remained folded at the foot of the bed. The nights were warm enough that it wasn't needed. He pressed a gentle kiss to Ally's forehead and retreated.

As she tucked in her niece, Jordan sensed him watching her. She suspected he'd picked up on her somber mood, concern for Ally's tender heart at the forefront of her thoughts. When her lips touched the spot the man had just kissed, awareness fluttered through her. Ally wasn't the only female whose heartstrings were being strummed.

Spence stepped into the well-lit hall as Jordan exited the room. He waited while she pulled the door partially closed behind her.

"It's a nice night," he said, keeping his voice low, though nothing would wake the sleeping girl in the bedroom. "Would you like to join me on the front porch?"

"I, um," Jordan fumbled for an excuse. With Caleb gone overnight at the Summers ranch, being alone with this man was not a good idea.

His fingers gently circled her wrist. "I have a few questions for you."

His firm look told her his intent was not romantic. Jordan felt heat warm her neck. The man was kind and considerate but had otherwise shown only a few vague signs of physical attraction to her. *Good,* she told herself, *that would make the stay easier*.

With a relieved sigh, she nodded, "Okay. Do you mind if I make a cup of tea first?"

A few minutes later, Jordan stepped outside, a mug of hot tea in hand. Spence sat at the top of the steps, leaning against the porch post with his one leg stretched across the opening and the other bent casually at the knee. He looked relaxed and far too inviting. Tamping down her embarrassing awareness of the man, Jordan chose the hanging double swing that faced the yard. Silence surrounded them, and neither was eager to break its calm hold.

"It's so quiet here," Jordan murmured after a time. She pushed her foot against the floorboards to get the swing swaying slightly. The soft rhythmic squeak mixed with night sounds all around them. Crickets chirped. The occasional croak of a frog or horse's nicker added to nature's soothing song. "I never realized before that the quiet to which I've grown accustomed is actually the steady hum of automobiles."

Spence nodded in agreement. "There seem to be more stars here, too."

Jordan gazed out at the dark sky, dotted with billions of tiny twinkling sparks. No amount of manmade lighting could ever compete. God had woven an awesome tapestry for his people to enjoy. "It's beautiful, Mr. Spencer," she whispered.

Spence plunked the bottle of beer he'd been sipping on the porch deck and glared at her.

Blinking in surprise at the startling noise, Jordan glanced at the man's shadowed face. She couldn't see clearly but knew he was staring. "What?" she asked a little defensively.

"Why can't you call me Spence, like everyone else?" he demanded gruffly. He didn't mind the mister normally but coming from her, it sounded much too formal. "Don't we know each other well enough to be on a first name basis? I've been calling you Jordan almost since we met."

"But Spence isn't your first name," Jordan countered. "It's what...I don't know...football buddies would say."

"Everyone has called me Spence for as long as I can remember," he argued

"I doubt your mother ever called you by that name," Jordan huffed, daring him to dispute her words. "Surely, she called you Carl."

"No, she didn't," he denied, shaking a finger at her in triumph. "She calls me C.J."

"Short for Carl Junior," Jordan stated adamantly, figuring she had to be correct. "That's practically the same thing."

"Unfortunately!" Spence blurted without thinking. She'd gotten him riled, and he didn't like the feeling.

"She called your father Carl then, right?" Jordan asked, surprised by the vehemence in his voice.

"That, and a few other things I won't repeat in your presence," Spence mumbled, wishing he hadn't brought up the subject. Why did she have to be so damned difficult?!

"Oh, I guess things weren't wonderful between them," Jordan surmised, tempering her exasperation. Perhaps she should let this go. Their relationship was tenuous and confusing enough, at least for her.

Spence looked into the blackness of the night, memories of the useless man who fathered him skating across his mind. He needed to give Jordan some sort of explanation. He'd revealed too much already.

"He was a drunk, who couldn't keep a job longer than a couple of months at a time. One night he went on a binge and never came home. My mom waited a few weeks, constantly watching the street for his beat up truck, hoping the door would open, and he'd return. When the rent came due, we moved to my uncle's ranch outside of Abilene." It was the condensed version, but all he was willing to share.

He spoke in a monotone, only the barest hint of emotion present. It was the lack of sentiment that affected Jordan the most. Her heart ached for the disappointed little boy he'd once been.

"I'm so sorry," she whispered. "How old were you?"

"Twelve."

Jordan's chin quivered at the irony. He'd lost his father at almost the same age Caleb had found his – as if God had arranged to repair the damage. Could two hurting boys heal each other's broken hearts? She wanted to say all these things to him but dared not for fear she'd start bawling.

Swallowing her emotions, she asked, "Did you ever learn what happened to him?"

"My uncle ran into him years later, when I was a Marine bent on killing myself. He got him sobered up, and they talked. My old man said he walked out as a favor to me and my mom, said he knew he'd never quit drinking and didn't want to drag us down with him," Spence replied, his previous ire weakening. "I guess I should thank him. It was sure better on the ranch than living with him."

Sliding off her swing to join him on the floor, Jordan reached across the distance between them and touched his arm. "There may be more truth to that statement than you realize, Mr. Spencer...Carl," she said softly, trying his name aloud for the first time. "Stepping out of your life may have been the only thing your father had to offer. You said yourself, he was a drunk, incapable of stopping. He appeared to know that. What kind of life would you and your mother have had if he'd stayed? Perhaps, God allowed him to leave for your own good, to help you become the man you are now."

Spence stared at her, surprised. "Do you really believe that? Do you think your sister's death was for the benefit of Caleb and Ally?"

Jordan shrugged. "I don't know God's plan. I only know that Caleb has you in his life now, and that wouldn't have happened if Tanya were alive. He's happier than I've ever seen him."

Spence's heart warmed at her observation. Was his son really happy? Was Caleb glad Spence was in his life?

"What about Ally?" he asked. Before the question was out, Spence knew the answer. "She has you," he said with conviction. "From what I've learned about Tanya, you're a far better mother."

Jordan shook her head, unwilling to drag her sister's memory any lower. "I don't think..."

"It's true, and you know it," Spence insisted, interrupting her protest. He covered the hand she'd laid on his arm with his own and held her gaze. "You are an excellent, loving, perfect mother for those two kids," he said, earnestly.

Jordan met his intense gaze as long as she could. When the undercurrents that always seemed to flow between them became too great, she turned away, carefully withdrawing her hand from beneath his, and returned to the swing. Deep down, she knew he was right about her sister. Tanya wasn't the best mother, rarely putting her children first in any decision she made. After Dad passed away, and Tanya no longer had him to leave Caleb with, she and her son bounced from one live-in boyfriend to the next, changing schools often, and turning the child into a nervous, distrusting wreck. Jordan had accepted God's plan in her life and the lives of the children, though she was far from perfect, as he'd suggested. She welcomed Carl Spencer as an answered prayer and a blessing. Could she convince him to see himself that way?

"May I make a recommendation?" she asked softly.

"Fire away," Spence replied, emotionally drained from this enlightening discussion. Anything else she said couldn't possibly surprise him.

"Forgive your father, and reclaim your name."

Or so he'd thought. "I can't forgive my father. He's already dead," he replied evenly. "I looked for him a few years ago."

"You can still forgive him in your own heart," Jordan explained. "Harboring all that anger can make a person bitter and unhappy, even sick. I was angry with Tanya over a great many things. Her untimely death was just one more item to add to the list. After a while, I realized that holding on to that anger was only hurting me and crippling my ability to care for her children. I had to let it go, or I'd end up damaging them, too. So, I forgave her. I gave my anger to the Lord, and I got on with my life."

Spence recalled his mother saying something similar a long time ago. She admitted struggling with anger toward her ex-husband. The difference was she hadn't quit going to church when Dad left. Eventually, she'd found peace there and, as Jordan suggested, got on with her life. A couple of years ago, she'd even remarried. Abe Hoffman was a very nice man with a squeaky clean background. Spence had personally checked.

"Just like that, huh?" he said, half joking.

Jordan nodded as she picked up her mug and stood. The discussion had sapped her energy. It was time call it a night.

"Jordan?"

She stopped on the threshold facing him and waited.

"You can call me Carl, but I'm still Spence to everyone else."

Jordan smiled, knowing how difficult this was for the man. "I'll consider it an honor," she replied softly.

Remembering Caleb's near slip of the tongue, she added, "What about your son? Are you Spence to Caleb, too?"

"We're still working on that," Spence replied.

"Goodnight, Carl."

"Goodnight, Jordan."

Chapter 12

The following day was spent with the Summers family. Elizabeth suggested packing a picnic lunch and riding to a nearby swimming cove along the river. After spending the morning in the hot sun, everyone was bound to look forward to cooling off in the water. She was also anxious to make the acquaintance of Caleb's aunt and sister.

Caleb was eager to show off his newly attained skills, but Spence wouldn't allow the boy to ride Dancer. The horse was still too edgy for an inexperienced rider. One of Jack's horses was chosen for the boy. At the last minute, Spence brought Dancer along, planning to reacquaint the animal with the saddle himself. A gentle mare was outfitted for Jordan, who had learned how to handle a horse during her years attending Girl Scout summer camps. Ally would take turns riding with Jordan and Spence. Since Dancer was responding so well, Carl took the little girl first.

A few minutes into the ride, Elizabeth guided her horse into position beside Jordan's mount. "We haven't had a chance to say much more than 'hello,'" she said with a smile. "Are you enjoying your visit?"

"Very much," Jordan replied with a returning smile. "This is a beautiful part of the country. I had no idea such open space and glorious quiet still existed."

"It is quiet here," Elizabeth agreed. "After living in crowded Southern California my whole life, I wasn't sure I'd adjust. You're not having any trouble?"

"None at all, but then, I'm on vacation. I want to slow down and appreciate God's handiwork," Jordan replied.

The two women compared notes on life in Orange County, discovering several restaurants and attractions they'd both visited. Naturally, Disneyland was a favorite. The conversation turned to careers, and Jordan explained that she was currently teaching preschool but hoped to progress to primary in the future. She'd earned her bachelor's degree in early childhood education a few years ago and was mostly finished with the requirements for a teaching credential. With the untimely death of her sister, she'd been compelled to postpone the student teaching portion of her education. Elizabeth mentioned her former life in real estate.

Jordan couldn't help asking. "Do you miss working full-time?"

Elizabeth laughed. "Believe me, I work harder now than I ever did as a relator. But, to answer your question, no, I don't miss it a bit. I love being home with my kids. The added blessing of having Jack close by most of the time is nice, too. I can't imagine how lonely I'd be if he were gone every day."

"Do you get off the ranch much?" Jordan wondered. She glanced around. Endless, untouched land stretched in every direction. Even the expansive homestead had vanished behind one of the many hills they'd passed. Could she live in a place that felt this remote?

"Oh, yes, every few days. My brother and his family live in town, along with a few friends. My good friend, Karen, defected the same year I did, and married Jack's childhood friend, Frank Wilson. Their ranch borders ours," Elizabeth replied. She cocked her head and studied the younger woman beside her, wondering whether she'd accept an invitation to worship with her family. "You're welcome to join us for church Sunday," she ventured softly. Spence had politely declined each and every invitation she'd extended to the hard headed man.

"Oh, thank you so much," Jordan replied enthusiastically. "We'd love to, that is, the children and I would," she hastily corrected. She couldn't speak for Carl.

Pleased with the woman's eager response, Elizabeth leaned over and whispered, "Maybe you can convince Spence to come, as well. He dodges my efforts at every turn."

"I'll certainly try," Jordan promised. Oh, but she wanted to enjoy the service! Would she be able to concentrate if Carl sat beside her?

The conversation ended when Jack asked his wife to take a turn supervising their five-year-old, Matthew. The boy was riding his own pony and needed constant surveillance. Since their youngest, Marie, was only two, she was spending the day with the Wilsons. Elizabeth excused herself and trotted off to ride with her son.

After being in the saddle for nearly an hour, Jordan couldn't wait to stop and get off. In her excitement to ride again, after almost a decade, she'd forgotten how doing so always aggravated her hips. Her bottom, she knew, wasn't going to fare well either. When they finally arrived, she discovered that dismounting was going to be harder than she'd anticipated. She needed help.

"Come get your sister, Caleb," Spence called as he took the drowsy girl from her aunt and set her on her feet. Ally reached for her brother's hand, and he led her away.

Spence turned to Jordan, who was still in the saddle, a pained look on her face. Assuming he knew what ailed her, he hid his smile. "Do you need a hand?"

Jordan bit her lower lip and nodded. The ache in her hips had advanced to a steady throb. Her legs felt numb. There was no way she'd be able to lift her right leg over the animal's back. She glanced around, embarrassed. Everyone else had dismounted and was busy gathering youngsters and picnic supplies.

"Come on," Spence said, his mirth shifting to sympathy. He wrapped his hands around her waist and urged her toward him.

Jordan leaned against his strong shoulders as he gently pulled her off the horse. "Don't let go yet," she whispered, after her feet touched the ground. She leaned against his tall frame and waited for the feeling to return to her legs, moaning helplessly with the discomfort.

Obliging her request, Spence drew her closer. Her warm skin and heavenly aroma sent his pulse racing. He breathed deeply, hoping to slow his body's zealous reaction before she noticed. "Are you going to be all right?" he asked, his words muffled against her hair.

Jordan nodded against his chest. If she weren't so focused on her own distress, the rapid beat of his heart beneath her ear might have warned her of his. After a moment, she cautiously stepped back. "I think I'm okay now," she said, massaging her jean clad hips and carefully stomping her feet. "But I'm not eager to get back on that horse."

Relieved to have her away from him, Spence tipped his hat like a gentleman cowboy and treated her to a lopsided grin. "We'll see that you get a nice long break, ma'am," he drawled.

Jordan laughed at his humorous antics, appreciating that he was trying to ease her suffering. When he offered his arm, she looped her hand through the crook of his elbow, and they joined the others.

Thirty minutes later, Elizabeth's carefully assembled picnic was thoroughly ravaged, and everyone was ready to cool off. Ally dozed off right after lunch, leaving Jordan with a little free time. She chose to take advantage of the rare opportunity and donned her swimsuit.

Elizabeth complimented Jordan on her modest, Hawaiian-print suit. The long top and high waist bottoms met at her middle, covering like a one piece. At thirty-five, Elizabeth's figure was still attractive in her modest, tank-style, black suit. If she had any doubts on that score, Jack's appreciative glances would have dispelled them. As she gingerly made her way down the steep embankment to the flat shore, Jordan didn't dare seek out the eyes of the other man present. When her toes touched the icy water, she instantly pulled back her foot.

"It's run off from the mountains," a deep, familiar voice said from directly behind her. "It'll stay pretty cold until late summer."

Jordan glanced up as Spence stepped beside her. He dropped his gaze from her lovely face, making a quick inspection of her shapely form. Her cheeks reddened, and he grinned mischievously. The modest suit covered entirely too much, he decided. "Pretty bathing suit," he whispered close to her ear.

"Thanks," Jordan managed to croak.

Still wearing his black T-shirt, now coupled with swim trunks in the same color, Spence waded into the water up to his waist. He turned and crooked his finger at her. "Come on in, Jordan," he said through teeth clamped against the cold. Knowing she'd see right through his blatant lie, he continued, "The water feels great."

"If it's so wonderful, go all the way under," she challenged.

"I will if you promise to join me."

"I won't be getting in that freezing water, no matter what you do," she replied, crossing her arms over her chest.

"In that case, I might have to help you," Spence replied with an impish smile. He slowly made his way toward her.

"You wouldn't dare," Jordan replied, suddenly worried that he might follow through with his threat. She dropped her hands to her sides and glanced over her shoulder, mentally calculating the amount of time it would take to get up the bank before he caught her.

Spence's eyebrows shot up, and he grinned slyly. "Is that a challenge?" he asked, executing a playful lunge toward her.

Before Jordan had time to react, ice cold hands circled her wrists. "Carl, no!" she pleaded softly, suspecting she was about to be dragged into the river.

Chuckling, Spence held her for a moment. "If we didn't have an audience, I'd toss you in on principle alone," he said, drawing her close enough for his wet bathing suit to drip cool water onto the tops of her feet. "I never turn down a dare, sweetheart. However, since Elizabeth would probably have my hide, I'll refrain – just this once, mind you." Her breath came in stuttering gasps. Her eyes, wide with the aftermath of fear, gazed up into his, and he glimpsed trust in their emerald depths.

When she smiled, his stomach did that annoying little flip again.

"You're not so tough, mister," Jordan whispered as she turned and strode away.

Jordan reached the safety of the picnic blankets none too soon. Feeling exposed, she pulled on a cotton skirt over her swim suit bottoms and dropped onto the blanket, exhausted. He'd managed to unnerve her again, and she trembled inside. Surely, everyone would notice. Her heart was pounding loud enough to shake the earth. How could he make her feel so terrified and alive at the same time? She rested her head on her bent knees. Her pulse slowed, and her eyelids drooped heavily. A nap would restore her confidence, give her much needed strength. Before she could seriously consider joining Ally in slumber, Elizabeth dropped down on the blanket.

"They sure are having a good time," the older woman commented, nodding toward the cove. Using a rope someone had hung from a tree growing along the edge of the river, the boys were taking turns launching themselves over the water and dropping into the deepest area. "Look, the men are going to have a turn."

They watched for a few minutes, laughing when Carl inadvertently did a belly flop.

"Something funny, ladies?" he hollered when he came up for air and heard them. He rubbed his red belly and shot them a pained look.

"Poor baby," Jordan whispered, snickering behind her hand. Carl pointed at her then made a gesture like he was dunking someone. Shaking her head vehemently, she waggled her index finger at him in warning.

Elizabeth watched the silent communication with interest. They seemed to get along well. Since they were bound by a child almost like a former couple, the positive relationship would likely prove to be a good thing. Every now and then, she caught the hint of something more. She glanced at the young woman beside her. Smiling, Jordan was dismissing Spence with the flick of her left hand.

Noticing the attractive silver band on Jordan's third finger, Elizabeth commented, "Your ring is very pretty."

"Thank you," Jordan replied, spreading her fingers to admire her ring.

"Did someone special give it to you?" Elizabeth knew she was prying but couldn't seem to help herself.

A small smile tugged at the corners of Jordan's lips. "My dad," she said softly, pleasant memories gliding across her mind.

Elizabeth leaned in to get a closer look. "Oh, it's a purity ring," she said, noticing the inscription. "I thought...well, never mind."

"You thought it was from a man," Jordan finished for her. "I quit wearing it for a long time because of that."

Elizabeth had assisted during a youth event at her church a few years ago. Similar rings were given out to any teenager who chose to make a commitment. She knew the ring represented much more than purity. It meant waiting, however long it took, for God to send along the right partner. Many people didn't have the patience. This young woman was well past the age when most gave up and gave in, yet clearly her vow was still important.

Patting Jordan's arm, Elizabeth said, "I applaud your decision to wait on the Lord. What made you start wearing it again?"

Elizabeth watched her new friend's gaze travel down to the water's edge and land on Carl Spencer. He looked up just then and Jordan hastily dropped her eyes, her cheeks flushed.

"Oh," Elizabeth said. "I thought I detected something."

"There's nothing going on, really," Jordan quickly clarified. "It's just that, well, he...unsettles me. I can't...we can't," she stuttered through the disjointed explanation. "Carl is my sister's former lover, the father of her son. I put the ring back on because I needed the reminder that God has someone for me."

"And you don't think he's the one," Elizabeth finished for her.

With absolute certainty, Jordan shook her head. A little physical attraction would not be enough to carry them through the long winters of their lives. Besides, Chris was waiting for her at home. Between him and Carl Spencer, Chris seemed far more likely to fulfill the role of partner in Jordan's life.

Elizabeth didn't miss the look of reluctant acceptance that displaced Jordan's previously cheerful expression. Taking her friend's hand, she gave it a tender squeeze. She knew Spence well enough to understand her friend's reasoning. At the same time, she recognized the recent changes in the man. He attended Bible studies with his son, even participating on occasion, according to Jack. He was taking his role as a father very seriously. Might he come around enough to prove himself worthy of a woman like Jordan?

Chapter 13

A tall shade tree outside Jordan's westward facing window kept the room in relative darkness until late morning. By the time Jordan opened her eyes, the sun was high in the sky. She stretched lazily, amazed at how nice it felt to sleep late. Voices and the occasional bark of a dog drifted up from the backyard.

Curious, Jordan crawled from beneath the warm covers, stole to the open window, and peered outside. Caleb held onto one end of what looked like an old sock. The terrier tugged eagerly on the other end. Ally stood a few feet away, giggling and petting the old dog which sat obediently beside her.

Smiling, Jordan tapped on the glass. Both children looked up and waved excitedly.

"Caleb's funny!" Ally called, pointing at her brother.

"Yes, he is," Jordan agreed. "Are you having a good time?"

Ally nodded and patted Lady's head. "Lady my friend," she said. The dog's eyes squinted closed with each vigorous thump on her brow.

"I can see that," Jordan said, glad the dog was so tolerant and gentle.

"Jordan, can Ally go for a walk with me and Butch?" Caleb called. When Jordan frowned uncertainly, he assured her, "We go every morning. I'll be careful."

"Okay, see that you are," Jordan relented.

Fifteen minutes later, Jordan sat on the bottom step of the rear porch. She'd found a full coffee pot on her way through the kitchen and helped herself. Left behind, Lady had decided to befriend her as well. The old dog lay beside Jordan, leaning against her thigh.

Jordan stared across the field beyond the backyard. Caleb's tall figure was easy to spot. With her head and shoulders barely higher than the tall grass, Ally was only partially visible. The only indication of the dog was the occasional eruption of birds escaping from the field in protest. Jordan couldn't help chuckling at the comical sight. She looked up when the door opened behind her.

"Morning," Spence said, holding up the coffee pot. "Do you need a refill?"

"Good morning and yes, thank you," she replied, holding up her mug.

Spence topped off her coffee, set the pot inside, and returned to the porch. "Did you sleep well?" he asked as he squatted down and sat on the stoop.

"Extremely well," she replied. "I'm embarrassed to show my face this late in the morning."

Spence smiled. "You had a busy day yesterday."

Lady laid her head in Jordan's lap and Jordan obliged by scratching the dog behind the ears. "Still, someone should have awakened me."

Not long ago, Spence had overheard Caleb telling his sister to do that and stopped them. "Nah, we figured you needed it. I don't imagine single parenthood allows for much sleeping in."

Jordan thought back over the last twenty-odd months. Ally was still a baby, only a little over a year old when Jordan became her surrogate mother. At three, she still required a good deal of supervision. She nodded, affirming the man's observation.

"How are things with you and Caleb," Jordan asked, changing the subject.

"Good," Spence replied. "He's coming around. Moving to this house has helped. He likes looking after the stock. The boy is compassionate when it comes to animals."

"I'd never noticed before," Jordan said, a bit remorsefully. "He's always lived in apartments, so being around animals is a new experience. The poor kid has never had more than a bowl of goldfish."

"It must be tough growing up that way." Spence observed, thinking about the ranch on which he'd been fortunate to grow up, and the dogs and cats he'd kept as pets. He'd never really appreciated how lucky he was.

"Is he staying out of trouble?" Jordan asked, certain she'd have heard by now if Caleb was being a problem.

"He doesn't have time to get into trouble," Spence replied with a chuckle. "Between helping out at the Summers ranch and keeping up this place, we both work pretty hard."

"He doesn't fight you on that?" Taking out the trash had been a weekly battle with the stubborn boy.

"At first, a little," Spence replied. "But I didn't give him much of a choice. After a while, he quit complaining and just did what needed to be done. Hard work is good for a boy."

"I suppose it is," Jordan agreed. Maybe part of Caleb's problems at home stemmed from not having enough productive activities to keep him busy. He'd had too much time on his hands. Would the boy fall back into the same bad habits when he returned?

As if reading her mind, Spence said, "Before he goes home, I'll have a long chat with him about what's expected."

Jordan glanced over her shoulder at Caleb's father and nodded. "That might be a good idea." When she looked back toward the field, she noted that the children were now walking toward the house.

"What do you say we go into town for breakfast," Spence suggested when the children returned. Everyone agreed heartily.

A short time later, the small group stepped inside the Bread Basket. Immediately, Ally announced she needed to use the potty, so Jordan herded the little girl to the ladies' room while the guys chose a booth. Only a few minutes passed before a plump, middle-aged waitress arrived with two glasses of water.

"Well, good morning, gentlemen," the woman said cheerfully. "I haven't had the pleasure of your company at one of my tables in a while. Where have you two been keeping yourselves?"

"Good morning, Tammy," Spence replied good-naturedly. "We've been eating at home lately."

"I heard you were taking care of Mrs. Hill's place while she's recuperating," Tammy said.

Spence spotted Jordan and Ally approaching and stood quickly. "We'll need a couple more waters, when you have a chance," he said, gesturing toward the girls.

"I'll get them right out, Spence," Tammy assured him. With a nod to the newcomers, she hurried off to fetch two more glasses.

Spence stood, and Ally bounced onto the cushioned seat and scooted over, clearly expecting him to sit beside her. Jordan took the seat opposite Spence, boxing the two kids in the middle of the corner booth. Picking up the children's menu, Spence began showing Ally her choices.

"Here you are, ladies," Tammy said, setting the additional glasses on the table. She smiled at Jordan. "Welcome to the Bread Basket and our humble community."

"Thank you," Jordan replied, pleased by the woman's friendly demeanor.

"I'm sorry," Spence blurted, realizing he'd forgotten to make introductions. Coming from busy Southern California, Jordan wouldn't think anything of it. "Tammy, this is Jordan Gray, Caleb's aunt. Jordan, our waitress and co-owner of the Bread Basket, Tammy…uh…"

"Just Tammy," the waitress said, reaching out to shake the young woman's outstretched hand. "Last names aren't necessary here." She turned to Ally, smiling at the adorable little girl. "And who might this be?"

"This is my sister, Ally," Caleb supplied before anyone else had the chance. "Jordan and Ally are visiting us," he added eagerly.

"Wonderful! I hope you all have a nice vacation. I'm sure these two gents are showing you a good time," Tammy said, gesturing to Caleb and Spence.

"Caleb gave me a kitty," Ally announced. "It's not real. It's pretend."

"How lovely," Tammy replied. Then, "Are ya'll ready to order, or do you need a few more minutes?"

A little while later, everyone was digging into their delicious homemade breakfasts with enthusiasm. Jordan couldn't believe the enormous meals Spence and Caleb were consuming. Their plates were loaded with steak, eggs, pancakes, and hash browns – the works. Ally worked with determination to finish her silver dollar pancakes.

Frowning, Spence glanced at Jordan's bowl of oatmeal and plate of scrambled eggs. "Is that going to be enough for you?" he asked, skeptically.

"Plenty," Jordan replied, adding in a teasing tone, "If it isn't, maybe I'll swipe one of your pancakes."

Spence pulled his plate of hotcakes closer and shot her a mock look of horror. Jordan was still trying not to laugh when a portly uniformed man stopped by their table.

"How are you doing, Spence," Sheriff Davies boomed, startling Ally. The little girl shrank against Spence's side and eyed the big man warily. "Oh, sorry about that, missy," Davies said, chagrined. He dropped his tone and added, "My wife's always reminding me to lower my voice. It scares the little ones. I'm afraid, I forgot."

"Don't worry about it, Sheriff," Spence said, patting Ally's shoulder reassuringly.

"Eat your breakfast, Ally," Jordan said softly. Ally nodded and returned her attention to her plate.

Spence made introductions again, and the sheriff tipped his hat to Jordan.

"I won't keep you from your breakfast," Sheriff Davies promised. "Spence, I wondered if you'd stop by my office later. There's something I'd like to discuss with you."

Spence caught Jordan's eye. "Are you and Elizabeth still planning on shopping this afternoon?"

"As far as I know," Jordan replied. Elizabeth had offered to show her around town.

Returning his attention to the sheriff, Spence asked, "Does two o'clock work for you, Sheriff?"

"Works fine," Davies replied. "I'll see you then." He tipped his hat to Jordan once more and took his leave.

Jordan and Ally enjoyed a busy afternoon in town with Elizabeth Summers and her niece. Ten-year-old Emily was a big help, entertaining Ally and her cousin, Marie, leaving the adults free to explore. Much of their time was consumed browsing in a lovely little shop co-owned by two of Elizabeth's good friends. Karen Wilson, an artist, and Elizabeth's sister-in-law, Andrea Nelson, who sewed beautiful quilts and other handmade items, had combined their talents four years ago, opening the store together. Their quaint establishment, Cottage Creations, had gained a reputation as a favorite location, even attracting shoppers from neighboring communities.

~ * ~

Spence surprised everyone by accepting Jordan's request to attend church. "If you don't want to go, I'll need you to drop us off," she'd explained. She wouldn't miss – couldn't, not with all she was struggling through. If he didn't want to drive her, she'd find another way to get there.

The service was excellent and Jordan had no problem focusing on the interesting sermon. The pastor spoke about waiting for God's perfect plan. How apt, Jordan thought, recognizing that her patience was growing thin in that regard. She felt particularly challenged lately, and asked God to strengthen her throughout the remaining days of her vacation in Montana.

Afterward, they enjoyed an afternoon barbeque with the Summers family and a number of their friends. The children played while the adults socialized. Jordan enjoyed becoming better acquainted with some of the women she'd met during her visit. By the end of the day, she was tired and happy, feeling she'd been accepted as one of the community.

Later that evening, Jordan came downstairs from tucking Ally in for the night. "She's already asleep," she announced softly.

"That didn't take long," Spence replied from his place on the sofa. He looked up from the outdated copy of Field and Stream he'd found in the bottom of Mrs. Hills china cabinet. "Have a seat."

Dropping into one of the two threadbare but comfortable wingback chairs, Jordan pulled her feet up and tucked them beneath her. She leaned her head against one of the side wings and glanced at the man across from her. He looked relaxed with his legs stretched out in front of him, his crossed feet propped on the coffee table. "How did you wind up in the FBI, Carl?" Jordan asked curiously.

Caleb heard his aunt's question as he came in from the kitchen. He'd been out back feeding the dogs. He quietly entered the room and sat in the other chair.

Spence looked from one expectant face to the other and smiled. "Well, it's sort of a long story," he said.

"We aren't goin' anywhere," Caleb replied, as he plopped his stocking covered feet on the coffee table beside his father's.

Raising his eyebrows, Spence pointed out humorously, "I think your aunt might be going to Slumberland." Jordan's eyes had drifted shut as soon as she sat down, the busy day catching up with her.

"I'm listening," Jordan said softly, keeping her eyes closed. "Go on."

With a nod, Spence thought over his past, trying to decide where to start. "Okay, I'll give you the short version," he finally said. "I'd been in the Marines a couple of years and was getting bored. We'd had a few skirmishes, been deployed a time or two. Mostly, being in the service meant watch and wait. Jack Summers was my commander at the time. He recommended me for advanced training, probably to get rid of my unruly butt," he added with a chuckle. "I was a real hothead back then, getting into trouble regularly. Jack basically gave me two choices – find something productive to do or plan on a dishonorable discharge, because that was the direction I was heading. He saw potential in me that I didn't."

"Mr. Summers helped you get into the FBI?" Caleb asked incredulously. "I'll bet Jeremy doesn't know that."

"Not directly," Spence corrected. "My time with the feds didn't happen for a while. In fact, Jack and I lost touch not long after that."

"Oh," Caleb muttered.

"What happened next," Jordan murmured, still peacefully resting her head against the chair.

Spence glanced at her closed eyes, studying the relaxed picture she presented. Her golden brown hair fell across her face in a soft wave. Long dark lashes fanned her cheek bones. Warmth spread in his middle and he forced his gaze away.

Clearing his throat, he continued, "I took a bunch of tests, and must have scored high because they accepted me – put me on the fast track for a college degree, gave me additional training in map reading, statistics, problem solving, stuff like that. I thought I was preparing for the officer program, and so did the Marines. About a year before my tour of duty was up, two guys dressed in dark suits knocked on my door. I guess the feds had been keeping tabs on me, while they waited until my commitment was finished. The job sounded interesting and definitely paid better. I left the military and joined the FBI. The rest, as they say, is history."

"Then you got shot and came here," Caleb added matter-of-factly, as he rose from his chair. He didn't see Jordan's eyes pop open. "I'm going to take a shower," he announced and headed for the stairs.

Caleb missed Jordan's intense reaction, but Spence didn't. He watched her previously smooth brow furrow deeply. Her tranquil expression was gone, replaced with one of apprehension.

"You never said you were shot," she said quietly.

Dropping his feet to the floor, Spence propped his elbows on his knees and studied the now tense woman across from him. No, he'd kept that minor detail to himself. "It was irrelevant," he replied evasively.

Blinking several times, trying desperately to assimilate what she'd just heard, Jordan slowly shook her head. "I don't think so," she breathed. From upstairs, she heard a door close, followed by the rumble of the water pipes when Caleb turned on the shower.

"Jordan..."

"Tell me, please," Jordan interrupted.

Spence sighed, knowing he couldn't avoid this any longer. He'd figured she'd find out sooner or later, especially with everyone in town being privy to the information. "During my last assignment, I took a bullet to the shoulder."

"The right one," Jordan stated. She'd noticed how he seemed to favor that side. It hadn't occurred to her to wonder why.

Spence nodded.

"When?"

"Nearly a year ago."

A year ago! He'd been on leave for a long time. "It must have been bad." Her tone was low, barely audible.

Spence's gaze held hers. She was too smart to accept any sugar coating. She'd already deduced that a year off work equated to a severe injury. He nodded again. "Several surgeries were needed to rebuild my shoulder, followed by over six months of physical therapy." He kept his tone neutral, his expression reserved.

Without conscious thought, Jordan rose and moved to his side. She sank to the sofa cushion on Spence's right. Her gut told her there was more, that he'd nearly lost his life. She raised her hand, laying it against the front of his shoulder. "Here?"

Spence stared at her for a long moment. The strong connection he felt with this woman was nearly overpowering. He wanted her comfort, her touch. And he needed to be completely straight with her. Leaning back, he reached for the edge of his T-shirt and tugged it over his head.

Jordan dragged her gaze from his intent face to the damaged flesh, her eyes widening at the disturbing sight. The scarring was extensive, covering several square inches and extending over his shoulder to his back. Angry fingers of raised, discolored flesh stretched across his chest in every direction. Some of the scaring reached his collarbone. Tears sprang to her eyes, as she lifted her hand again and gently touched his wound.

Spence watched her expression shift from the initial horror to deep compassion. Moisture glistened in her eyes. Her fingers lightly brushed his skin, setting off tiny sparks of sensation. Warmth flooded his scarred shoulder. His eyes never left her face. A tear slid free and coursed down her cheek. Spence reached up and brushed it away, his fingers lingering on her soft skin, his thumb gliding over her cheekbone. When she turned her tender gaze to his face, his chest tightened and his breathing slowed.

"It must have been horrible," Jordan whispered. "I'm so sorry, Carl."

Spence covered her hand with his and pressed it to his scarred skin. "It was, but I survived," he responded, suddenly anxious for her to understand.

His words triggered uncertainty in the back of Jordan's mind. *I survived.* It almost sounded like others hadn't.

"We weren't expecting trouble," Spence said, as though he'd heard her thoughts. "Gunfire seemed to come from every direction. My partner didn't make it. He left behind a wife and two children."

Jordan felt suddenly light headed. Her vision blurred, and she swayed. Closing her eyes, she felt Carl's arms loop around her, felt his bare skin against her damp cheek. Images coursed across her mind – Carl bleeding, another man lying dead, a sobbing woman in a black dress, grieving children clinging to her hands. *Grieving children! A flower draped casket!* Caleb's tear-streaked face hovered in her mind, and then Ally's. *Oh, God!*

Spence held Jordan for several minutes, his heart aching as he listened to her weep, felt her shuddering against him. When she suddenly stiffened and pushed away, he wasn't sure what to make of it. He watched as she withdrew both physically and emotionally, her pale expression turning passive. His eyes held hers for only a moment before she looked away. She stood and rushed up the stairs.

"Jordan?" he called before she reached the top, worried about the abrupt change.

"Goodnight, Carl," she called back without turning.

~ * ~

Over the next few days, Jordan avoided Carl. Fear kept her moving, constantly disappearing anytime they might end up alone. Two months ago, when she'd first learned that he was an FBI agent, she hadn't given it a second thought. He had a good job, worked for a respectable organization. If anything, she'd been impressed and fascinated. She'd been oblivious to the dangers he faced daily, had no idea that people shot at him. She shuddered each time she thought of it.

With disgust, she recalled the way she'd silently commended herself on finding him. Now, she worried she'd set Caleb up for the ultimate heartbreak. As if he hadn't been through enough, she reminded herself. Had she brought them together only to have the boy lose his father in some senseless, tragic way? Was he destined to attend another parent's funeral? Her throat thickened at the mental image.

Spence stood near the barn door, quietly watching Jordan. Deep in thought, she leaned on the corral fence, absently stroking Dancer's neck. The horse loved her. Whenever she came within his view, he trotted along the fence, nickering and making a nuisance of himself until she went to him. Spence had to bribe the animal with a carrot or an apple to lure him near enough to touch.

Dancer pushed his sides against Jordan's hand, shamelessly begging for a scratch, and Jordan obliged, raking her fingernails into his thick coat.

"Careful," Spence said from behind her, making her jump. He felt devious sneaking up on her, but it seemed the only way he was going to get her alone. There were things between them that needed to be cleared up.

"Y-you scared me," Jordan cried, yanking her hand through the slats. Dancer emitted a noisy exhale, protesting the disruption of his massage.

"You're spoiling that horse," Spence said with a grin. "He'll be impossible to live with..." He started to add 'after you go home' but caught himself. In two days, he'd take Jordan and Ally back to the airport. He didn't like to think about them leaving.

"I'm sure Mrs. Hill will forgive me," Jordan replied. She felt it prudent to remind herself that this wasn't his home, that one day soon he'd be going back to New Jersey and his job.

Spence watched her eyes shift from him to the house. She was planning her escape. When she stepped in that direction, he reached out and grasped her forearm. "Jordan, we need to talk."

Jordan kept her eyes averted, her mind spinning, searching for an excuse that would delay this conversation. Finding none, she sighed in resignation and nodded.

"About the other night..." he began softly.

"How many times have you been shot?" she blurted, suddenly anxious to have all the facts.

"Jordan..."

"How many, Carl?" she demanded sharply. "How long before Caleb loses his father, too?" She'd lain awake every night wrestling with this thought, fearing that the day would come. Another knock on the door, another funeral – *Please God!* She couldn't bear to go through it again. "You can't do that to him!" Anger gripped her, and she yanked her arm free.

"Jordan, stop!" Spence grabbed her upper arms and held her, facing him. She flinched a couple of times, trying to pull away and then stilled. "Look at me!" he commanded, his tone stern.

Jordan lifted her face and stared into his anguish-filled eyes. Her anger fled as quickly as it had come, her throat closing as sorrow took its place. She started to cry. Spence drew her into his arms.

"I'm not planning to die any time soon," he whispered against her hair. "I only just found my son. I have no intention of leaving him."

"Your job..." Jordan rasped.

Spence sighed. The job – that seemed to be the million dollar question lately. He still hadn't arrived at a decision, didn't even know his choices yet. "I might not be able to go back into the field," he said, hoping to alleviate some of her worries. He stroked his hands up and down her back, soothing his own emotional turmoil with the touch, as well as hers.

"What do you mean?" Jordan whispered.

"My shoulder will never fully recover," he replied softly. "Depending on how well it heals, how much movement it regains, they may pull me from field duty."

Even as he voiced the truth, he grimaced at the thought. He loathed the idea of being a desk jockey. At the same time, he understood Jordan's fears, recognizing the realities of his job. In eight years, he'd taken three bullets. The other two weren't serious, but this last one had nearly killed him. If the medics hadn't been able to transfuse him en route to the hospital, he'd have died. Jordan was right; he couldn't put his son through another loss. He'd have to learn to be content behind a desk, or find another line of work.

As Jordan leaned against the hard chest of the man, strong arms encircling her, warm attentive fingers comforting her, she recognized that it would be extraordinarily easy to fall in love with Carl Spencer. His very presence awakened something in her that she'd never felt before, feelings she wanted to explore.

Shoving all that aside, she forced herself to remember the conversation from the other night. She squeezed her eyes shut, letting in the ugly images of the past – Tanya's funeral, the casket bearing her sister's remains resting at the front of a cold anteroom, Caleb's pale, shocked face, Ally's confusion and tears as she responded to the emotional tension all around. The child was so young; she didn't even know why she cried. Jordan's thoughts turned to Carl's scarred shoulder, and the knowledge that he could be shot again. Next time, it might be his body lying in the ornate box, waiting to be lowered into the ground. Jordan resolved to control her reactions to this man. Her future held too many uncertainties, too many hazards to risk adding a shattered heart.

A picture of Chris's handsome face slipped into her mind. He worked as an engineer – a nice, safe job with no risk of death. She was ashamed to admit he'd hardly entered her thoughts in the last week and a half. That would change now, she decided. She could imagine a future with him, a long, happy life filled with…living.

Jordan sniffled and inhaled, bringing her emotions under control. She pushed gently against Carl's firm chest. When his hold loosened, she stepped out of his embrace. Dragging her wrist over her checks, she wiped away most of the dampness. "I'm sorry," she said.

Spence held her arm as long as he could, finally letting go when she moved beyond his reach. His hand dropped to his side. "Are you okay?"

She nodded. Not meeting his eyes, she replied, "Yes, just…worried about Caleb's heart."

What about yours? a voice inside his head whispered. He pushed the question to the back of his mind. A woman like Jordan deserved more than he could offer. Yes, he'd try to keep himself safe. He'd even seriously consider the desk, for his son's sake. He couldn't make any promises to Jordan. He knew himself too well. When it came to women, he wasn't the staying kind. He couldn't see that changing, no matter how beautiful and alluring the woman standing before him, no matter how painfully his gut twisted each time she looked at him, no matter how often his heart told his mind that he needed her.

Chapter 14

Spence tapped on the partially closed door to room 2B. A metal frame mounted on the wall beside the door held a white card on which was printed *Mrs. Adele Hill*, confirming he was at the right place. Caleb was enjoying a day with Jeremy. Jack had been the one to suggest the boy stay behind while Spence took Jordan and Ally to the airport. It provided an ideal opportunity to stop in for this overdue visit to Mrs. Hill.

The nurse had suggested that it might take a few tries to get the elderly woman's attention. Her hearing wasn't at its best. He knocked again.

The sound of a throat being cleared reached him, followed by a faint, "Come in."

Spence pushed the door open and stepped inside the dimly lit room. The hospital smell wasn't quite as strong here as it was in the hall. He glanced around, quickly noting the homey touches to the otherwise antiseptic room. A vase filled with fresh flowers, along with several potted plants, rested on a shelf below the window. A knitted throw draped the foot of the bed. Get well cards were propped here and there.

"Can I help you?" the woman's scratchy voice asked.

"I'm sorry to disturb you, Mrs. Hill," Spence said, moving farther into the room. "My name is Carl Spencer. Sheriff Davies said..."

"My, aren't you a sight for sore eyes," she cried, smiling and reaching a hand out to him. "Come on over here and let me look at you."

Surprised, Spence walked to the bed and took the elderly lady's bony hand. She gave his fingers a surprisingly firm squeeze and let go.

"Have a seat, young man," she said, gesturing to a chair beside her, "And tell me, how are my babies doing?"

"The animals are all doing fine, ma'am," Spence said, perching on the edge of the seat.

She waved her hand, a look of disgust pinching her wrinkled face. "You can dispense with the ma'ams and the missus. I'm Adele, son. After all, you're living in my house."

Spence smiled. He liked the old bird already. When Sheriff Davies said she wanted to speak to him, he'd been a bit uncertain, wondering why. The man had given no reason, just shrugged his ample shoulders as if that explained it.

"Okay," Spence replied. "Adele it is."

"And what do they call you?"

"Most people call me Spence," he replied.

"Spence?!" she exclaimed uncertainly. "Well, I don't like it. What did you say your first name was?"

"Carl," he offered, remembering Jordan's similar response to his nickname.

"Alright, Carl. Tell me about my place. Is Buster giving you a bad time?"

Spence spent the next few minutes telling Adele about her zoo. Buster had yet to warm to him, he told her, though he hadn't given up on the old mule. Shasta was content to hang out in the paddock. He described how happy she seemed when he picked up Ally and plopped the little girl on the old mare's back one morning.

Gentle as can be, as tough she knew she carried precious cargo, the horse had strolled patiently around the perimeter of the corral with Ally clinging to her mane, and Spence walking beside her.

"She always was good with the little ones," Mrs. Hill said, her voice growing soft with things remembered. "I'll just bet your daughter loved her, too."

"Ally is my son's sister," Spence explained. "She was visiting with their aunt." At her confused expression, he shook his head and said, "It's a long story."

Mrs. Hill flipped the edge of her blanket over exposing a glimpse of the cast that encased a quarter of her body and kept her bedridden. "I've got no place to go," she said. "I could do with a long story."

Chuckling at the woman's direct approach, Spence began at the beginning, when he first learned that someone was searching for him. It took an hour, with the woman asking questions periodically. She was thrilled to hear that Dancer had not only been ridden but also made friends.

"He always was a ladies' man," she commented, referring to her horse's affection for Jordan.

Spence concluded his story with this morning's trip to the airport then quieted.

Mrs. Hill stared at him, seeing things in his face he probably wished to keep hidden. "You like the girl, don't you, Carl?" she said, her tone serious.

He knew she referred to Jordan. "She's very nice," he replied, pretending to misunderstand her meaning.

"Yes, I can tell," she commented. Guessing that she wasn't going to get him to admit anything exciting, she changed the subject. "Have you given any thought to the sheriff's proposal?"

Spence blinked in surprise. Now, why would the old coot tell Mrs. Hill about the discussion they'd had? Her hearty guffaw stunned him further.

"When Davies was still a deputy," she explained, "his superior pulled him aside, and let him know he was impressed. The sheriff could see leadership potential in his young deputy. You see, he was thinking on retirement and didn't want to leave the town to fend for itself. A good lawman wants to see his shoes are filled properly. Don't you think that's wise?" she asked cryptically.

Spence nodded, curious to see where this discussion was going.

"As do I," she continued. "Davies knew he'd have his boss's endorsement if he chose to run for sheriff, when the time came. And it did come, just a year later, when Sheriff Hill announced his intention to step down."

Spence's eyes widened as understanding dawned. "Your husband."

"One and the same," Mrs. Hill replied, clearly pleased with herself. "My William was ready to take it easy, travel maybe, play checkers at the feed store with his buddies." Her wistful smile waned. "He only got in a couple of good years. I'm so glad he retired when he did, that he chose not to put it off."

Spence stared at the floor, imagining what had happened. "What took him?"

"Cancer," she replied softly. "He was a lifelong smoker, as were many of his friends. He wasn't the first to go that way, nor the last, I'm sorry to say. I'm thankful the Lord saw fit to take him quickly. The day the pain got so bad he couldn't bear it, he went to sleep and didn't wake up."

"I'm sorry."

"So am I," she said. "We had a wonderful marriage, lasted nearly fifty years. I wouldn't trade one day. The good Lord called my William home for a reason, and I'm not one to question Him. I loved being married, but I've also enjoyed being alone. William never liked maintaining the property, so we'd sold off a good deal of it. He didn't much care for raising animals, so we never had any more than a dog while he was alive. As you can see, I've indulged myself a bit," she said with a wink.

"But the mule?" Spence asked in pretend disgust, returning her wink with one of his own.

"Buster's a dear, but he can be a pain," she agreed. "I've been considering selling him, especially now." She tapped on her hard cast meaningfully. At her age, it would be foolhardy to think she'd bounce back completely. It was time she faced reality. "On that note, I've got a proposal of my own for you. It might make the sheriff's a bit more tempting."

Spence gave her his full attention.

~ * ~

With Ally in tow, Jordan stopped by the market on her way home from work. They'd been back several days, and she hadn't been on a real grocery run. She checked her list as she made her way through the big store. When they finally finished, she paid and headed home.

As she carried in the last bags, the telephone started ringing. Hastily setting her packages on the kitchen table, she rushed to answer the call before it went to voicemail. It was Caleb.

"Hi, Jordan," the boy said.

"Caleb, how are you?" She hadn't expected to hear from him so soon. There were still a couple of weeks of summer left. Spence wasn't planning to bring his son home until just before school was scheduled to start.

"I'm fine. Guess what?" Caleb said excitedly. "Me and Jeremy are gonna try bronco riding. If we're good, we might even get to compete in a junior rodeo!"

Jordan's head spun. Bronco – as in a wild horse trying to buck its rider off? What was that man thinking?! "That sounds – interesting, Caleb," Jordan stammered, hoping her anxiety wasn't too obvious.

"Come on, Jordan! Don't sound so worried. It's gonna be fun! Mr. Summers has a friend who raises horses for rodeo competitions," he explained. "My dad said we'll meet at the ranch right after church on Sunday and drive over together. That's two days away, and I can't wait!"

Jordan had never heard him sound so happy, so excited about anything. But, did it have to be something dangerous? She made a mental note to pray for him on Sunday afternoon, while he was risking his neck. As she listened to her nephew expound on his upcoming adventure, she began putting her groceries away.

"Hold on, Jordan," Caleb finally said breathlessly. "Spence wants to talk to you."

Jordan paused, listening to the muffled noises of the phone exchanging hands.

"Hello, Jordan."

Carl's deep voice rumbled over the line and instantly set her pulse racing. Ignoring the unwanted physical reaction, she cried, "Are you crazy?" Laughter was the only reply, adding anger to her already disgruntled mood.

"The boy will be fine," Spence finally replied. Her reaction was exactly what he'd expected. Her city girl lifestyle wasn't acclimated to such activities. The fact that she'd never had any brothers, probably added to her cautious nature.

"You're going to encourage him to get on the back of a wild horse whose goal is to get him off by any means necessary?" she groused.

"The man who raises the horses does this all the time. He'll choose a mild animal for the boys. Jack and I will also be there. Believe me, it's a very controlled environment," he assured her. "Caleb will be perfectly safe."

"And who is going to demonstrate how it's done?" she asked sarcastically. "You?"

Spence grinned, thinking that might not be a bad idea. "I just might," he replied, as he mentally considered the question. "I haven't been on a bronco in years. A ride would be a good test for my shoulder."

Jordan instantly regretted goading him. "Oh no you won't!" she blurted, her previous worry escalating to fear. "You'll hurt yourself, Carl. Your shoulder hasn't had enough time to heal for something like that."

The concern in her voice slid into Spence's heart, leaving a warm ache. "Are you worried about me, Jordan?"

"Yes!" Jordan cried, and then realized how that sounded. "I mean, no! Well, yes!" Her thoughts spun; her mind felt confused, overtaxed. She dropped onto a dining room chair and hung her head.

"Which is it, Jordan?" Spence pressed playfully. "Yes or no?"

Sucking in a deep breath, Jordan said, "Yes, I'm worried about you, but only because of Caleb." Her heart thundered so loudly, it was a wonder he couldn't hear it. If Carl was hurt… She couldn't finish the thought.

"I'm not going to get on the horse, Jordan," Spence gently assured, guessing that he'd pushed too far and upset her. She was frightened – and she cared about him.

The knowledge that she struggled with the same attraction as he, didn't really surprise him. He'd known it from that first embrace months ago, when she melted into his arms, a virtual stranger, at the time. "You *are* worried about me," Spence breathed. "And not only because of Caleb."

Jordan forced the softness from her voice, remembering her resolve to keep her distance. "You're wrong, Carl," she countered firmly, hoping to convince herself, as well as him.

"Jordan, when I bring Caleb home, maybe we should talk." *Damn!* he swore silently. Where had that come from?

"There's nothing to talk about," Jordan replied, suddenly panicked. "I'm seeing someone, Carl. I'm afraid you've misinterpreted..." she paused, hating herself for lying so blatantly, "...things."

The words felt like a sucker punch. She'd said nothing about a boyfriend before. Obviously, he'd been around for a while, definitely prior to her visit to Montana. *Had* he misunderstood her reaction to him? Was he only seeing what he wanted to see, because he felt something, and the idea that she didn't was just too close to...rejection?

"I have to go, Carl," Jordan's small voice filtered into his thoughts. "Goodbye."

"Bye, Jordan," he muttered.

~ * ~

Sunday morning, Spence looped his arm around his boy's shoulders and headed across the parking lot toward the sanctuary. Anyone watching might assume church attendance was a regular occurrence in his life, such was his relaxed demeanor. In fact, it was only his second or third service in the past two decades.

When he was growing up, going to church and Sunday school were a routine part of his week. His mom's commitment never wavered. After his dad left, he'd quit attending willingly. During his teen years, he'd sit in church with his arms crossed, and his mind closed. He refused to let even one positive word penetrate his angry, bitter heart. Since coming to Silver Springs, Spence had changed. People like the Summers family, Sheriff Davies, and Jordan Gray had shown him what a lived-out faith looked like, and he yearned for a taste of that peaceful contentment.

His own son, his beloved lost boy, was the greatest influence, by far. Caleb was the spitting image of himself at the same age. Not only did they look alike but Caleb's attitude when they first met was identical to Spence's as a young teenager – sarcastic, ugly, and angry. Spence had blamed all his problems on others – God, his mom, his deserter father – anywhere except where they belonged – on himself. It had taken two long, agonizing decades, a near-death experience, and a great many caring people willing to look beyond the broken man whom he'd become, before he realized that the majority of his problems were brought on by his attitude.

The last Bible study he'd attended with Caleb on Tuesday focused on attitude. 'Circumstances *are* what they *are*, and often can't be changed,' the booklet read. 'How we react to those circumstances is up to us. We have a choice.' During the discussion that evening, Spence learned that he wasn't the only man there who'd suffered great loses. Two men had lost their first wives to cancer. Several had buried children, taken from them much too early through disease, accident, or for no known reason at all. All had lost parents.

One man saved the life of his young sister by becoming her bone marrow donor. At only twelve years old, the girl had faced certain death. Greg Cooper talked about how his sister had refused to let fear win. Before finding him, an unknown brother from her father's first marriage, she'd faced her own mortality bravely. Her strong faith, along with the knowledge that she was going to heaven, was firmly implanted in her heart. She'd chosen to be content in her circumstances, even unto death.

That night, Spence silently made a commitment to change the way he reacted to the difficulties life threw his way. The following day, he had a long talk with Jack about God. Spence told his friend that, at the age of eleven, he'd accepted the Lord's free gift of salvation with a child-like faith, just as the Bible commanded. He wasn't sure that meant anything today. Jack assured him that his relationship with God was secure, that the Lord hadn't forgotten about him. Then Jack did something Spence could never imagine his former commander in the Marine Corps doing. He folded his six-foot-three frame into a kneeling position and prayed for a hurting friend.

Moved to tears, Spence dropped to his knees beside the man, bowed his head, and listened. When Jack finished, he patted Spence's hunched shoulders and left, with the parting words, "You can recommit your life to God whenever you choose. For me, that knowledge didn't come until I'd gained and then nearly lost my greatest earthly treasure, my wife. You don't have to wait until you're at the lowest point with your heart bleeding to make the change."

Spence stayed there in the quiet of Jack's deserted barn for a long time. He wrestled with the idea that he could hand over all his problems to God. He struggled to understand that the Lord was willing and able to forgive even a sinner like him. His heart warmed with the knowledge that, though his earthly father had deserted him, his heavenly Father never would.

His conversation with Sheriff Davies came back to him. Adams' death wasn't his fault, so why was he carrying around such remorse for being alive? Closing his eyes, he gave the guilt to God and asked Him to be with his partner's grieving family. He remembered Jordan's admonishment to forgive his father and move on. He added that burden to the pile. Caleb's shining, youthful face drifted into his mind, and he sent a heartfelt prayer of thanks heavenward. He also asked forgiveness for the part he played in adding to Tanya's difficult life, and for being unable to tell his boy that he'd been conceived in love. He apologized for all the wrong things he'd done and said over the years, the people he'd hurt both intentionally and accidentally, and promised to mend his ways. He felt suddenly free. The weight on his shoulders was gone; the darkness that had always surrounded his heart and mind lifted. He'd laid it all at the foot of the cross, and God carried it away.

Today, he walked into the sanctuary of the Friendship Christian Church a new man. With a smile, he greeted people he'd met since coming to Silver Springs, shaking hands, enjoying the fellowship. He felt Caleb's eyes on him, noted the curious look on the boy's face. As the music started, Spence clapped a hand on his son's thin shoulder and guided him to a seat. There'd be time to talk later.

Chapter 15

Jordan stared in surprise at the buzzing phone in her hand. Chris had hung up on her. He was mad because she'd waited nearly a week to call and tell him she was back. He'd made accusations that she was cheating. *Cheating?!* They'd only been on three or four actual dates, had never discussed any sort of commitment. He was making assumptions for which he had no right. Her hand shook as she replaced the receiver on its base.

It was late Sunday night by the time her plane landed, and she'd had to work first thing Monday morning. There were almost no groceries in the house when she returned. She'd spent the week getting back into the groove, hardly talking to anyone. Why was it that she felt she needed a vacation to recover from her vacation? She'd finally called him on Friday, leaving a message. He didn't return her call until tonight, Saturday. Did she have a right to be irritated with him for waiting twenty-four hours? Probably, but she wasn't.

She ought to call Chris back and try to mend this rift. They'd gotten along so well, until now. She should be upset with his attitude but mostly what she felt was...annoyance. Carl drifted into her thoughts, and her pulse quickened. *Stop!* she silently scolded, forcing her mind to remember his dangerous job, his intimacy with her sister, anything to push him from her mind, to make him seem less appealing.

"Ugh!" she groaned.

"What's wrong?" Ally asked, glancing up from the floor. Surrounding her were several stuffed animals, the black and white cat Caleb had given her among them. She rarely went anywhere without the life-sized toy.

"Nothing, sweet pea," she replied, using Carl's endearment for the little girl. Jordan cringed inside. How was she supposed to keep the man out of her heart when she couldn't put him out of her mind? "How about we go to the movies tonight?" she asked, recalling that a new Disney movie had recently been released. She'd hoped to have a date, but that wasn't going to materialize.

"Yay!" Ally cried, clapping her hands and dancing around Jordan.

Hours later, Jordan carried her sleeping niece inside and took her straight to the bedroom. It was a good forty-five minutes past the little girl's bedtime. Thankfully, they'd visited the restroom at the movie theater before heading home. She gently changed Ally into her pajamas, deciding to forego brushing her teeth, just this once.

As she tucked the blankets around the little girl, an early night became more appealing. She was tired, drained from thinking about the uncomfortable conversation with Chris and entertaining a three-year-old. She retreated to the bathtub, a mound of bubbles and a glass of wine her only indulgences. When she finished, she performed her nightly routine, walking through the apartment and checking to make sure the windows and doors were locked. Satisfied, she was about to retire when she spotted the silently blinking light on her answering machine. She clicked the play button.

"Hello, Jordan," Carl Spencer's voice greeted her. "I'll be bringing Caleb home late Saturday night. I'm planning to stay a few days to help him get ready for school. See you then."

Jordan's brow creased. Was summer over already? Caleb would be home in a week. The machine announced the commencement of a second message.

"Jordan. It's Chris." Next was a pause in which she detected the soft sounds of fretting, like he didn't know what he wanted to say. Finally, "Listen, babe, I'm really sorry for earlier. I didn't mean the things I said. I hope you'll let me make it up to you." Another pause, including a sigh, and then, "I'm gone on a business trip until Thursday. Let's go out Saturday night. I'll call you this week to give you the details. Bye."

Babe, Jordan thought with uncertainty. He'd never called her that before. She wrinkled her nose, trying to decide if she liked it or not. Finally, she shrugged indifferently. It seemed she had a date next week. She chose to attribute her lack of enthusiasm to the difficult day that just passed. By Friday, she'd be her old self again, she felt sure.

~ * ~

Spence's last week with Caleb was his busiest this summer. In preparation for their eventual departure, he'd agreed to handle the relocation of Mrs. Hill's stock. The mule was sold to a pack outfit that specialized in taking groups into the mountains on horseback for an extended wilderness experience. Mrs. Hill felt Buster would be much happier if he was put to work. Jack offered to board Dancer and Shasta temporarily, while the woman continued recovering. He also agreed to look after the dogs. The birds were given to a friend of Mrs. Hill's. The two barn cats were rounded up and delivered to a woman in town who rescued and cared for abandoned animals. She planned to rehabilitate the mostly wild creatures and find homes for them.

Spence walked around the yard, checking to be sure everything was secure. After delivering Caleb into Jordan's care, he planned to head back to his apartment in New Jersey. He needed to check in – come to terms with his future. He assumed there was a psych evaluation awaiting him, along with a physical and probably some interviews. The Bureau would be taking a long hard look at him. He'd be doing the same.

As the sun sank low in the sky, Spence stopped on the far side of the barn, and looked across the fields toward the distant peaks. Jordan was right; this was a truly beautiful place to be. During his self-imposed exile, he'd grown to love the wide open spaces, the quiet, the magnificent sunrises and sunsets. He was going to miss Silver Springs and Montana.

"Dad! Dad!"

Caleb's frantic cries jerked Spence from his silent reverie. Fear sliced through him. With his heart pounding, he sprinted around the barn and across the yard. Nearly colliding with the backyard gate, his hand shook as it forced up the latch.

"Caleb!" he called anxiously, rushing into the yard. "What is it?" The boy knelt beneath the old oak tree.

Caleb glanced briefly over his shoulder at his approaching father. "Oh, no," he cried, his voice quivering with emotion. "Dad...I think..."

Spence reached his son's side and squatted. Before them, lay the still body of Lady, the old shepherd. Caleb glided his fingers through the fur on the dog's neck; his other hand rested on her side. Spence's thundering pulse slowed as he comprehended the reason for his son's anguished cry. He reached down and pressed a palm against the dog's chest in search of a heartbeat. He bent his head near the dog's mouth, listening for breathing. Detecting nothing, he slowly shook his head, meeting his son's sad eyes.

"She's gone, Caleb," he whispered, slipping an arm around the boy's shoulders.

"Oh, no," Caleb squeaked, his voice fading.

A choked cry tore from the boy, and Spence pulled him into his arms, his throat painfully thick with sympathy. Caleb sobbed against his father's chest. Fighting for control of his emotions, Spence comforted his son. A few tears managed to escape the man's eyes – not for the loss of the dog, but for the connection with his son. Caleb had called him 'Dad' for the first time. Spence prayed it wouldn't be the last.

After a while, the boy pulled away, wiping his face on his shirt. Together, they dug a deep hole beneath the dog's beloved tree, her final resting place. Spence found some scraps of wood and fashioned a simple cross to mark the grave. In Caleb's lopsided print, the word *Lady* was scrawled in permanent marker on the cross section. Butch stayed on the porch, quietly watching, and seeming to understand the importance of what was taking place.

Few words were spoken during the little funeral, though Spence's thoughts stayed with his aching son, and the many similar lessons he'd had in his short life. Jordan's heartfelt words drifted back to him. Caleb shouldn't have to go through this again.

~ * ~

Spence brought the rental car to a halt at the curb across the street from Jordan's apartment complex. They'd just come from the airport. He'd opted to fly, leaving the Porche in Jack's care. Spending two weeks zigzagging across the country in the uncomfortable sports car wasn't his idea of a good time. Plane fare cost more but required less time. He'd deal with the Porche later. Winter would be here before long and the Range Rover, currently parked in his condo garage, would be his vehicle of choice anyway.

Caleb squirmed beside him, still clearly unhappy. He didn't want to be dumped with his aunt, as he put it, for the school year. He wanted to go to New Jersey with Spence.

It had taken all summer, but they'd finally come to see each other as father and son. The road was a hard one, particularly for Caleb. From the start, he tried to dislike Spence. He'd wanted to hate his father for being absent all these years, blame someone for the tough upbringing he'd experienced thus far.

After Spence's commune with the Lord in Jack's barn, he'd had a long talk with the boy. He told Caleb about his life. He explained the circumstances of his disappointing childhood, pointing out that it was actually pretty darned good. He'd grown up around a large extended family, spent lots of time on his uncle's ranch, and had a loving, caring mother who would do anything for him. But he hadn't seen any of that back then. It was only recently that he'd come to recognize the positive aspects of his tumultuous beginnings. He'd tried to make the boy understand that his own attitude was the reason for missing those good things. He didn't want his son to make the same mistakes.

Thankfully, Caleb did understand some of what his father was saying. He gradually began to understand that he was doing exactly the same things Spence had done – blaming others for his unhappiness. They talked a long time, each promising to discuss their difficulties before they festered.

Then, it was time to head back to Southern California, and Caleb balked.

"Why can't I go with you, Dad?" he'd pleaded yesterday evening. They'd spent the day cleaning the house, locking up the out buildings, and packing. "I'm not a little kid. You can still go to work and everything."

The squeak in his son's voice speared straight through Spence's heart. Caleb was trying not to cry.

"It isn't a good time, son," Spence explained. "There are things I need to settle before we can live together permanently." He wondered briefly what his son's aunt would think about this discussion. Would Jordan be happy or distressed? And what about Ally?

"What things?" Caleb demanded. "My mom managed as a single parent. Jordan does, too. Why can't you?!" Tears welled in his eyes, and he turned away from his father, more hurt than angry.

Spence gripped his son's trembling shoulders, his own heart breaking with Caleb's. "I promise you, Caleb," he murmured close to the boy's ear. "I'm going to work things out. I don't want to move you to New Jersey with me now. I might not be staying there. It's best if you go back with Jordan until I make some decisions." He turned the boy around and wrapped his arms around him.

Caleb wept quietly against his father's chest for a few minutes then forced his emotions under control. Raising his head, he asked, "How long will it take, Dad?"

Spence sighed deeply. It was a step in the right direction, at least. "Do you think you can give me a few months? By Christmas, I should have a plan."

Caleb thought about that. Christmas wasn't too far off, plus it would give him time to hang out with his friends – well some of them anyway. He wasn't planning to reconnect with the ones that helped get him into trouble. He'd also have to explain things to Ally. He felt a pang of uncertainty at the thought of his little sister. Jordan wasn't going to be happy about this either, he reasoned.

Finally, he nodded. "Okay, Dad. Will I see you before Christmas?"

"Your aunt assures me that you have a week off for Thanksgiving," Spence replied with relief. "I'll see you then, Caleb. Maybe sooner."

As he sat in the car pondering the conversation, a black BMW pulled into the empty space in front of the apartment complex. Spence glanced across the street as the driver's door opened and a casually dressed man got out. He hurried around the front of the late model car and opened the passenger door. To Spence's surprise, Jordan emerged.

"Look, there's Jordan!" Caleb cried, reaching for the door handle.

Spence caught his son's arm. "Wait," he said quietly, still watching the couple. Jordan laughed at something the man said. Spence's gut twisted when the man slid his arm around her waist.

"What's wrong?" Caleb asked, eyeing his father's furrowed brow and wondering at the strange look in his eyes.

Spence watched the couple stroll through the gate. "Nothing, Caleb," he replied. Clearing the gruffness from his tone, he added, "Let's get your bags inside." He was suddenly anxious to make the acquaintance of Jordan's boyfriend.

"Sure, Dad," Caleb replied curiously.

A few minutes later, Caleb pushed the door to the apartment open and stepped inside, followed by his father. Jordan's date stood alone near the living room windows.

"Hi," Caleb said, staring at the stranger. He turned to Spence in time to glimpse a brooding expression.

Jordan suddenly appeared from the kitchen carrying two mugs of coffee. "Oh my goodness!" she exclaimed in surprise, immediately setting the cups on the nearest end table. "Caleb, your home!"

Much to the boy's embarrassment, she rushed to her nephew and pulled him into her arms, hugging him fiercely. When she spotted Spence standing behind him, her happy smile slipped. Why did he look so odd?

"Jordan," Caleb whined, protesting the too long embrace.

"I'm sorry," Jordan said as she released the boy. Oh, but it was good to have him back, she thought. Then, remembering the two men in the room, she turned and made hasty introductions.

Reaching for Chris's arm, she said, "This is my nephew, Caleb, and his father, Carl Spencer. Carl, this is Chris Oliver, my...friend," she stammered nervously. She watched Chris step forward and extend his hand.

"Nice to meet you, Mr. Spencer," he said with a hesitant smile, pulling his gaze from Jordan's pink cheeks to the stern looking man before him.

"Likewise," Spence replied, forcing the hardness from his face and shaking the younger man's hand. There was absolutely no reason to be irritated. She was free to see whomever she chose.

Silence settled over the room. Jordan's discomfort turned to disbelief as she watched the two men assessing one another. What was going on?

"I wasn't expecting you until later tonight," she finally said, hoping to bring the uncomfortable moment to an end.

"Our flight got canceled, and they moved us to an earlier one," Caleb explained, also wondering at the sudden tension in the room.

"I hope that isn't a problem," Spence said, turning to Jordan. He studied her for a second, noting her flushed complexion, her hands clenched nervously in front of her. Had his and Caleb's unexpected arrival interrupted anything significant? His gaze drifted past her toward the hall leading to her bedroom.

Jordan detected a hard edge in his tone. When his gaze shifted to the entrance to the hall, her anger spiked. Though he hadn't said a word, she knew exactly what he was thinking. How dare he assume such a thing!

"No problem at all," she said, tempering her tone and glancing at Chris. Her forced smile slipped when she saw the look of annoyance on his face. Now what? Turning toward the kitchen, she said, "I'll just get another cup of coffee. Would you like something to drink, Caleb?" She hurried off, not waiting for an answer.

Caleb's gaze bounced from one man to the other, trying to comprehend why they both looked sort of pissed off. Shrugging, he followed Jordan.

Jordan's heart hammered against her ribcage. Her hands shook as she poured coffee into a third cup. What had just happened in there? She felt like she'd just been caught doing something wrong. She replaced the carafe on its warmer and leaned on the edge of the counter, thinking and trying to calm her nerves.

"Where's Ally?" Caleb asked as he walked into the kitchen. His aunt stared blankly through the window that overlooked their tiny patio.

Jordan blinked away her confusion and turned to her nephew. "Ally's with Deborah. I'm going to pick her up in a little while," she replied, reaching for his arm. "She'll be so glad to see you, Caleb. She's been beside herself waiting for your return."

After helping himself to one of the full mugs Jordan brought in earlier, Spence sat down on the couch and took a sip. It wasn't hot anymore, but he drank the warm brew anyway. Over the rim of the mug, Spence's practiced gaze examined the other man. Jordan's boyfriend was good looking, probably around thirty, tan and fit. His blonde hair was perfect, the light streaks a little too even to be natural. Did pretty boy visit the hair dresser to make that happen? Spence hid a smile. He'd bet on it.

Following Spence's example, Chris grabbed the other mug, sloshing a few drops on the back of his hand, and sat in the easy chair opposite the sofa. He didn't like this guy. He was smug, a little too sure of himself.

"What do you do for a living, Chris?" Spence asked casually.

"I'm an engineer for an aerospace company," Chris replied. He mentioned the name of the company and boasted about the big defense project to which he was currently assigned.

Spence nodded and asked a few questions. He sipped his coffee and let the guy talk. Chris was clearly impressed with himself, Spence decided. The guy never asked a single question. In fact, his initial annoyance had all but vanished in his eagerness to talk about himself.

When Jordan finally returned to the living room, carrying her coffee and the full carafe, she felt a measure of relief. The men were chatting and appeared relaxed.

Good! She hoped the previous tension was in the past. She refilled everyone's mugs with hot coffee and sat in the only seat available, beside Spence on the small couch. Caleb opted to take his bags to his room and telephone a friend, gladly leaving the adults and their strange behavior behind.

Spence leaned back and stretched his arm across the back of the sofa, his fingers coming to rest behind Jordan. Chris continued to dominate the conversation, with occasional nods and smiles from his audience. After a while, Jordan checked her watch and rose.

"I need to pick up Ally," she announced.

Chris stood as well, looking at his watch and grimacing. "I need to get moving, too," he said, heading for the door.

Spence remained on the sofa, aware of every move the couple made. For a Saturday night, it seemed awfully early to be ending a date. He couldn't imagine what pressing appointment would send this guy running from the side of a beautiful woman like Jordan. *If it was me...*but he shoved the thought aside.

"Jordan, do you mind if I hang out here for a while?" He still needed to check into a motel but wasn't in a big hurry.

"Not at all," Jordan replied from her place beside Chris. "Ally can hardly wait to see you."

Jordan didn't see the look of irritation return to her boyfriend's face, but Spence did. Smiling broadly, he said, "I'd like to see Ally, too. I'll be here when you return." When Chris's jaw hardened further, he added, "We'll all go out for an ice cream cone – my treat." His gaze held Jordan's as he sipped his coffee.

Jordan grew uncomfortable under Carl's unwavering stare. A throat clearing behind her dragged her attention away.

"I'll walk you to your car," Chris said brusquely.

As soon as the door closed behind them, Spence pulled his phone from his pocket and started typing. His text was short – a license plate number and the word 'tonight.'

Fifteen minutes later, he stared at the response, surprised. His inquiry was routine. He'd expected nothing problematic, but the message he received definitely warranted further scrutiny.

~ * ~

Later that night, Spence sat on the queen-sized bed in his hotel room, staring at the screen of the muted television. True to his word, he'd taken Jordan and the kids out for ice cream. They'd strolled around a nearby park enjoying their treats and the mild weather.

Ally yammered away about anything and everything, captivating Spence with an adorable combination of intelligence and innocence. Jordan was compelled to remind the girl to lick her ice cream before it melted. When she finally held it out, barely touched, and said she didn't want anymore, they'd all laughed. While Caleb finished her cone, Jordan took the little girl to the restroom for a quick wash.

When they returned, Ally begged her big brother to push her on the swing. Caleb obliged willingly, letting Ally take him by the hand and lead him to the playground. Spence took Jordan's arm and guided her to a nearby bench. Leaning against the wooden slats, he laid his arm along the edge of the seatback and propped one ankle atop the other knee.

"How'd you meet him?" he asked casually.

"Who? Chris?" Jordan replied.

Spence nodded.

She told him about being set up by her friends, including her initial annoyance. "He's a really nice guy, though," she'd said. Something in his expression must have hinted at his skepticism because she'd playfully punched his arm and admonished, "He really is, Carl. Give him a chance."

That remains to be seen, Spence thought, but asked, "Was that his Beamer parked in front of your place?" Of course, he already knew the answer.

"Yes, Chris bought it last month," she replied, clearly pleased to impart something positive to counter Spence's suspicion. "It's a really nice car…"

She went on to describe the BMW's features, undoubtedly parroting Chris's boasting. Her words seemed forced to Spence, like the car wasn't really all that important to her, but she didn't have much else to share.

At one point, Jordan leaned back against his arm. When she didn't shift away, he'd cupped his palm around her shoulder and continued the conversation. He chuckled now, thinking how juvenile the action must have appeared, like a teenager on a first date trying to find a way to move things to the next level. He'd even been tempted to slide across the bench and close the distance between them. He'd refrained, kept things casual, two close friends out for the evening. Doing more would have opened a can of worms, and he wasn't planning to go fishing.

Jordan Gray was off limits, at least to him. However, that didn't mean he'd leave her to the wolves.

Chapter 16

The following morning, Spence arrived at the apartment in time to take the family to church. Since Jordan wasn't teaching Sunday school at this time, she directed Spence to accompany her to the adult class. The chairs were arranged in a circle around the perimeter of the room. As they sat down side by side, Jordan noticed, for the first time, the Bible in Spence's hand. Her brows arched inquisitively.

"Jack and Elizabeth gave it to me," he said by way of explanation.

"Any particular reason?" she asked curiously. She watched his expression turn serious, and his Adam's apple rise and fall as he swallowed emotions. "Never mind," she whispered in surprise. "It's none of my business." Embarrassed now, she stared at her hands, wishing she'd kept her questions to herself.

Spence watched her cheeks redden. His emotional discomfort had shocked her as much as it had him. He inhaled a deep breath, regaining control. Reaching for her hands where they lay clasped in her lap, he gave them a gentle squeeze, and whispered thickly, "Sometime, I'll tell you about it."

She slowly raised her head. Their gazes met and held. Spence wasn't sure exactly what he saw in the green depths of her wide, compassionate eyes, a tender glimpse of something he couldn't identify. A good 'something,' he felt certain. She glanced away before he could explore further. The instructor began to speak, and the moment was lost.

Stunned by her reaction, Jordan discreetly blinked away tears. She'd nearly started crying. Had something significant happened in Montana? Carl was different somehow. His hard edges weren't quite as sharp.

Later, during the worship service, Jordan was uncomfortably aware of the man beside her. Every brush of his arm prickled her skin and fired her senses. When he'd given up trying to contain his broad shoulders in the narrow seat and rested his arm across the back of her chair, the sensitive hairs at the nape of her neck tingled. Agitated fingers constantly spun the ring on her finger. The pastor's words sailed over her head, her ability to pay attention obliterated by her proximity to Carl Spencer.

When the service came to a merciful end, though her body yearned to bolt from his presence, Jordan walked out sedately. She felt completely undone, exhausted from the effort of merely sitting beside the man. Caleb met them at the exit.

"Hey Jordan, a bunch of people are going to the beach," the boy announced. "It's sort of an end of the summer celebration. Can we go?" Though his request was directed at his aunt, his eyes rested on his father.

Feeling incapable of making a decision, Jordan dodged the question, desperate to escape. "I'm going to pick up Ally from her class."

"But Jordan..." Caleb called as his aunt hurried away.

Spence smiled at Jordan's retreating back. All through the service, he'd sensed her discomfort. He reached for his son, tugging him to his side. "Give her a minute to think, Caleb," he said. "Why don't you get the details, and we'll talk about it?"

Caleb nodded and hurried off to find out what he could about the beach trip. Jordan returned a few minutes later, Ally in tow. Spence noted that she looked much more composed, less agitated. When Ally spotted Spence, she pulled her hand from Jordan's and raced toward him.

Jordan watched as Carl opened his arms and caught Ally in mid-flight, lifting her into the air and swinging her around. The little girl shrieked happily. Carl's broad grin responded in kind, and Jordan's heart swelled. *If only...*

"Jordan, what do you say to a beach party?" Spence called, closing the distance between them. Ally's short arms draped his neck, and she bounced in his arms.

"I want to go!" Ally shouted, making her opinion known in no uncertain terms.

Caleb returned then, and the vote was three to one for the beach. Jordan sighed and finally agreed, if somewhat reluctantly. When she ran into Deborah in the parking lot and learned that she and Gary were also going, she felt relieved. At least, she'd have a distraction.

~ * ~

In the state beach parking lot, a sign propped against the rear window of someone's car directed them to the space between lifeguard stations 24 and 25. With a canvas bag slung over her shoulder and a blanket tucked beneath her arm, Jordan trudged across the hot sand toward a good sized group. Ally dragged her bucket full of sand toys about halfway before abandoning it and skipping ahead. Grinning, Spence shifted the two beach chairs and hooked Ally's bucket with an index finger. His other hand effortlessly carried Jordan's hastily packed cooler. Hauling a couple of body boards, Caleb brought up the rear.

Deborah waved them to a space to the right of her blanket. As Jordan came to a stop, her friend's curious gaze gravitated to the approach of a handsome man. Deborah glanced at Jordan, her brows raised curiously, and Jordan made introductions.

"I'm so pleased to finally meet you, Spence," Deborah gushed. "I've heard so much about you."

Shaking the hand of the pretty brunette, Spence replied with a wink, "All good, I hope."

"Well, interesting anyways," Deborah said, a mischievous glint in her eye. "I wouldn't exactly say 'good'."

"Behave, wife," Gary warned with a chuckle, coming up behind her. "I'm Gary Olsen."

"Spence, Caleb's dad." The two men shook hands.

"In a little while, we're going to get a volley ball game going, if you're interested," Gary suggested. He gestured to a group of men in the process of setting up the net several yards behind them.

"Sounds good," Spence replied. Gary jogged off, and Spence started unfolding the chairs they'd brought.

Jordan shook out her blanket, preparing to spread it on the sand. The wind fought her, whipping it around and tossing sand in the air. Each time she thought she'd won the battle, a corner would fly up, undoing her efforts. Spence saw her struggling and chuckled at the comical sight. Taking pity on her, he grabbed an edge and together, they defeated the brisk, warm breeze and laid the blanket flat. When their eyes met, Spence winked playfully before Jordan looked away.

"I'm going in," Caleb announced. Tossing his towel on top of one of the body boards, he grabbed the other and headed for the water. Resting on their floating boards, a number of friends waved at him from several yards out.

"Be careful," Jordan called, echoing Spence's thoughts.

"I go, too," Ally said as she raced toward the surf.

"Wait for me, Ally," Jordan said.

"I'll keep an eye on her," Spence offered. Not waiting on a response, he jogged after the small girl.

Deborah moved to Jordan's side and stared after the pair. Ally stopped and said something they couldn't hear. Spence smiled and reached for her hand as they stepped into the water.

"Wow, he's...wow!" Deborah said, her eyes still fixed upon the man now ankle deep, a squealing little girl at his side.

"You're married," Jordan said, her tone a mixture of annoyance and understanding.

"Yeah, but you're not," Deborah reminded her. "Speaking of which, how are things between you and Chris. Still good?"

Jordan thought about Chris for a moment. His boyish charm and warm smile, the fun they had when they got together, the very infrequent dates. She sighed.

"Yes, still good," she replied. Relationships take time, she mentally chided herself.

"But he's not here today," Deborah pointed out the obvious. "What will he think of you coming to the beach with," she nodded toward Spence, "him.

"I didn't come to the beach with him," Jordan said pointedly. "He came with his son."

"Oh," Deborah said, feeling suitably reprimanded. Her friend was out of sorts today, that much was clear. She turned and quietly walked away. Returning to her blanket, she picked up the magazine she'd been flipping through earlier.

Jordan wanted to kick herself for snapping. She never should have reacted so strongly. She felt wound up, confused. She needed to sort out her feelings for Carl, and for Chris. How could she claim to care for one man, while practically turning inside out over another? And why did Carl seem so different? Why now, when her relationship with Chris was heading in the right direction? Chris was the man God had for her, she felt certain. She didn't want to feel anything for Carl!

Jordan dropped to the blanket, pulled her knees up to her chin, and stared at the distant horizon.

"You want to talk about it?" Deborah asked softly. She didn't have to guess that something was bugging Jordan. It was pretty easy to tell.

Jordan turned to her friend, and laid her cheek on her bent knees. "That obvious?"

"I'm afraid so." Deborah reached over and patted Jordan's back, giving her a small, sympathetic smile.

Returning the smile with an uncertain one of her own, Jordan murmured, "It's complicated."

"Isn't everything."

Jordan turned back to the sea. While Spence held both her hands, Ally jumped in the deeper water, coming up much higher than she should, clearly not under her own power. Jordan smiled.

Deborah watched her friend and understood. She felt something for Caleb's father.

"You're torn between him and Chris," she said softly.

Jordan considered that possibility. It wasn't exactly right. "No," she said, shaking her head. "Carl's going to leave in a couple of days. He won't be around. It's just,

I...I feel so...so..." Giving up, she heaved a sigh. "He's not the man for me, Deborah."

"But you're attracted to him," Deborah said. "Maybe it'll just take a while."

"That's just it," Jordan said in exasperation. "It's a chemical thing, nothing more."

"How do you know there's nothing more?" Deborah asked.

"For one thing, if he was interested in me, he'd ask me out," Jordan replied. "I mean, there have been plenty of opportunities, you know?"

"Well, maybe he doesn't because he knows you're seeing Chris."

"I don't think that would stop a man like Carl," Jordan replied with a sigh. Carl Spencer seemed like the kind of man who did what he pleased without apology. He was tough, determined, and fearless. She'd figured all that out within the first few days after they met. If he had any romantic intentions, he'd have made them known by now. He didn't, at least not the type that would interest Jordan. She remembered his remark months ago, 'Do you like what you see?' The innuendo was pretty direct. He'd made no such comments since, either rude or respectful.

A short while later, Spence brought Ally to the blanket. The little girl rubbed her eyes with salty fists and yawned. Sitting in a beach chair, Jordan immediately wrapped a towel around her and pulled her onto her lap. She was asleep in seconds.

"I'm going to join Caleb," Spence said, picking up the second body board.

Jordan nodded, watching him jog down the sand and into the water. His swim trunks were soaked from playing with Ally, but the blue T-shirt he still wore was dry. He waded out beyond the breaking waves then used the board to float the remaining distance. His left arm did most of the work, Jordan noted, a reminder of the major reason to guard her heart from this man with the dangerous job.

The afternoon passed almost too quickly. Ally awoke and wanted to build a sand castle. Jordan and Deborah helped her for a while. A volley ball game was announced, and Deborah raced off to play. Several others, including Spence emerged from the water to join a team. Jordan stayed with Ally until she said she was hungry, and then they moved their chairs and ice chest into a better position to watch the game.

The game ended, and new teams were organized in preparation for the next. Everyone was drenched in sweat, and many people ran to the water for a quick dip to cool off. Caleb joined the second game, whipping off his shirt, as many others had done.

Spence's soaked shirt had expanded in size after his refreshing dip in the water. After the first round, he yanked it off and tossed it in the sand at Jordan's feet. He served the ball with much more skill now, and it was passed back and forth over the net several times before being hit out of bounds.

"Holy cow! What happened to your shoulder?" a teenager asked, as Spence retrieved the ball and returned to the sand.

Hearing the question, Jordan's gaze automatically settled on Carl's wound. The sensitive area surrounding the white scars was rapidly turning pink. *He's getting a sunburn*, she noted with concern. That couldn't be good for the still tender skin. She reached down and picked up his wet, sand-covered T-shirt.

"Oh man!" someone else exclaimed. "Did you get speared or something."

"My dad got shot," Caleb piped in, anxious to get the inquiry over with and restart the game. For him, the novelty and intrigue had worn off long ago. Now, he preferred not to think about his dad's damaged shoulder.

"Shot?" the first kid said. "With what, a grenade launcher?" Several of the boys laughed.

Jordan approached Spence. He stood with his hands on his hips, listening to the teens and smiling. *Smiling?!* She thought. *But, why?*

"It was a hollow point round," he said, and went on to explain how the bullet breaks apart on impact.

Jordan felt suddenly weak and sick to her stomach. No wonder his injury was so extensive.

"Cool!" another boy said. Caleb's shocked look wiped the impressed expression from his face. "I mean, that must have hurt."

Spence nodded. "It did," he said, his gaze moving from face to face. They were impressed and interested, all but Caleb. He looked uncomfortable. Spence frowned, worried about his son. The conversation had gone too far. Where was his shirt? Ignoring the continued inquiries, he turned.

"Jordan," he said, surprised to find her almost directly behind him. She held out his shirt.

"You should put this on," she murmured. "You're getting burned."

As Spence reached for the wet, sandy wad, her pale face didn't escape his perceptive eye. She'd heard the entire conversation.

"Come on," he said, taking the shirt and grasping her arm. "You should sit down." He guided her back to her chair then opened the ice chest and fished out a water bottle. "Drink this." He twisted off the cap and handed it to her.

Jordan took a long drink of the cold water. Spence smiled, pleased to see the color slowly returning to her cheeks. "Better?" he asked.

She nodded and pointed at his shirt. "Your scars are getting sunburned," she said again.

"I'll go rinse this in the water and put it back on," he said with a nod. "And I'm ready to go when you are." They'd been at the beach several hours, and she looked wiped out.

"I'm ready now," Jordan replied. "Would you let Caleb know? I think he went back in the water."

Spence looked around. Sure enough, the volley ball teams had disbanded and disappeared. With a nod to Jordan, he moved off toward the surf. He waded in up to his knees, swished his shirt in the breaking waves, and pulled it on over his head. Shielding his eyes from the sun's rays, he scanned the body boarders, searching for Caleb. Spotting the boy, he waved, motioning for him to come in soon. Caleb's hand came up in acknowledgement.

In the meantime, Spence would help Jordan pack up. As he turned with that goal in mind, something caught his eye. In the distance, apart from the other swimmers, a lone arm waved above the surf. He watched as a boy's head broke the water. The youth's mouth was open and his eye's wide with fear. A second later, a swell rolled over him, and he disappeared beneath the wave.

The boy's in trouble, Spence thought with a jolt as he strode deeper into the water, his eyes glued to the spot where he'd last seen the kid. A wave rose in front of him, and he dove under it, feeling it break on his back. He came up, caught a glimpse of a hand in the distance and swam directly for it. His muscular shoulders flexed powerfully as his hands shoveled through the water. The first time Spence's arm rounded the top of his head, a loud pop exploded in his right shoulder, followed by a sharp pain. Ignoring the discomfort, he continued to butterfly swim at a rapid pace until he reached the location where he'd last seen the struggling swimmer.

He dove beneath the water, opened his eyes in its murky green depths, and searched. Seeing nothing, he came up for air then dove again, this time deeper. The pale skin of a leg drew his attention, and he pushed himself toward it.

Jordan stood on the shore, craning to see where Carl had gone. Seconds ago, someone started yelling that a boy needed help. Along with everyone else, she'd watched the lifeguard jump from his tower and sprint toward the distressed boy. Her eyes shifted until they fell on Carl, swimming rapidly toward the boy. The determined and well-trained lifeguard was way behind him. Now she watched the spot where Carl had disappeared under the water, praying silently that he'd find the person. Seconds felt like minutes, as everyone waited. All around her, members of her church and other's she didn't know bowed their heads and petitioned the Almighty to intervene.

Jordan lifted her head as Carl broke the surface. His arm was wrapped around a body, the head bobbing above the water. The people on the beach cheered. Two lifeguards reached Spence and relieved him of the boy.

Minutes later, Spence dragged his weary body from the water and joined the crowd surrounding the rescued boy. A lifeguard hovered over the still body, administering CPR. A sobbing woman sat in the sand near the boy. *His mother*, Spence assumed. The boy started to cough up water, and the lifeguard immediately turned him to his side. Clapping and cheering broke out all around the scene.

As Spence turned away, he felt the weight of a beach towel drop over his shoulders. Jordan stood beside him.

"Will he be all right?" she asked softly.

"I think so." Spence adjusted the towel more securely. "They got to him in time."

"No, they didn't," Jordan said, her tone incredulous. "*You* got to him in time. He would have drowned waiting for the lifeguards."

"Then I guess he was lucky I saw him."

"There's no such thing," a man interjected, his voice raspy with emotion.

Spence turned to the stranger.

"God put you there for the purpose of saving my son's life," the man explained. Wiping his tears on a towel, he extended his hand. "Thank you."

Spence took the father's hand, emotion suddenly clogging his throat. The boy was about Caleb's age. It could just as easily be him thanking someone. Sheriff Davies's words flooded his mind, 'Man knows not his time.'

"You're welcome," he said, his voice made deeper by the poignant moment. "But if you truly believe that, you should be thanking Him." He glanced upward, and the man nodded.

"I already did."

Several others came by to thank Spence, including the two lifeguards who couldn't have gotten to the boy in time to save his life. Though Spence accepted the praise graciously, he couldn't wait to get away. As quickly and politely as they could, the small group packed up and headed for the car. While Caleb talked about the incident all the way home, the pain in Spence's shoulder decreased to a steady throb.

As soon as they got inside the apartment, Jordan searched her freezer for a bag of frozen peas and handed it to Spence. He looked at her in surprise. Had his discomfort been that obvious?

"Sit there." She gently pushed him toward a living room chair.

"I'm filthy," he pointed out, glancing at his sand-coated calves.

"I'll vacuum later. You need to get that shoulder iced down before it swells. Can I bring you some ibuprofen?"

Spence knew the swelling had already begun. Maybe he could lessen it with the painkillers. He accepted three tablets and a glass of water.

While Jordan rushed off to help Ally with a much needed bath, Spence relaxed back in the chair. The words of the rescued boy's father kept repeating in his mind – 'There's no such thing as luck.' Was that true? Had God used Spence to save the life of that boy today? The idea was compelling.

Spence had always taken the credit for his good fortune. Was he wrong to do so? Was it really God, who orchestrated the close calls that ended in his favor, the times when he happened to be in the right place at the right time? In the last few months, he'd come to understand that God allowed bad things to happen in order to further His plan for our lives. The concept that He also controlled the good things seemed to be the opposite side of the same coin.

Jordan made a batch of grilled cheese sandwiches and heated tomato soup. It wasn't a fancy meal, but it would suffice. Ally ate then went to bed for the night. It was still early, but the sun and water had sapped the little girl's energy. Caleb ate two sandwiches then went to take a shower. Spence dozed on Jordan's sofa throughout the evening.

The inviting aroma of a hot meal dragged Spence from an exhausted sleep. Opening his eyes, he stared at Jordan's ceiling, slowly remembering where he was and the events of this odd day. As he pushed himself to a sitting position, a soggy bag of frozen vegetables slid from his sore shoulder. He caught it and smiled. He'd said nothing about hurting, but Jordan had figured it out.

He headed for the kitchen. Jordan stood at the sink, rinsing dishes and placing them in the open dishwasher at her side. She'd changed into a sundress, Spence noticed. The narrow straps failed to conceal her pink-tinged shoulders. She'd burned today, too.

"You might want to treat that sunburn before you go to bed tonight," he said. She jumped, and he winced.

Jordan's heart pounded as she turned to the man. "Must you make a habit of scaring the life out of me?" she scolded.

Spence shrugged, grinning innocently. He really hadn't intended to startle her. "Sorry."

"Are you hungry?" she asked over her shoulder. She'd returned to the dishes.

"Starving," Spence replied. "But I think I need a shower worse. Do you mind if I use yours?"

"Go right ahead. The towels are in the hall cupboard."

To save time earlier, he'd swung by his motel for his beach wear and changed his clothes at the apartment. He retrieved the bag containing the clothes he'd worn to church. For fifteen minutes, he scrubbed away the sand

and the salt, the stress of the day. Between the nap and the shower, he felt refreshed. Jordan's agitated voice greeted his return to the living room. She was on the phone.

When she saw him, she covered the mouth piece and whispered that his dinner was on the table. Spence nodded and headed that direction.

"Who were you talking to?"

Jordan returned her attention to the caller. Chris had telephoned just a few minutes ago. When he heard that she'd spent the afternoon at the beach with Spence, he hadn't been happy. Now, she was trying to explain.

"That was Carl," she said matter-of-factly. "I was just letting him know his dinner is on the table."

"He's eating with you, too?" Chris asked, clearly annoyed.

Jordan turned her back and walked to the farthest end of the room. "No, he's actually eating alone," she said, keeping her voice low so Carl wouldn't hear her talking about him. "The kids and I ate while he slept on the couch. He had a hard day..."

"What do you mean, he slept on the couch?" he practically shouted, interrupting her.

Jordan stared at the ceiling in exasperation. A headache was forming at the base of her skull. She hadn't had one all summer. Why now? "Chris, he saved a boy from drowning today. The man was beat!"

"Then he should have gone back to his motel," Chris grumbled angrily. "Why are you letting him sleep on your couch?"

And he took a shower here, too! Jordan was tempted to point out. She held her tongue. There was nothing to be gained by aggravating the man. How could she have ever thought his jealousy was sweet?

"Chris, you're making a big deal out of nothing," she said, keeping her tone calm and even. "Please, stop. The man is Caleb's father. He's going to be around for a few more years, at least."

"Not if the kid moves in with him," Chris challenged.

He was right, of course. Jordan had worried over that quite a bit lately. It seemed the same thought had crossed Chris' mind. Was Caleb's presence in her life a deciding factor in the relationship?

While Spence discretely watched, Jordan reached behind her head and pressed her fingers to the base of her skull. She was tense. He'd heard enough of the conversation to know he was the subject. He also figured the caller was her boyfriend. The guy was acting like a jealous idiot. Why wasn't he the one with her at the beach today? It seemed strange. If Chris was so enamored, why didn't he spend his weekends with her?

His thoughts strayed to the results of the license plate check he'd asked a buddy to run. The BMW Chris claimed he'd recently purchased wasn't registered under his name. Not only that, the vehicle was leased. The name on the paperwork was Terry Shatner. He hadn't planned to do a full investigation on the guy. Now, he was reconsidering.

Jordan ended the call, discouraged. He'd refused to be placated. What was she supposed to do, throw Carl out? Was she destined to go through this turmoil every time the man visited his son? She replaced the telephone on its base.

"I take it that was Chris," Spence said as he pushed his empty plate and bowl away.

Dropping into the chair across from him, Jordan nodded. "He doesn't like that you're here," she explained, assuming he'd already figured that out.

"That was obvious."

He studied her expression. She didn't look heartbroken by the fight. She appeared more annoyed, and maybe a little angry. It made him wonder just how deep her feelings ran for the guy. Chris acted jealous and possessive, but not exactly like a man in love. Spence recalled Jordan's behavior in church this morning. Sitting beside him, she'd been distracted and nervous. Her skin flushed regularly, and goose bumps had spotted her arms. He smiled. There was a definite spark there, and today wasn't the first time he'd detected it. Did she respond the same way with Chris? Was there a way to test her without hurting her?

"Do you really like him?" Spence asked, folding his arms across his chest and watching her.

"Yes, I do," Jordan responded immediately.

That was a little too fast. "So, there's fire between you," he stated, smiling at her, trying to goad her. "He turns you on."

Jordan's face flushed. She surged forward in her chair, palms pressed to the table top, and speared the man across from her with a fierce look. "That is none of your business!"

Got her! "I don't agree," Spence replied, keeping his voice even. "It is my business who spends the night here, in the same home as my son." He watched her rise from the chair, her face even redder.

"No one is sleeping here!" Jordan seethed. Gesturing toward the living room, she added, "Except you, on my couch!"

"Who said anything about sleeping?"

Jordan rounded the table, fuming now. "You have no right to interrogate me!" She stopped at his side and stared daggers at him.

"I'm just trying to be a dutiful father," Spence explained, matching her glower. "Maybe I should talk to Chris."

"Don't you dare!"

"Why not? I'll ask him what his intentions are toward you. I mean, as far as I can tell, there's more electricity crackling between you and me than you and him."

Stunned, Jordan could only gape at him in muted shock. "That's not true," she finally managed to articulate, though her voice squeaked unnaturally. "Th-there is nothing between us!" She glared, daring him to contradict her.

"Really!?" Spence said, his tone mocking. He slowly rose from the chair, facing her. The look on her face screamed, *'You've got to be kidding!'* and the old Spence, the one who never backed down from a fight, emerged.

His hands shot out and grasped her shoulders, pulling her against his chest in one swift motion. His mouth crushed hers in what was meant to be a forceful, intimidating kiss. She resisted for only a beat or two before her lips softened beneath his and parted. When she melted against him, he was lost in the moment. He couldn't have pulled away if his life depended on it. One hand moved to the nape of her neck, the other wrapped around her waist, molding her supple body to his. His lips moved over hers, urgently at first. When he felt her hands glide over his chest and around his neck, the kiss became a gentle, searching caress.

Jordan was powerless to stop what was happening. She'd lost control of the situation and had no desire to regain it. With the passing of the initial shock came an even more troubling reaction, her body's eager and wholly spontaneous response. Her brain ceased to function. Some unknown, natural instinct held her in its grip. The feel of his lips and the touch of his hands left her weak. His fingers caressing the back of her neck electrified her senses. His tongue grazed hers, igniting a blaze inside her. Coherent thought fled, replaced by a blurry longing she'd never known.

Spence knew this had to end – now. Things had already gone much too far. His hands moved back to Jordan's shoulders, and he gently eased her away, breaking the kiss at the last possible moment. The urge to pull her back into his arms was strong. He resisted, holding her away from himself. He should apologize, but he wasn't sorry. Not yet, anyway.

He looked down at her closed eyelids, her swollen, moist lips, and knew he'd made his point. He'd given her a means of measuring her attraction to Chris. Had he severed the tenuous cord of their friendship in the process?

"Jordan," he rasped, his voice husky.

Jordan opened her eyes and gazed up at Carl Spencer – at his unsmiling face, his stern gaze. Her knees felt wobbly, and her pulse hammered. They'd kissed. She blinked, trying to clear her muddled head. No, he'd kissed her – by force. She'd been given no choice. In fact, he'd pushed her and aggravated her and thrown accusations in her face. He was no better than Chris. How could he do that? She thought Carl respected her.

Spence watched the dreamy, passion-induced haze give way to confusion. When her expression grew angry, he knew he'd stepped over the proverbial line. Her next words didn't surprise him.

"Get out!"

"Jordan..."

She clamped her teeth together and pointed toward the front door.

Spence pushed agitated fingers across his scalp and nodded. It was no less than he deserved.

Chapter 17

Late into the night, Spence lay in his motel room unable to sleep. He shouldn't have kissed her. That ranked as one of the stupidest things he'd ever done. It got high marks in another category, as well, but he refused to go there. Two things were likely to come about because of that kiss – she'd never forgive him, and it would always stand between them. Why did he do it?

Because you wanted to, you fool! It was true. He'd wanted to get close to her for a long time. But engaging in a casual relationship with his son's guardian was a bad idea on too many levels to list. He knew that. He couldn't begin to predict the damage that could result. Kissing her wasn't going to be good for his state of mind either, he admitted. He already knew that forgetting about it wasn't going to be easy. Well, there was nothing to be done about it now.

Would she break things off with Chris? She damn sure should! Spence didn't trust him. The guy was self-centered and cocky. Not to mention, a liar. He'd lied to Jordan about owning the Beamer. Not a big lie, to be sure. After all, what guy wasn't guilty of bending the truth to impress a girl?

Spence glanced at the clock – three in the morning. A quick mental calculation told him that it was seven on the east coast. He pushed himself off the bed and scrubbed a hand over his eyes. Sleep wasn't coming soon; he might as well work.

He fired up his laptop. The connection at this motel was decent, not great, but okay. *Especially in the middle of the night*, he thought sarcastically. No one else would be sucking up bandwidth at this hour.

Jordan's sleep was nearly as troubled as Spence's. Her thoughts continuously strayed to the kiss. The anger was gone now, replaced with a heavy dose of self-recrimination. Yes, Carl had forced the kiss on her but, had she resisted even a little bit, he would have stopped. He'd received no such signals from her. She'd melted. She'd quivered. She'd definitely returned his passion. But resist? – No, not in the slightest. She could hardly blame the entire episode on him.

As they had a hundred times tonight, her fingertips strayed to her lips. Focusing her thoughts, she was desperate to recall the details of the kiss – Carl's demanding mouth, the total control he had over her for those few seconds. Left only with the memory, her pulse raced, even now. It was the single most amazing kiss she'd ever experienced.

How would she ever face him again? This one indiscretion would always remain between them. Did Carl struggle with such innocent worries? Will he be able to pretend it never happened or worse, forget about it? The thought was equally sad and frightening.

What about Chris? The little voice in the back of her head reminded her that there was a third party in all this. Should she continue seeing Chris? Would it be fair? Should she tell him about the kiss, about the attraction she'd been struggling with even before the two of them started dating? Did he have a right to know? Her mind wrestled with the difficult questions until fatigue set in.

Finally, utterly exhausted, her eyes drifted closed, and she slept.

Monday morning, Jordan awoke with a raging headache. Ally was up earlier than usual, watching television and begging for breakfast. Dragging herself from bed, Jordan popped several painkillers first then poured cereal and milk in a bowl for her niece and left them on the table. She hoped a shower would revive her.

Last night's tumultuous events continued to plague her throughout the day. She managed to get herself and Ally to school on time. She'd teach her class and take a long afternoon nap when she got home.

While Jordan struggled through her day, Spence was hard at work. By six a.m., he'd learned all he could via the Internet and his agency contacts. Jordan's boyfriend owned a beat up Nissan – paid for, and little else. His credit card debt was about average. His student loans were almost paid off. He worked as an engineer where he'd said. His salary was decent.

Besides the car, the only fact Spence had found that raised any red flags was his residence. His DMV records showed the same home address as the one listed on the BMW's registration. So the question Spence needed answered was, 'Who is Terry Shatner?' Was this person a roommate who didn't mind lending his expensive car to Chris? A sibling? Or something more?

The only way Spence knew to find out, without calling in favors at the Bureau, was to stake out Chris's condo. At half past six, he parked his rental in front of the condominium complex, unit number twenty-one within his range of view. At five to seven, Chris exited, walked to his blue Nissan, and left for work. No surprise there.

The Beamer was parked in the condo's one designated space, also within sight. When no one came out for the next hour and a half, Spence began to think the car's owner might be out of town. He even considered knocking on the front door of the unit. But then, Chris's roommate stepped outside, and he had his answer, or at least part of it.

An hour later, Spence walked into a real estate office. An attractive young woman seated at the front desk looked up and smiled.

"Can I help you?"

"I hope so," he replied, turning on his most charming smile. Though it hadn't been trotted out much recently, her pretty blush proved it still worked. "I'm considering relocating to this area, and a friend recommended your agency."

"Wonderful!" she exclaimed.

"He suggested I ask for Terry Shatner."

The receptionist stood, tugged her mid-thigh length, snug-fitting skirt down, and assured him she'd be right back. Spence glanced around the small front office. A white, faux leather sofa offered a few seats below a wide window. A variety of magazines fanned out along a coffee table. Several framed photos mounted on the far wall caught his eye and he walked over to take a look.

They were all flattering head shots of the company's real estate agents. Spence's gaze went straight to the pretty brunette he'd followed here. A name was engraved on a brass plaque attached to the bottom of the frame, along with the words 'Top Seller.'

"Excuse me."

Spence pasted on a smile and turned around.

"I'm Terry Shatner," she said, extending her hand. "And you are?"

"Carl Spencer." He took her hand and gave it a firm shake. "You're much prettier in person," he said, gesturing to her photograph. "It must be true what they say about a woman glowing when she's expecting."

Beaming, Terry Shatner's fingertips brushed her rounded abdomen. "Thank you!" She invited him into her private office and asked the receptionist to bring him a cup of coffee.

While Spence sipped his coffee, he recited his made up story about planning a move to the area. He said he was looking for a condominium. She asked lots of questions about his space requirements, his budget, how many residents, and so forth.

"It's just going to be myself and my wife," he explained.

"So you're thinking a bedroom and a computer room, or two bedrooms, plus?" she asked, trying to draw him out.

Pretending to consider the question, Spence rubbed his chin and discreetly glanced around. Several framed photos sat on her desk facing away from him.

"Two bedrooms would probably do, and I think we'd like something near the mall," he said. "In fact, there's a nice looking complex on Main Street near Lemon Avenue. Do you know if anything is available there?"

Her eyes widened in surprise. "Oh, that's where I live! My fiancé and I love the place. Our unit has two bedrooms and two full bathrooms, but the best feature is a small alcove off the dining room. We call it the office."

Spence smiled. He was finally getting somewhere. "So, you're going to remodel the extra bedroom into a nursery soon?"

"Very soon," she said with a happy smile. "We're finding out the baby's gender next week, I hope. I want a little girl, but Chris is convinced we're having a boy."

Spence felt a small jolt, not that the revelation surprised him. This was going to hurt Jordan, and that unpleasant fact wedged uncomfortably in his gut. Pushing the feeling aside, he said, "Well, if the baby gets your lovely hair, she'll be beautiful."

Ms. Shatner practically blushed. "I'd be happy if she, *or he*," she added pointedly, "Had Chris's blonde hair."

Impulsively, she reached for one of the frames on her desk and turned it slightly, admiring the couple in the picture. Spence leaned forward and peered at the smiling face of Chris Oliver with his arm wrapped around Terry Shatner's waist.

Five minutes later, right on schedule, the alarm on Spence's phone buzzed. He made a point of extracting the device from his pocket and glancing at the screen.

"I'm afraid we'll have to finish this conversation at a later date," he said apologetically. "I've got a plane to catch." He stood and shook the woman's extended hand once again.

"Let me give you my card," she said, reaching for the small rack on her desk. "I'll find out if any of the units in my complex are for sale. Do you have a phone number where I can get in touch with you?"

He gave her the contact information he used at times like this. If she called, she'd get a recorded message stating that the number was no longer in service. Most people assumed they'd jotted it down incorrectly.

~ * ~

Spence debated what to do with this piece of information. Should he go straight to Jordan, warn her about the kind of man with whom she'd been spending time – before she did something regrettable? She might not be ready to listen to him. What he'd like to do was find Chris Oliver and give him the thrashing he deserved. He should have told Terry Shatner why he was really there – that her fiancé was a lousy, cheating... He would have, if she wasn't pregnant.

His phone rang as he pulled away from the real estate office. The smiling face of a teenager appeared on the screen.

"Hello, Caleb."

"Hey Dad, are you coming over today?"

Spence checked the time. It was almost eleven. Jordan wouldn't be home for several more hours. Her anger from last night replayed in his memory. Maybe he should give her another day or so to cool off.

"How about if I pick you up?" he replied. "We can hang out at the hotel and maybe swim, if you want."

"That's sounds cool, Dad. I'll leave Jordan a note, just in case we aren't here when she gets home."

After swinging by the apartment to retrieve Caleb, they picked up lunch at a burger joint and brought it back to the hotel. Between bites of cheeseburgers and fries, they chatted. School started for Caleb on Thursday, and Spence wanted the boy to have a handle on what was expected. After a while, they headed for the pool.

Later that evening, when Spence returned Caleb to his aunt's home, they were surprised to find Jordan dozing on the sofa.

"Auntie gots a headache," Ally announced. She held an index finger to her pursed lips and, with rounded eyes, whispered, "Be real quiet."

Somewhat hesitantly, Spence followed Caleb into the living room, wary of the type of reception he'd receive. Jordan was stretched out on the couch, a thin blanket covering her still form. Concerned, Spence sat on the edge of the coffee table. Her face looked pale. Frowning, he placed his palm against her forehead.

"Does she have a fever?" Caleb whispered, leaning over his shoulder.

Spence felt a rush of relief at the cool feel of her skin. "I don't think so."

Jordan's eye lashes fluttered, and she peered up at them. Frowning, her narrowed gaze slid past Carl and landed on his son. "Caleb, will you make Ally something to eat?" she rasped weakly.

"Sure," Caleb replied. Turning to find his sister missing, he called, "Ally, what do you want for supper?"

Spence shushed his son, albeit a little too late. Jordan winced at the loud volume. Her hands came up and cupped around her pounding skull.

"Sorry," the boy muttered as he went looking for his sister. She'd gone to the hall closet to look for a game.

"Is it a migraine?" Spence asked, keeping his voice low.

"The doctor calls them stress headaches," she replied, her voice weak and breathy. "They don't usually last very long."

"When did it start?"

"Last night...well, not really until this morning," she corrected. "I should have stayed home today."

Last night, he thought with an internal grimace. Had the incident between them caused this? He hoped not. "Have you taken anything?" When she gave a slight nod in response, he asked, "When?"

"Lunchtime," she replied.

"That was nearly six hours ago," Spence pointed out. He asked her what she was taking. "Where do you keep them?"

She told him where to find the bottle of ibuprofen, the same medicine she'd given him yesterday. Since his shoulder still throbbed, he popped several tablets while he gathered things for her, returning a few minutes later with a glass of water and the bottle of pills. Jordan pushed herself to a sitting position. With one hand pressed to her forehead, she managed to down the tablets, along with a few swallows of water. This was a bad headache, the kind that sometimes made her throw up. She hoped that wouldn't happen.

"Thanks," she whispered.

"You're welcome. I'm grateful for the opportunity to pay you back for taking care of me yesterday," Spence replied.

She eyed him warily, no doubt remembering other things about the previous day. Spence smiled and patted her on the back. She might want to throw him out again, but she was in no condition to do so.

"Now, why don't you go to bed?" he suggested. "Caleb and I can hold down the fort here."

Jordan squinted at the man beside her, debating whether to let him help her. She had no doubts about his ability to take care of things. He was quite capable of handling just about anything, she decided. But did she really want him handling her? The jack hammer in her head started again, and she squeezed her eyes shut.

"Okay," she whispered, conceding defeat, at least for now. She stood slowly, keeping her head tilted down. Somehow, it didn't hurt as much that way.

Spence jumped to his feet and looped an arm around her waist. "Let me help," he murmured.

In her bedroom, he pulled the covers back on the double bed she and Ally obviously shared. Several stuffed animals lay under the sheets, and Spence hastily pushed them aside. He waited while she eased to the edge of the bed and lay down on her side. As Spence pulled the sheet and blanket over her, he wondered at this very domestic role he was playing. He'd never taken care of anyone before. It was a new and not unpleasant experience.

Kneeling at her side, he asked, "Can I get you anything else, Jordan?"

"A big plastic bowl," she muttered, "just in case."

"Do the headaches usually make you sick?" he asked, surprised.

"Sometimes."

"I'll bring one."

He returned a couple of minutes later with the bowl, a dry hand towel, and a damp washcloth. Jordan was already asleep. The sight of her looking so fragile, so delicate, triggered an unexpected tightening in his chest. An image of Chris Oliver popped into his head, fueling a fierce anger. His jaw stiffened. The guy was using her, misleading her in the worst way. Before he left this area, Spence would make sure Oliver was painfully aware of his transgressions. The man was going to wish he'd never met Jordan Gray. He cleared a spot on her nightstand and left everything there, within easy reach. He'd check in on her later.

Spence spent the remainder of the evening eating macaroni and cheese and playing Candy Land with Ally. The little girl never tired of the game. She was a good sport, always expressing sadness for Spence when he drew a card that set him back.

"'t's okay, you catch up," she'd say, patting his knee in sympathy.

When Ally's bedtime rolled around, Caleb volunteered his bed so Jordan wouldn't be disturbed. He didn't mind roughing it on the living room floor. While the boy tended his sister, Spence made a run to his hotel. Since he was leaving the next day anyway, he packed up his things and checked out. He'd be sleeping on Jordan's couch tonight.

~ * ~

Jordan awoke to a silent apartment. She glanced at the clock on her nightstand. It was a quarter of six in the morning, early even for Ally. The little girl wasn't in the bed, though that wasn't unusual. Ally was often the first one up. Lifting her head cautiously, Jordan waiting for the hammering to start anew. It didn't. Thank heavens! Tossing off the covers, she swung her legs over the side of the bed and stood. She felt great, a little weak perhaps, but otherwise, really good.

She crept across the hall and found Ally sound asleep in Caleb's bed. After a quick peek in the living room, she stepped back in disbelief. Caleb was stretched out on the floor on top of a sleeping bag, snoring softly. The real surprise was the sight of Carl on the couch.

A sheet had been spread over the cushions, but only the knitted throw from the back of the sofa covered him – barely. His lower half was concealed beneath the small blanket, leaving his unclothed upper body exposed. Her gaze started at his chest – the dark, curly hair, the strong muscles, the tapered waist. In sleep, he'd thrown his left arm over his head, like a child. His right hand rested on his abdomen just above the navel. She couldn't see his damaged shoulder from this view; his left side faced her. When he suddenly shifted, startling her, she jumped and then froze. He inhaled deeply and became still.

Jordan turned and bolted from the room. The last thing she needed was to be caught ogling the man. A shower would clear her head and calm her nerves. After that, she'd march through the living room, keeping her eyes directed straight in front of her until she reached the kitchen, and make coffee.

For the second time in as many days, the smell of cooking lured Spence from slumber. He inhaled deeply, breathing in the delicious aroma of frying bacon. In response, his stomach rumbled ominously, last night's macaroni and cheese dinner a distant memory. Soft music drifted from the region of the kitchen. He tossed the blanket onto the back of the couch and sat up. Jordan's lilting voice accompanied the radio's song, a pleasant reminder of where he was, along with his present state of undress. Being caught in his boxers wouldn't do at all. Grabbing his jeans from the floor, he made a hasty dash for the bathroom.

Five minutes later, he stepped around the corner and peered into the kitchen. Jordan stood at the stove with her back to him. The bacon that awoke him sizzled in a skillet in front of her.

He smiled at the picture she made, snug fitting denim shorts, a pink tank top, and checkered apron. Secured in a ponytail, her light brown hair reached the middle of her back. She looked like a girl, not much older than Caleb. And she looked damned good to him just now. He considered slipping up behind her and tugging the apron strings loose. The thought of bacon grease burns kept him in check.

He cleared his throat, hoping to avoid starling her. She jumped anyway.

"Good morning," he said. "Are you feeling better?"

"Much better," Jordan replied over her shoulder. She piled the last of the bacon strips on a paper towel covered plate and switched off the burner then turned toward him. "Thank...you..." the halting words stuttered from her lips. Wearing faded jeans and nothing else, Carl leaned casually against the wall a few feet away, his arms crossed over his powerful chest. Recalling her earlier perusal of his person, she averted her now pink face and continued, "...for looking after things last night."

Spence smiled, accurately assessing her sudden discomposure. With wry humor, he told himself it was the handsome cut of his manly figure that caused the hitch in her voice, not the ugly scars.

"You're welcome," he replied then, gesturing to the breakfast she was obviously preparing, asked, "Is there anything I can do to help?"

Put a shirt on! Jordan's addled nerves begged. "No, nothing. I'm just about finished." She hoped he'd think her flushed skin was caused by the hot stove at which she'd been standing. "Coffee's made," she added. Using the spatula still gripped in her hand, she gestured toward the pot.

After reluctantly donning a T-shirt, Spence helped himself to a mug. Why did her discomfort in his presence please him? He should be encouraging distance between them, not provoking her. His current train of thought reminded him of yesterday's revelations. He still needed to have a talk with Jordan about her boyfriend. It was a discussion to which he wasn't looking forward. With the apartment so quiet, now seemed like as good a time as any.

"Jordan, we need to talk."

The serious inflection in his tone made Jordan pause. Her heart beat quickened. What did he want to talk about? Did it have anything to do with their intimate kiss from the other night? Was he going to suggest they forget it ever happened? *As if I ever could!* a soft voice whispered in her mind. *Maybe he wants more.* Hope flickered in her heart. She'd come to care for Carl. The other night, when he said there was a spark between them, he was right. She'd known it, at the time. Fear kept her from admitting the fact, even inside her own head. But, after he kissed her...

She could no longer deny her attraction to Carl Spencer. With that revelation, she'd also come to the conclusion that she couldn't continue seeing Chris. It wasn't fair to either of them. She'd meant to contact him yesterday, but the debilitating headache had prevented it.

All these thoughts skated through her mind in seconds. With her pulse racing, she set the stack of plates she was still holding on the table, and nodded.

Spence stood and pulled a chair out from the table. "Sit down, Jordan."

Before Jordan could comply, Ally bounded into the room. "Mornin' Auntie, mornin' Spence," she said with a smile as she climbed into the chair Spence still stood behind. "Auntie, you feel better?"

Spence's eyes met Jordan's over the little girl's head. "Later," he whispered. She nodded and resumed her tasks.

Ally's chatter roused Caleb and soon the boy was sitting at the table devouring everything in sight.

"You'd better hurry," Jordan said. "We need to be at the school by eight." Today was freshman registration at the high school.

"I'll take him," Spence volunteered with a solemn expression.

Jordan opened her mouth to protest, closing it again at the pained expression on the man's face. Carl was leaving this afternoon. He probably wanted to spend as much time with Caleb as he could. All the paperwork was completed, everything signed by both her and Carl. She'd taken the day off to be with her nephew. Resting at home was beginning to sound much more appealing than standing in line at the school.

Chapter 18

Spence and his son slowly made their way around the perimeter of the sunny high school quad. Surrounded by low buildings, the open square was dotted with picnic tables and immature trees. Three flag poles rose at its center. The long line they stood in would end at the registration windows. Afterward, there were other lines – for school pictures, physical education uniforms, textbooks, yearbook purchase, etc.

Caleb chatted with friends who happened by. Most wanted to know where he'd been all summer. He indulged their curiosity with stories of horseback riding, rodeos, and fishing. The other teens appeared awed by what sounded like an incredible vacation. Caleb eagerly introduced each kid to his dad. The father was equally proud to be on the receiving end of his son's many happy glances.

When Spence caught a glimpse of himself as a young teen reflected in Caleb's actions, his breath hitched. How proud and excited he would have been to have his own father at his side during even one of the milestones of his life. Those important occasions were long passed, the wish never to be realized. He prayed a silent thank you that his son wouldn't have to grow up with similar regrets. He was here, standing with Caleb at his induction into high school. He couldn't imagine wanting to be anywhere else in the world!

Spence made a careful study of each boy he met, determining which he thought might be good influences and which didn't impress him. His near perfect memory cataloged each name with a matching face. Mumbled greetings from several boys brought up images from the past. He'd seen the other two boys Caleb was with the night he was arrested, and they'd seen him. Their parents had bailed them out. Spence made a point of attracting their attention now and holding their gazes for a few moments, until they turned away.

One familiar boy shot him a dirty look. When a carefully aimed curse word reached his ears, Spence excused himself, telling Caleb he'd be back shortly. He didn't waste any time. He followed the boy around a corner. Out of sight of his son, he clamped a hand on the insolent boy's shoulder and spun him around.

"Was there something you wanted to say?" he asked in a quiet tone, his expression stern.

"N-no," the kid stammered, all his previous bravado vanished.

He tried to shrug off the heavy hand on his shoulder. Spence clamped a little harder, holding the boy steady.

"What's your name, son?"

"Tom Graham," the boy muttered, glancing around fearfully.

"Well now, Tom," Spence began, loosening his grip and patting the kid's shoulder. "I want to offer you a piece of advice. If you find yourself on the wrong side of the law again, they aren't going to do you the favor of driving you home. You'll be headed to juvenile hall, and a hearing before a judge." Spence shifted nonchalantly, letting his jacket fall open just enough for the boy to glimpse his concealed handgun.

"Are you a c-cop?" Tom asked, his eyes wide in surprise.

"Something like that," Spence replied evasively. "But, like you, Tom, I was once a tough, angry kid. I had my share of scrapes with the law."

The boy looked like he was about to faint. Spence forced down his mirth and clapped a hand on Tom's shoulder again. "Don't throw away your future, son. You can be anything you set your mind to."

When the boy nodded hesitantly, Spence smiled and turned away. Several other boys stood around watching curiously.

~ * ~

At noon, looking very pleased, Caleb toted a heavy stack of textbooks into the apartment. He was going to like high school. The only thing that would have made the experience better, in his opinion, was attending school with Jeremy Summers and Jeff Edwards. He missed his newest friends far more than the guys he'd left behind when his dad took him to Montana.

Before he carried the load to his room, Jordan inspected her nephew's books. She remembered taking biology and literature as a young teen. Algebra II seemed advanced for a ninth grader.

"He takes after me," Spence said, when she mentioned the math class.

"Do I detect a note of pride in your voice?" Jordan replied playfully.

Spence ginned. "Absolutely! Have I ever thanked you for looking for me?"

"I don't believe you have," Jordan said, still teasing.

Spence's tone turned serious. "Well, thank you." His voice was suddenly husky with emotion. "Thank you for giving me my son."

Jordan understood. This man loved his boy; that was clear. She tilted her head in acknowledgement. "You're welcome, Carl."

"Jordan, check this out!" Caleb called, returning to the living room. With a huge smile, he held up a smart phone. "Dad bought it for me for my birthday."

Jordan glanced from her nephew's excited expression to his father's. Carl looked just as pleased. Caleb's fourteenth birthday would arrive in just a few weeks, before the end of September, she recalled with shame. Why hadn't she thought to organize a celebration for this weekend?

"I'm so sorry, Carl," she began. "I should have planned something while you were here..."

"Don't worry about it," Spence replied, cutting off the unnecessary explanation. "You have no reason to apologize. I would have waited, except he needed one," Spence explained. "I don't want him stuck somewhere without a way to call for help."

Jordan nodded, recalling several incidents last year in which a cell phone would have been handy. The late-night vandalism spree came to mind. Caleb handed her a white plastic bag.

"Dad got you one, too," he announced.

Surprised, Jordan turned to Carl. "I can't..."

"Yes, you can!" Spence cut her off, anticipating her protest. "Your safety is an integral part of Caleb's. Plus, what good would his phone do him if he couldn't reach you?"

Jordan nodded hesitantly, still unconvinced that such a costly item was necessary.

"Here," Carl said, reaching for the small bag that dangled from her fingertips. "Let me show you how it works."

For the next fifteen minutes, Jordan learned how to operate her new phone. The new technology was overwhelming. "I'll never remember all this," she protested.

"I'll help you, Jordan," Caleb assured her. "It's easy. Here, let me show you how to use the camera, and save a photo to go with a phone number." He pointed his phone at Jordan and said, "Smile." He pressed the touch screen, and the camera made a clicking sound. "Look, now I'll save it under your phone number. Dad already programmed it into my phone."

Jordan watched, amazed that the boy had picked up all this in such a short period of time.

"There, now you take my picture with your phone," Caleb said. He made a funny face, and Jordan snapped his photo. Then he walked her through the process.

"Take a picture of me!" Ally shouted. Minutes ago, she'd awakened from a nap and wandered into the living room, curious about all the commotion.

"Come here, sweet pea," Spence called, holding out his hand. Smiling, Ally climbed onto his lap.

Jordan turned her phone toward them and took their picture. Caleb helped her save the photo under Spence's phone number.

"Now, whenever Dad calls you, this picture will show on the screen," Caleb explained. "And mine will show when you get a call from me. Neat, huh?"

"Yes," Jordan agreed. "It is pretty neat." Turning to Carl, she said, "Thank you."

He nodded in acknowledgement. "There's no contract with these. I'll make sure you both have plenty of minutes. By the way, the text feature on Caleb's phone only works with your number and mine." He glanced at his son. "You might want to tell your friends that," he suggested."

"I will," Caleb replied. "Thanks for the phone, Dad."

"You're welcome." Spence smiled and glanced at his watch. He still needed to have that talk with her, and time was running out.

"When is your flight?" Jordan asked, noticing his concern.

"Not for a few hours yet," he replied. "I need to speak with you in private."

She nodded, remembering their missed opportunity this morning. "Caleb, would you mind taking Ally to the playground for a little while?"

"No problem, Jordan," the boy replied, glancing from his aunt's odd expression to his dad's serious one.

Jordan whipped up several sandwiches and handed the plate to her nephew, along with a can of soda for Caleb and a juice box for Ally. The pair trouped through the front door and passed in front of the picture window facing the courtyard. The playground stood in the center of the small complex.

When she saw them sit down on a bench, Jordan turned and joined Carl in the living room. He sat on the sofa, one arm stretched along the back, watching her closely. His serious expression bothered her. Inhaling a fortifying breath, she chose the chair across from him. The coffee table would provide a much needed a barrier.

"What did you want to talk to me about?" she asked hesitantly.

"Chris." The single quiet word spoke volumes.

Her heart skipped a beat. "W-what about him?"

Spence debated the best approach to this difficult subject. Finally, he said, "Have you ever been to his place?"

"No," Jordan replied uncertainly.

"Why not?"

"He's never suggested it," she said. "Why do you ask?"

Leaning his elbows on his knees, Spence laced his fingers together in front of him. He stared at his hands for a long moment before responding evenly, "Because he isn't the man you think he is."

Jordan sighed, suspecting he had something to say and wishing he'd just say it. "What does that mean?"

Spence heard the annoyance in her tone. He needed to get to the point before she was too angry to listen. "The car he claims to own isn't his at all. It's leased to...someone else."

Jordan stared at him, stunned. "How do you..." She didn't need to finish the question. She already knew the answer. He had access to resources not available to the general population. He worked for the FBI. "You had him investigated," she accused, her eyes narrowed and angry. "Why?"

Spence stood and shoved his hands in his pockets. Should he admit he just didn't like the guy? Why not? His instincts were rarely off the mark. "Because I don't trust him," he replied evenly. "He's arrogant, self-centered, and possessive."

"You gathered all that from the one time you met him?" she asked incredulously. Even though she wasn't planning to see Chris anymore, she wouldn't sit by and let Carl berate him. "You could be talking about yourself?"

Ignoring the barb, Spence replied, "I'm trained to spot the bad apples, Jordan, and I'm very good at the job. I knew the guy was hiding something from the first moment I laid eyes on him."

"So, he's driving a leased vehicle, and naturally that's a cardinal offence in the FBI handbook?"

"The lease wasn't the part that bothered me, sweetheart," Spence replied, picking up on her sarcastic tone and throwing it back at her. "It was the name on the lease, and the fact that the address matched the one listed in his DMV records."

Jordan stood now and threw her hands in the air, exasperated. "That doesn't mean he's bad, Carl. He told me he has a roommate. I assumed that was the reason he never invited me to his home." She walked to the front window and back again, frustrated. "Why are you so suspicious? Why don't you just talk to him?"

Oh, I plan to! His jaw stiffened, and he stepped toward her. "My suspicions have saved my ass on more than one occasion," he pointed out. Only a few inches stood between them now. The anger sparking in her green eyes worked on his temper like a challenge. He wanted to wipe it away, to justify himself in her judgmental gaze. "His so called roommate is a pregnant fiancé."

The quiet words cut into Jordan like a sharp blade. Her angry stare shifted to shock. She stepped back and turned away. Her hand went to her open mouth, covering the gasp she couldn't keep from emitting. She'd been dating an engaged man? Why would he do such a thing?

Spence watched the results of his brief foray into Chris Oliver's life. Jordan's shoulders hunched and quivered. Was she crying, heartbroken over that worthless pile of manure?! Had he underestimated her affection for the man?

"Jordan, I'm sorry," he began, speaking softly to her back. "When I ran his plates, I didn't really expect anything to turn up. It was routine."

Jordan stared through the slatted blinds at the flowering shrubs growing outside her window. She was still processing the shocking news about Chris, still trying to come to terms with his actions, when Carl's apology threw her thinking off again. Something clicked. What had Carl just said? *It was routine* – like he did this sort of thing all the time. It wasn't just Chris. He didn't trust *anyone*. She slowly turned and looked at his contrite expression. Surely, he didn't feel regret about exposing Chris for the cheating cad he was? That hardly seemed appropriate now. Or was the remorse something he'd experienced in the past? Had he delved into the background of others without their knowledge and been sorry for what he'd uncovered? *Did he investigate me?*

"Do you scrutinize everyone you meet, Carl?" she asked, her hands clamped tightly at her belly.

"No, not everyone," he replied, missing the carefully controlled tension that hummed through her words. "Only people who might affect my life or the lives of people close to me. I don't like surprises."

Jordan nodded slowly, understanding – no surprises. "You checked me out, didn't you?"

Her unemotional tone caught him off guard. In his experience, a woman who sounded like that was dangerous and unpredictable. He couldn't read her at all. She'd closed herself off, wiped her normally open expression clean.

"Jordan," he said on an exhale, rubbing his fingers across his forehead. This wasn't going as planned. "I started the investigation before I knew you." Worried now, he backpedaled to the beginning. "Before I knew your name, before Caleb." It was true.

"You could have asked me anything, Carl, anything at all," she murmured, barely registering his excuse.

"The results didn't come in until after I'd returned to Montana with my son."

"When you knew I wasn't a threat," she countered. "But that didn't stop you from looking, did it?" Accusation filled her tone. She stepped away from him, moving to the couch and putting the coffee table between them once again. "Did you find anything interesting?"

Spence cringed at the saccharine tone, like she knew the answer to her question. Of course, he'd reviewed the background check. He knew what was there, the secret she kept deeply buried. He looked at her but said nothing.

"Ah, so you did discover something," Jordan surmised from his wary expression. The pitch of her voice was a little higher than she wanted.

She realized she'd prepared herself to hear something entirely different. That he'd somehow intended to declare himself, to tell her the kiss meant something to him. At the knowledge that she'd fooled herself, a tiny fissure opened in her heart. She was becoming ever so good at doing that – fooling herself. First Chris – engaged, and the woman expecting a baby! How could she be so naïve? And Carl, a man who kissed like Casanova but offered nothing more.

Her gaze returned to Carl's face. He looked stricken, the kid caught with his hand in the cookie jar. Well, that was just too damned bad! She'd been taken in by a two-timing jerk. She wasn't about to be lulled to complacency by a man who didn't know how to trust.

"Jordan, what turned up isn't as important as you think it is," Spence said, hoping to ease her mind. This was the twenty-first century, a time filled with single parents. Her circumstance was no different than fifty percent of the other women out there.

"What turned up..." Jordan repeated quietly, staring past him at a photo of Ally propped beside the television – a precious, innocent child, her supposed secret. She smiled and shook her head. "Your powers of deduction failed you, Carl."

Suddenly exhausted, Jordan sank to the edge of the sofa and dropped her head into her palms. Her heart ached, her head hurt. Her world spun around her, and she was helpless to keep up.

Spence watched her slowly deflate. His chest felt suddenly tight, and he wanted to go to her, to offer comfort. He resisted. She wouldn't welcome his touch right now. She was angry with him, furious that he'd had her investigated, that he'd read the file, that he knew things about her – private things that weren't his business. She needed time. He checked his watch again.

When she muttered, "Don't you have a plane to catch?" he knew he was being dismissed. With one last look at Jordan's defeated form, he grabbed his bags from their place by the door and stepped outside. He'd just toss these in the trunk of his rental then say goodbye to Caleb and Ally.

~ * ~

"I've got to hit the road."

Jordan watched Carl approach the children, as the words floated through the front window. He knelt and Ally launched her body into his arms, her little hands circling his neck. He spoke softly to the little girl, and she shook her head with determination, her lower lip extended. She was going to cry. With an effort, Jordan controlled her recently developed motherly instinct to go to the child. Carl talked quietly for a few minutes, patting her back. Finally, Ally nodded and kissed his cheek. Jordan's throat tightened, and she barely held back her tears.

When Carl stood and turned to the somber face of his son, Jordan moved away from the window. This was a private moment for Caleb, one he wouldn't want her to see. He'd developed a bond with his father, and saying goodbye, even a temporary one, wasn't going to be easy.

Spence cupped a hand on his son's shoulder and stared at the boy's glistening eyes. This was going to be hard on both of them.

"Dad," Caleb rasped.

Unable to look at the anguish in his son's face, Spence hauled the boy to his chest and wrapped his arms around him. Caleb wept, and Spence's thick throat swallowed hard to keep from joining him. When he'd mastered his emotions better he spoke.

"I'll see you soon, son, probably before the Thanksgiving recess. I don't think I can wait that long." He rubbed his hands up and down the boy's back, unwilling to break the contact.

"Okay," Caleb muttered against his father's shirt. There was more he wanted to say but didn't know how. Instead, he clung to his dad's strong body like a little boy – and he didn't care who saw them.

Closing his eyes, Spence savored the intimate moment. So much could happen, once they were apart. The boy had lost his mother unexpectedly. Spence's partner fell without warning. It made them both aware of how quickly their lives could be changed by one insignificant event, a single mistake, the Master's plan.

He couldn't leave without telling his boy how he felt. "I love you, Caleb," he whispered. Why were those three words so hard to say, even when they were meant so sincerely? He pressed his lips to son's head.

With a muffled sob, Caleb tightened his arms around Spence's waist. "I love you, too, Dad."

The raspy, emotion-laced words sailed into Spence's heart and filled it to overflowing. He couldn't imagine a better sentiment to carry him through the lonely weeks and months to come.

~ * ~

Spence had one last errand to run before heading to the airport. He parked his rental across from the blue Nissan and waited. He didn't need to check in until five o'clock. Chris Oliver got off work at three. What Spence had to say wouldn't take long.

When he saw the man exit the company's main entrance, Spence opened his car door. He intercepted his quarry as the man reached his parking space.

"Hello, Chris." Spence stood a few feet behind the younger man, his arms folded across his chest.

Halting in surprise, Chris turned. "Mr. Spencer," he said, wondering why he was here. The man's determined, almost menacing, expression raised his guard. "Is there something I can do for you?"

In two strides, Spence closed the distance between them. He'd like to draw this out a bit just to watch Oliver squirm, but there wasn't time. Clamping a hand on the younger man's shoulder, Spence leaned in close.

"Yes, there is," he said in a quiet, firm tone. "You can stay away from Jordan."

Hackles raised, Chris reached up and shoved Spence's hand off his shoulder. He'd known from the start that this guy had a thing for Jordan. That was one of the reasons he didn't like him hanging around her, sleeping on her couch, eating dinner at her apartment. It didn't matter now but, obviously, Spencer wasn't aware of that fact.

"You don't have a say," Chris seethed. "It's you who should leave her alone. She's my girl."

Spence straightened and smiled. The guy was too cocky for his own good. "That so?" he said. "Seems like one woman is enough for any man, but you think you need two?"

Anxiety flushed through Chris. "What do you mean?"

"I had a nice chat with your girlfriend yesterday," Spence replied. "From my place, it sure looks like you've got a full plate. Tell me, why are you sniffing around another woman's skirt?"

Chris turned away. Terry had said nothing about talking to this guy. She had a notorious temper. If she was pissed off, he'd be the first to know. He turned back and stared at the man behind him. He had to be bluffing.

"You're full of it, man," Chris said, his previous confidence returning.

Spence braced his hands on his hips and glared. He'd love to pop this guy in the mouth, knock a few teeth down his throat. If he had time to deal with the local police right now, he'd indulge himself.

Instead, he said, "I'm going to give you fair warning. If you so much as text Jordan, you'll be dealing with me. I've squashed bugs much larger than you."

Still trying to get a bead on him, Chris returned the man's glare. Spence was supposed to be leaving town;

Chris knew that much. He'd be gone, after today. "Aren't you going back to wherever you came from soon?" Not waiting for a response, he spun around and headed for his car.

The mocking sneer pushed Spence beyond his usual limits. This guy had no intention of leaving Jordan alone. He'd probably be calling her tonight. Should he give the fiancé a call, let her know her beloved's intentions? No. Spence worried that if that relationship split, Chris would have no reason to heed the very useful advice he was receiving now. He glanced around the parking lot. There were no other people nearby.

Quick as lightning, Spence grabbed the collar of Chris's shirt and slammed him against the side of his car. His right shoulder protested the sudden movement with an agonizing jolt. Using his free hand, he reached into his pocket and withdrew his wallet. The temptation to bring out his sidearm was strong. It was also a very bad idea, under these circumstances.

Chris's initial instinct was to fight the man off, but Spence's bigger, stronger frame pinned him chest first against the car. Every move Chris made was expertly blocked.

"I'm trained to track down and neuter little turds like you," Spence seethed in the man's ear. "If you think I'm kidding, go ahead and test me!" He slapped his billfold open on the top of the car, inches from Chris's nose.

"Get off me, you son of a..."

The expletive lodged in his throat, when got a look at the wallet that had practically hit him in the nose. For several shocked seconds he stared at the FBI badge, before shifting his focus to the photo identification beside it. Spence's face glared back at him, erasing any doubts he still may have harbored about the authenticity of what he was seeing. Clearly, the man wielded some serious power.

"Do you need any more proof that I'll carry out my promises?" Spence asked. "Or do you want to see my gun, too?" He pressed hard, curbing the man's attempts to free himself.

As Chris stared at Spence's picture, he noticed the edge of a familiar, peach-colored card tucked haphazardly behind the FBI credentials. The last few letters of a name were visible – TNER. Shatner, as in Terry Shatner. He closed his eyes, and envisioned his fiancé's face. Spence had been to see her, had apparently gotten pretty close.

"Why didn't you tell her?" Chris said, his voice flat and the fight gone.

Spence heard the defeated tone. He glanced at his wallet and spotted the business card. Evidently, Chris had seen it, too. Spence gave one last push against the car and stepped back, jerking the guy around to face him.

He countered with a question of his own. "Why are you bothering Jordan? You're engaged to a nice looking woman who is about to have your baby."

Spence watched the color drain from the man's face. So, that was it. He wasn't ready for fatherhood.

"I don't know," Chris replied, leaning heavily against his car. "It just came out of nowhere. Here I am, in this fun, laid-back relationship, and Terry gets pregnant." Agitated, he pushed both hands over his scalp, mussing up his usually impeccable hair. "I'm just not ready for that."

Shocked by the honest admission, Spence stared at him, wondering if he would have reacted the same way. If Tanya had tracked him down fourteen years ago, how would he have taken the news of Caleb's impending arrival? Maybe he should cut the guy some slack, at least regarding his cowardice. He could do that. But where Jordan was concerned, Chris was way out of line.

Ignoring the sympathetic leanings in gut, Spence demanded, "Why did you involve Jordan?"

"I don't know," Chris replied. "She was just so nice, so simple and uncomplicated. I guess I was looking for a little mental escape." He glanced at the angry man in front of him and cringed. "I never intended to leave Terry. Jordan was just – a diversion."

Stunned, Spence grabbed Chris by the front of his shirt and shoved him against the car again. "You son-of-a..."

"I know!" Chris interrupted, holding up his hands and ready to take whatever punishment the man meted out. "You're right! I'm a weasel. I don't deserve either of them."

Letting go, Spence shoved himself away again, his jaw clamped, his shoulders taut. "The only reason I didn't tell Terry everything is because she's pregnant. You're right; you don't deserve her. And you damn sure don't deserve Jordan," he pointed out, walking a few steps away. His time was up. He turned and jabbed his index finger at Chris. "Go fix your relationship. Man up! You're about to be a dad, ready or not."

"I know," Chris said, staring dejectedly at the ground.

The guy looked like he was going to puke. For Spence, becoming a father was the best thing that had ever happened to him. Recalling the painful goodbye he'd just come from, he released a deep sigh. "Be glad you get to know your kid from the start," he said, his voice growing solemn, his head drooping. "Mine is thirteen and we only met a few months ago."

Chris stared at the man, noting the deeply etched regret in his face. Maybe this wasn't the jail sentence he'd feared. "You don't have to worry about me bothering Jordan again," he said, giving the man the assurance he was seeking. "She left a voicemail this morning telling me she didn't want to see me anymore. I guess you must have already spoken to her."

The moment Chris's words registered, Spence's head snapped up. Jordan had called him this morning? But they'd only talked a little while ago. "What time?"

"What time?" Chris repeated, confused.

"What time did she send the text message?" Spence demanded.

"I don't know...I guess around ten o'clock. I was in a meeting at the time and couldn't respond. Why?"

Spence smiled. He hadn't swayed her decision at all, at least not in the way he'd thought. By the time they had their discussion, she'd already dumped him. Was the amazing kiss the catalyst? As he boarded his flight two hours later, he was still pondering the news.

Chapter 19

A nurse showed Spence into the physician's private office and gestured to one of the two chairs. A thick file folder rested in the center of the desk. Several x-rays hung against an unlit light board on one wall. Ignoring the chairs, Spence walked over to have a look. A sticker in the corner of each scan read, Spencer, C. Printed below his name was a date. These were the latest pictures of his shoulder, taken last week. He switched on the light, and the outline of his shoulder became clear. He studied them, trying to determine if there was any new damage.

Dr. Phillips came in and found his patient at the lighted board. This man was one of his more inquisitive clients. Carl Spencer was intelligent and preferred to know everything.

"It's easier if you have the previous films to compare against," the doctor said. He grabbed an oversized, brown paper sleeve from his desk and carried it across the room.

Spence turned and held out his hand. "Hello, Doc."

"Mr. Spencer."

The two men shook hands then the doctor extracted two additional films and attached them to the light board beside the ones already there.

"Look here," Dr. Phillips said, pointing to a gray area on one of the older x-rays. "This region shows extensive scar tissue. There's more here and here," he added, gesturing to other gray and white splotches.

Spence nodded.

"Now, that popping noise you heard when you overextended your arm," the doctor continued, "was probably caused by stressing the largest section of scar tissue." He gestured to one of the newer films.

Spence could see small fissures in the largest mass.

"I don't see any further damage to the rotator cuff, or any of the tendons. The pain you're experiencing is probably just a byproduct of overstretching the muscles and tendons," Phillips explained.

"But I haven't been able to accomplish that sort of reach since, Doc," Spence stated. "Why is that?"

Dr. Phillips flicked off a switch, and the light boards darkened. He gestured toward the chairs opposite his desk, and the two men sat down.

"The adrenaline rush you experienced is my best guess. Your brain told your body what needed to be done, and your body complied – burning right through that scar tissue," the doctor explained. "That fact gives me confidence I didn't have before, Mr. Spencer."

"Go on," Spence said.

"I'd like to go back into your shoulder, arthroscopically, of course. If we break up and remove as much scar tissue as possible, you stand a good chance of making a nearly complete recovery."

Spence leaned forward and stared at the doctor. "What are we talking about here, Doc, in percentages?"

"It's hard to say. Perhaps, seventy to eighty percent. Maybe more," Phillips guessed. "There's no way to know for sure, and I can't offer a guarantee. We can make your shoulder better, though."

Spence leaned back and contemplated the man's predictions. If he could regain eighty percent of the natural mobility in his shoulder, he might not be confined to the desk. He could go back into the field. That's what he wanted, right? He waited for a feeling of elation. None came.

"When can we get it done, Doc?"

"You're fortunate, Mr. Spencer," the man replied. "I have an opening next week."

~ * ~

Jordan's daily life quickly settled into a predictable routine. She and Ally spent their weekdays at her church, Jordan teaching her *fours* and Ally happily pursuing the simple joys in the *threes* class. After work, they'd do their marketing or play in the park or visit the public library. Ally loved checking out piles of picture books and bringing them home. Many were returned the following week, untouched. She usually discovered the ones she preferred rather quickly. These would be read and reread until both Ally and Jordan could recite their stories by heart.

Whenever the weather was clear, which was most of the time, they'd hit the park. A fifteen or twenty minute stop would usually placate the little girl for a few days. Jordan didn't mind unwinding on a park bench or lounging on the blanket she always kept in her trunk.

It was at unhurried times like these that her thoughts often turned to Carl. She'd come to terms with his prying, finally understanding that he couldn't switch off the inquisitive part of his nature. Knowledge gave the man peace. He liked to solve puzzles, thrived on it. Being taken by surprise was unsettling, even dangerous, particularly in his line of work.

She realized that the investigation into her background was prompted by her initial search for him. After discovering his son, he'd probably forgotten all about it. He'd tried to tell her that, but her overloaded brain hadn't heard. Then, when the information came in, he couldn't keep himself from looking. *And why not?* she reasoned. After all, she'd been caring for his son for the last year and a half. If the tables were turned, if it were she who had access to information about him, she'd look. It was human nature.

~ * ~

Caleb's first weeks of high school were mostly uneventful. Meeting new teachers, figuring out what they expected from him, learning to get from class to class in less than four minutes. All these daunting challenges were faced with a combination of eagerness and boredom. He wanted to please his dad but, at the same time, he wanted him here. He hated that they had to be apart.

Caleb exchanged emails with Spence almost daily. He knew his dad was seeing a doctor about his shoulder again, and that his boss was pushing for him to return to work. Caleb wasn't sure what to think about that. He kept reminding himself that something would give by Christmas. He could wait that long. He had to.

~ * ~

With the busy summer behind them, Deborah was eager to invite Jordan over for dinner. After extracting a solemn promise that Gary would be the only man present, Jordan finally agreed. The Friday evening arrived two weeks into the new school year. Caleb opted to stay home. His math was harder than expected. He was planning to talk with his dad about it over the phone, maybe scan the textbook pages and email them to Carl. Deborah's step daughter was available to entertain Ally.

"Come in and have a glass of wine," Deborah said, taking Jordan's arm and leading her into the living room.

Ally had already disappeared down the hall in search of Kiera.

Jordan sat down on the sofa. A few minutes later, Gary appeared with an open bottle and two glasses.

"Hi, Jordan," he said, as he poured Cabernet into a glass and handed it to her. "It's nice to see you. Did Caleb's father make it home okay?"

"Thank you," Jordan said. "And, yes, he did. Caleb's been mourning his departure ever since. I'm sure Carl feels the same."

"That's probably a good thing," Gary pointed out. Several times last year, Gary had offered wise counsel regarding the troublesome youth. His advice helped Jordan see things from a male point of view. "It's good to know they've bonded. Caleb really needed him."

Jordan nodded. She agreed completely.

He poured his wife a glass and excused himself to the kitchen. He was playing the role of chef tonight and had pots and pans on the stove to attend.

Deborah watched her husband go then turned to her friend. "Okay, spill it. What happened between you and Caleb's dad?"

Jordan practically choked on her wine. "W-what? Nothing, Deborah," she sputtered in surprise.

"Nothing? Really? I figured, well...never mind." She looked away and then down.

Jordan watched her normally overconfident friend fidget uncomfortably, and she couldn't help it. She started laughing. When she couldn't seem to stop, she set her glass on the table. Deborah joined her and before long they were both holding their stomachs and wiping away tears. Responding to the boisterous sounds, Gary stuck his head into the room, stared in surprise at the out of control women for a moment, and then disappeared, shaking his head.

"I...I think...we scared him," Deborah said between breaths, reaching for a tissue. She wiped her face and winced at the sight of the residue covering the white material. Her carefully applied makeup was ruined. Oh well, seeing Jordan laugh was worth the sacrifice.

Nodding her agreement, Jordan started coughing...and then crying. And, like the earlier mirth, she couldn't seem to stop.

"Oh, heavens," Deborah whispered, when she noticed the change. All levity was now gone, instantly replaced with concern. She moved to the sofa and pulled her friend into her arms. Jordan wept, and her friend soothed with meaningless phrases. "It'll be okay, Jordan. Go ahead and let it go. Everything will work out."

Gary peeked into the living room again and frowned when he saw what was going on. His wife waved him away.

After a while, Jordan forced her emotions down and lifted her head from Deborah's now damp shoulder. "I'm sorry," she squeaked.

"Honey, everyone needs a good cry once in a while," Deborah replied, handing her the box of tissues.

Jordan pulled out a handful and mopped her face. What had just happened to her? After she'd blown her nose three times and wiped away most of the smeared mascara that blackened her eyes, she turned to her friend and offered a tenuous smile.

"Is this because of Chris?" Deborah asked hesitantly, patting Jordan's knee.

"Chris?" Jordan repeated uncertainly, as though she'd never heard the name before. "No. I haven't seen him in weeks. Why?"

"Well, I just assumed you'd heard about…um…" she trailed off.

"About what, Deb?" Jordan asked. She'd hardly given Chris a thought since the day she ended their relationship. What had happened to the man? Remembering Carl's anger toward him, she wondered for a brief, terrifying second if he'd done something rash.

"He's getting married next week," Deborah replied sheepishly. "Gary found out a few days ago. Needless to say, we weren't invited to the wedding." She chewed her lower lip anxiously then reached for Jordan's hand. "I'm so sorry, Jordan. We never should have set you up like that. The man's a creep. I swear, we had no idea! Did you know his fiancé is seven months pregnant? I feel like such an idiot!"

Jordan covered her friend's hand with hers and said, "It's okay, Deb. I couldn't care less."

"Really? I thought you were falling for him."

"I thought I was, too. I had myself convinced that he was the one," she admitted, looking suitably embarrassed.

Deborah had really worried about talking to Jordan tonight, fearing their friendship might have suffered because of that horrible man. She was immensely relieved to discover that it hadn't. Reaching for her wine, she asked, "What made you change your mind?"

Jordan picked up her glass. For a long moment, she stared unseeing at the glossy, red liquid, debating how to answer the question. "Carl," she finally said with a sigh. "He made me realize I could feel so much more for a man than I did for Chris."

Deborah studied her friend. Ever since Carl Spencer left town, she'd looked sad, sort of far away and lost. She rarely smiled and her usually lively personality had all but vanished, even the preschoolers seemed to notice. Deborah had assumed her breakup with Chris was the cause. Clearly, that wasn't the reason – but it did have something to do with a man. There was really only one explanation.

"You're in love with him."

Jordan's head snapped up, and she stared at her friend, stunned. Was she? Admittedly, she was attracted to Carl and missed him – but love? Her stomach clenched, and a cold sweat washed over her. She didn't want to be in love with Carl Spencer. There was a mile long list of reasons why that was a bad idea.

"I...I can't be, Deb," she whispered, fearing her friend was correct.

"Why not? Isn't he single, too?"

Jordan shook her head. Everything was so simple with Deborah. One single man plus one single woman automatically equated to a perfect couple. "He doesn't feel that way about me," she explained. "He loves his son. Ally has him wrapped around her finger. With me, there's a lot of spark, but he's never indicated he wants anything permanent." She looked away and sipped her wine.

"Well, spark is something, Jordan," Deborah stated eagerly. "You have to start somewhere."

Jordan loved her friend's optimism. Though she could use a little positive thinking these days, it wouldn't change the facts in this case. "Don't forget, he lives three thousand miles away."

"And you are raising his son," Deborah countered. "You have to see each other occasionally."

"Maybe," Jordan replied. "But Caleb plans to live with his father. Carl has promised him they'd work things out by Christmas." The thought of her nephew leaving stimulated a fresh wave of emotion. Jordan blinked the tears away. She didn't want to cry anymore.

"He told you that?"

"Caleb did, and he's convinced it'll happen," Jordan replied, grabbing a clean tissue and dabbing at her damp eyes.

Deborah moved closer and slid her arm around Jordan's shoulders. She'd been through far more than her share of turmoil. Life just wasn't fair.

~ * ~

Bartholomew Peel glanced at the four walls of his cell for the last time. His mattress was rolled up, awaiting a new resident. The small cardboard box containing all his worldly possessions, at least the ones he'd been allowed to keep inside this place, rested on the bunk. His roommate of the past few months stood well back. He was silent and no doubt, relieved. When Bart heard the guard coming his way, he turned to the scrawny kid and sneered. Good riddance! He couldn't wait to get out of here.

He silently counted each and every step he took through the cold, echoing hallways toward freedom. He feared that some last minute glitch would close the doors before he could pass through them. That would be paradoxically cruel.

It was through a twist of fate that he was being released today. Overcrowding, the news report had stated. He'd read it himself in the library. California's prisons were overflowing with inmates, with new arrivals being admitted daily. The worst offenders would stay – the murderers, rapists, some of the sex offenders. Others, less violent sorts who had already served most of their sentences, were evaluated for early release. Somehow, even though his crime was assault with a deadly weapon, he'd fallen into that particular category. He wasn't about to correct the powers that be. If they wanted to let him go, he was happy to oblige.

A guard at the final exit searched his box. For what, Bart could only imagine. Were they worried he was making off with the good silver? Satisfied that none of his possessions were contraband, he handed a thick manila envelope to Bart, followed by a clipboard with a pen dangled from one corner.

"Sign here," he said pointing to the signature line at the bottom of the sheet. "It states that you received the same clothing and personal items you arrived with."

Ignoring the clip board, Bart took the envelope. He tore it open and looked inside – his ratty shirt, still stained with blood from the fight that put him behind bars, an old pair of ripped jeans, even his boxers. Gross. He dumped the contents on top of the other things in his box. His wallet dropped out onto the pile, along with his watch, a very dead cell phone, and several pieces of jewelry.

Bart smiled, picking up the snake earring he'd always worn. One end, the snake's tail, formed the long, pointed hook that slid through the hole. Without preamble, he positioned the sharp point against the now closed hole in his lobe and shoved it through. Blood spurted onto his fingers. The two nearby guards groaned. One of them covered his mouth and gagged, almost vomiting. Bart grabbed the old bloody shirt, wiping his earlobe and his hand.

"That's better," he said with satisfaction, reaching for the clipboard. He scrawled something indecipherable on the line and dropped the board onto the counter with a loud bang. A few minutes later, the final locked gate was opened, and he stepped outside. Free at last.

Chapter 20

Not long after his medical consultation, Spence spoke to his supervisor. If his recovery was as good as the doc predicted, the man assured him, they'd keep him in the field. He'd also set up a lunch date with Agent Jefferson.

He and Jefferson had joined the Bureau at almost the same time. They'd known each other nearly eight years. Brent was a computer analyst. He drove a desk. His weapon of choice was a very sophisticated laptop, coupled with an off the chart IQ. He wasn't the guy you wanted literally watching your back. You went to him when you needed information. The extremely thorough dossier on Jordan was assembled by Jefferson. He knew where to look for answers to questions that had yet to be asked. He was also a friend.

"You look like crap, man!" Jefferson said with a broad grin.

Spence approached the thin black man with his hand extended. "Thanks, Brent," he said with a smile. "You're not so bad yourself."

The two men shook hands then walked through the front door of the small Italian restaurant they both frequented. Spence hadn't eaten at Antonio's in nearly a year, and the thought of a meatball sandwich had his mouth watering. Almost instantly, a small, round waitress, Antonio's wife, showed them to a table in the back.

"What have you been up to, Spence?" Brent asked, after they'd placed their orders. "I haven't heard from you in months – not since you requested info on that woman. What was her name?"

"Jordan Gray," Spence replied, as his mind conjured a picture of her pretty face. He smiled.

Noting his friend's suddenly pleasant expression, Jefferson asked, "And she turned out to be?" Since running the background check, he'd had one brief text from Spence. It said simply, *everything is fine.*

"My son's aunt."

Spence used the next hour to bring his friend up to speed on the latest events in his life. He told about finding his son, the trouble the boy had gotten himself into, the summer in Montana. The only major detail he left out was the powerful attraction he felt for Jordan. He'd yet to figure out what to do about it and wasn't ready to share.

"Wow!" Jefferson exclaimed quietly when the explanation came to an end. "So, you're a dad now, and starting off with a teenager, no less. My wife would be impressed! Are you planning to make it a full-time gig?" He'd guessed that Spence had taken a liking to his new role.

Spence heaved a sigh. The waitress came by to collect their plates and refill their water glasses, giving him a moment to consider his friend's question. "I'd like to," he finally replied.

"But…" Brent said, picking up on Spence's uncertainty.

Spence scraped a palm over his eyes. He'd thought of little else beyond what he was about to share with his friend. "The kid lost his mother last year, a few months before I was nearly killed in the line of duty. Jordan –

Caleb's aunt, worries I'll get shot again and, frankly, so do I. The boy doesn't deserve to go through that again." There, he'd said it out loud.

"So, you take the desk job, Spence," Brent said matter-of-factly. He shrugged. "No one has ever taken a shot at me." But he knew Spence wasn't cut out for an office job. His friend preferred the action, liked being outside, enjoyed poking around crime scenes and conducting investigations.

"Maybe," Spence replied. His thoughts drifted back to his last conversation with Sheriff Davies. The offer was practically guaranteed, though the pay stunk. He'd almost laughed when Davies told him the salary. He made more than twice that amount now.

While Spence mulled something over in his mind, Jefferson waited. "What is it?" he finally asked.

"While I was in Montana licking my wounds, I was offered a job," Spence replied, chuckling.

"What kind of job?"

"Small town sheriff's deputy."

As an image of Don Knott's came to mind, Brent couldn't help smiling. "Barney Fife," he said, staring at his friend. He tried to picture Spence manning a speed trap in order to make his quota, or directing traffic around such highway disasters as an overturned fertilizer truck. He shook his head, his shoulders shaking with mirth. "I just can't see it."

The men were still laughing when they signed their credit card slips and left the restaurant.

~ * ~

Jordan fought the Friday afternoon traffic all the way to the campus. She parked as close to the building as she could and hurried inside. The instructor was in the process of writing her name on the white board. Good,

Jordan thought with relief. She wasn't late. She'd be here until nine, then again Saturday morning for an all-day session. The weekend long course would fulfill the second to the last requirement she needed to earn her teaching credential. She chose not to think about the last requirement – student teaching. How was she going to manage working fulltime without pay? *One problem at a time*, Jordan reminded herself.

She sat through four hours of utter boredom. As the instructor droned on, Jordan continuously dragged her wandering thoughts back to the subject. When the class finally ended, she practically sprinted to the door.

Caleb was babysitting Ally tonight. Jordan didn't like to leave him in charge for long periods of time. He tended to forget that he was the one responsible. Tomorrow, she'd be leaving Ally with Deborah for the day. Caleb had plans with a friend, an extra credit project in his world history class. It wasn't Caleb's favorite subject, a fact that his scores already reflected.

His dad was the one who suggested doing the additional work, Jordan recalled, as she steered her car onto the freeway. Too late, she realized she was thinking about Carl again.

She desperately needed peace. *Time,* she kept reminding herself. *Time heals all wounds.* Over the next weeks and months, her feelings for him should dry up and blow away like dandelion fluff. She'd convinced herself it would happen. But four weeks had already gone by, and she still felt the same painful yearning. Her heart ached. Her thoughts were jumbled. She was unable to focus long enough to finish a novel or sit through a movie. After a while, her mind wandered, and she'd find herself at the end of the story, with no idea what had happened in the middle.

What if Deborah's observations were right? Maybe what she felt wasn't mere physical attraction or infatuation. Maybe she was in love with him.

Jordan pulled into the last available spot on her street. God must be smiling on her tonight, she decided, because it happened to be right in front of her apartment complex. She grabbed her tote bag and purse and climbed out, glancing around cautiously. As her gaze skimmed over the vehicles parked across the street, a match sparked inside one. For a split second, she glimpsed a person sitting behind the wheel. An involuntary shudder vibrated through her. Swallowing the irrational fear, she hurried to the low gate leading into her complex's courtyard. An engine started, and she turned in time to see the black car pull away from the curb and drive off. It was nothing, she thought, willing her racing pulse to relax, just someone on their way out. She opened the gate and walked inside, glad to be home.

~ * ~

She had no way of knowing the black vehicle had been parked on her street, in one place or another, most of the evening. Nor could she be aware that the occupant was waiting for her to arrive. He needed to get a look at her, verify her identity. During her cautious sweep of the surrounding area, she'd held her car door open long enough for the interior lighting to reveal her pretty face. It matched the photograph he'd printed earlier.

Bart smiled, glad he'd availed himself of an education while doing time. Before he joined the general population at the state pen four years ago, he'd never touched a computer. Thankfully, courtesy of some well-intentioned do-gooders concerned with the rights of the incarcerated, the prison boasted a few late model desktops. He'd become quite proficient. Discovering nearly identical equipment at the public library was nothing short of extraordinary. *Your tax dollars at work*, he mused with a wry grin.

Finding her was easy. Months ago, he'd run across her sister's obituary. That had been a stroke of luck. It made everything much less complicated. It also provided him with the vital information he required, her name, for example. Google was an amazing tool. He'd been able to narrow down her location fairly quickly. The church where she worked was a big help, he had to admit. Had they neglected to list their preschool teachers' names, along with very nice color photographs, things wouldn't have gone so smoothly. Of course, he couldn't be a hundred percent sure she was the right Jordan Gray. He'd never actually met her, had only seen a couple of ancient photos, and that was years ago. But then, the kid showed up. Caleb. He'd grown quite a bit but still had that same strawberry-blonde hair, same freckles across the bridge of his nose.

At four o'clock, when the backpack-toting boy got home, Bart took his leave. He couldn't afford to be spotted in the middle of the day. He was a night owl by nature, preferring to do his thing in the dark. He'd decided to come back later and check her out. He wanted all his bases covered, all the angles explored before things went down.

~ * ~

Compared to Spence's previous surgeries, the two hour procedure he'd recently undergone was simple. The general anesthetic the doctor insisted he receive was the only reason he'd been admitted to the hospital. After an overnight stay, he'd come back to his condo. His shoulder hurt like crazy for the first few days, just as the doc warned him it would, but ibuprofen took care of the pain. Spence was no wimp. He didn't even bother to fill the prescription for heavy duty meds. He'd traveled that perilous road a year ago. The lack of control brought on by the hard stuff was unnerving. It also muddled his thinking. And right now, he needed full use of his brain.

More than a week had passed since his lunch appointment with Jefferson. Spence often replayed the conversation, carefully considering his friend's suggestion to join the office team. He was no closer to making a commitment now, than the day they talked. He'd suffered many sleepless nights, weighing the pros and cons.

By the first of the year, the doc assured him, they'd know the results of his latest surgery. Just five days post-op, Spence could already feel a difference. Though his shoulder ached, movement was far easier. His physical therapist was amazed. Each day, he could lift his arm a little higher. Prior to the procedure, a barrier seemed to hold the limb down. That wall had been removed. He could go back into the field.

You can't do that to him! Jordan's heartfelt admonishment haunted his mind. That day in Montana, when she'd come apart emotionally and cried in his arms, felt like yesterday. Her anguished tears and desperate plea speared his heart and challenged his conscience. By going back to his field agent job, he'd be putting himself in harm's way. He risked making his son an orphan.

Jordan was right – he couldn't do that to Caleb. Going back to the field wasn't a viable option. The danger was too great. There were other choices. For the sake of his son, he'd adapt.

A weight seemed to lift from his shoulders. His churning stomach calmed. He sucked in a deep breath and relaxed. Dropping into a leather easy chair, he contemplated this new state of mind and body. He'd come to a decision, and it felt absolutely right. He wasn't going back.

He glanced around the plush living room of his condominium. The spacious two bedroom unit was located in a nice part of town – safe, good schools, quality shopping and entertainment options. He'd purchased the unit five years ago, shortly after the housing market collapsed. It was a bargain. He wondered what it might be worth now.

The following day, Spence lounged in his recliner, studying a printout left by the relator. Wow! The comps suggested his place was worth nearly twice what he'd paid. If he dumped it now, he'd net a tidy profit, more than enough to set up housekeeping elsewhere. She'd assured him it would move quickly. Properties in his zip code rarely stayed on the market longer than a week or two before someone snapped them up. That was encouraging.

He could move away from here. The Bureau had offices all over the country. He could relocate to California, and buy a place near Jordan. Caleb could live with him, and still be able to see his sister and his aunt. What did a condo cost there? He chuckled, remembering his brief meeting with Terry Shatner. He should have asked her.

He glanced through the window facing the street. Buildings blotted out most of his view. If he could see through them, the picture wouldn't be enticing – smog, taller buildings, congestion. Around here, traffic was atrocious twenty-four-seven. What had Jordan said? In Southern California, the silence she thought she heard was actually the steady hum of automobiles. It was an equally appropriate description for this area.

He closed his eyes, allowing his mind to linger on that long ago evening – the two of them sitting on the front porch of Mrs. Hill's house, chatting, relaxed. His months in Montana were peaceful. He'd been refreshed and renewed. After Caleb joined him, he'd enjoyed it even more. While Jordan and Ally visited, it began to feel like home.

If he could live anywhere in the world, he'd choose Montana – but only if Caleb was there. *And Jordan and Ally,* his heart whispered. That pleasant dream stayed with him as he dozed in the chair.

Chapter 21

Caleb spent most of Saturday working on his history poster. He and a friend were combining their talents to create a giant map of the world as it was during the last five hundred years. It would include basic geography, along with a key listing major world events in each region. They hoped the detailed project would earn them enough extra credit points to offset their mediocre test scores. Jordan pointed out that doing the optional assignment would probably infuse so many facts into their memories that tests would no longer present a problem – and she was usually right.

They'd finished early and Caleb opted to return to the apartment rather than hang out playing video games. He was tired, plus his dad was supposed to call. He wanted to tell him about the map.

Using his house key, he let himself into the apartment and headed straight for the bathroom, another reason he'd decided to come home. By the time he finished, his stomach was grumbling. Before leaving for her class, Jordan reminded him that there were leftovers in the fridge. She wouldn't be home until after six. He pulled out the plastic container of lasagna, piled some on a plate, and stuck it in the microwave. While his dinner heated, he kicked off his shoes and turned on the television.

CNN flickered across the screen. That's weird, he thought. His finger was poised over the button, ready to change the station. He hesitated. As he stared at the slick looking anchorman, a sense of foreboding settled over him. Before leaving this morning, he'd been watching cartoons. Jordan's class started early so she and Ally were long gone by then. He was the last one to leave the apartment.

Had he locked the door? Yes, he'd needed his key to get in a little while ago. Might Jordan have come back for some reason? That seemed unlikely. He remembered seeing her grab her tote bag on the way out the door. Ally wouldn't have forgotten anything crucial, warranting a return trip. Even if Jordan needed something, she wouldn't have turned on the TV. She hardly ever watched it.

All at once, Caleb remembered the slow drain in the kitchen. Just yesterday, Jordan mentioned that she needed to call the manager about fixing the problem. Mr. Ableman must have come today. It did seem odd that he'd turn on the television, though.

Caleb clicked the button and a teenager appeared on the screen, the laugh track playing over the speakers. *Great, I haven't seen this episode.* As he eased back against the sofa cushions, the microwave beeped, letting him know his dinner was ready.

~ * ~

Damn kid! Bart grumbled. He'd nearly gotten caught. If the boy hadn't gone straight for the bathroom, he might not have made it out. The patio door was a handy escape. He'd slipped outside and then over the fence. Thankfully, the house bordering that side of the complex was empty. He hid out in the backyard for a while, listening through the wooden slats of the fence. Not that there was anything to hear. Stupid jokes and fake laughter flowed from the ridiculous kid's TV show Caleb had on.

During his search, a photograph was the only useful item he'd found. They wanted other documentation, but he hadn't located anything. If she kept a filing cabinet or a safe, it was concealed well. He'd looked through the closets, under the beds, in bottom dresser drawers, all the usual places. At least, he thought those were the usual places. None of the other B&Es he'd done involved looking for paperwork. Jewelry and electronics had value. In the past, the only paper that concerned him was covered with green ink and presidents' faces.

This time, the treasure came in a completely different form, one that would earn him a big pile of cash. However, he needed to make it happen. He'd already met with Rodriguez. The man was in the process of setting up the delivery system. Bart was warned that there'd be a window. These things were meticulously arranged. People had to be in place at each juncture of the transfer. If he acted prematurely, he might screw up the entire operation. He'd have to be ready to move when Rodriguez gave him the go-ahead.

~ * ~

It only took a few days for Spence to pack up his personal belongings and bring in a cleaning service. By Monday evening, the condo was ready to be listed. He made an appointment with a real estate agent for the following day. The unit would be sold furnished. He didn't want to deal with transporting anything. Whatever he needed, he'd buy. Besides, he didn't know where he'd end up.

Arriving at a decision was both liberating and terrifying. He was moving, that was a given. Whether he wound up in California or Montana was still in question.

Other people would affect that part of his future. Since he was on medical leave, time was on his side. He was still an FBI agent receiving a biweekly paycheck. He could afford to explore his options, talk to his son. He wouldn't make any final plans until he got to California. He intended to be on the road Wednesday morning.

He needed to speak to Jack. Since his Porche was already there, he hoped he could ship a dozen or so boxes, as well, however, Jack would have to find a place to store them. Spence didn't think he'd mind. There was something else he wanted to pick Jack's brain about as well.

He called on Tuesday night. Jack was fine with Spence sending his boxes. There was room in the garage.

"I'll stuff them in your car," Jack teased.

"If you do that, you won't be able to use it to take your lovely wife out to dinner in style," Spence reminded him. He'd left them the keys and encouraged them to avail themselves of the Porche.

"We've driven it a couple of times. Elizabeth thinks we're too old to be crawling around on our hands and knees to get in and out of such a low profile car. I agree."

"Point taken," Spence replied with a laugh. They were right. The sleek vehicle was too low to be comfortable. Maybe it was time to trade it in. Besides, if his plans worked out, he'd no longer need the two-seater. "There's one other thing, Jack. I wonder if you can help me figure out a particular Bible verse."

"I can try, although I'm not much of a theologian," Jack replied with a chuckle. "Maybe we can sort it out together. You want to tell me the verse?"

"Sure, it's Jeremiah 29:11," Spence said. "My version reads like this, *'For I know the plans I have for you,' declares the LORD, 'plans to prosper you and not to harm you, plans to give you hope and a future.'"*

Jack looked up the verse in his Bible and read it through silently. "Jeremiah's ministry took place at a time when Israel was rebelling against God," he explained. "He was trying to get them to repent and turn to the Lord."

Spence nodded. His Bible included an introduction to the book which provided the same information. "Yeah, I read that and I get what's going on."

"Then what's your question?" Jack asked, sensing his friend's reluctance. Maybe Elizabeth...

"The verse is engraved on a ring," Spence blurted. Man, he didn't want to sound like a sap! He cringed, suddenly wishing he hadn't started this conversation.

"A ring? You mean the kind you'd wear?" Jack asked, surprised.

"Yes, a woman's ring."

Jordan's ring, the one she fidgeted with whenever they were alone together. The day of her headache, when she was too sick to function, he'd seen the ring in a dish on the window sill above her kitchen sink, along with her watch. She must have taken them off to cook or wash dishes. He'd picked up the ring and studied it. It was a fairly simple, inexpensive piece of silver jewelry. He figured it cost less than fifty bucks. For some reason, it was important to her, and he wanted to know why. *Jer. 29:11* was engraved on the inside edge, offering the only clue.

As Jack pondered this piece of information, he realized he was out of his league. He knew next to nothing about women's jewelry and only slightly more than that about Bible verses that might be important to the opposite sex. Elizabeth was the resident expert on both. He put Spence on hold.

"Hi, Spence!" Elizabeth said, clearly pleased. "We've missed you around here. When are you coming back for a visit?"

Spence grimaced when he realized Jack had handed him over to his wife. He really didn't want this conversation to get back to Jordan; and he knew she and Elizabeth had become friends. "Hello, Elizabeth. Listen, I don't need to bother you with this."

"Wait a sec, Spence," she said, detecting his discomfort. "Jack said you wanted to know about a Bible verse engraved on a woman's ring. Are you referring to Jordan's?"

Spence closed his eyes and turned his face heavenward. How in the world had she come to that conclusion? Was his attraction to the woman that obvious, even two months ago? He cleared his throat, and replied sheepishly, "Yes."

"What do you want to know?" She shot her husband a look that told him just what she thought of him – the coward!

Jack shrugged and headed for the coffee pot. Curiosity kept him in the room.

"I'm not sure, actually," Spence replied. "I guess I'd like to know why she wears a ring with that verse engraved on it."

"That's simple," Elizabeth said, warming to the subject. If Spence was asking about Jordan's ring, maybe there was hope for them yet. She really loved the man he'd become. He deserved to be happy, to have a lovely young woman like Jordan in his life. "The ring represents a promise she made a long time ago. She chose the Jeremiah verse as her reminder."

Spence reread the verse. Okay, he understood that God had plans for his people. He just didn't understand the significance of it being engraved on a ring. Elizabeth said it represented a promise.

Curious now, he asked, "What sort of promise? And to whom?"

Elizabeth smiled. Spence was innocent in so many ways. "She made the promise to herself and to God."

Spence still didn't quite get it. Did she promise to let God make her prosperous, according to his plan? Isn't that what everyone wanted?

She could tell he was still confused. It would be easy enough to lay it out for the man, but it might be more meaningful if he figured it out for himself. "Spence, think about the ring," Elizabeth continued. "What shape is it in?"

"It's a rose," Spence replied. What did that have to do with anything?

"An unblossomed rose," Elizabeth corrected. "That's what the companies that sell those rings call that particular style."

"Okay." He wished she'd just tell him. This guessing game was getting on his nerves.

"I'll give you one more hint. I hope you can figure it out from there," Elizabeth said. "Jordan made a promise, or a vow, if you prefer, to God and to herself when she was a teenager. It was also a promise to her future husband. The vow is represented by an unblossomed rose."

Spence silently repeated Elizabeth's explanation. Jordan made a vow a long time ago. She made a vow to God, to herself, and to her future husband. And the rose bud represented – what? The only thing he could come up with was...her virginity?

When his ragged exhale resounded in her ear, Elizabeth knew he'd solved the mystery. "Jordan wears a purity ring, Spence," she said, her voice soft with emotion. "It serves as a reminder that God has a life partner chosen for her, and He will bring the two of them together in His timing and according to His plan."

"I get it," Spence replied quietly. "Thank you, Elizabeth. You know, you could have just told me that from the start."

"But wasn't it more fun to come to it yourself?" Elizabeth replied with gentle humor. "Before you go, Spence, I'd like you to know something. You're a fine man, even finer since you rediscovered the Lord."

"Thanks." He was suddenly anxious to get off the phone. He needed to think about all this. Things weren't adding up.

"One more thing before you go," Elizabeth said, sensing his desire to be alone. "God's timing is always perfect. Remember that."

"I will, Elizabeth."

Chapter 22

As Jordan finished reviewing the alphabet with her class, she heard a quiet jingle coming from the region of her desk. Caleb must have sent her a text. She kept the phone on the lowest volume during the school day, not that she received many calls.

"Okay, you have fifteen minutes of free play," she announced. "Do you want to set our clock, Becky?"

Today's little assistant nodded eagerly as she raced to the wooden pretend clock that rested on a shelf below the real one. Jordan helped her determine where to set the hands. The children knew their free time was over when the two clocks matched. After they finished, the little girl scampered off to play house with her friends.

Jordan opened the cupboard on the side of her desk where she kept her purse, extracted the phone, and pressed the unlock button. An image of Caleb's dad with Ally perched on his lap, filled her screen, and her heart swelled in response. Would she never be able to control her body's spontaneous reaction to this man? With a sigh, she pressed the text icon.

'I need to talk to you. Be there this weekend.'

She reread the message several times to be sure she understood it. Carl was coming here. He'd be in town in a few days. While she held the phone, it jingled again. She touched the back button, and Caleb's picture appeared on the screen. She smiled, not at all surprised. His text read, 'Dad is coming this weekend!' Carl had sent them both the same message. The boy hadn't seen his father in over a month. He'd be impossible to live with for the next few days, she surmised. She sent them each a reply, impulsively offering Carl the use of her sofa, so he wouldn't have to pay for lodging elsewhere.

~ * ~

While he was stopped at a red light, Spence read Jordan's message. She'd invited him to stay at the apartment, he noted. That was a good sign. He wondered how eager she'd be to host him after she learned he was homeless. The condo was listed, an open house for this weekend already scheduled. The agent felt confident she'd have an offer by Sunday. On his way out of town, he dropped by a shipping company and sent his boxes to Montana. The back of his SUV held his two suitcases, a sleeping bag, and a few other things – everything he'd need for the foreseeable future.

He planned to drive straight through to Abilene, spend one night with his mother, and then finish the journey in as short a time as possible. It was going to be a grueling trip, but he was impatient to get to the west coast – anxious to see Jordan and his son. There was much to talk about, decisions to make.

He was glad to have these next days to straighten out his jumbled thoughts. Learning about Jordan's ring had thrown him into a tailspin. The feeling was disconcerting. He had her figured out, or so he'd thought. He liked her, and she liked him. They had chemistry. Turning all that into a partnership seemed like a logical plan. He'd intended to ask her to live with him, or something along those lines. Cohabitation was the norm nowadays, the method couples used to test their compatibility before jumping into marriage.

After learning about Jordan's vow, Spence did some further investigating. His search for information on purity rings took him from websites that sold the jewelry to pages which discussed God's plan for marriage. He read dozens of inspiring testimonials from couples who'd abstained from sex until after they were married. Spence was astounded to discover that such people still existed. Even more shocking was the knowledge that the woman who occupied his thoughts night and day was one of them. The idea that Jordan was holding out for marriage had his stomach tied in a knot.

Spence was still processing the information when his car left the city behind. He pressed the accelerator, and the car sped up to seventy. There was one thing that nagged at the back of his mind. According to Elizabeth, Jordan's vow was made long ago, when she was still very young and undoubtedly naïve. Yet Ally was three and a half years old. Had Jordan lost hope in finding a mate for a time? Obviously, she wasn't still protecting her nonexistent virginity. He still couldn't fathom why she insisted the child was her niece. Was her moral stumble so mortifying that she'd deny her own daughter?

Another idea came to him, one that was far more disturbing. Could Ally's conception have taken place against Jordan's will? That thought sent fingers of burning rage racing though his body. At the same time, he recalled her reaction following their one and only kiss. Though she'd clearly enjoyed the experience, she'd been furious afterward.

Because you forced her! his conscience rebuked. He shoved the private reproach aside. He'd deal with his own shortcomings later. This mental wrestling match was about Jordan.

Though her anger at being kissed like that was certainly justified, her prior behavior didn't support the rape theory. She should have fought him but instead, offered no resistance. She was a trusting person. Spence was good at reading people. Jordan didn't act like a victim.

'Your powers of deduction failed you.' Her parting words during their last discussion popped into his head. She'd been referring to her background check. Clearly, his investigation had missed something and somehow, Ally was at the center of it. Maybe he'd give Jefferson a call and ask him to take another look.

~ * ~

The week flew by. Caleb's enthusiasm rubbed off, and Jordan found herself scrubbing floors and cleaning out closets in anticipation of Carl's return. Why she felt these tasks were important she couldn't begin to fathom. She just couldn't seem to sit still.

On Thursday night, they received a call. Carl was at his mother's house in Texas. He'd stopped there to get some rest and tell her in person about finding his son. She was thrilled, insisting on speaking with the boy. Blushing fiercely, Caleb complied. He mostly listened at first, but eventually answered a few of his new grandmother's questions. She couldn't wait to meet her only grandchild.

Jordan spoke to Carl for a few minutes. At first, the brief conversation was stilted and uncomfortable. Both seemed preoccupied. Jordan inquired about the long drive, and cautioned him to take it slow.

"Sleep when you get tired," she suggested. "Don't push yourself."

"You sound like my mother," Spence teased. "She's trying to talk me into staying a few days."

Jordan's heart skipped a beat. She didn't want him to be delayed and longed to tell him so. "Caleb wouldn't like that," she murmured, grasping a safe means of expressing the wish.

Detecting a hint of emotion in her soft voice, Spence asked, "Would Jordan like it?"

Jordan's breath hitched at the searching question. Was he trying to tell her he'd missed her? "Um...no," she whispered. "No, I wouldn't like it either." She closed her eyes and prayed she hadn't misread him.

Spence smiled. "Good," he said on a relieved exhale. "That's good."

Ally vied for her turn on the telephone, saving the couple from any more uncomfortable admissions. Jordan said goodbye then handed the phone to her niece. Spence kept Ally chatting and giggling for several minutes. When they finally disconnected, the little girl was brimming with excitement.

~ * ~

Friday afternoon, Rodriguez finally called and gave Bart the go-ahead. Everything was in place for a Monday delivery. It was about damned time! He'd hoped to have his business completed by now. He'd lain awake many nights dreaming about spending the money. He was thinking of going to Mexico, maybe buying a little shack on the beach and a senorita to keep him company. After this job, leaving the country might be a really good idea.

Weekends were tough – too many people around. He'd have to handle this at night. No way was he doing anything in broad daylight.

If he'd found the paperwork, he might have been able to negotiate with the woman. That was the original strategy. They liked having the paperwork. Personally, he couldn't see the importance, considering the whole outfit was crooked. Having a document didn't make what they were doing legal.

He'd yet to disclose that little detail. Rodriguez would have to figure something out. He'd done it before. Creating phony documents wasn't that big of a deal. Heck, he could probably do it himself at the public library!

His backup plan involved more risk – lots more. He'd have to break in during the middle of the night, snatch the package, and get out without being followed. Or identified, he reminded himself. The kid might recognize him, but he slept in a separate bedroom. As long as Bart was quiet and didn't wake Caleb, he'd be fine. He didn't like to think about what he'd do if the boy marked him. He'd committed plenty of nasty deeds before, but he'd never killed anyone.

~ * ~

Startled awake, Jordan glanced around the dark bedroom. As usual, something had disturbed her sleep. She lay there for a moment listening to the night sounds through the cracked window above her bed. From the street, she heard the approach of a vehicle and then the diminishing sound of it passing. Voices filtered in, carried on the breeze from neighboring apartments, other open windows. A dog barked in the night.

She rolled to her side and peered at the clock on her nightstand. It was three a.m. Carl was supposed to arrive sometime tomorrow, probably around noon, he'd estimated. Her pulse quickened with the thought. She looked forward to seeing him again, to discovering what, if anything, was happening between them.

As she closed her eyes, a muted thump resonated from somewhere in the apartment. Caleb must be up. She listened for the sound of a door closing or the toilet flushing. The boy was oblivious to the noise he made, especially in the middle of the night when he was half asleep. All was silent. She tossed and turned once or twice more, then sighed in frustration. She might as well get up and use the bathroom before trying to fall back asleep.

Careful not to wake Ally, Jordan pushed off the blanket and got up. She straightened her twisted pajama bottoms and tugged the top into place. Comfortable now, she headed for the partially closed door.

As she stepped into the hall, an odd sensation came over her. Something felt off. What was it? She moved quietly down the hall, growing more cautious with each step. Her hand brushed the wall settling on the molding that bordered the opening into the living room. Glancing around, she noticed nothing out of place. Were the shadows and night sounds causing her imagination to run away with her?

She inhaled to calm her nerves and suddenly realized what was wrong. It was an odor. She smelled...cigarettes? Behind her, the bathroom door hinges squeaked, startling her. She turned suddenly, and a tall man loomed in front of her. There was no time to scream before a hand closed over her mouth.

Chapter 23

On Saturday night, Spence sailed through Phoenix, nixing his plan to rent a hotel room. He wasn't tired and thought he might drive straight through. By midnight, he'd come to regret that rash decision. Since he could hardly keep his eyes open, he decided it would be wise to heed the advice of the women in his life and pull over. A rest stop near Palm Desert provided a safe location at which to get a few hours shuteye. At four, he was back on the road, roaring his way to an uncertain but exciting future.

Two hours later, he brought the car to a halt and peered through the early-morning haze at the front gate to Jordan's complex. It was six a.m., probably too early to knock. He pulled out his phone, opting to wake his son, if that were possible, instead of the entire apartment complex. It rang six times then went to voice mail. He disconnected and dialed again with the same results.

On the third try, he heard a groggy, "Hello?"

"Wake up and open the door, sleepy head," Spence said as he climbed from his vehicle. "I'm outside."

"Dad? You're here?" Caleb cried, mostly awake now. "I'll be right there."

Spence pressed the disconnect button and tucked the phone inside his jacket pocket on the way to the apartment. As he stood on the front stoop, he heard his son mutter, "That's weird." Then, the door opened and the boy was in his arms.

His heart swelled as he hugged his son. He'd missed him more than he realized. "Hey, kid," he finally managed through a tight throat. "It's good to see you, too."

Caleb stepped inside the apartment. "Come in," he urged. Moving back and holding the door open.

"What's weird?" Spence asked, as he walked past.

"Huh?"

Spence turned to the boy. "Before you opened the door, you said, 'That's weird.'"

Caleb thought for a second, then replied matter-of-factly, "Oh, yeah. The door was unlocked." He rubbed the sleep from his eyes and mumbled that he needed to use the bathroom.

Spence nodded and stepped out of his son's way. He needed to do the same. As he pushed a hand across his scalp and made for the couch, Caleb's words repeated in his mind.

"Is that unusual?" he asked when the boy returned a few minutes later.

Caleb looked at his dad. "Is what unusual?"

"The door being unlocked," Spence clarified.

Caleb shrugged. "Sort of. Jordan's pretty fussy about locking up at night. She doesn't even like me leaving my window open."

Spence stared at his son, pondering the explanation. His gut tightened uncomfortably, instincts shifting into high alert.

"Caleb, go take a look in your aunt's bedroom," he directed, pushing hastily to his feet. "No, wait, I'll do it!"

He stuck his head in the kitchen, verifying that the room was empty and then headed for the hall. Turning left, he stood in front of Jordan's closed door. Did she normally sleep with her door shut? He reached for the knob and twisted. It was locked.

"Everything all right?" Caleb asked from behind him. He'd never seen his Dad like this.

Spence glanced over his shoulder. "Does Jordan always lock her bedroom door?"

"N-no," Caleb said, his voice faltering. "Why?"

The note of uncertainty in his son's tone gave credence to his suspicions that something was wrong. Spence knocked loudly, calling Jordan's name. When there was no response, no sound of movement coming from within, his nerves spiked.

Grabbing the nob, he slammed his shoulder against the hollow panel. Pain shot through his right side as the wood splintered and the door exploded into the room, bouncing off the side wall. Heavy curtains covering the window made it impossible to see. He felt for the light switch and flipped it up. A rush of fear blazed in his chest at the sight of the empty bed. Scanning the room anxiously, he stopped at the oddly cocked closet door.

In two strides, he crossed the room, grabbing the derailed sliding panel, and shoving it aside.

"Oh God, no!" The oath ripped from deep inside him.

Jordan was slouched in the corner of the closet, her eyes closed. Dropping to his knees, Spence reached for her bound hands, extended painfully above her head and tied to the wooden rod above. In a desperate search for a pulse, he pressed his fingertips to her wrist. "Thank God," he breathed when he detected the faint thump-thump of her heartbeat. Extracting his pocket knife, he called over his shoulder, "Caleb, call the police!"

The shocked boy stood frozen, staring at his aunt's colorless face. "Is she...?"

"She's fine," Spence assured the boy. "Go!" He slashed through the rope that secured her bound hands to the closet rod. Dangerously white with blood loss, her hands and arms dropped into her lap. How long had she hung here like this? Next, he cut through the scarf that gagged her mouth and pulled it away. Still, she didn't move.

"Jordan," Spence said, gently slapping the flat of his hand against her cheek. "Talk to me, sweetheart."

Getting no response, he scooped her body into his arms and carried her to the living room, where he gently laid her on the sofa. After removing the final bindings that held her hands together in front of her, he resumed patting her cheeks and talking to her.

"The police are coming," Caleb said, holding out his phone. "The lady wants to talk to you."

"Too bad," Spence replied, ignoring the phone and focusing on the unconscious woman in front of him. "Jordan, talk to me, honey."

Jordan's lashes fluttered open. Her glassy stare rested on Spence, and he decided she was the most beautiful sight he'd ever seen. Close to tears, he gathered her against his chest and buried his face in her hair. "Thank you!" he murmured. He'd never known such torment as he'd felt in the last few minutes.

"Carl..." Jordan's voice was a raspy, painful whisper. She'd cried in that closet for hours, the gag stifling the noise and absorbing the moisture inside her mouth. "Carl...Ally..."

Spence's heart froze. Ally! Where was Ally? His mind screamed the question. He lifted his head and barked, "Caleb, find Ally!" He laid Jordan down and hurried to join his son on a frantic mission that he already knew was fruitless. If Ally were here, they'd know it by now.

When the police arrived, Jordan was sobbing in Spence's arms. Caleb stood back and watched, the shock of the morning still ringing in his ears. Ally was gone. Someone had broken in and kidnapped her during the night, and he hadn't heard a thing. He listened to his dad question Jordan, heard what she had to say.

Introducing herself as Yates, a female police officer came in, prepared to take a statement. Spence gently eased Jordan from his arms and down to the sofa. Snatching the blanket from the back of the couch, he draped it around her quaking shoulders. Jordan looked at the officer, recognizing her from the incident at Caleb's school last year. Bowing her head slightly, Officer Yates acknowledged that she'd come to the same realization.

While a paramedic assessed Jordan's condition and treated the abrasions on her wrists, the officer asked the same questions Spence had posed, arriving at the same conclusion he'd reached. The little girl had been kidnapped. Her partner radioed his superiors. A detective would be arriving shortly.

"Did the man sexually assault you, Ms. Gray?" Yates asked. The medic quietly awaited his patient's response. Though her injuries were minor, a trip to the hospital might still be warranted.

"Caleb, can you refill your aunt's water?" Spence abruptly asked, retrieving the glass from the side table and handing it to the boy. Caleb took it and left the room. Spence hadn't had time to get to that particular inquiry. The fact that Jordan still wore her pajamas was a good sign.

Jordan shook her head then looked away, her cheeks flaming red. Tugging the sofa blanket more snuggly around her shoulders, she replied in a soft voice, "He talked like he wanted to."

She mentally recalled the terrifying minutes when she'd assumed that was his intention. He'd held her against the wall in the hallway and put his free hand under her top. The other remained over her mouth, pinning her head back. The vulgar words he used still echoed through her mind. She'd pushed against his chest, tried to fight him, but he was much bigger and stronger than she.

"Ally," Jordan whispered tearfully. "Please, you need to find my little girl."

Spence's jaw stiffened as his blood boiled. He knew more went on than she was telling – but she was right, Ally was their concern right now. As the medics packed up and left, Caleb brought him the glass. Spence took a seat on the coffee table in front of Jordan and handed her the water.

"Drink this," he said, his voice gruff in an effort to temper his rage. "Then we'll talk."

Jordan's gaze shot to his face, noting the hard planes, the anger flashing in his eyes. "Thank you," she said, taking a long swallow of the much-needed liquid. When she handed the glass back to Spence, he set it on the table.

"All right, Jordan," he began, more in control now. "You need to think, sweetheart. You're the only person who can tell us who took Ally."

The second officer tapped him on the shoulder. "Excuse me, sir," he said, "It'll be better if you let us handle this. We know what questions need to be asked."

Spence stared up at the police officer in understanding. To this man, he was only a concerned friend. He reached inside the jacket he hadn't had time to shed earlier and withdrew his wallet, handing it to the man.

"I know what to ask, too," he said, leaving the stunned man to examine his credentials. Turning back to Jordan, he said, "Tell me about the man. Was he alone?"

She nodded hesitantly. "I think so."

"Did you see his face?"

"He wore something over his head," she said. "Panty hose, I think. I could see his face, but it was distorted."

"And you don't remember ever seeing him before?" She shook her head with certainty. "Not even an inkling of familiarity?"

"No."

The two officers jotted notes on their pads and let the federal agent ask the questions. Occasionally, one would interject something, but mostly they listened. They had the kidnapper's hair color down as dark blonde or brown. He was a smoker. The agitated woman managed a description of his clothing.

"How tall was he?" Spence asked.

On trembling legs, Jordan slowly stood and reached for Spence's hand, gesturing for him to join her. Leaning against his chest, she tried to gauge the difference between him and the man who stole Ally. "He's taller than you by two or three inches," she whispered, her voice cracking on the last words. She squeezed her eyes shut and pressed against him as a wave of anguish swept over her. "Find her, Carl."

Spence wrapped his arms around the weeping woman and held her as long as he dared. With his heart in his throat, he promised, "I will, sweetheart. I will."

The two officers exchanged concerned glances. FBI agent or not, he shouldn't have said that. These cases were never that simple.

"Sir!" the woman said, a note of caution in her tone.

The detective arrived at that moment, along with a fingerprint expert. One of the officers handed him Spence's wallet and gestured to the FBI man.

"He's a friend of the victim," he pointed out.

Detective Barns' brows arched in surprise. For a moment there, he thought he'd stumbled into a federal investigation. In fact, Agent Spencer was a mere civilian. He stepped forward and introduced himself.

"Excuse me, ma'am, Agent Spencer," he said, acknowledging the FBI agent with a brief nod. "My name is Detective Barns. I'll take over from here."

Spence's hackles rose at the apparent dismissal. He gently eased Jordan down to the sofa and turned to the newcomer, shaking the man's hand. He understood – this was the man's jurisdiction. Today, Spence was a private citizen. At the same time, he wanted Detective Barns to know he wasn't going anywhere.

The detective took a moment to look over his officers' notes. Then, turning to Jordan, he said, "I know this isn't easy for you, Ms. Gray, but I want you to think about the man again. Did you notice anything unusual – tattoos, scars, piercings? Did he speak with an accent?"

Jordan suddenly nodded vigorously. "He wore an earring!"

"Describe it."

"It was odd, a U-shape, I think. A long, squiggly U that looped through his earlobe," she said, surprised she remembered that much. "When he turned his head, I saw it flattened against his neck. It reminded me of a..."

"Snake!"

Several pairs of eyes turned to the speaker of the anxiously whispered word. Standing near the front window, Caleb stared at the group, his face white as a sheet.

Spence strode to his son's side. "Caleb, have you seen the man before?" he asked, looping an arm around the boy's shoulders, worried he'd pass out.

Closing his eyes, Caleb nodded slowly. Dread soured his stomach, and he suddenly felt like throwing up. Swallowing hard, he turned to his dad. "He called himself Snake," he said. "Dad, he was mean – really, really mean! If he has Ally…" He let the words trail off in a choked whisper, unable to voice what was in his head. Horrible memories surfaced, and he shuddered involuntarily.

Everyone's focus shifted to Caleb. Spence guided the boy to the sofa, sitting him down beside Jordan. "Tell me about him," he said.

"He was my mom's boyfriend, a long time ago," Caleb began. "He liked to drink, and he got meaner when he did. He used to…hit…Mom." Jordan reached for her nephew's hand and squeezed gently. Caleb barely noticed. "Sometimes, he'd hit me, too. Mom would try to stop him, but then he'd take it out on her. He broke my arm."

Jordan suddenly remembered the manila envelope she'd found in a bottom drawer of Tanya's dresser, where she'd located the kids' birth certificates. 'Important stuff' was written on the outside in bold black letters. She recalled thinking that some of the things her sister deemed important really weren't, at least not anymore – concert ticket stubs, Tanya's high school student body card, and a five-year-old emergency room record from when Caleb broke his wrist. No wonder she'd hung on to that paper.

"Caleb, how long ago was that?" Spence asked, an odd sensation niggling at the back of his mind.

"It was before...Ally..." Caleb halted mid-sentence. "I think he's Ally's father."

Like a club, the words seemed to smack Spence across the head. He stood suddenly and walked away, his mind working to fit this statement around other facts he knew. *If the guy who grabbed Ally is her father...* He pushed the thought aside. Right now, he needed to focus all his energy on finding Ally.

Caleb stood and went to his father's side. "Dad..."

Detective Barns cleared his throat and pinned his stare on Jordan. "Ma'am, if this is a domestic issue, we need to know that right now. Is this kidnapper your ex-husband, or a former boyfriend?"

Spence rounded on the man, but before he could speak, Caleb intervened. "Jordan is my aunt. She's never met him," he said. "We lived in Indio at the time and, well, my mom wasn't speaking to Jordan then. Snake was my mom's boyfriend, and he's supposed to be in prison."

"What do you mean, Caleb?" Spence asked, reaching for his son's arm.

"He got arrested for beating up some guy in a bar," Caleb explained. "I was there when the cops came and took him away. They said the guy was in the hospital. As soon as Snake was gone, my mom threw our clothes into bags, and we left, too. She'd tried to leave before, but he...he always made her come back." He looked down, remembering those awful times, the way Snake had hurt her.

"Then what happened, son?" Spence asked. "How do you know he went to prison?"

"We went to stay with some people my mom knew in Phoenix," Caleb continued. "I remember my mom talking to her friend, saying she'd heard Snake was charged with attempted murder or something like that. She was so happy that he was going to prison. Not long after that, Ally was born and we came back here."

Angry with himself, Spence's jaw hardened. He'd missed something alright – a falsified birth record. Caleb's story went a long way toward explaining why Tanya put her sister's name on the document.

Jordan stood and walked to Caleb's side, wrapping an arm around his quivering shoulders.

Now they were getting somewhere, Detective Barns thought. "What was his name, son?"

Caleb shrugged. "I don't know," he replied. "Everyone just called him Snake, because he had this big rattlesnake tattoo. It started at his shoulder and wound around his arm to his wrist. The head was even tattooed on the back of his hand, and the fangs were on his fingers. He liked to show it off."

Jordan shuddered. "I remember seeing something dark on his left hand. I couldn't tell what it was."

"We need a name," the detective muttered. "Ms. Gray, I'm going to need you and your nephew to come to the station to look at some photos. We need access to the criminal records database."

Jordan nodded then turned away. Over her nephew's head, her eyes met Carl's, her expression pleading. "Please, Carl," she whispered. "Find her." If anyone could figure this out, she knew he could.

Spence nodded and pulled out his phone.

Chapter 24

While Jordan changed her clothes for the trip to the station, Spence stepped outside and telephoned Jefferson. His friend should be able to get the needed information much quicker than the locals. He'd barely finished relaying Snake's description and the few facts they knew when Detective Barns approached.

"Mr. Spencer," the man said. "I appreciate your interest in this case, and I understand where it's coming from. But you need to remember, this is my jurisdiction. You're far too close to the situation to be objective."

From the start, Spence knew this lecture was coming. He'd made a few similar ones himself in the past. Barns were right; he was too close – but he wasn't backing off, either.

"Detective, I'm afraid you're stuck with me on this one," he replied gruffly. "It's personal. This creep messed with my family."

"That is precisely why you need to take a step back, sir," Barns pointed out firmly. "You'll end up getting in the way, putting my men in danger."

Spence slowly shook his head. "I'll take a backseat, Barns, act as a consultant, if that's what you want. But I'm not going away. We can work together or apart – your call."

The detective's spine stiffened. Of all the insolent, stupid... "You're forcing me to go over your head, agent."

Spence's phone rang. "Do whatever you have to do," he said as he pushed the answer button. "Talk to me."

"His name is Bartholomew Peel," Jefferson said without preamble. "He was discharged from Ironwood State Prison last month as part of an early release program, after serving less than four years of a ten year minimum for assault with a deadly weapon. The guy he beat up spent two months in the hospital. Apparently, the state of California judged Mr. Peel non-violent." The last was stated with a heavy dose of sarcasm.

"How do we find him, Brent?" Spence's overtired brain wasn't firing on all cylinders. Right now, he needed his friend to think for him.

"His last cellmate was only with him a short time," Jefferson said, reading off the printout he'd made in anticipation of the question. "Peel shared his ten by ten with the previous roomy for three years, a guy named Miguel Ramos. Ramos got out in July. I'd suggest starting with him."

"I'm assuming you know where I can find Mr. Ramos," Spence replied.

"I'm sending a file containing photos of both men, along with all the pertinent information, as we speak. Can you get to a computer?"

With rapt attention, Detective Barns listened to one side of the conversation. They'd finished questioning Ms. Gary less than thirty minutes ago. It would have taken half the day to get the information the FBI agent was receiving.

An unwelcome Sunday morning telephone call was placed to the parole officer assigned to Miguel Ramos. Fifteen minutes later, an unmarked police car was dispatched. A tired but focused Agent Spencer accompanied Detective Barns and a second plainclothes officer to a coffee shop located in the foothills, twenty miles away. Their target, Miguel Ramos, was supposed to be working the morning shift.

After a brief audience with the manager, Barns and Spence were escorted to a private booth. As a precaution, the third member of their party was stationed at the rear door of the establishment. Coffee was delivered, Spence's first cup of the day. As he sipped it gratefully, a young, slightly built Hispanic man wearing a white apron approached their table. Spence recognized him immediately.

"Boss says you want to talk to me," he mumbled uncomfortably, taking in the casual attire. One man screamed plainclothes cop. The other, he couldn't peg. He was tough looking and solidly built; a man who could hold his own in a fight. He wouldn't want to cross him. What did they want?

Detective Barns stood and made introductions. "Mr. Ramos, I'm Detective Barns and this is Agent Spencer. We'd like to ask you a few questions." He gestured to the booth. "Please, have a seat."

Spence noted Ramos' body language. When Barns offered him a seat, he seemed to visibly recoil, though he hadn't moved an inch. The fact that he didn't make a run for it indicated he probably had nothing to hide. The uneasiness was a habit.

Ramos hesitated. "Wh-what's this about?"

Barns clapped a hand on the man's shoulder, letting him know this was going to happen whether or not he cooperated. "Sit."

His nervous gaze shifted from one man to the other, though he complied, sliding into the booth. Barns dropped onto the cushion beside him, boxing him in.

"We need to ask you about your stay at Ironwood," Barns said.

"What about it?" Miguel slid farther into the booth and folded his hands on the table top in front of him.

"Have you seen or been in contact with your former cellmate?"

Miguel grimaced. "Hell, no! What, you think I'd go back there to visit him?"

Barns said, "That's one of the things we're trying to determine."

"No way, man. Me and Snake, we weren't friends or nothing. He was..." Miguel paused, curious now. "Listen man, you want to know about Snake, why don't you go visit him yourselves?"

"He was released last month."

"No kidding! Man, I thought he'd be in for a long time," Miguel mumbled. "So, he's out a month, and you guys are already looking for him. What'd he do?" He stared at the man across from him. So far he'd done nothing except drink his coffee and watch. No, not watch, Miguel decided, feeling suddenly like he was being studied.

"That's not important," Barns said.

Spence carefully set down his mug. This was taking far too long. They should be asking questions, not answering them. The window of time for finding an abducted child unharmed was typically small. He exchanged glances with Barns, and the detective nodded slightly.

"Did Snake ever mention people he might know in this area?" Spence asked.

Miguel shrugged. "Not that I recall but, like I said, we weren't friends. The guy was cruel, and not real talkative. I tended to avoid him."

Spence knew Snake had never received visitors, phone calls, or mail at Ironwood. That information had been verified. Four years in the slammer with no one to talk to must be lonely. "Who did Snake socialize with on the inside?"

Suddenly wary, Miguel squirmed in his seat. If Snake was out, and the cops were looking for him, he'd gotten into some pretty deep crap. That probably meant he was still involved with Crypto. Handing out information wasn't wise. The inside and the outside were well connected. Word of his involvement could easily find its way to the wrong person. An involuntary shudder rippled through him, and he shifted again to cover it.

Spence weighed the man before him. With the last question, Ramos' brown complexion lost some of its color. The barely perceptible tremble that shook his hands was telling. The guy was scared.

"I don't know nothing more," Ramos said firmly. "Like I told you, we weren't buds. He did his thing and I did mine."

"Surely there was someone Snake hung out with regularly," Barns tried again.

"Not that I know of," Miguel replied. He glanced at the other man. The detective introduced him as agent something. Agent of what? A fresh wave of uneasiness left him feeling weak and sweaty. "Listen, man, I got a job to do here, you know? I can't be sitting in this booth jawing with you. I've got nothing else to offer."

"You're sure you don't remember..."

"I don't know nothing, man," Miguel replied forcefully. No way was he putting himself in danger because of Snake. "I need to get back to work."

Thirty minutes later, Miguel Ramos quietly slipped through the backdoor of the restaurant. His shift was over. After glancing around nervously, he headed for the street. He lived eleven blocks away and usually walked. Today, he felt like taking the bus. It picked up just up the block.

Spence watched the man leave. Ramos knew more than he was letting on, and they needed whatever was inside his head. Spence switched places with the driver and got behind the wheel, following slowly. The bus stop half a block away appeared to be his quarry's target. He couldn't let him reach it. He sped up, passing the man. With a jerk of the wheel, he turned the car right and blocked Ramos' path. The startled man, stopped for only a second before taking off at a run between the buildings.

"Stay here," Spence ordered, as he jumped from the car and gave chase.

Ramos raced down the short space and turned left into the alley behind the buildings. He was fast, and would have outrun the older man on his tail except for a kid on a bicycle. The boy zipped out from a backyard gate on the opposite side of the alley and straight into the fleeing man's path. Ramos put on the brakes, knowing he couldn't stop in time.

Reaching for the back of his target's jacket, Spence jerked him to the right. The startled boy looked up for a moment, spotted a gun in the second man's hand, and kept going. He didn't want to be in the middle of whatever was going down.

Breathing hard, Spence pressed Ramos face first against a high, ivy-covered fence and jabbed his weapon into the gasping man's ribs.

"What the hell, man!" Ramos grunted, when he'd regained his breath enough to speak.

"You know more than you're saying, Ramos," Spence barked close to his ear. "I need all the information I can get, and I'll use whatever means are necessary to get it. Understand?" He holstered his weapon then forced the man's arm behind his back. Ramos grunted as pain shot into his shoulder.

"I know my rights, man!" he mumbled against the foliage. "I don't have to tell you nothing!"

"Now, you see, that's where you're wrong," Spence replied in a deceptively calm tone. "At the moment, you don't have any rights. We're just two guys having a chat."

"You're a cop! I'll have you charged with police brutality!"

"I'm not a cop, Miguel. I'm a federal agent," Spence corrected, his tone menacing. He didn't have time for twenty questions. "But at the moment, I'm on leave, so I'm just a guy like you."

Fear shot through Ramos. What was going on? "What'd Snake do?"

"He kidnapped a little girl, someone close to me. So you see, this is personal," he grunted. "I need the information you have, Miguel. We can do this the easy way, where you just tell me what I want to know. Or we can do it the hard way. The choice is yours."

Miguel flinched. He didn't need to think about what the hard way might entail. He'd seen more than his share of nastiness in his twenty-four years. "Listen, man, I don't want trouble. I don't want nobody thinking I'm in bed with the cops. It's...unhealthy, know what I mean?"

"Whatever you say is between the two of us," Spence assured him, adding in a low, harsh tone, "However, if you lie to me or waste my time, you'll be more sorry than you can imagine!"

Miguel could imagine a whole lot of ugliness. He suspected this guy could make him disappear, and no one would ever bother looking. "Okay, man," he said with resignation.

Spence slowly let up and released Ramos. The man pushed himself off the fence, brushing leaves from his clothes. He rubbed his aching shoulder and elbow and turned, eyeing the other man with cautious respect.

"What do you want to know?"

~ * ~

"What do you mean you don't have the birth certificate?" Rodriguez barked through the telephone. "I told you, man, they won't deal if there's no documentation."

Grimacing, Snake pulled the phone away from his ear until the shouting stopped. "I couldn't find it!" he whined. "Can't you create one? Come on, dude! How hard can it be?"

"That wasn't part of the agreement. It was your responsibility," Rodriguez pointed out. This deal was getting worse by the minute. First, the girl is much older than they liked to have. That automatically pushed the exchange out of the country. Crossing borders added risk. Now this! "I thought you said she was your kid?"

"She is my kid," Snake grumbled. Crap! What was he going to do now? He sure as heck didn't want to be stuck with her. He remembered the library. "I'll handle it, but I need a babysitter."

Rodriguez could picture the pathetic excuse for a fake this idiot might attempt. He had too much invested in this exchange to drop it now. It would cost a few bucks, but he knew a forger who might be willing to do a rush job. "Forget it, Snake. I'll take care of it, but the fee is coming out of your cut."

"Fine, fine," Snake agreed, relieved. "Will that mess up the schedule?"

"I hope not," the annoyed man replied. "I'll get back to you later."

"Hey, man, you think I can get that babysitter?" Snake pleaded. "I need a decent meal."

Rodriguez scowled. He couldn't wait to be rid of this creep. "I'll send someone over this afternoon," he replied, annoyed.

Snake hung up the hotel phone and glanced at the little girl sitting on the bed. She stared back for a moment then returned to the cartoon playing on the television. At least she wasn't asking when she could go home. Man, was he sick of hearing that question!

She was pretty, like her mother. He'd always known he'd make cute kids. The aunt was a looker, too. It was a shame he didn't have time to explore more of her.

It was a stroke of luck, the kid's mother being dead. Tanya was a spitfire, one of the toughest women he'd ever met. He'd enjoyed keeping her in line. If she'd been around, he probably couldn't have pulled this off. As it was, things went far easier than he had anticipated. That sliding glass door had one of the flimsiest locks he'd ever jimmied. He was in and out in less than thirty minutes, and that included tying up the woman. Too damned easy, he mused.

Chapter 25

It took a few more hours to process what they'd learned from Miguel Ramos into usable information. Snake had gotten in tight with a guy who called himself Crypto. Crypto was in for the long haul, doing time for double murder. He controlled the illegal drug trade, along with any other contraband that made its way inside. Not long after Snake's incarceration began, he started doing Crypto's dirty work. He was the debt collector, the leg breaker.

Calls were placed to the prison and pressure exerted in the right places. They needed a list of known associates on the outside. From whom did Crypto receive mail, what telephone numbers did he call the most, and who took the time to visit him? A list was compiled, and the names that appeared repeatedly were the ones on which they focused. Black and whites were dispatched to visit Crypto's mother and sister, and another to check in with a former girlfriend who was also the mother of his son. Spence and Barns headed to Santa Ana to look into a cousin named Albert Rodriguez. Rodriguez was Crypto's most frequent visitor. Oddly enough, he'd even paid a call on the day Bartholomew Peel was released. Coincidence? Not likely.

After circling the block once to verify the address, Barns brought the unmarked SUV to a stop a few lots down from the house listed as Rodriguez's residence. They chose to park in front of a home with a realtor's sign in the yard, the uncovered windows suggesting no one lived there.

Through tinted windows, they studied the house across the street. It was a typical example of homes in this area – single story, Spanish style with arched windows, and a detached garage at the rear. A low brick and iron fence surrounded the small front yard; a sliding gate stretched across the narrow driveway. An older dark green Lincoln Continental was parked inside the gate; and an unremarkable black Chevrolet sedan sat at the curb.

Usually on a Sunday afternoon, the yards would be filled with activity. A steady rain had begun to fall earlier, sending everyone inside. The street was relatively quiet, though that would change if they started flashing badges or making arrests. These people didn't trust the authorities and looked out for their own.

When Spence unlatched his door, Barns reached over to stop him. "Where are you going?"

"Just taking a walk, detective, don't worry," Spence replied. He wanted to get a closer look, maybe listen for the voice of a small child. He knew it was unwise to expose himself, but time was running out.

"Wait!"

The attention of both men shifted to the front of the house. Obscured from view by several tall, flowering shrubs, someone had just stepped onto the porch. Voices drifted through Barns' open window – a man and a woman, both speaking Spanish. He strained to hear.

"Sounds like his mother reminding him to be home for supper," Barns translated. "Also, something about taking a package to her sister in Mexicali."

"Mexicali!" Spence's heart skipped a beat.

A second later, a man stepped off the porch and walked across the yard. They recognized Rodriguez immediately. He looked neither left nor right, but headed straight for the Chevy, a file folder gripped in his hand.

Barns started the engine of the SUV and pulled slowly away from the curb as Rodriguez rounded the front of his car and climbed behind the wheel. The unconcerned man never looked up. He had no idea he was being watched.

At the end of the block, Barns made a U-turn and followed the other vehicle at a modest distance. They didn't have far to go. Ten minutes later, Rodriguez pulled into a strip mall, jumped out, and headed for a small copier store in the corner. Barns parked beside the Chevy, keeping Rodriguez in his sights while blocking the man's view of his car.

Spence hopped out and circled the Chevy, glancing in each dirty window as he moved around the car. The floor of the front seat bore the remains of a fast food meal. He peeked through the rear window and found more of the same. His careful inspection slowed at a red cardboard carton – the kind that held a kid's meal. It could belong to anyone, though Rodriguez didn't have any children. Spence's search moved to the floor – more trash, a discarded newspaper, soda cans. His eyes riveted on a black and white object poking out from beneath the backside of the front passenger seat. As he stared through the murky glass, his mind filled in the hidden parts. It was a stuffed cat, striped. His heart lodged in his stomach.

He climbed back into the SUV. "He's our man," he said through clamped teeth.

The door to the copier store opened and Rodriguez walked out, a cell phone pressed to his ear. He was arguing with someone in Spanish, waving the same file folder in the air in exasperation.

When Rodriguez got to his car, Barns backed out of the parking space and stopped behind the Chevy. He'd already called for backup. The moment the suspect laid aside the phone, Spence leaped out and charged the driver's side of the Chevy, yanking open the door. The guy didn't know what hit him, as he was hauled violently from the car.

"Hey, what the hell!" Rodriguez yelled as he was shoved against the side of the car.

Barns arrived and cuffed the man before he could make a move. He started reading him his Miranda rights.

As the man protested that they had the wrong guy, that he hadn't done anything wrong, Spence searched the car. The cell phone should prove useful, he decided as he stuffed it in his pocket. Next, he grabbed the file folder and brought it out to the hood of the car. He flipped it open and froze. It contained an official-looking birth certificate, plus several photo copies of the same. He stared at the name – Allison Peel and felt sick to his stomach. The date of birth didn't match Ally's though it came within a month. He stared at the document uncertainly, trying desperately to understand how this fit in with the kidnapping.

"Hey, what do you think you're doing? That's my niece's birth certificate," Rodriguez grumbled nervously. "I was making copies for my sister. I don't know who you guys are looking for, but you've got the wrong man."

Spence stared at the man, barely controlled rage bubbling in his gut. He longed to drive a fist into the smug mouth that openly lied to him. Turning his back, he focused his attention on the cell phone, pressing a button to reveal the recently made and received calls. A woman's name appeared beside the most current one – Carmen. She'd called three times in the last hour. Prior to that, there were several back and forth calls to a local number with no identification.

Spence turned back to Rodriguez, clamping a hand on his shoulder. "Where's Ally?"

"I don't know an Ally," Rodriguez replied, suddenly worried. The man's fingers pinched painfully around the tendons in his neck. His set jaw and narrowed eyes looked ominous.

Spence slowly shook his head. "Sure you do. She's the little girl your friend Snake kidnapped." He watched the man's face pale, his eyes blinking rapidly.

Kidnapped! Snake said nothing about snatching the kid! He said she was his daughter. Suddenly filled with fear, he shook his head, staring at the angry man before him.

"I don't know anything about a kidnapping," he replied. Half a second later, a fist to his gut doubled him over and knocked the wind out of him.

"Enough!" Barns barked, surprised by the agent's quick action. He pulled Rodriguez to the side. "You better start talking!"

~ * ~

Carmen paced from one side of the small hotel room to the other, her gaze turning occasionally to the little girl sleeping in the bed. She couldn't figure out why she was here, babysitting that creepy guy's kid. What did Albert and this Snake character have going? Her boyfriend didn't usually associate with men like him.

She pulled out her cell phone and verified the time – almost four o'clock. Albert promised she'd only be here an hour. Two had already passed. She pulled back the curtain and peered across the parking lot to the street. Seeing no sign of Snake, she dropped the curtain and groaned. Albert was going to owe her big for this!

~ * ~

The unidentified calls on Rodriguez's cell phone were quickly traced to a local motel. Within minutes of learning the address, several unmarked cars were dispatched to the location. A plainclothes officer verified that Peel was room one-twelve's current resident. The desk clerk had no idea whether the man was there at the moment. The phone number Peel wrote on his registration form belonged to Rodriguez's cell phone, further proof of their involvement.

They needed eyes inside that room. It was decided that a female officer posing as housekeeping would approach the door. Officer Yates was outfitted with a borrowed maid's uniform and a stocked cleaning cart. Her weapon was tucked under a stack of towels, her finger poised over the trigger.

Under the pretense of utilizing the hotel, Barns and another officer parked and made for the room next door. Spence waited in a car at the rear of the lot.

~ * ~

Carmen was clicking through the stations on the television when a knock sounded on the door. Without thinking, she rushed to answer.

"It's about time…" the words dissolved at the sight of the white-aproned maid.

"Housekeeping," Yates announced in accented English. She purposefully stepped to one side so the others could get a look at the woman who answered.

"The room is fine," Carmen said, still standing in the doorway. She didn't want to deal with this! Where was Albert? He should have been here by now.

Continuing the charade, Yates said, "I bring clean towels." Carrying a stack of folded linens, she stepped past the woman. A quick look to the right and left revealed no other adults. As she headed toward the open vanity area, she noted the small child tucked beneath the bed covers. After a hasty search of the toilet and shower room, she whispered into the microphone beneath her collar, "Suspect is not here. The kid is."

Bored, Carmen watched the maid drop the towels on the counter beside the sink and turn. Her eyes rounded in surprise at the sight of a raised weapon. Before she could do more than utter a surprised grunt, two men entered the room, weapons drawn. Feeling suddenly dizzy and faint, she collapsed into the chair she'd been using earlier.

~ * ~

Snake finished his steak sandwich and washed it down with the last of his beer. The meal was delicious, the best he'd had in over four years. He tossed a few bills on the counter, conveniently forgetting the tip. Cash was a scarcity, and he couldn't afford such unnecessary extras right now. He'd make up for the oversight soon enough. The meager advance Rodriguez had given him was going quick. Grabbing the bag of goodies he'd picked up earlier, he headed out.

He fished the list from his pocket and double checked that he'd gotten everything – hair dye for the kid – he'd chosen dark brown, a couple of instant lunch kits for the drive to Mexico tomorrow, water bottles. He'd added that item himself, remembering the raging case of the runs from the last time he'd partied across the border.

The last item was his meds. He'd stood in the pharmacy, weighing the cost of the pills against the few remaining bills in his pocket. Frugality won, and he skipped the drugs. He didn't need them anymore, he decided. Living behind bars for so many years had taught him to control his impulses. As long as he stayed away from the booze, he'd be fine.

He rounded a corner and headed in the direction of the motel, still a couple of blocks away. As he drew closer, his pace slowed. Visible at the end of the block, police cruisers were parked along both sides of the street. *Probably nothing*, he told himself. This was a rough neighborhood. The presence of cops was not unusual. All the same, he wasn't taking any chances.

Turning abruptly, he made his way down an alley behind a long strip of small businesses. He moved stealthily to the end of the building, rounded the corner, and entered the convenience store that occupied the farthest space. The front windows afforded a decent view of the motel parking lot on the opposite corner. Picking up a magazine from a rack, he flipped through the pages, keeping his head down, and discreetly watched the activity outside.

Everything appeared normal for several minutes. He'd almost decided he was overreacting when all hell broke loose at the motel. Cops emerged from various locations and ran toward the building. From his vantage point, he could see a uniformed man on the roof. It didn't take a rocket scientist to realize his plan was blown. As a flood of rage engulfed him, he slammed a fist on the shelf in front of him, rattling several items placed there. His heart thundered, and his vision contracted for a moment before returning to normal. Breathing deeply, as the counselor had taught him, he yanked his hood over his head and slipped outside.

~ * ~

From several yards away, Spence watched the scene. His gaze continuously roamed the parking lot and street, scrutinizing every window, every dark alcove, for the kidnapper. A signal from Barns had him jogging toward the hotel room.

He stepped through the doorway and heard, "'Pence!"

Ally sat on the bed, Officer Yates by her side. She scrambled to her feet and ran across the mattress. Spence grabbed her, pulling her little body into his arms.

Through an emotion-thickened throat, Spence asked, "Are you okay, sweet pea?"

Burrowing her face against Spence's neck, she murmured, "Want Auntie." Weeping accompanied the soft plea. Under the circumstances, the little girl had borne up well. Though she'd been confused, she hadn't cried. The scary man kept promising he'd take her home. After a while, she'd stopped asking. She thought he was fibbing. Then the lady came and made her drink some red medicine that made her sleepy.

"She needs a medical examination," Detective Barns said as Spence carried Ally outside. "And we'll need to ask her some questions."

"Jordan and Caleb need to see this little girl," Spence replied firmly. "The rest can wait."

Barns studied the determined look on the man's face and knew arguing would be hopeless. He'd gathered that the boy was his son. He still hadn't quite figured out the relationship between the woman and the agent. Spence acted possessive, though no concrete proof of involvement had been offered.

"Fine, I'll have my men bring them to the hospital. We can take care of the questions and the examination at the same time."

~ * ~

Jordan wasn't told where they were going, so when the cruiser turned into the hospital parking lot, her pulse began to race. Frightening visions of both Ally and Carl rushed through her mind. Whispering a soft prayer for their safety, she shook off the disturbing images and reached for Caleb's hand. The few minutes it took to get to the private room on the second floor felt like hours.

The door opened, and Spence stood and walked toward her, Ally tucked safely in his arms. Jordan couldn't speak as she reached for the precious girl. Ally's arms and legs wrapped around her aunt in a desperate hold.

"Where were you, Auntie?" the small, accusing voice whispered.

Spence watched Jordan sway unsteadily. When her knees buckled, he had her in his arms in an instant. Through tear blurred eyes, she looked up at him and whispered, "Thank you."

Unable to form a reply, Spence nodded. Spotting his weeping son behind her, he reached a hand out and drew Caleb into the embrace that now held the three most important people in his life. His throat ached as a full gamut of emotions engulfed him. Today, he'd experienced the worst kind of terror – and discovered his full capacity for love. In this moment, he came to the realization that he'd do anything to keep these three people safe and in his life.

Chapter 26

The ensuing investigation uncovered Peel's intention to sell his daughter through an illegal adoption ring. Because Ally was not an infant, she was supposed to be delivered through the organization's Mexico City connection. She would have eventually been adopted by a foreign family, most likely in Europe.

Insisting that he had no knowledge of the kidnapping, Rodriguez agreed to provide information. In exchange for a lesser charge, he was willing to help shut down the adoption ring.

Due to the international nature of the crime, the FBI was now officially involved. Naturally, Agent Spencer's connection to the case caught the attention of the local Bureau chief. Spence was questioned thoroughly. His relationship to the kidnap victim was now common knowledge.

"We'd like you onboard with this investigation, Agent Spencer," Mr. Grant said.

"Thank you, sir, but I'm currently on medical leave," Spence replied. "I'm in California to visit my son."

"Well, I'd be very interested in having you work for me," the man said. "Get in touch when you're ready to get back in the game. Our weather is much nicer here," he pointed out with a smile.

Spence almost laughed. He'd been back in the game for the last few days. His injured shoulder still hurt, but it hadn't prevented him from doing the job. He wasn't quite ready to make that information public. There were still decisions to be made.

"Sir, what about Peel?" he asked, his focus on the still at-large felon.

"We'll be watching for him, but I've got to be honest with you," the man replied sympathetically. "Peel isn't our top priority. His part in this was small. He isn't likely to be of any use to us when it comes to nailing the adoption ring."

Spence's jaw stiffened angrily. "So, you're just letting him walk?"

"No, not at all. Like I said, he's still on the radar," Grant assured him. "Detective Barns and his men are actively searching for him. Don't worry, he'll be found. We want him put away as much as you do."

I doubt that, Spence thought sarcastically. He wondered if the man would be more motivated if it were his child Peel had taken.

~ * ~

Later, Spence met with Barns at the police station and posed the same questions to the detective.

"We're doing what we can," Barns said. "His photo is posted in every squad car. My men are showing it in every bar, every seedy motel – anywhere the guy might frequent. We've already overturned a bunch of rocks, but he hasn't slithered out." He gestured to the chair opposite his desk.

Discouraged, Spence dropped into the seat. They'd recovered Ally four days ago. Since then, Jordan and the children had been staying at an undisclosed location, a safe house the local police occasionally used. Though he was staying at the same house, he'd yet to manage a full night's sleep. Knowing that creep was out there, that Ally and Jordan might still be in danger, had kept his mind running full speed.

"Have you turned up any leads?"

"Nothing that's panned out," Barns replied leaning back in his chair. "You want my advice?"

"Sure."

"If it was my family in jeopardy," he began. "I'd get them out of the area for a while."

Nodding, Spence stared at the floor. For more reasons than one, he'd been thinking along those lines. Jordan was constantly agitated, rarely letting Ally out of her sight. She needed some peace and rest before she came apart at the seams.

"I'm not completely sure Jordan would go for that," he said, recalling her comment the previous evening about needing to get back to work. She was worried about money, an unfortunate reality, whether or not there was a kidnapper on the loose. He'd tried to reassure her, telling her he'd take care of things. She'd blanched at the idea but remained silent.

Barns picked up a folder from his desk and handed it to Spence. "Maybe this will help convince her."

~ * ~

After losing the girl, Snake had been forced to conserve his cash. He slept wherever he could find a safe place, including behind the bushes beside an overpass, twice. The third night, he stumbled upon a homeless man's residence. The man had broken into a boarded up gas station and made himself a little house there. Snake produced a bottle of wine, and the man willingly offered to let him stay the night. That was pure luck for Snake. Unfortunately, the other man hadn't fared as well. When he caught Snake going through his belongings, he'd put up a fight. One drunken old man was no match for

Snake's temper. When he left, the guy lay on the floor, unconscious and bleeding. Too bad he'd only had a few dollars. That was two days ago.

With nowhere else to go and the nighttime temperatures hovering in the low fifties, he'd come back to the vacant house next to Jordan Gray's apartment complex. He'd grabbed the girl nearly a week ago. The authorities would have conducted a neighborhood search during the first few days. They wouldn't be back.

Snake gloated at the irony. Here he sat, right next door, and no one was the wiser. Just for fun, he'd snuck back into the apartment a couple of times. The place looked like they'd left in a hurry —unmade beds and dirty clothes on the floors. In the woman's bedroom, the closet door was off its track and the entrance door looked like someone had kicked it in. He smiled, mentally patting himself on the back for deciding to lock it.

During one of his forays into the apartment, he located her files on the top shelf of a linen cabinet. She kept her papers in a red box with a Christmas tree printed on the side. No wonder he'd missed it the first time. The kid's original birth certificate was there. He almost whooped out loud, stopping himself just in time. Alerting the neighbors to his presence was unwise. He stuffed the folded document inside his shirt, intending to look at it later, and returned the box to its cupboard. A minute later, he'd slipped silently through the patio door and over the fence.

He was relieved now that he hadn't let Rodriguez control everything. The shifty-eyed guy had treated him with disdain, like a dimwit. Snake didn't trust him and had insisted on talking to the Mexico City contact, a man named Gomez, over the phone. The man's English was passable and Snake managed to negotiate the contract himself. Twenty-five grand was going to be his cut. Then Rodriguez screwed everything up!

Snake's vision suddenly blurred as a surge of anger claimed him. Without thinking, he slammed a fist into the wall of his borrowed bedroom. The unfinished sheet rock cracked in several places. Surprised, Snake drew back his hand and glanced around. Half a dozen similar distortions marred the walls around him. He shook his head, trying to clear his jumbled thoughts. Maybe he should get that prescription filled, after all.

~ * ~

The three bedroom townhouse where Jordan and the children were staying was leased by the county. The front of the gated complex was monitored by a twenty-four-hour guard and a continuously active surveillance system. Each unit had a separate entrance. The police officer staying on the premises provided additional security.

With mixed feelings, Jordan wondered how long they'd be expected to remain here. Would she be held captive until Ally's kidnapper was located and arrested? What if they never found the man? Surely, the budget didn't allow for a lengthy stay.

Partially closing the door to the bedroom she and Ally shared, Jordan proceeded down the hall and stopped at the entrance to the living room. Yates was the current officer on duty. When Jordan spotted the attractive female officer chatting with Spence over a cup of coffee, she felt a twinge of annoyance.

Spence glanced over his shoulder and smiled. "Everything all right?" he asked, pushing his cup of decaf aside and standing. He'd been brainstorming with Yates, hoping to expose some pertinent fact they'd overlooked. Unfortunately, nothing new came to light.

"Ally's down for the night," Jordan replied evenly. The little girl had fretted every night, and Jordan was compelled to lie down with her, rubbing her forehead until she dozed off. Brushing past Spence, she headed for the kitchen. She needed a glass of water.

Concerned about the odd expression she wore, Spence followed. "Is Caleb still watching his movie?" he asked, coming up behind her. Officer Yates had thoughtfully brought several movies with her, hoping they'd help combat the boy's boredom. A second story loft boasted a television and DVD player.

Staring at the water pouring into her glass, Jordan nodded. As usual, Carl's close proximity sent her nerves spiraling. She didn't welcome the feeling, especially now. Confusion reigned in her heart and mind. Since coming here, he'd become distant toward her. She knew part of the reason was his preoccupation with the investigation. Was the other part to do with Officer Yates, or was he simply over his mild infatuation? *Perhaps there never was such a feeling for him*, she scolded herself. A palm closing over her shoulder brought the troubling thoughts to a stop.

"Jordan, can we talk in private?" Spence asked softly. Her distress bothered him. She stood at the sink, shoulder's tensed, and clearly uneasy. Was it only the case?

Jordan exhaled a long breath and nodded again as she turned around. With a hand at her back, Spence guided her to an enclosed courtyard, drawing the sliding glass door closed behind him.

Jordan stood stiffly to one side, until Spence took her hand and gently lead her to a patio chair. Without releasing her fingers, he dragged another chair closer and sat facing her.

"When I drove by your apartment today to pick up Caleb's backpack," he began, reaching into his pocket. "I found this on the windowsill in the kitchen."

Spence turned her hand palm up and placed something in it. Her fingers closed around the small object.

"My ring," Jordan said softly, pleased and surprised. She gazed down at the simple treasure then slipped the promise ring on her finger. "Thank you."

"You're welcome," Spence replied. He was mentally debating how to broach the next subject when she spoke.

"When do you suppose this will be over." Since the apartment was considered a crime scene, she'd been forced to do without the majority of her clothing and other personal items. "I'd like to go home."

Spence reached for her hands, thoughts of what he'd learned today solidifying his resolve. "Jordan, I don't think you should go back anytime soon."

"I can't stay here forever, Carl!" she exclaimed, pulling her hands free and gripping the arms of her chair. "I have bills to pay, a job to get back to – a life!"

Resisting the urge to recapture her hands, Spence clamped his together in front of him. "We found papers in Peel's personal effects, stuff he left in the motel room."

With a sense of foreboding, Jordan asked, "What…papers?"

Spence held her gaze, desperate to absorb the shock he knew she'd feel. "He had a some papers – information from the preschool's website, including your picture. There were photos of you and Ally taken through the chain-link fence surrounding the school playground, Ally playing in the park, you sitting on a blanket and watching her, and you and her getting out of your car in front of the apartment."

Jordan gasped, her breath stuttering as he explained. A ghostly white replaced the previously pink hue in her cheeks. She raised one hand to her mouth, covering her stunned expression. Spence chose not to share all of what he'd seen – the close-up shots that zeroed in on only Jordan. Peel's goal wasn't simply information gathering for a job. There were other unsavory things on his mind. Anger spiked, and he pushed it down. Right now, he needed to be calm – for Jordan.

"I can't keep you safe here," Spence said, knowing he was heading into this backwards.

Jordan blinked, forcing her mind to focus on the words and not on the disturbing disclosures she'd just learned. "You shouldn't feel responsible for keeping us safe, Carl. Um, at least, not Ally and me. Surely, the police..." she said, but stopped when he shook his head.

"There's only so much they can do. If Peel isn't caught soon, they'll have to move the case to the back burner." At her appalled expression, he added, "Don't get me wrong, sweetheart, they'll keep looking, but they don't have unlimited resources."

Jordan nodded her understanding. These were the same thoughts she'd been wrestling with earlier. There had to be an end. "We'll just have to...move, maybe," she stammered, feeling suddenly overwhelmed. She looked away. She'd never find an apartment with rent as low as she paid now, not in the same school district, at any rate.

"Or you can go to Montana with me," Spence said, anxious to offer her a viable alternative.

As the suggestion slowly penetrated, Jordan studied his earnest expression. The offer was genuine. They could go, for a short time. However, eventually he'd have to return to his job in New Jersey, probably fairly soon. What would happen then?

"But you don't live in Montana, Carl," she said softly.

"That's true," he replied with a smile. "In fact, I don't currently live anywhere."

"Wh-what do you mean?" she stammered. How could he be homeless?

"Before driving out here, I put my condo up for sale and packed away all my belongings," he explained. "I'm not going back."

"But...your job... What are you going to do for work?"

"Actually, I came here with a couple of ideas in mind. One possibility is transferring to the local office," he explained, purposefully omitting the fact that he'd already been offered a position.

"To be near Caleb," Jordan whispered. "Or were you going to move him in with you?" She'd given that idea substantial attention. Her worry was that he'd move the boy away. If they stayed in Orange County, Ally and she would be able to remain close to Caleb.

Spence shrugged. "That's one possibility."

"Oh," Jordan murmured. "You mentioned a couple of options for work."

"Right. Last summer, Sheriff Davies offered me a deputy position in Silver Springs."

Shocked, Jordan's heart constricted uncomfortably. If he moved to Montana, wild horses wouldn't keep Caleb here. The distance was almost as far as New Jersey! Grasping the first thing that came to mind, she blurted, "Wouldn't that be a step down for you?"

"Initially," Spence replied, noting the troubled look on her face. "Not that I care about maintaining a certain status."

"I'm sorry," Jordan said quickly, embarrassed now to give voice to such a frivolous thought. "I didn't mean it like that."

Spence smiled and reached for her hands again. "I know you didn't," he said softly. "And besides, the deputy position would be a stepping stone. The sheriff wants to retire in the next year or two. He's looking for his replacement and seems to think I'd do a good job."

"I see," Jordan whispered, her gaze resting on their joined hands. His right thumb was making little circles around her promise ring. Did he know he was doing that? Her pulse quickened at his gentle touch and tendrils of heat shimmered across her skin. "Which job do you think you're likely to pursue?" she asked breathlessly.

Spence gazed at the top of her head. She was keeping her head down, hiding her emotions, and he really needed to look into her eyes during the next part of the discussion. He placed one hand under her chin and lifted, until she faced him.

"That decision depends on you."

Jordan blinked in surprise. "Me?"

Spence slowly nodded.

Jordan studied his open expression. In his eyes, she glimpsed a vulnerability she'd seen only once before, the night Caleb learned he had a father. Memories of the embrace they'd shared when Carl felt such deep and emotional hurt drifted across her mind. She didn't understand what made him feel that way now, or what part she played in it. She could only respond. Raising a hand to his face, she cupped his cheek.

"What is it, Carl?"

Spence covered her hand with his and pressed it to his stubbly skin. Turning his head, he kissed her palm, his eyes closing as he savored the moment – this deep closeness he'd never felt with anyone else. When he opened his eyes, hers were closed. She looked serene, beautiful and he leaned forward, touching his lips to hers in a tender kiss.

"Will you marry me, Jordan?" he whispered against the softness of her mouth.

The tender words filtered through the fog that muddled Jordan's thoughts. *Will you marry me?* Had she heard him correctly? Surely not! Why, they'd never even been on a date! Her eyes popped open and she sat up straight, pulling away from him, severing the warm touch that always seemed to leave her disoriented.

"Carl...why?" she stammered, confused and uncertain. "I...we..." Unable to transform her erratic thoughts and emotions into words, she stood suddenly and moved away from him. She needed distance – air and space. *Please, Lord*, she prayed silently, *help me know what to say.*

Stunned by her unexpected flight, Spence could only watch her flee. *Damn!* He'd bungled this badly. He shouldn't have blurted out the proposal like that. She was a cautious woman, not prone to making rash decisions or jumping into water without first knowing its depth. He'd given her no clue as to how he felt, nor had he afforded her the opportunity to share her thoughts. He stood and followed, coming to a stop behind her.

"I'm sorry, Jordan," he said to her back. "That didn't go the way I'd envisioned. I hadn't intended to..." He paused and heaved a heavy sigh. "I'd hoped to woo you, court you a while – do it right. This thing with Ally really threw my plans out the window."

With her heart pounding, Jordan listened to the explanation. Carl had planned to date her, but Ally's kidnapping, and now their need to leave the area, pushed everything into overdrive. She wrapped her arms around herself, a useless gesture that offered little comfort. What should she tell him? *No, I can't marry you, even though I'd like to very much?* Was it wise to rush into marriage? He hadn't declared his love for her. He'd never really expressed any emotion other than...attraction, and that wasn't an emotion at all.

Spence began to doubt his assumptions about Jordan. Did she even feel anything for him? He pushed tense fingers through his hair and turned away. *Just tell her!* The annoying voice inside his head shouted. *Tell her what?* He argued back.

"Tell her you love her."

The whispered words drifted across the cool, dewy night air and straight into Jordan's heart. Turning, her gaze came to rest on Carl's broad back. Tense muscles rippling under his shirt, one hand rested on the back of his neck in a posture of agitation. He was mumbling, unaware that his words were audible. She walked forward and hesitantly touched his back.

"What did you say?" she asked softly.

Spence's inner dialog halted. Had he spoken aloud? He spun around and gazed down at Jordan's upturned face. It was his turn to discern vulnerability in her expression. She could have pretended not to hear. The question in her eyes gave him a boost of courage.

"I said I love you."

Could he really believe that? Jordan wondered. They'd spent so little time together. Instantly, her own heartfelt revelation came blasting into her memory. *You're in love with him,* Deborah's voice whispered through her mind.

"But...how...when?" she stammered.

"I don't know when or how, exactly," Spence replied, reaching for her hands. "But after I returned to New Jersey, I was miserable. I missed Caleb, I missed Ally, and I missed you. In fact, I couldn't get you out of my thoughts. When I'd finally decided to move away from there, it wasn't to be near my son. It was to be near you." He hesitated, studied her still confused expression and then continued. "If it's too much to answer my question right now, Jordan...if it's too soon, please just tell me. I can wait until you're ready." He realized as he said the words that she hadn't said anything to indicate she felt the same. She hadn't moved away or interrupted his speech either. He chose to look at those small things as a positive sign.

As Jordan stared up at his earnest expression, joy seeped into her heart, filling it with a sweet ache. Thoughts of her emails back and forth with Elizabeth gave her peace. More than once, her friend had mentioned Carl's walk with the Lord. She'd expounded on the father-son Bible study Carl attended and later, alluded to a soul searching experience. His church attendance had also continued after Jordan returned to California. That part, she'd seen firsthand when Carl accompanied her to a worship service last month. He'd grown close to the Lord, and the Lord had allowed them to grow close to each other.

She dropped her gaze to her left hand, to the ring he'd delivered to her moments ago. Was there hidden meaning in that gesture? She prayed often that God would bring the right man into her life. She'd never felt this close to any of the few men she'd dated in the past.

Spence watched her stare at her ring. Was she weighing his proposal against her long-ago vow? He brought her left hand to his lips and kissed her fingertips.

"Jordan, I know what this ring represents to you," he said quietly. "I'm far from perfect, sweetheart, and not nearly so arrogant that I'd pass myself off as God's ideal husband – or yours," he added with a smile. "But I'm prepared to do the best I can, with His help, if you're willing to take a chance on me."

Jordan's breath hitched at the sincerity in his voice. With tears shimmering in her eyes, she raised her head and whispered. "I love you, too, Carl."

Spence's smile broadened as he dropped his face and kissed away first one tear and then another. After a moment, his lips found hers, and his arms enfolded her. The kiss was tender and sweet, filled with promises for a future that they could neither predict nor anticipate.

"Is that a yes?" he asked when he finally lifted his head.

"Yes," Jordan replied dreamily. This might be the shortest, oddest courtship in history, but she was ready.

Chapter 27

First thing in the morning, Spence contacted Sheriff Davies to make sure his offer still stood. It did, the older man assured him.

"Let me know when you get to town," he said. "In the meantime, I'll look into the particulars of getting you hired on. There might be some tests required by the state. Can't see them being a problem, what with the training you've already had."

"Neither can I," Spence replied. "I won't be ready to start until the first of the year, though. I'm on medical leave from the Bureau until then. The doc's not likely to release me early. I'm also getting married and wouldn't mind having the time to get my family settled."

"Well, congratulations then!" Davies exclaimed. "January will to be fine. We ought to have the red tape cleared up by then."

When he put in a call to Mrs. Hill at her care facility, he was informed that she'd been released. He dialed her home number. After the initial greeting, he broached the subject of his call.

"I was wondering if you're still interested in selling your property, Adele."

"If you're the buyer, I might be," she replied, adding, "with a few conditions."

"Okay," Spence said, knowing this was part of the deal.

She wouldn't let her place go to someone who would bulldoze it or turn it into a shopping mall or some other atrocity. "There'll be a provision in the contract stating that the property is never to be parceled out or sold for development purposes. I'd like the remains of my grandfather's mill to be preserved as an historical site. Perhaps someday, it can be restored, and school children will come to visit," she said, her voice taking on a dreamy quality. "I've always thought that would be nice."

"That sounds like a fascinating project, Adele," Spence replied in earnest. He made a mental note to look into the possibility when time permitted. "Anything else?"

"Are you willing to keep the animals, as we discussed?" Her pets were her first priority.

"Yes, ma'am," Spence replied with a chuckle. "Caleb would be disappointed if we came back and the horses weren't there. In his mind, they're part of the place."

"I like the boy already," Adele said. "What about your young lady, Carl?"

Spence smiled, remembering how the perceptive old bird had honed in on his preoccupation with Jordan, even before he understood it. "I'm marrying her in a few days."

"Wonderful!" she exclaimed, pleased to detect wonder and happiness in the man's tone. "There is one catch to our plan," she added. "I'm going to be staying here for a while. My sister-in-law wants me to move to the retirement village where she lives, but I'm not quite ready. I'm thinking sometime this spring."

Spence's hopes slipped a little, as he said, "We can find someplace else, until then."

"No, Carl! I won't hear of it!" she hastily replied. "I'd like all of you to stay here at the house. The whole upstairs is unused, as you know. Besides, if you and your family were here to help out, we'd be able to bring home the animals." She missed her horses and even the little yappy dog. Having children in the house again, after all these years, sounded like an exciting adventure, as well.

"We wouldn't want to get in your way, Adele," Spence said hesitantly. Yet, the prospect sounded good to him.

"You won't," she assured him.

So it was settled. He relayed the plans to Jordan, and she agreed. Everything should work out fine.

~ * ~

Clearing out the apartment was the most pressing and challenging task they needed to conquer. They chose to attack the job very early Monday morning arriving at six before most people were up and about. Ally promptly positioned her still drowsy body on the sofa with the early-morning cartoons playing on the television.

A charity pickup was scheduled for later in the day. They'd promised to send a crew to pack up and haul away whatever remained in the apartment. All the furniture, along with most of the kitchen items and linens would be donated. Detective Barns had arranged to purchase Jordan's old Ford for his teenaged daughter.

With Spence at her side, Jordan packed up the rest of hers and Ally's clothing, tossing many worn out or outgrown garments in a separate bag. She set aside her mother's jewelry box and the few trinkets with which she couldn't bear to part. Spence wrapped these in paper and packed them in a box.

By eight, they'd moved into the kitchen. Jordan grimaced at the enormous task before her. The very thought of filtering through the many cupboards was daunting. She opened the refrigerator and promptly slammed it shut again, sealing in the smell of sour milk.

"I'll handle the fridge," Spence volunteered, chuckling as he opened the kitchen window. He grabbed a trash bag and dove in. Within minutes, the interior of the appliance was bare, and Caleb was hauling the bulging trash bag outside.

Jordan stared at the open cupboards, overwhelmed. She'd inherited most of her dad's kitchenware after he passed away. Though it had once belonged to her mother, she didn't think anything was heirloom quality.

"Would it be sacrilegious to just leave it?" she muttered absently.

Watching her fret over the decision, Spence said, "Sweetheart, we'll buy what we need."

"Silver Springs doesn't have much in the way of shopping," Jordan pointed out. Thinking of the ancient slow cooker she used weekly, she added, "Especially kitchen appliances."

"Then we'll make a trip to Bozeman," he countered with a smile. "You don't need to worry about any of this. Remember, Mrs. Hill's place is well-stocked."

"But that seems so wasteful, Carl," she replied, glancing over her shoulder and pausing to admire him.

He leaned against the counter, arms crossed over his broad chest, and smiled. The warm expression on his face told her how much he cared and reminded her that soon they'd be man and wife. As she turned to face him, he reached for her hand and pulled her close.

Caleb returned at that moment and groaned. "Kissing again!" he complained in exaggerated disgust.

Spence lifted his head and gazed at his future wife's content expression. Jordan snuggled under his chin and sighed.

"Someday, son," Spence replied. "You'll understand."

He only hoped it wouldn't take the boy as long to get there as it had his dad. The moment the thought expressed itself, Spence changed his mind. No, that wasn't right. *God's timing is always perfect,* Elizabeth's reminder rang in his head. He was pleased the Lord had chosen Jordan for him, and that had meant waiting. He prayed his son would someday experience a similar blessing.

~ * ~

Snake woke slowly, his mind heavy from an alcohol induced sleep. Voices filtered through the broken window above his head. He sat up and listened, surprised when he realized they weren't drifting down from the upstairs apartment this time. The conversation was coming from the one right next door.

He moved closer to the cracked glass and focused. It sounded like the woman, Jordan Gray, was talking to a man. They were cleaning the kitchen – no, not cleaning, packing. The man called her sweetheart, and then said something about buying what they needed. When a location was mentioned, Snake felt a surge of excitement.

"Yes!" he cried then immediately clamped a hand over his mouth. "Don't mess this up!" he quietly scolded himself.

He stayed near the window for the next two hours, catching snippets of the conversation. By the time they left, Snake knew Tanya's sister was getting married in a few days and moving to Montana next week. What a lucky break! He pulled out his wallet and hunted through the scraps of paper for the one on which he'd written the phone number. He stared at the long row of digits beginning with the international code for Mexico. It was his winning lottery ticket!

Chapter 28

Jordan asked Deborah to be her matron of honor at her informal wedding to be held the following Tuesday. When her friend learned that Jordan planned to repeat her vows wearing a simple, everyday dress from her closet, the woman had a fit.

"That is unacceptable!" Deborah protested. "You're only doing this once, and you'll do it right."

She arranged for Spence to bring Jordan to her home. Deborah's wedding gown was brought out for Jordan to try, along with several gowns borrowed from generous friends. Jordan modeled five dresses and chose the one she liked the best. A few minor alterations were required, which Deborah handled. Since they were still under police protection, a cruiser remained parked outside during the fitting.

On Tuesday afternoon, the happy couple met at the church Jordan had attended since she was a teen. This would be her last visit, for the foreseeable future. The guest list was minuscule, with only twenty people Jordan knew from teaching preschool and Sunday school in attendance. At Spence's insistence, no big announcement was made. Several police officers were present, including Detective Barns and Officer Yates.

The brief ceremony took place in the main sanctuary. Deborah made all the arrangements, from flowers to a short reception in her home following the event. She'd insisted that Jordan enter the sanctuary in the traditional manner, walking down the center aisle. A friend was recruited to be the photographer.

Spence stood at the front of the chapel with Caleb, his best man, at his side. The boy shifted nervously, his hand fingering the two rings in his pocket. When his dad asked him to be his best man, he hadn't fully understood what that entailed. Keeping the wedding rings safe and secure seemed like an immense responsibility. But then, they'd gone to get fitted for tuxedos, and Caleb realized he'd also be expected to stand at the front of the church. When he pictured a typical Sunday morning crowd, he became light-headed. Thank heavens only a few rows were currently filled.

An organist began to play the wedding march and all eyes turned to the rear doors. Holding a small basket of pink carnations and wearing a new chiffon dress, Ally walked down the aisle, as slowly as her three-year-old legs could manage. When she reached Spence's side, she happily stood on tiptoes for a kiss then skipped to the first row to sit with the preschool director.

Deborah came next, equally sedate and beautiful in a pale pink dress that matched Ally's. The tiny bulge under her gown, a secret she'd finally shared with Jordan, was hidden behind a bouquet of baby roses.

Anxious for a glimpse of his bride, Spence kept his eyes glued on the foyer doorway. When Jordan stepped into view, all the nervous energy that had kept him going these last few hours evaporated. Adoration took its place as he watched her move toward him. She wore an ivory colored, off-the-shoulder gown that stopped at mid-calf and hugged her trim figure. Her hair was piled loosely atop her head with curly tendrils dancing around her face. Attached to a wreath of white roses, a slip of tissue-like fabric veiled her face. Ignoring Deborah's husband, Gary, who guided Jordan to the front, Spence only had eyes for his bride. He unconsciously held his breath until she reached his side.

Before taking Jordan's hand, he lifted the veil and held her gaze. Moisture shimmered in the emerald depths of her eyes, tears of joy to match his own feelings. Impulsively, he dropped his head and pressed a kiss to her startled lips. A throat clearing behind him, along with snickers coming from various locations throughout the room, reminded him of the purpose of this day. Jordan's content smile reassured him that this was exactly where she wanted to be, and he shared the desire. Tucking her hand into the crook of his elbow, he turned toward the minister.

"Dearly beloved..."

Many hours later, as Jordan snuggled against his side, happy and content, Spence pondered what he'd discovered tonight. She'd kept her vow, coming into their marriage untouched. That long ago promise was important to her; she'd never faltered.

Until now, he hadn't considered how such a gift might make him feel. He was awed, yet at the same time, felt honored and humbled. He could imagine the pressure she must have felt to conform to the world's view of love, perhaps even suffering ridicule. He'd once been the type of man who wouldn't have appreciated her sacrifice. He may have even mocked her because of it. Thankfully, that man no longer existed. He would have loved her no matter what choices she'd made in the past, however, knowing her this way, made him respect her all the more.

Jordan shifted and sighed. "What are you thinking, Carl?" she asked, sensing his restlessness. His arm around her tightened and he leaned over and kissed her forehead.

"About you – about what you've given me." Spence whispered, as he lay back on his pillow. "You know, for a time, I thought Ally was your daughter. I thought you'd lied to me."

"I know," she replied softly. "I was a fulltime college student in the midst of final exams when Ally was born. I was surprised you didn't connect the dots."

Spence chuckled, equally stunned he'd missed the obvious. "I'm sorry I doubted you, sweetheart," he said. "I hope it never happens again. Did you know your sister was going to do that?"

"No," Jordan replied. "I discovered it by accident after she died, and the children came to live with me."

Gliding his hand from her bare shoulder down her arm, Spence said, "I guess we know why she did it."

"To protect Ally," Jordan replied. "Knowing that man must have forced Tanya to face the consequences of her choices. It was a very unselfish act. I'm glad she chose me," she added softly.

"Me, too," he agreed. "You're Ally's mama in every way that matters."

They'd discussed changing Ally's birth certificate, even running their concerns by Detective Barns to get his opinion. The man had shaken his head, reminding them of the trauma the little girl had recently experienced. She needed all the stability they could offer. Instead of changing it, he suggested making it a reality. Becoming her parents served the dual purpose of eliminating confusion and giving her a much needed anchor.

A few days ago, they talked to Ally, asking if she'd like to call them mama and daddy. Her happy squeal had confirmed that they were doing the right thing.

"Everybody at schools gots a mommy and daddy, 'cept me," Ally explained. From that moment on, she happily used the new titles.

Caleb had also agreed to the change, though he didn't intend to participate. His memories of his mother were volatile and unsettling. He preferred to leave her in the past. Jordan had always been his fun, happy, grounded aunt and he like her best in that capacity.

After four days of driving with occasional stops to see the sites, the Range Rover pulled into Mrs. Hill's driveway. The elderly woman promptly stepped onto the front porch and waved. Spence had made a point of calling her earlier with an estimated time of arrival. Using a cane, she hobbled down the steps and pulled him into a one-armed embrace.

"I wondered if you'd make it in time for dinner," she said after introductions were made. "I've got a big batch of fried chicken just waiting to be devoured."

Before Spence could respond, Caleb announced, "I'm starved. When do we eat?"

Jordan and Adele Hill liked each other from the start. The older woman enjoyed having another female with whom to socialize. For Jordan, Mrs. Hill filled a gap in her life. Her mother had died when she was only nine, and she'd never known her grandparents. Her sister had never been a great role model. Conversing with Adele was both stimulating and educational.

One afternoon, a few days after they arrived, Jordan sat in the living room enjoying a cup of coffee and chatting with Adele. The house was quiet, for a change. Ally was upstairs napping. In anticipation of the horses' scheduled return the following day, Spence and Caleb had driven to town to purchase feed and supplies.

Jordan's gaze roamed the room, taking in the various photographs placed here and there. One eight by ten rested in a place of honor atop a curio cabinet. Wearing the dress uniform of a Marine Corps private, the unsmiling young man posed next to an American flag. The photo's colors had faded slightly over the years. Jordan learned that the young man was Adele's only son, Corbin. One month after being deployed during Desert Storm, he made the ultimate sacrifice for his country. Recalling Carl's eight years in the military, Jordan couldn't help feeling blessed, yet visions of his scarred shoulder overshadowed the sentiment. Though he'd been away from such danger for a while, he would soon be reentering that volatile field.

"Do the lawmen around here face…many dangers?" she asked haltingly.

"Oh, they have their share of problems," Mrs. Hill replied. "A few years back, we had an arsonist to contend with and before that, the incident out at the Summers place. There's always the occasional bad apple, sometimes a drifter but often the homegrown variety. Crime happens in small towns, same as the large cities."

Jordan's heart sank. Perhaps she'd been hasty in agreeing to spend her life as Carl's wife. Would she worry every time he left for work? Did her future include another unexpected knock on the door?

Adele sensed the younger woman's unease and longed to relieve it. Turning sympathetic eyes to Jordan, she said, "Honey, my husband was lawman in these parts for over thirty years. The only time he was injured on the job was when old man Higgins ran the stop sign at the corner of Fourth and Main and broadsided his patrol car," she chuckled over the memory. "William was hopping mad, hobbling around on crutches for three months. After he returned to work, the first thing he did was confiscate the old codger's pickup truck. Higgins was nearly ninety years old, could barely see or hear, and hadn't carried a valid driver's license in a decade."

Jordan offered a weak smile at the humorous story. She still felt uncomfortable with Carl's job. "I just wish he did something else for a living," she muttered.

"Now, don't you go thinking that way, young lady!" Adele scolded gently. "Your man is a lawman through and through. My husband was the same. It isn't something they can change, nor should they try. The community needs men like them." Grasping her cane for support, she pushed herself up, and shuffled to the sofa. She seated herself beside Jordan and patted the young woman's hand. "Carl could just as easily be injured unloading those bales of hay as behind a badge. Your job is to have faith, to keep praying, and to support your man. Life on this earth isn't for wimps."

Jordan smiled, appreciating the woman's candor. She was right. None of us is in control, but God would always be there, if only we allowed Him. In the past, she'd had few problems accepting these truths. However, she'd never loved anyone as deeply as she loved Carl. Could she accept whatever the future held, and still hold onto her faith? She resolved to add to her daily prayer list an appeal for strength in this area.

~ * ~

After visiting the feed store and market, Spence stopped in at the Bread Basket for lunch. The restaurant was running at full capacity, but he and Caleb managed to grab the last two seats at the counter. Without the usual fanfare, a harried waitress he'd never seen before took their orders for hamburgers and sodas. Ten minutes later, she returned with two loaded plates.

"Dad, when are you going to pick up the Porche?" Caleb asked between enormous bites.

"I promised Jack I'd get it out of his garage by the end of next week," Spence replied. "Snow's going to fly soon, and we'll need a second vehicle."

"The Porche won't be much good in the snow, though," the boy pointed out. Didn't his dad know that?

"Nope, it'll have to go. We're going to need a pickup," he replied evenly, eyeing his son and waiting for the explosion. It didn't take long.

"What?! You're not going to get rid of it, are you?" When his dad nodded, Caleb pleaded, "Awe, Dad! I was hoping you'd let me have it when I'm old enough."

Spence's loud guffaw turned a few heads at nearby tables. In a lowered voice, he said, "Son, you couldn't afford the insurance." He chuckled over the thought of a sixteen-year-old boy behind the wheel of the overpriced sports car – way too much testosterone between the two of them. Plus, *he'd* be the one writing the tickets.

"Yeah, well," Caleb mumbled. "I'd look cool in that car."

"You'll look cool in a truck, too, Caleb," Spence replied, clapping a hand on his son's back. "And everyone around here will be a lot safer, including you."

Caleb rolled his eyes. When had his dad become...well, a dad? He was about to ask when Tammy, their usual waitress, walked over.

"How'd the new gal do?" She nodded toward the waitress who served their food.

"She did fine," Spence replied. "Especially considering how busy you were when we came in."

"Boy, ain't that the truth!" Tammy agreed with a smile. "Hey, that reminds me, had a fella in here this morning asking how to find the Hill place, said he was inquiring about a job. Did he ever show up?"

Spence pushed his plate away and picked up his glass of root beer, taking a drink. "I wouldn't know. Caleb and I have been in town all morning picking up supplies and running errands," he replied. Adele hadn't said anything about looking for help. Had she put out feelers before he'd been in touch? "What was his name? I'll let Adele know when we get home."

Tammy chewed her lower lip, thinking. "Well, I don't rightly know. I'd never seen him before."

A stranger? Spence felt the hairs on the back of his neck prickle. "Do you remember what he looked like?"

"Well, he was tall," Tammy said, staring at the ceiling and trying to recall details. "Kind of cagey, if you ask me. Didn't strike me as the type Adele would want around – sort of dirty looking, like he'd been sleeping in his clothes. I just couldn't see her being interested in hiring him."

A feeling of unease trickled into Spence's stomach. "Did he have any earrings or tattoos?"

"Not that I recall, but then, he wore his leather jacket the whole time he ate his breakfast," she replied. "I noticed his hands shook a bit when he was paying."

Spence was up in a flash. He didn't like the sound of this. Shoving a twenty into Tammy's hand, he urged Caleb out the door. As though the very devil was on their heels, the car flew the ten miles to the Hill place.

~ * ~

Jordan felt her husband's agitation the moment he stepped through the door. The peck on the cheek he greeted her with seemed like an afterthought as he rushed past. She followed him into the kitchen. Mrs. Hill stood at the sink peeling potatoes to add to the pot roast she was getting ready to put in the oven.

"Adele, were you advertising for help around here?" he asked, hoping his worries were groundless.

Mrs. Hill glanced over her shoulder, surprised by Spence's brusque tone. "I was," she replied. "There's an ad on the bulletin board inside the feed store. Did you see it? I guess I should have Ernie take it down, now that you and Caleb are here."

Spence's anxious heart calmed. She'd been advertising. Good! "Did a man come by today to inquire about the job?"

"No, I don't think so." She turned and glanced at Jordan. "Honey, did anyone stop by while I was resting my eyes."

Jordan shook her head. "Is anything wrong, Carl," she asked, reaching for his forearm. The muscles beneath her palm were tense. She searched out and held his gaze for a few seconds before he turned away.

"Everything's fine, sweetheart," he said, leaning close and pressing a kiss to her lips.

He refused to give her any cause to worry. She'd finally begun to relax. He couldn't rob her of that. Besides, his suspicions appeared to be unfounded.

Chapter 29

The following day, Jack delivered the horses. Spence and Caleb had spent the morning preparing the stalls and making sure the corral was secure. Fresh hay and water, along with a couple of excited children, awaited the two animals.

When the passenger door of the truck opened, a very excited little dog tumbled out, followed by Jeremy. Both headed straight for Caleb. The boys spent a few minutes getting reacquainted while the men unloaded Dancer and Shasta. When the task was finished, the horses trotted across the corral, seemingly happy to be home.

"You'd best put them in the barn before dark," Jack suggested, gesturing toward the storm clouds to the north. The temperature had dropped several degrees since this morning.

Spence nodded. He'd already thought of that. He smiled as Butch danced on two legs around Caleb's knees. "I think the dog is happy to be back."

Jack laughed. "Dumb animal spent the first two weeks at our place moping around like he'd lost his best friend." He shook his head. When Spence and Caleb left, he'd figured they'd inherited the dog. Now, it appeared the terrier would have no problem transitioning back to the Hill place.

Ally appeared on the porch wearing a brand new coat buttoned to the throat. She squealed at the sight of the dog and stumbled down the steps to get to him. A moment later, she was knocked on her butt, giggling as he lathered her face with wet kisses.

Jordan stepped outside and waved at Jack. "Would you like to come in for a cup of coffee?" she asked, adding the further enticement, "Adele's made a batch of homemade donuts."

Jack laughed and rubbed his stomach. "I'm afraid I'll have to take a rain check," he replied, clearly disappointed. "With this storm rolling in, I've got stock of my own to get settled. Come on, son," Jack called to his nephew. "Let's get a move on."

Spence and Jack closed up the horse trailer, while Jeremy said goodbye. As Jack climbed behind the wheel, Jordan appeared carrying a paper plate and handed it through the open window.

"A gift for your trouble," she said with a smile.

Jack lifted the paper towel and admired the five chocolate donuts. "Jeremy, we'll have to dispose of these before we get home," he said in mock disgust.

Grinning, Jeremy reached for the plate. "No problem!"

"That reminds me," Jack said as he fired up the engine. "Elizabeth wants all of you to come for supper after church next Sunday. She made me promise to issue the invitation."

Jordan glanced at Spence, who nodded. "We'd love to come," she replied. "Tell her I'll give her a call. Adele and I will want to bring a dish."

"Will do." Jack nodded and executed a mock salute as he put the truck in gear. He circled the yard and headed back down the long driveway.

Spence slipped an arm around his wife's waist and watched until the truck was out of sight. For some reason, the return of the livestock validated their arrival. The move felt permanent. Together, they returned to the house. Caleb and Ally had taken Butch into the backyard and were tossing a stick for the spirited little dog.

~ * ~

From the trees to the west of the house, Snake enjoyed a clear view of the front door and yard, along with the side of the barn. The kids were still outside. He could hear their laughter carrying across the fields. They must be in the backyard, he decided. He couldn't see the rear of the house, or the corrals from his hiding place.

He debated how to handle the grab. He could do it right now. Knock the boy over the head and snatch the kid. He should just walk right in and take her. She belonged to him, regardless of what it said on the birth certificate! His mood darkened at the memory.

He'd figured having the original would make the trade less complicated – until he'd gotten a look at it. She hadn't put either of their names on the document! That stupid...! He almost wished Tanya was still around. He'd show her what he thought of her deviousness.

Everything was set up for the trade. He'd promised to have the kid in Mexicali by Sunday. That gave him less than four days to get there. He needed the girl tonight! He glanced over his shoulder, verifying that the car he'd stolen in Fresno was still well hidden. The California plates wouldn't be a problem. He wasn't going back through the state. He planned to cross the border in Arizona then make his way to the drop location from there. He had it all figured out in his head. He only needed the girl.

~ * ~

The delicious aroma of chicken stew invaded every corner of the house, and Spence's stomach growled its approval. He was ready for a hearty meal. Glancing through a window, he noted the unnatural darkness outside. The storm clouds were overhead. He pulled the backdoor open and stuck out his head.

"Caleb," he called over the noise of the dog's barking. "Let's go get those horses bedded down."

The terrier ran along the side fence, yapping excitedly. Spence remembered him doing that every time a rabbit bounced across the yard.

"Be right there, Dad," Caleb replied. "I'm gonna feed Butch first."

"Okay, don't take too long," Spence said, pulling the door shut and heading toward the front to retrieve his heavy coat from the peg in the entryway.

He dragged on the Shearling jacket and headed down the porch steps. The dog continued to bark as he reached the corral. The horses stamped around the gate, agitated by the noise. Spence held out his hand for Dancer, the more restless of the two.

"You doing all right, boy?" he murmured. The horse nudged his hand then pulled away, trotting to the side several yards off. "Butch!" Spence shouted at the dog. "Enough already!"

The dog quieted for about three seconds before resuming his discourse. With a sigh of resignation, Spence unlatched the gate, deciding he'd move Shasta first. Grasping her lead, he guided her through the opening and slid the gate closed behind him.

As he entered the dark interior of the barn, Spence flipped a light switch on his right. When nothing happened, he frowned. The bulb was working fine yesterday. After pushing the door open all the way to let in as much light as possible, he led Shasta toward her stall at the back. Without warning, she emitted a high-pitched whinny and abruptly sidestepped, nearly stepping on his boot.

"Whoa, girl," Spence crooned soothingly, tightening his grip on the halter and stroking the horse's neck. Tense muscles rippled beneath his fingers. "What's got you so spooked?"

As the words left his lips, a chill skittered down his spine. The dog, both horses...before Spence could examine the thought further the air shifted behind him and something hard slammed into the side of his head. The world went dark and he crumpled to the floor.

Snake stepped from the shadows and stared down at the prone man. The horse neighed loudly, startling him. The large animal loomed close, and he moved away in fear. He'd never been around horses before. Creeping forward, he slapped its hindquarters. The animal grunted and trotted to the back of the barn.

"Good," he muttered. "You just stay there and we won't have any problems."

Snake glanced at the man at his feet. This must be the guy she married, though he'd never seen him before. He briefly considered using his blade to slit the man's throat. Wouldn't want him to wake up and interrupt things. Shuddering at the thought of all that blood, he forced down bile rising in the back of his throat. Tying him up should do the trick, he decided with relief. If the guy came to, he'd still be helpless.

"What's this?" The man's coat had fallen open revealing the leather strap of a shoulder holster. "Who is this guy?" Snake mumbled as he released the snap and withdrew the Glock. He glanced at the grapefruit sized rock gripped in his other hand and let go. It thumped to the floor and rolled a few inches away. Snake didn't much care for firearms, preferring to conduct business with his bare hands. In this situation, however, a gun might prove useful.

~ * ~

When Caleb reached the corral, he was surprised to see Dancer in the far corner. Why wouldn't the horse want to come in from the cold? He whistled and called. Dancer snorted and threw his head around, making his opinion known – he wasn't coming. With a sigh, Caleb stomped toward the barn. Dad would have to deal with the ornery animal.

The moment he stepped inside, he sensed that something wasn't right. "Dad?" he called softly. As his eyes adjusted to the dim interior, he spotted a dark mound on the floor. "Dad!" He ran toward the still body.

A hand shot out and clamped his upper arm, bringing him to a halt and swinging him around at the same time. Caleb suddenly found himself face-to-face with his mother's former boyfriend. The instinct to flee surged in him, and he attempted to jerk his arm free, but the man's grip only tightened.

"Dad!" Caleb shouted over his shoulder, still straining against the force that held him. "Dad, are you all right?!"

Anger furrowed Snake's brow. He struck the boy across the face with the back of his hand. As Caleb stumbled backward, only the strong grip on his jacket kept him from falling. Snake dragged him closer until they were mere inches apart. "Shut up!" he hissed.

"Wh-what did you do to my dad?" Caleb stuttered, terrified but unable to hold back the question.

"Your dad?" Snake teased. "Is he your latest father project, Caleb?"

Caleb stared at the man but remained silent.

"I remember you wanting to call me dad once," Snake continued teasing.

"Before I knew you!" Caleb spat without thinking.

Snake's hand went up again, his eyes sparking with fury. Caleb remembered that look well. He ducked, covering his head with his arms, as the man's fist came down. Caleb grunted, as pain shot through his forearm. Releasing a curse, Snake pulled his bruised hand to his chest. He needed to stop doing that.

"Come on, kid," the sadistic man growled, yanking the boy toward the barn door. "We're going to have a little chat with your aunt."

Fear for his family exploded inside Caleb, and he jerked backward, out of the man's grip. "You leave her alone!" he screamed. "Go away! Leave us alone!" Snake lunged, but Caleb dodged him. He continued yelling at the top of his lungs, hoping to warn Jordan.

"Shut up!" Snake shouted. Suddenly remembering the gun in his pocket, he pulled it out and pointed it at the motionless man on the floor. "Shut up or I'll make sure he's dead!"

Caleb's breath hitched, and he instantly quieted, his heart racing. He watched Snake wave his dad's gun around. "No! Please!" he pleaded. "I'll stop. I'll do what you want." He moved closer, inching around the wild-eyed man and positioning himself in front of his dad's body.

Snake grinned maliciously. "Then get over here so we can get this over with!"

Caleb nodded and moved closer. Snake grabbed him by the collar and dragged him out of the barn.

Voices drifted in and out of Spence's consciousness – Caleb's and another he didn't recognize. He tried to focus, to comprehend what he was hearing, but his head ached. Caleb was shouting... His boy sounded scared. When

Spence attempted to open his eyes, the pounding inside his skull intensified. Darkness suddenly closed in, and the voices faded to nothing.

Jordan placed the last of her clean clothes in the dresser drawer then turned and stared at the window overlooking the backyard. What was making that dog so agitated? Butch's barking had grown worse since she'd come upstairs. Striding across the room, she pushed up the window and leaned against the screen, hoping to get the dog's attention.

Before she could shout anything, she heard Caleb calling her name.

"Jordan?"

He sounded far away.

"Jordan, come to the front door."

She straightened, speculating at the strange undertones in her nephew's voice. He almost sounded...

"Jordan, Dad's hurt!"

Fear – that's what she detected in Caleb's tone. She turned from the window and sprinted from the room. "Stay upstairs, Ally," she called as she raced down the stairs. Ignoring the coat rack, she yanked open the front door and rushed outside. Caleb stood in the middle of the yard a dozen feet from the porch. The shadowy figure of a tall man loomed behind him. Jordan froze, staring at the somehow familiar person. The man shifted to the side, and recognition dawned.

"No!" she whispered, taking an involuntary step back. Alarm surged painfully in her chest.

"Hey, babe," Snake called. "Did you miss me?" He smiled and winked at her, clearly enjoying her shocked reaction.

Jordan felt rooted to the porch decking, oblivious to the ice cold wind that puckered her skin. She could neither breathe nor speak. How had he found them!? Her eyes darted around the yard. Where was Carl? *Please help us*, she prayed fervently, the mantra repeating over and over in her mind.

"You got something that don't belong to you, babe," Snake said casually. When her face paled, he grinned. "I want my kid."

Jordan spotted the black gun in the man's hand. She recognized it – Carl's gun. Her eyes slid across the yard to the open barn door. Was he in there? Was he injured – or worse? Fear mixed with alarm as she peered into the darkness inside the building, desperate for a glimpse of her husband. *Please, God! No!*

Spence's thoughts drifted through a thick fog. Voices slowly faded in and out. He wanted to stay awake, struggled valiantly to do so. Sleep lured him, longing to reclaim him. Only agitation kept him from succumbing. Something was wrong. He was needed – he could feel it! The hovering darkness turned a dull gray, and he pried his eyes open, blinking, and squinted into the dim light. The incessant hammering inside his head made his eyes slam shut again, and he yielded to the exhaustion that permeated his entire body.

Something pressed against his shoulder, dragging him back to consciousness. Grumbling, he attempted to wave away the disturbance. He struggled with the simple movement. His hand felt heavy.

As he shifted to his side, a soft, wetness mushed against his ear, startling him. He shook his head, and a wave of nausea washed through him. Pinching his eyes shut, he lay still while the sensation passed. Taking shallow breaths, he slit his eyes. The muzzle of a horse hovered above his face then pressed against his cheek. A soft nicker vibrated through his skull, and he winced. That sound shouldn't cause pain. What had happened?

Caleb's voice cut through the open barn door. He was calling for Jordan. Spence cautiously turned his head and gazed across the dusty wooden planks toward the opening. Why was he lying on the floor? He forced his mind to remember. He'd brought Shasta inside. Someone was here. He was struck on the head.

Caleb! Jordan! His family was in danger! He reached automatically for his gun. Bound together in front of him, his hands couldn't to get to it. As he shifted, he realized the holster under his arm was empty. Whoever knocked him unconscious had relieved him of the weapon! Think, Spence!

The horse nickered again and nudged his boot. That was it! Ever since Ally's abduction, he'd begun carrying a small handgun in an ankle holster. Ignoring the pain rampaging through his skull, he shifted around until his bound hands neared his ankles. He pulled up his pant leg with one hand, while the fingers of the other retrieved the compact weapon. Now to get to the door...

Chapter 30

"Bring my kid outside and we'll make us a little trade," Snake called, giving the boy a shake to emphasize his demand. "My kid for your nephew."

"Jordan, no!" Caleb shouted frantically. "Don't do it!"

He fought, trying to pull away, but Snake's grasp only tightened. Infuriated, Snake cursed angrily then whacked the flat of the gun against Caleb's temple. The boy howled and dropped to his knees, holding his head.

"That'll teach you to keep your mouth shut!" Snake raged. Waving the gun in the air, he returned his attention to the woman on the porch and bellowed, "Get the kid! Now!"

~ * ~

Using his elbows for leverage, Spence belly crawled to the barn doorway. *Peel!* That revelation shouldn't surprise him. He should have listened to his gut when Tammy told him about the stranger.

Peel and Caleb were less than ten yards away. Caleb knelt beside the man with his head in his hands, crying. A stab of anguish pierced Spence's heart and with it, a sudden bout of dizziness. He dropped his head, breathing deeply. Blackness narrowed his vision. He closed his eyes, forcing it back. His family needed him!

As Spence slowly lifted his head, blood dripped down his face and obscuring his vision. He swiped the back of his hand across his brow. The shouts had grown louder and more crazed. The guy was losing it! Peel whipped the Glock around madly.

Raising his weapon, Spence took aim at Peel's head. His finger hovered over the trigger. Suddenly the guy shifted, jerking Caleb to his feet. Startled, Spence eased his finger up and slowly let out his breath. His heart thundered. He'd nearly pulled the trigger! He couldn't get a clean shot now, not without risking hitting his son. He had to get the boy to move!

He needed a distraction. With no other choice and time running out, he pointed the gun high above Peel's head and pulled the trigger.

The deafening crack reverberated across the empty yard, starling Snake and making him jump. He turned, swinging his head around wildly, searching for the source. Caleb felt the hold on his jacket loosen and instantly leapt away from the demented man, scrambling rapidly for the shrubs beside the porch.

At the sound of the blast, Jordan ducked beneath the porch railing, shaking and terrified. It couldn't have been Peel. The shot came from her right – from the barn. Was it Carl? She crawled across the planks and peered through the slats, searching the dark entrance, praying for a sign of him. Sirens screamed far in the distance.

It had to be the guy in the barn! Shrieking a string of expletives, Snake swung around and pointed his weapon at the porch.

"I'll kill her!" he shouted in a high-pitched screech. "I swear! I'll kill her!" Not waiting for a response, he fired at the front of the house. The kick of the weapon jerked his hand back, and he stumbled. A second later, he'd regained his footing and was advancing on the porch, holding out the Glock in front of him. "Throw the gun out, or I'll ki-"

A second blast rent the air. With a surprised squeal, Snake jerked involuntarily and grabbed his left thigh. Before he could raise the weapon again, a third shot, much louder, exploded across the yard. Peel's body hurled backward several feet and landed with a thud, spread eagle across the ground. The handgun flew from his grip and skidded across the dirt.

On quaking legs, Jordan slowly stood, her eyes riveted on the still form of the man who'd threatened her family. He didn't move, would probably never move again. Her pulse raced erratically. She turned her stunned gaze to the barn, her attention settling on a dark form lying in the doorway. Carl! Her heart lurched as she sprinted down the steps and across the yard, skidding to a stop on her knees beside the face-down body of her husband.

"Carl!" she called. "Carl! Answer me!"

When he didn't move, she put her hands on his shoulders and shook him, calling his name again. Tears streamed from her eyes, blurring her vision. Grabbing his thick upper arm, Jordan lifted with all her strength until he rolled over. The sight of his bloody head and face ripped an tortured gasp from her throat.

"Oh my God!" she cried. "Carl, please! Please!"

Desperate pleas penetrated the fog that swirled in Spence's head. Jordan... He forced his mind to focus, to push back the curtain of darkness and get to her. She needed him. Jordan... He swam through the mist toward her voice.

Jordan shook Carl, frantic to make him respond. With each passing second, her hope weakened. Sobbing now, she gripped the front of his shirt. "Carl!" she begged. "Carl, don't you dare leave me!" Her voice faded and she closed her eyes, slowly dropping her head to his chest and wept. "Don't leave me..."

As Spence listened to her anguished sobs, felt her body quivering against his chest, his heart constricted. With one final heave, he pushed through the murky fog and sucked in a deep breath.

Detecting faint movement beneath her, Jordan raised her head and stared down at the closed eyes of her husband.

"Carl?" she whispered, searching his face. The faintest beginnings of a smile tilted his lips.

"Sweetheart," he rasped weakly. "You know I never back down from a dare."

His eyelids fluttered and he squinted up at her. Crying in relief, Jordan's heart soared as she cupped his face between her palms and kissed his goofy grin.

~ * ~

Two sheriff's vehicles, followed by the local paramedics, pulled into the storm darkened yard, stopping when their headlights landed on the body of a man. A rangy boy stood over him, a handgun gripped in his fist. Brandishing their firearms, the sheriff and two deputies approached with caution.

"I'm fairly certain he's the only one," Adele Hill called from the porch, pointing at the dead man. "Carl Spencer's been injured," she added, gesturing to the couple huddled in the barn doorway.

Deputies Tucker and Atkinson began a careful search of the property. Sheriff Davies directed the medics to the barn. He stayed with the body. The gaping hole in the prone man's chest confirmed his condition. He wouldn't be in need of medical attention. Davies main concern, at the moment, was the trembling boy.

"You all right, son?" he asked gently.

"He – he hurt my Dad. He tried to take my sister," Caleb stuttered, clearly in shock.

Assuming this was related to the recent problems Spence had discussed with him before the family's arrival, Davies nodded. He pulled a photograph from his pocket and compared it to the dead man. He was the suspect wanted for the little girl's kidnapping. This was most likely a case of self-defense.

"You want to give me the gun?" the sheriff asked, holding out his hand. "I'll make sure he doesn't move while you check on your dad."

Caleb stared at the lawman for a couple of beats then slowly nodded. Davies reached for the handgun and slid it from the boy's grip. Caleb's eyes seemed to clear as he turned and sprinted toward the barn.

The sheriff glanced at the front porch. Leaning on her cane, Adele Hill stood beside the door, a rifle propped beside her. His gaze shifted to the dead man once again, understanding. His sprawled position indicated the direction from which the fatal shot had originated. The elderly woman was the one to bring him down.

~ * ~

Two days later, Spence sat in Mrs. Hill's parlor while his wife fussed over him. His head injury had required an ambulance ride to the hospital for x-rays and suturing. He considered himself lucky to get off with only six stitches, a black eye, and what the doctors deemed a mild concussion. The fist-sized rock Peel had used to incapacitate him could have killed him. From his run-in with the madman, Caleb sported a bruised temple and a black eye to match his father's.

Several federal agents arrived the day after the incident. Apparently, they'd intercepted a telephone call to the Mexican contact they'd begun monitoring after Rodriguez started talking. The fact that the call was made from a Montana payphone had put them on alert. Agents were dispatched, though not in time to prevent Peel from making his move.

Statements were taken from all the parties involved, and the killing was recorded as self-defense. Spence learned that the Bureau planned to take advantage of Peel's arrangements and send a decoy in his place, with the hope of bringing down the illegal adoption ring.

Jordan set down two mugs of coffee then adjusted the blanket covering her husband's knees. "Are you feeling okay?"

"I'm fine, sweetheart," Spence replied reaching for his wife's hand and pulling her down to his lap. He was much more concerned for her wellbeing than his. The past few weeks were a whirlwind of emotion and change. "How about you?" he asked, gently stroking her cheek. "Are you all right?"

"Mm hmm," she replied, as she closed her eyes and shuddered faintly.

With an effort, Jordan kept her mind from dwelling on the recent past. Right now, she wanted only to be with Carl and the children, know they were safe and well. Spence pulled her closer. With a sigh, Jordan laid her head against his shoulder and slid her hand across his chest. Of their own accord, her fingertips swirled gently over the damaged area.

In the past few weeks, she'd prayed more than she had during the last decade. She'd also worried far more than she ought. She'd always considered her faith strong. Giving her problems to the Lord, asking for His help, used to be easy, routine. Now, she realized, though she'd faced trials, they'd never been ones she couldn't handle.

Even dealing with Tanya's death had not been insurmountable. She'd prayed for God's help with each difficulty but, in a sense, took care of things without truly relying on Him. Facing a real threat, one over which she had no control at all, had forced her to acknowledge her own helplessness. Even then, she'd turned to Carl rather than the Lord. However, when he lay unconscious in that barn, when she didn't know whether he was dead or alive... she discovered true dependence. God was in control.

Later, while Carl was being treated at the hospital, she'd found a quiet corner and silently given up her supposed control. Immediately, the heavy burden she wore like a mantle slipped from her shoulders. Adele was right. Her job was to have faith, to keep praying, and to support her man. From this day forwards, she intended to leave the rest in more capable hands.

Spence glided his palm along Jordan's arm and kissed her forehead. "We've been married...let's see now...ten days. Are you ready to get rid of me yet?" he asked jokingly, though he was a little concerned she might feel she'd made a mistake by allowing herself to be rushed to the altar.

"I think I'll keep you around. You'll need some training, to be sure," she teased back. At Carl's chuckle, she lifted her head and smiled. She stroked a finger along his jaw and across his lips. "Besides, what would God think if I rejected you after all the trouble He went through to bring us together?"

Spence reached for her hand and pressed her fingers to his lips in a gentle kiss. "Do you really believe that?"

"With all my heart," Jordan whispered, suddenly tearing up. Equally moved, Spence leaned forward and captured her lips in a deep kiss.

A few moments later, Caleb walked in, Ally by his side, and found them that way, locked in a passionate embrace, oblivious to everything and everyone around them.

Ally giggled. "Mama and Daddy are kissing again."

Caleb rolled his eyes and groaned. "Guess we'd better get used to it," he replied with a long-suffering sigh.

EPILOGUE

Independence Day – Eight months later

The banner across the top of the booth read simply, *Vittles.* Beneath, in smaller print, were the words, *Sponsored by the Silver Springs Sheriff's Department.* Deputy Chase Tucker flipped patties onto waiting buns and pushed the two paper plates down the table. Adding napkins and bags of chips, Spence carried the lunches to the customer. Marissa, the office dispatcher, was in command of the cash register. Reminiscent of their official uniforms, each volunteer wore a tan apron, emblazoned with the words, *Here to protect and serve.*

"Thanks, Sheriff," said an elderly gentleman, as he accepted the meals. "Sure was glad to learn you won," he added with a chuckle.

"Thanks for your vote, Mr. Jones," Spence replied with a broad grin.

In March, Davies announced his intention to retire. Elections were called and held in June. With Davies' endorsement, as well as that of Adele Hill and the local Cattlemen's Association, Spence agreed to run. During the six months he'd lived in Silver Springs and worked as a deputy, he'd made a name for himself. Most people remembered him from the previous summer and many from his stint in town five years ago. His impressive background, coupled with the fact that nobody had run against him, pretty much guaranteed him the position. His official installation would take place later this afternoon. In the meantime, he was doing his part to support the community event.

When Deputy Atkinson and two other men arrived to replace the present crew, Spence saluted and left the booth. Spotting his family waiting at a nearby table, he grabbed the plates he'd prepared in advance and headed that way. Setting down the meals, he dropped a kiss to his wife's soft lips. As he raised his head to break the kiss, Jordan pushed upward and kept him from doing so. He gladly obliged, ignoring the snickers from friends and neighbors occupying the other tables. When she finally drew away, her warm gaze held his for a long moment.

"Look what Caleb won for me, Daddy," Ally suddenly cried, breaking the mesmerizing spell.

Dragging his eyes from his lovely wife, Spence glanced at the stuffed animal his daughter held. It was identical to the black and white cat she'd lost last fall during the kidnapping. He looked at his son's beaming face.

"I won it at the shooting gallery again," Caleb eagerly explained. "I checked the guns and figured out the best way to make the shot, just like you showed me last summer."

"Good job!" Spence replied, giving his boy an encouraging pat on the shoulder and adding with a grin, "How much did it cost me?"

"Fifteen dollars," Caleb admitted sheepishly. "It took me a while to determine where to aim."

"Not too bad," Spence replied with a nod, impressed that the boy had managed to outsmart the dishonest game. "We'd better dig in before these burgers are cold."

He passed around the plates, his hands slowing when his eyes met Jordan's. She still wore that soft, inviting expression. He raised his eyebrows in a silent question, but she only smiled and began to eat.

At dusk, Spence was called to the stage area and sworn-in as the new sheriff of Silver Springs. The town also honored Sheriff Davies and thanked the other deputies and staff for their valuable and selfless service. Afterward, the whole community was dismissed to the high school parking lot. Spence and his family sat on folding chairs in the bed of his late model, black Ford pickup, for which he'd traded the Porche, and enjoyed the fireworks display. Numerous other trucks filled with spectators did the same, including the Summers family parked beside them.

Much later, the families headed for their various homes, tired but happy. While Spence gathered a sleeping Ally from the backseat, Caleb headed for the corral to look after the horses.

"I'll be out in a minute to give you a hand," Spence called after his son.

"I can handle it, Dad," Caleb called back. "Um, I mean – Sheriff Spencer," he added with a mock salute. "You can go on in."

"You're sure, Caleb?"

"Yup!"

His son's self-assured response left Spence with a melancholy feeling. He'd missed so much. At nearly fifteen, Caleb was mostly grown. Before long, the boy would be a man – dating, driving, going off to college. That sobering thought stayed with him as he carried his little girl upstairs and tucked her into bed. Jordan had gone ahead to draw back the bed covers.

In May, Mrs. Hill moved into the small retirement village in town, taking some of her furniture with her. Her former sewing room had been redecorated for Ally.

Caleb's room remained the way it was before, complete with the same pair of twin beds. He'd added a couple of posters depicting Christian rock bands, along with the usual clutter associated with a teenaged boy. Adele's downstairs bedroom was restored to its original purpose, a sunroom. Jordan arranged to have the hardwood floors refinished then added an area rug and comfortable furniture.

As Spence finished tucking the blankets around Ally, he turned to find Jordan standing in the doorway watching him. That same soft look from earlier graced her lovely face. With a full heart, he stepped forward and tugged her into his arms. His gaze drifted longingly across the hall to their bedroom door. Was it too early?

"What pleasant thought has you looking so lovely tonight?" he whispered in her ear.

Wrapping her arms around Carl's back, Jordan sighed against his throat. "I was just wondering how you'd feel if I put off teaching for a while?"

Spence lifted his head in surprise. She'd been adamant about completing her final requirements and getting started on her career. The last hurdle, student teaching, was scheduled for the fall semester.

"You don't want to teach?"

"Yes, I do," Jordan replied hastily. "But...well, I'm not going to be ready to accept a position immediately. That is, unless you think we need the money." Jordan cringed. She'd only just thought of that. She knew he'd taken a substantial pay reduction by moving here and changing jobs. Would changing her plans upset Carl's? Her heart fell, and she pulled away.

Spence felt the abrupt change in her mood and wondered at it. When she brought up money, he was further confused. He reached for her hand as she backed into the hall.

"Jordan," he said, pulling Ally's door closed behind him. "Have I ever given you the impression that you're expected to work because we need the second income?"

"Well, we haven't really talked about it," Jordan replied hesitantly. "I know you don't make as much as before..."

Spence's jaw stiffened. "My salary is more than adequate to take care of our needs," he said, stunned by this unexpected conversation. When her brow furrowed, the lovely expression now completely gone, he tipped her chin up and asked, "Sweetheart, what is this really about?"

Jordan closed her eyes and tried to recapture the good feelings she'd been savoring all day. *Please let this be all right,* she prayed silently. *Please, let him be as happy as I am.* When a peaceful sensation stole over her, tears promptly banked behind her eyes, and she smiled.

Spencer watched as the stress disappeared from her face, replaced with the pleasant expression she'd worn earlier. He drew her into his arms once again and murmured, "I love you, Jordan. You can tell me anything."

Jordan slid her arms up his chest and around his neck. Holding his gaze, she whispered through her tears, "We're having a baby."

Stunned, Spence continued to stare down at his wife's moist eyes. The words slowly seeped into his head, wound through his mid-section leaving a trail of butterflies, and wrapped around his heart like a warm blanket. Emotion blocked his throat. "We are?" he asked, his voice husky and too deep.

Smiling, Jordan nodded.

"When?"

"Next February."

The feelings churning through Spence's body were similar to what he'd experienced the day he learned about Caleb. Jordan had been the bearer of that news, as well, and he'd walked out on her. Not this time! He dropped his face to her neck, burrowed into her silky hair, and inhaled a deep, ragged breath. His arms tightened around her, molding her body to his as he worked to bring his emotions under control.

Jordan felt the mixture of physical strength and emotional vulnerability raging inside him. He was overwhelmed. She smiled, remembering their first embrace, so like this one.

"Are you happy?" she asked softly.

"Yes!" came the raspy, desperate sounding reply. When he raised his head and gazed at her, tears slid freely down his cheeks.

Jordan brushed her fingers over his face, wiping away the moisture. She pushed up on her toes and kissed his cheeks, his nose, his chin. When she reached his mouth, he responded with enthusiasm, attacking with vigor and drawing out the intimate kiss until her insides had melted and her legs no longer provided support.

With a groan, Spence scooped his wife into his arms and headed for their bedroom. It was definitely not too early to go to bed. She was pregnant with his child, after all, and, as any good investigator knew, it was only prudent to revisit the scene of the crime.

Midnight, seven months later

Spence lounged in the upholstered recliner beside his wife's hospital bed. His tender gaze drifted from

Jordan's angelic face, relaxed in sleep, to the precious bundle snuggled in his arms. Earlier this afternoon, after eleven exhausting hours of labor, his son had come into the world. Before dozing off, Jordan pronounced her eight pound baby perfect.

As he cradled the newborn, Spence pondered how anyone could fall in love so instantly and so completely. The moment the baby slid from Jordan's body, his emotions had morphed from fear and worry to awestruck wonder. Baby Adam, named after his fallen partner, was the most amazing gift he'd ever received. Sheer joy swelled his heart to near bursting.

The tiny bundle suddenly shifted. Gazing down, Spence watched one small arm wriggle free of the constricting blue blanket. Adam stretched his hand far above his head and yawned, displaying toothless gums and a pink tongue. Peering through heavy eyelids, his gray eyes seemed to study the unfamiliar face above him.

"Well, hello there, mister," the proud new dad murmured.

Blinking, Adam scrunched up his face and let go a tiny squeak. A moment of panic seized Spence when he thought the baby might cry. His eyes shot to Jordan. He hated to interrupt her much-needed slumber but if his son was hungry, there wasn't much he could do to help. When he looked back, the baby's eyes were closed, and he'd settled down.

Careful to keep a firm hold on the baby, Spence leaned back with a relieved smile. For the umpteenth time tonight, he thanked God for the priceless gift of a second son, whom he wouldn't have if not for the existence of his firstborn. With emotion blocking his throat, he offered thanks for the beautiful, remarkable woman who was his wife, chosen especially for him by God, and for Caleb and little Ally, their precious children.

He acknowledged the trials of the past two years with the absolute certainty that he would not have his wonderful family or his strong faith had those hard times been absent from his life. *God works in mysterious ways.* Spence was a living example of the cliché's truth. The bullet that nearly killed him was a catalyst, setting off a chain of events that were destined to change him forever. Gone was the cynical, lonely man he'd once been. Love filled his formerly damaged heart. Blessed with a perfect family, good friends, and a growing relationship with his heavenly Father, for the first time in his life, Spence was whole.

Once again, he marveled at the promise Jordan had kept for so many years, along with the promises he'd made to himself and to the Lord since she came into his life. Gazing at his beautiful wife, he vowed to be worthy of her, to protect his family to the best of his ability, and to continue striving to become the man God wanted him to be.

#####

Dear Reader,

Each morning, before I turned my attention to the creation of this novel, I spent a few minutes in a daily devotion, reading a few passages of scripture, and asking the Lord to bless my work. As a result, Keeping Promises practically wrote itself. I believe the Lord gave me the words and I simply put them down in print. I would be remiss if I did not give Him all the credit.

Thank you for choosing Keeping Promises. I hope you found the story uplifting and, perhaps, gained something from the moral and spiritual struggles the main characters encountered and overcame.

Be sure to check out one of my favorites, <u>No Regrets,</u> a story of second chances. It's a love story filled with twists, turns, and misconceptions. And, as always, it is a clean read. (<u>No Regrets</u> is a mainstream romance novel and is not listed under the Christian category.)

I love to hear from readers and welcome contact at my email address <u>ginamcoon@gmail.com</u>.

Sincerely,
Gina Marie Coon

Please enjoy the following excerpts.

No Regrets
a tale of second chances
By Gina Marie Coon

"So, what brings you here, Liv? And don't tell me you happened to be in the area? It's a hundred and five degrees outside," she pointed out calmly. "No one comes here without a reason."

Olivia grimaced. Yesterday, she'd only thought of escaping, not actually talking about the reasons why. Finally, she simply said, "Men!" as if that would explain everything. She was surprised to discover that the single word actually did a pretty fair job, according to her mother's life experience.

Helen Griffin nodded her very knowledgeable head. As far as she was concerned, this lesson was long overdue for her naïve, nearly thirty-year-old daughter. She smiled and asked, "Just one, or all of them in general?"

Olivia chewed her lower lip, weighing how much she wanted to share. "I guess just one," she said softly, adding, "so far." After all, her baby could be a boy!

"Do you want to talk about it?" Helen asked gently. She sensed her daughter's distress. Whoever this man was, he was important to her.

Olivia shrugged and sipped her lemonade. Evade and ignore, that was her battle plan.

Helen searched Olivia's face, finding both pain and anger there. Definitely man related, she thought. "Would this particular gentleman have anything to do with the baby you're carrying?" She softened her words purposefully. Her role was to counsel not judge.

Olivia's eyes shot to her mother's. "How...?" If her mother knew about the pregnancy after thirty minutes in the same room with Olivia, would anyone else have guessed yet?

Helen smiled. "You look different. It wasn't hard to figure it out." Then she said, "Tell me about him."

Olivia started at the beginning and told her mother everything, well the condensed version of everything. It felt good to get it off her chest. "The thing is, mom, I've known him for years and years, but not really well until…" Her face reddened as the memory of their intimacy entered her mind. "Anyway, I guess I'd built up this idea of who Mason was in my mind, but then…"

Helen heaved a sigh. "Then he didn't live up to your high expectations. Believe me, honey, they never do," she said sarcastically. "You have to remember, they're human, just like us."

Suddenly embarrassed, Olivia swallowed and nodded. "I know. I guess, in a way, I wasn't fair with him. I've made a few mistakes in this non-relationship, though I've laid most of the blame on Mason."

"What do you want from him?"

It was an excellent question; one Olivia didn't have an answer for. At one time, she might have said love or marriage, but not now. The way he'd behaved in their recent history, she wasn't sure she wanted anything to do with him.

"I don't know," she finally answered honestly. "Maybe I just want his respect. I mean, the man treated me like I was after his wallet! I was so angry!"

"Olivia, you've always had more than your share of pride," Helen pointed out lovingly. "I have a feeling you'll be hearing from him. And you might have to swallow some of it."

Olivia groaned and flopped back on the sofa. That was one of the many things she feared.

(No Regrets is a full-length novel of approx.. 250 pages.)

Mail Order Bride
Silver Springs Settlers Series, Book 3
by Gina Marie Coon

"Good morning, Mr. Cooper," Sarah said, the evidence of her recent and still ongoing illness very prominent in her faint tone.

Whipping off his hat, Tom replied in kind. Eliza hastily vacated the only other chair and gestured for Tom to take it. He hesitated.

"Please, Mr. Cooper," Sarah implored softly. "I'd like to speak to you."

Tom sat and a moment later a mug of steaming coffee was placed in front of him. He nodded a thank you, and Eliza smiled in reply then moved off to help Ling with the chores.

Seated in the artificial privacy afforded by the drying clothes, Sarah said, "I've not had the opportunity the thank you, sir. You've done so much for my sister and me. I owe a debt I fear I can never repay."

Raising his hand to ward off the woman's gratitude, something he felt he didn't deserve, Tom said, "Miss Marshall, please. You don't owe me a thing. I was only doing as my conscience directed."

"I know that, sir," Sarah replied earnestly. "The Lord sent you. I've already made my acknowledgments to Him," she stated in complete seriousness.

Tom studied the brown liquid swirling in his cup, a little surprised and embarrassed by her declaration. "You believe God sent me to your rescue?" he asked skeptically.

Sarah's eyes rounded, surprised by the doubt she detected in his question. "Absolutely!" she replied with a firm nod. "His hand has been on our journey, even before we left."

"Since before...?" Tom repeated, astounded by what she was implying.

"It was God's plan for us to come west," she explained. "I didn't want to believe that at first, but once I accepted it, I felt wholly at peace with the move." She watched the man's expression change from bewilderment to a scowl.

"What about Bradford?" Tom asked, his jaw clamped painfully. "Was that God's plan for you and your sister?" he hissed, careful to keep his voice down.

Ignoring his vehemence, Sarah merely smiled. "Mr. Bradford was simply a means to an end," she explained, having already come to terms with the rancher's role in her circumstances. "In the Bible, there are countless examples of God using evil men to accomplish His will. A man's consent is not required."

Tom set his mug down with a clunk and stared hard at the woman. Was her brain still muddled by the fever? "What kind of God would send you into the hands of a man like Bradford?" he asked harshly.

Sarah started at his fierce tone. "He didn't, Mr. Cooper," she replied intently. "Why, I've never even met the man. On two different occasions, the Lord used *you* to intervene. You said it yourself – your conscience directed you," she reminded him of his own words. Then, leaning forward, she reached for his hand where it rested on the table and laid her palm over it. "Just what do you think your conscience is?" she asked gently.

Tom didn't know what to say, had no idea how to respond to her. He had no argument. As much as he wanted to discount her explanation, he couldn't. She made it seem sensible; and more importantly, she believed what she was saying with all her heart. There'd be no convincing her otherwise. Was Sarah Marshall right? Did God select him for the job? Did He choose Tom Cooper to save the Marshall women?

(Mail Order Bride is a full-length novel of approx. 280 print pages)

Both ebooks, along with all the others in the Silver Springs Settlers Series and the Silver Springs Contemporary Series, are available now.

The three books in the Settlers series are also available in print.

ABOUT THE AUTHOR

Gina Coon resides in Southern California with her husband and children. When she isn't writing she enjoys sewing and crafts, as well as volunteering at her church, scouts, and kids' schools.

For more than a decade Gina was defined as a (crazy) homeschool mom. After retiring from homeschooling, she found herself at loose ends, unaccustomed to having time on her hands. As a little girl her head was filled with made up stories and that hasn't changed. An avid reader, she's always loved books and the idea of writing one. Deciding to capitalize on all those years of teaching and editing her kids' essays, she quietly started a project. She had no idea if she'd produce a decent paragraph, let alone a whole story. Her first book, Elizabeth's Hero, was a huge personal achievement that launched a love affair with writing.

Her Christian faith is often reflected in her stories. The main characters are generally good people with strong values and, of course, *there is always a happy ending!*

Made in the USA
Monee, IL
12 September 2023

42478385R00225